I, Mona Lisa

JEANNE KALOGRIDIS

ST. MARTIN'S GRIFFIN

New York

I, MONA LISA. Copyright © 2006 by Jeanne Kalogridis. All rights reserved. Printed in the United States of America. No part of this book may be used or reproduced in any manner whatsoever without written permission except in the case of brief quotations embodied in critical articles or reviews. For information, address St. Martin's Press, 175 Fifth Avenue, New York, N.Y. 10010.

www.stmartins.com

Library of Congress Cataloging-in-Publication Data

Kalogridis, Jeanne.
    I, Mona Lisa / Jeanne Kalogridis.—1st U.S. ed.
        p. cm.
    ISBN-13: 978-0-312-34139-8
    ISBN-10: 0-312-34139-3
    1. Florence (Italy)—History—1421–1737—Fiction. I. Title.

    PS3561.A41675I25 2006
    813'.54—dc22

                                        2006047659

First published in the United Kingdom by HarperCollins*Publishers* under the title *Painting Mona Lisa*

First U.S. Edition: November 2006

10 9 8 7 6 5 4 3 2 1

FOR GEORGE, FOREVER

ACKNOWLEDGMENTS

I am extraordinarily indebted to the following people:

My husband, who not only survived cancer, chemotherapy, and complications this past year but, far more impressively, survived the writing of this novel with good humor and good grace;

My brilliant agents, Russell Galen and Danny Baror, who have both survived having me as a client for well over twenty years;

My friends Kathleen O'Malley and Anne Moroz, who bravely waded through this daunting manuscript and kindly offered their comments; and most of all:

My editors, Charles Spicer at St. Martin's Press and Emma Coode at HarperCollins UK, both consummate professionals gifted with infinite patience. Charlie and Emma each went to extraordinary lengths so that I could spend time caring for my husband during his illness. The book was, as a result, abysmally late. I wish I knew words that could convey the depth of my gratitude for their kindness, and my regret that they were pushed to the limit in order to ready the manuscript for the printer. For them, I have these words: Thank you, Charlie. Thank you, Emma.

Things that happened many years ago often seem close and nearby to the present, and many things that happened recently seem as ancient as the bygone days of youth.

—Leonardo da Vinci
Codex Atlanticus, fol. 29v-a

PROLOGUE

Lisa

JUNE 1490

I

My name is Lisa di Antonio Gherardini, though to acquaintances I am known simply as Madonna Lisa, and to those of the common class, Monna Lisa.

My likeness has been recorded on wood, with boiled linseed oil and pigments dug from earth or crushed from semiprecious stones and applied with brushes made from the feathers of birds and the silken fur of animals.

I have seen the painting. It does not look like me. I stare at it and see instead the faces of my mother and father. I listen and hear their voices. I feel their love and their sorrow, and I witness, again and again, the crime that bound them together; the crime that bound them to me.

For my story begins not with my birth but a murder, committed the year before I was born.

It was first revealed to me during an encounter with the astrologer two weeks before my birthday, which was celebrated on the fifteenth of June. My mother announced that I would have my choice of a present. She assumed that I would request a new gown, for nowhere has sartorial ostentation been practiced more avidly than my native

Florence. My father was one of the city's wealthiest wool merchants, and his business connections afforded me my pick of sumptuous silks, brocades, velvets, and furs.

But I did not want a gown. I had recently attended the wedding of my uncle Lauro and his young bride, Giovanna Maria. During the celebration afterward, my grandmother had remarked sourly:

"It cannot last happily. She is a Sagittarius, with Taurus ascendant. Lauro is Aries, the Ram. They will constantly be butting heads."

"Mother," my own had reproached gently.

"If you and Antonio had paid attention to such matters—" My grandmother had broken off at my mother's sharp glance.

I was intrigued. My parents loved each other, but had never been happy. And I realized that they had never discussed my stars with me.

When I questioned my mother, I discovered that my chart had never been cast. This shocked me: Well-to-do Florentine families often consulted astrologers on important matters, and charts were routinely drawn up for newborns. And I was a rare creature: an only child, the bearer of my family's hopes.

And as an only child, I was well aware of the power I possessed; I whined and pleaded pitifully until my reluctant mother yielded.

Had I known then what was to follow, I would not have pressed so hard.

Because it was not safe for my mother to venture out, we did not go to the astrologer's residence, but instead summoned him to our palazzo.

From a window in the corridor near my bedroom, I watched as the astrologer's gilded carriage, its door painted with his familial crest, arrived in the courtyard behind our house. Two elegantly appointed servants attended him as he stepped down, clad in a *farsetto*, the close-fitting man's garment which some wore in place of a tunic. The fabric was a violet velvet quilt, covered by a sleeveless brocade cloak in a darker shade of the same hue. His body was thin and sunken-chested, his posture and movements imperious.

Zalumma, my mother's slave, moved forward to meet him. Zalumma was a well-dressed lady-in-waiting that day. She was devoted to my mother, whose gentleness inspired loyalty, and who treated her slave like a beloved companion. Zalumma was a Circassian, from the high mountains in the mysterious East; her people were prized for their beauty and Zalumma—tall as a man, with black hair and eyebrows and a face whiter than marble—was no exception. Her tight ringlets were formed not by a hot poker but by God, and were the envy of every Florentine woman. At times, she muttered to herself in her native tongue, which sounded like no language I had ever heard; she called it "Adyghabza."

Zalumma curtsied, then led the man into the house to meet my mother. She had been nervous that morning, no doubt because the astrologer was the most prestigious in town and had, when the Pope's forecaster had taken ill, even been consulted by His Holiness. I was to remain out of view; this first encounter was a business matter, and I would be a distraction.

I left my room and stepped lightly to the top of the stairs to see if I could make out what was going on two floors below me. The stone walls were thick, and my mother had shut the door to the reception chamber. I could not even make out muffled voices.

The meeting did not last long. My mother opened the door and called for Zalumma; I heard her quick steps on the marble, then a man's voice.

I retreated from the stairs and hurried back to the window, with its view of the astrologer's carriage.

Zalumma escorted him from the house—then, after glancing about, handed him a small object, perhaps a purse. He refused it at first, but Zalumma addressed him earnestly, urgently. After a moment of indecision, he pocketed the object, then climbed into his carriage and was driven away.

I assumed that she had paid him for a reading, though I was surprised that a man with such stature would read for a slave. Or perhaps my mother had simply forgotten to pay him.

As she walked back toward the house, Zalumma happened to glance up and meet my gaze. Flustered at being caught spying, I withdrew.

I expected Zalumma, who enjoyed teasing me about my misdeeds, to mention it later; but she remained altogether silent on the matter.

II

*T*hree days later, the astrologer returned. Once again, I watched from the top-floor window as he climbed from the carriage and Zalumma greeted him. I was excited; Mother had agreed to call for me when the time was right. I decided that she wanted time to polish any negative news and give it a rosier glow.

This time the horoscopist wore his wealth in the form of a brilliant yellow tunic of silk damask trimmed with brown marten fur. Before entering the house, he paused and spoke to Zalumma furtively; she put a hand to her mouth as if shocked by what he said. He asked her a question. She shook her head, then put a hand on his forearm, apparently demanding something from him. He handed her a scroll of papers, then pulled away, irritated, and strode into our palazzo. Agitated, she tucked the scroll into a pocket hidden in the folds of her skirt, then followed on his heels.

I left the window and stood listening at the top of the stairs, mystified by the encounter and impatient for my summons.

Less than a quarter hour later, I started violently when, downstairs, a door was flung open with such force it slammed against the wall. I ran to the window: The astrologer was walking, unescorted, back to his carriage.

I lifted my skirts and dashed down the stairs full tilt, grateful that I encountered neither Zalumma nor my mother. Breathless, I arrived at the carriage just as the astrologer gave his driver the signal to leave.

I put my hand on the polished wooden door and looked up at the man sitting on the other side. "Please stop," I said.

He gestured for the driver to hold the horses back and scowled sourly down at me; yet his gaze also held a curious compassion. "You would be the daughter, then."

"Yes."

He appraised me carefully. "I will not be party to deception. Do you understand?"

"No."

"Hmm. I see that you do not." He paused to choose his words carefully. "Your mother, Madonna Lucrezia, said that you were the one who requested my services. Is that so?"

"It is." I flushed, not knowing whether my admission would anger him further.

"Then you deserve to hear at least some of the truth—for you will never hear the full of it in this house." His pompous irritation faded and his tone grew earnest and dark. "Your chart is unusual—some would say it is distressing. I take my art very seriously, and employ my intuition well, and both tell me that you are caught in a cycle of violence, of blood and deceit. What others have begun, you must finish."

I recoiled. When I could find my voice, I insisted, "I want nothing to do with such things."

"You are fire four times over," he said. "Your temper is hot, a furnace in which the sword of justice must be forged. In your stars I saw an act of violence, one which is your past and your future."

"But I would never do anything to hurt someone else!"

"God has ordained it. He has His reasons for your destiny."

I wanted to ask more, but the astrologer called to his driver, and the pair of fine black horses pulled them away.

Perplexed and troubled, I walked back toward the house. By chance, I happened to lift my gaze, and saw Zalumma, staring down at me from the top-floor window.

. . .

By the time I returned to my chamber, she was gone. There I waited for half an hour until my mother called for me.

She still sat in the grand hall where she had received the astrologer. She smiled when I entered, apparently unaware of my encounter with him. In her hand she bore a sheaf of papers.

"Come, sit beside me," she said brightly. "I shall tell you all about your stars. They should have been charted long ago, so I have decided that you still deserve a new gown. Your father will take you today into the city to choose the cloth; but you must say nothing to him about this. Otherwise, he will judge us as too extravagant."

I sat stiffly, my back straight, my hands folded tightly in my lap.

"See here." My mother set the papers in her lap and rested her fingertip on the astrologer's elegant script. "You are Gemini, of course—air. And Pisces rising, which is water. Your moon is in Aries—fire. And you have many aspects of earth in your chart, which makes you exceedingly well balanced. This indicates a most fortunate future."

As she spoke, my anger grew. She had spent the past half hour composing herself and concocting a happy falsehood. The astrologer had been right; I could not expect to find the truth here.

"You will have a long, good life, wealth, and many children," my mother continued. "You need not worry about which man you marry, for you are so well aspected toward every sign that—"

I cut her off. "No," I said. "I am fire four times over. My life will be marked by treachery and blood."

My mother rose swiftly; the papers in her lap slipped to the floor and scattered. "Zalumma!" she hissed, her eyes lit by a fury I had never seen in her before. "Did she speak to you?"

"I spoke to the astrologer myself."

This quieted her at once, and her expression grew unreadable. Carefully, she asked, "What else did he tell you?"

"Only what I just said."

"No more?"

"No more."

Abruptly drained, she sank back into her chair.

Lost in my own anger, I did not stop to think that my kind and doting mother wished only to shield me from evil news. I jumped to my feet. "All that you have said is a lie. What others have you told me?"

It was a cruel thing to say. She glanced at me, stricken. Yet I turned and left her sitting there, with her hand pressed to her heart.

I soon surmised that my mother and Zalumma had had a terrible argument. They had always been on the most amiable terms, but after the astrologer's second visit, my mother grew cold each time Zalumma entered the room. She would not meet her slave's gaze, nor would she speak more than a few words to her. Zalumma, in turn, was sullen and silent. Several weeks passed before they were friends once again.

My mother never spoke to me again of my stars. I often thought of asking Zalumma to find the papers the astrologer had given my mother so that I could read for myself the truth of my fate. But each time, a sense of dread held me back.

I already knew more than I wished.

Almost two years would pass before I learned of the crime to which I was inextricably bound.

PART ONE

APRIL 26, 1478

III

*I*n the stark, massive Cathedral of Santa Maria del Fiore, Bernardo Bandini Baroncelli stood before the altar and fought to steady his shaking hands. He could not, of course—no more than he could hide the blackness in his heart from God. He pressed palms and fingers together in a gesture of prayer and held them to his lips. Voice unsteady, he whispered, pleading for the success of the dark venture in which he found himself entangled, pleading for forgiveness should it succeed.

I am a good man. Baroncelli directed the thought to the Almighty. *I have always meant others well. How did I come to find myself here?*

No answer came. Baroncelli fixed his gaze on the altar, fashioned of dark wood and gold. Through the stained-glass windows in the cupola, the morning light streamed down in golden rays, glittering with dust as they glinted off the golden fixtures. The sight evoked unsullied Eden. Surely God was here, but Baroncelli sensed no divine presence, only his own wickedness.

"God forgive me, a most miserable sinner," he murmured. His quiet prayer mingled with the hundreds of hushed voices inside the cavernous Church of Saint Mary of the Flower—in this case, a lily. The sanctuary was one of the largest in the world, and built in the

shape of a Latin cross. Atop the juncture of the arms rested the architect Brunelleschi's greatest achievement: *il Duomo*. Dazzling in its
sheer expanse, the huge dome had no apparent means of support. Visible from any part of the city, the orange brick cupola majestically
dominated the skyline and had, like the lily, become a symbol of
Florence. It stretched so high that when he first set eyes upon it,
Baroncelli thought it surely touched the Gates of Heaven.

Baroncelli dwelled in a far lower realm this particular morning.
Though the plan had seemed simple enough to be foolproof, now the
painfully bright day had dawned, he was overwhelmed with foreboding and regret. The latter emotion had always marked his life: Born
into one of the city's wealthiest and most eminent families, he had
squandered his fortune and fallen into debt at an advanced age. He
had spent his life as a banker and knew nothing else. His only choices
were to move wife and children down to Naples and beg for sponsor-
ship from one of his rich cousins—an option his outspoken spouse,
Giovanna, would never have tolerated—or to offer his services to one
of the two largest and most prestigious banking families in Florence:
the Medici, or the Pazzi.

He had gone first to the most powerful: the Medici. They had rejected him, a fact he still resented. But their rivals, the Pazzi, welcomed him into their fold; and it was for that reason that today he
stood in the front row of the throng of faithful beside his employer,
Francesco de' Pazzi. With his uncle, the knight Messer Iacopo,
Francesco ran his family's international business concerns. He was a
small man, with a sharp nose and chin, and eyes that narrowed beneath dark, disproportionately large brows; beside the tall, dignified
Baroncelli, he resembled an ugly dwarf. Baroncelli had eventually
come to resent Francesco more than the Medici, for the man was
given to fits of temper and had often loosed a nasty tongue on his
employee, reminding Baroncelli of his bankruptcy with stinging
words.

In order to provide for his family, Baroncelli was forced to grin
while the Pazzi—Messer Iacopo as well as young Francesco—insulted
him and treated him as an inferior when in fact he came from a fam-

ily with equal, if not more, prestige. So when the matter of the plot presented itself, Baroncelli had a choice: risk his neck by confessing everything to the Medici, or let the Pazzi force him to be their accomplice, and win for himself a position in the new government.

Now, as he stood asking God for forgiveness, he felt the warm breath of a fellow conspirator upon his right shoulder. The man praying just behind him wore the burlap robes of a penitent.

Standing to Baroncelli's left, Francesco fidgeted and glanced right, past his employee. Baroncelli followed his gaze: It rested on Lorenzo de' Medici, who at age twenty-nine was the de facto ruler of Florence. Technically, Florence was governed by the Signoria, a council of eight priors and the head of state, the gonfaloniere of justice; these men were chosen from among all the notable Florentine families. Supposedly the process was fair, but curiously, the majority of those chosen were always loyal to Lorenzo, and the gonfaloniere was his to control.

Francesco de' Pazzi was ugly, but Lorenzo was uglier still. Though he was taller than most and muscular in build, his fine body was marred by one of Florence's homeliest faces. His nose—long and pointed, ending in a pronounced upward slope that tilted to one side—had a flattened bridge, leaving Lorenzo with a peculiarly nasal voice. His lower jaw jutted out so severely that whenever he entered a room, his chin preceded him by a thumb's breadth. His disturbing profile was framed by a jaw-length hank of dark hair.

Lorenzo stood awaiting the start of the Mass, flanked on one side by his loyal friend and employee, Francesco Nori, and on the other by the Archbishop of Pisa, Francesco Salviati. Despite his physiognomic failings, Lorenzo emanated profound dignity and poise. In his dark, slightly protruding eyes shone an uncommon shrewdness. Even surrounded by enemies, Lorenzo seemed at ease. Salviati, a Pazzi relative, was no friend, though he and Lorenzo greeted each other as such; the elder Medici brother had lobbied furiously against Salviati's appointment as Archbishop of Pisa, asking instead that Pope Sixtus appoint a Medici sympathizer. The Pope turned a deaf ear to Lorenzo's request and then—breaking with a tradition that had existed for generations—

fired the Medici as the papal bankers to replace them with the Pazzi, a bitter insult to Lorenzo.

Yet today, Lorenzo had received the Pope's own nephew, the seventeen-year-old Cardinal Riario of San Giorgio, as an honored guest. After Mass in the great Duomo, Lorenzo would lead the young Cardinal to a feast at the Medici palace, followed by a tour of the famed Medici collection of art. In the meantime, he stood attentively beside Riario and Salviati, nodding at their occasional whispered comments.

Smiling while they sharpen their swords, Baroncelli thought.

Dressed unostentatiously in a plain tunic of blue-gray silk, Lorenzo was quite unaware of the presence of a pair of black-frocked priests standing two rows behind him. The tutor to the Pazzi household was a youth Baroncelli knew only as Stefano; a somewhat older man, Antonio da Volterra, stood beside him. Baroncelli had caught da Volterra's gaze as they entered the church and had glanced quickly away; the priest's eyes were full of the same smoldering rage Baroncelli had seen in the penitent's. Da Volterra, present at all the secret meetings, also had spoken vehemently against the Medici's "love of all things pagan," saying that the family had "ruined our city" with its decadent art.

Like his fellow conspirators, Baroncelli knew that neither feast nor tour would ever take place. Events soon to occur would change the political face of Florence forever.

Behind him, the hooded penitent shifted his weight, then let go a sigh which held sounds only Baroncelli could interpret. His words were muffled by the cowl that had been drawn forward to obscure his features. Baroncelli had advised against permitting the man to assist in the assassination—why should he be trusted? The fewer involved, the better—but Francesco, as always, had overridden him.

"Where is Giuliano?" the penitent whispered.

Giuliano de' Medici, the younger brother, was as fair of face as Lorenzo was ugly. The darling of Florence, he was called—so handsome, it was said, that men and women alike sighed in his wake. It would not do to have only one brother present in the great cathedral.

Both were required—or the entire operation would have to be called off.

Baroncelli glanced over his shoulder at the shadowed face of his hooded accomplice and said nothing. He did not like the penitent; the man had injected an undertone of self-righteous religious fervor into the proceeding, one so infectious that even the worldly Francesco had begun to believe that they were doing God's work today.

Baroncelli knew God had nothing to do with this; this was an act born of jealousy and ambition.

On his other side, Francesco de' Pazzi hissed. "What is it? What did he say?"

Baroncelli leaned down to whisper in his diminutive employer's ear. "Where is Giuliano?"

He watched the weasel-faced Francesco struggle to suppress his stricken expression. Baroncelli shared his distress. Mass would commence soon now that Lorenzo and his guest, the Cardinal, were in place; unless Giuliano arrived shortly, the entire plan would evaporate into disaster. Too much was at risk, too much at stake; too many souls were involved in the plot, leaving too many tongues free to wag. Even now, Messer Iacopo waited alongside a small army of fifty Perugian mercenaries for the signal from the church bell. When it tolled, he would seize control of the government palace and rally the people against Lorenzo.

The penitent pushed forward until he stood almost alongside Baroncelli; he then lifted his face to stare upward at the dizzyingly high and massive cupola overhead, rising directly above the great altar. The man's burlap hood slipped back slightly, revealing his profile. For an instant, his lips parted, and brow and mouth contorted in a look of such hatred, such revulsion, that Baroncelli recoiled from him.

Slowly, the bitterness in the penitent's eyes eased; his expression gradually resolved into one of beatific ecstasy, as if he could see God Himself and not the rounded ceiling's smooth marble. Francesco noticed, and he watched the penitent as though he were an oracle about to give utterance.

And give utterance he did. "He is still abed." And, coming back to his senses, the man carefully drew the hood forward to conceal his face once more.

Francesco clutched Baroncelli's elbow and hissed again. "We must go to the Medici Palace at once!"

Smiling, Francesco steered Baroncelli to the left, away from the distracted Lorenzo de' Medici and past a handful of Florentine notables that comprised the first row of worshipers. They did not use the nearby northern door that led out to the Via de' Servi, as their exit would more likely have drawn Lorenzo's attention.

Instead, the pair moved down the outermost aisle that ran the intimidating length of the sanctuary—past brown stone columns the width of four men, which were connected by high, white arches framing long windows of stained glass. Francesco's expression was at first benign as he passed acquaintance after acquaintance in the first few rows, nodding greetings as he went. Baroncelli, dazed, did his best to murmur salutations to those he knew, but Francesco pushed him along so swiftly, he scarce could catch his breath.

Hundreds of faces, hundreds of bodies. Empty, the cathedral would have seemed infinitely vast; filled to capacity on this fifth Sunday after Easter, it seemed cramped, crowded, and airless. Each face that turned to meet Baroncelli seemed filled with suspicion.

The first group of worshipers they passed consisted of Florence's wealthy: glittering women and men weighed down by gold and jewels, by fur-trimmed brocades and velvets. The smell of the men's rosemary and lavender water mingled with the more volatile, feminine scent of attar of roses, all wafting above the base notes of smoke and frankincense from the altar.

Francesco's velvet slippers whispered rapidly against the inlaid marble; his expression grew sterner once he moved past the aristocracy. The aroma of lavender increased as the two men walked past rows of men and women dressed in silks and fine wool, embellished with the glint of gold here and silver there, even the spark of an occasional diamond. Unsmiling, Francesco nodded once or twice to lower-ranking business associates. Baroncelli struggled to breathe; the onrush of faces—witnesses, all of them—triggered a profound panic within him.

But Francesco did not slow. As they passed the middle-class tradesmen, the smiths and bakers, the artists and their apprentices, the smell of fragrant herbs gave way to that of perspiration, and the fine fabrics to the coarser weaves of wool and silk.

The poor stood in the final rows at the back: the wool carders, unable to muffle their coughing, and the fabric dyers, with their darkly stained hands. Their garments consisted of tattered wool and rumpled linen, perfumed with sweat and filth. Both Francesco and Baroncelli involuntarily covered their mouths and noses.

At last, they made their way out of the huge open doors. Baroncelli took a great sobbing gasp of air.

"No time for cowardice!" Francesco snapped, and dragged him down into the street, past the clawing arms of beggars planted crosslegged on the church steps, past the slender, towering campanile to their left.

They made their way through the great open piazza, past the octagonal Baptistery of San Giovanni, dwarfed by the Duomo. The temptation to run was great, but too dangerous, although they still made their way at a pace which left Baroncelli breathless despite the fact that his legs were twice the length of his employer's. After the dimness of the Duomo, sunlight seemed harsh. It was a gloriously beautiful, cloudless spring day, yet to Baroncelli it seemed ominous all the same.

They veered north onto the Via Larga, sometimes referred to as "the street of the Medici." It was impossible to set foot upon its worn flagstones and not feel Lorenzo's iron grip upon the city. The wide street was lined with the palazzi of his supporters: of Michelozzo, the family architect, of Angelo Poliziano, poet and protégé. Farther down, out of sight, stood the church and convent of San Marco. Lorenzo's grandfather, Cosimo, had rebuilt the crumbling cathedral and founded the convent's famous library; in return, the Dominican monks revered him and provided him with his own cell for those times he was given to contemplation.

Cosimo had even purchased the gardens near the monastery, and Lorenzo had transformed them into a sculpture garden, a luxurious training ground for young architects and artists.

Baroncelli and his co-conspirator approached the intersection with the Via de' Gori, where the cupola of Florence's oldest cathedral, San Lorenzo, dominated the western skyline. It had fallen into ruin, and Cosimo, with the help of Michelozzo and Brunelleschi, had restored its grandeur. His bones rested there now, with his marble tombstone set before the high altar.

At last, the two men reached their destination: the rectangular gray bulk of the Medici palazzo, somber and stern as a fortress—the architect, Michelozzo, had been given strict instruction that the building was not to be ornate, lest it rouse suspicion that the Medici considered themselves above plain citizens. Yet the modest design still emanated sufficient magnificence to be suitable for entertaining kings and princes; Charles VII of France had dined in the great hall.

It struck Baroncelli that the building resembled its current owner: The ground floor was made of rough-hewn, rustic stone, the second floor of even brick, and the third was crafted of perfectly smooth stone capped by an overhanging cornice. The face Lorenzo presented to the world was just as polished, yet his foundation, his heart, was rough and cold enough to do anything to maintain control over the city.

It had taken barely four minutes to reach the Palazzo of the Medici, which dominated the corner of the Vias Larga and Gori. Those four minutes passed as though they were hours; those four minutes passed so swiftly Baroncelli could not even recall walking down the street.

At the southern corner of the building, closest to the Duomo, stood the loggia. It was covered from the elements, but broad archways offered its shelter to the street. Here, citizens of Florence were free to meet with others and converse, ofttimes with Lorenzo or Giuliano; a good deal of business was conducted beneath its stone ceiling.

On this Sunday morning, most folk were at Mass; only two men lingered in the loggia, talking softly. One of them—wearing a wool tabard that marked him as a merchant and possibly one of the Medici's own bankers—turned to scowl at Baroncelli, who ducked his head, nervous at the prospect of being seen and remembered.

A few steps more, and the two conspirators stopped at the thick brass doors of the palazzo's main entrance on the Via Larga. Francesco pounded adamantly on the metal; his efforts were finally rewarded by the appearance of a servant, who led them into the magnificent courtyard.

Thus began the agony of waiting while Giuliano was summoned. Had Baroncelli not been in the grip of fear at that particular moment, he might have been able to enjoy his surroundings. At each corner of the courtyard stood a great stone column connected to the others by graceful arches. Atop those was a frieze, adorned with pagan-themed medallions alternating with the Medici crest.

The seven famous *palle,* or balls, were arranged in what looked suspiciously like a crown. To hear Lorenzo tell it, the *palle* represented dents in the shield of one of Charlemagne's knights, the brave Averardo, who had fought a fearsome giant and won. So impressed was Charlemagne that he allowed Averardo to design his coat of arms from the battered shield. The Medici claimed descent from the brave knight, and the family had borne the crest for centuries. The cry *"Palle! Palle! Palle!"* was used to rally the people on the Medici's behalf. Of Cosimo the Elder, it had been said that he had branded even the monks' privates with his balls.

Baroncelli let his gaze follow the path from one medallion to the next. One showed Athena, defending the city of Athens; another remembered the winged Icarus, soaring for the heavens.

At last he dropped his gaze to the courtyard's centerpiece, Donatello's bronze *David.* The sculpture had always struck Baroncelli as effeminate. Long curls spilled out from beneath David's straw shepherd's hat; his naked, curving form bore no masculine muscularity. Indeed, one elbow was crooked with the hand resting on the hip in a girlish posture.

On this day, Baroncelli drew a totally different impression from the statue. He saw the coldness in David's eyes as the boy stared down at the head of the slain Goliath; he could see the keenness of the great sword in David's right hand.

Which role shall I play today? Baroncelli wondered. *David, or Goliath?*

Beside him, Francesco de' Pazzi was pacing the floor with his hands clasped behind his back and his small eyes glaring downward at polished marble. Giuliano had best come soon, Baroncelli reflected, or Francesco would begin muttering to himself.

But Giuliano did not appear. The servant, a comely youth, as well oiled as every part of the Medici machinery, returned with a look of practiced sympathy. "Signori, forgive me. I am so sorry to tell you that my master is currently indisposed and cannot receive company."

Francesco barely managed to replace his fright with joviality in time. "Ah! Please explain to Ser Giuliano that the matter is most urgent." He lowered his tone as if confiding a secret. "Today's luncheon is in the young Cardinal Riario's honor, you see, and he is sorely disappointed that Ser Giuliano will not be attending. The Cardinal is at the Duomo now with Ser Lorenzo, asking after your master. Mass has been delayed on this account, and I fear that should Ser Giuliano fail to come with us now, the Cardinal will take offense. We would not want him to report this to his uncle, the Pope, when he returns to Rome. . . ."

The servant nodded graciously while wearing a small frown of concern. Yet Baroncelli sensed he was not quite convinced he should further disturb his master. Francesco clearly sensed the same, for he pressed harder. "We are here at the behest of Ser Lorenzo, who bids his brother come, and swiftly, as we are all waiting. . . ."

The youth signaled his understanding of the urgency with a quick lift of his chin. "Of course. I will relay all that you have said to my master."

As the lad turned, Baroncelli gazed on his employer, and marveled at his talent for duplicity.

Soon footsteps sounded on the marble stairs leading down to the courtyard, and then Giuliano de' Medici stood before them. Though his brother's features were imperfect, Giuliano's were without flaw.

His nose, though prominent, was straight and nicely rounded at the tip, and his jaw was strong and square; his eyes, large and golden brown, were framed by long lashes that were the envy of every Florentine woman. Delicate, well-formed lips rested atop even teeth, and his hair was full and curling, parted down the middle and brushed back to better show his handsome visage.

At twenty-four, life was good to Giuliano; he was young, lively, fair of face and voice. Yet his good nature and sensitive character ensured that he never made another feel inadequate. Indeed, his cheerful, generous nature made him generally loved by Florence's citizens. While he might not have shared his brother's painful brilliance at politics, he was astute enough to use his other attributes to gain public support. Were Lorenzo to die, Giuliano would have no difficulty in taking up the reins of power.

Over the past few weeks, Baroncelli had tried hard to despise him, and failed.

This morning the faint light that had begun to paint the bottoms of the columns revealed that Giuliano's glory was sorely dimmed. His hair had not been combed, his clothes had been hastily donned—and his eyes were noticeably bloodshot. For the first time in Baroncelli's memory, Giuliano did not smile. He moved slowly, like a man weighed down by heavy armor. *Icarus,* Baroncelli thought. *He soared too high and has now fallen, scorched, to Earth.*

Giuliano spoke, his normally melodic voice hoarse. "Good day, gentlemen. I understand Cardinal Riario has taken offense at my absence from Mass."

Baroncelli felt a strange sensation in his chest, like that of his heart flipping over. Giuliano looked like a beast resigned to the slaughter. *He knows. He cannot possibly know. And yet . . . he knows. . . .*

"We are so sorry to disturb you," Francesco de' Pazzi said, his hands clasped in an apologetic gesture. "We have come at the behest of Ser Lorenzo. . . ."

Giuliano released a short sigh. "I understand. God knows, we must take care to please Lorenzo." A glimmer of his old self returned, and he added with apparently genuine concern, "I only hope it is not too late to reassure the Cardinal that I hold him in the highest regard."

"Yes," Baroncelli said slowly. "Let us hope it is not too late. Mass has already started."

"Let us go, then," Giuliano said. He gestured for them to move back toward the entryway. As he lifted his arm, Baroncelli took note that Giuliano had dressed so hurriedly that he wore no sword at his hip.

Out they went, the three of them, into the bright morning.

The scowling man who had been waiting out in the loggia glanced up as Giuliano passed. "Ser Giuliano," he called. "A word with you; it is most important."

Giuliano looked over and clearly recognized him.

"The Cardinal," Francesco urged frantically, then addressed the man himself. "Good man, Ser Giuliano is late for an urgent appointment and begs your understanding." And with that, he took Giuliano by the arm and dragged him away down the Via Larga.

Baroncelli followed. He marveled that although he was still terrified, his hands no longer shook, and his heart and breath no longer failed him. Indeed, he and Francesco joked and laughed and played the role of good friends trying to cheer another. Giuliano smiled faintly at their efforts but lagged behind, so the two conspirators made a game of alternately pulling and pushing him along. "We must not keep the Cardinal waiting," Baroncelli repeated at least thrice.

"Pray tell, good Giuliano," Francesco said, catching the young man by his sleeve. "What has happened to make you sigh so? Surely your heart has not been stolen by some worthless wench?"

Giuliano lowered his gaze and shook his head—not in reply, but rather in indication that he did not wish to broach such matters. Francesco dropped the subject at once. Yet he never eased their pace, and within minutes, they arrived at the front entry of the Duomo.

Baroncelli paused. The thought of Giuliano moving so slowly, as though he were heavily laden, pricked at him. Feigning impulsiveness, he seized the young Medici and hugged him tightly. "Dear friend," he said. "It troubles me to see you unhappy. What must we do to cheer you?"

Giuliano gave another forced little smile and a slight shake of his head. "Nothing, good Bernardo. Nothing."

And he followed Francesco's lead into the cathedral.

Baroncelli, meanwhile, had laid one concern to rest: Giuliano wore no breastplate beneath his tunic.

IV

*O*n that late April morning, Giuliano faced a terrible decision: He must choose to break the heart of one of the two people he loved most in the world. One heart belonged to his brother, Lorenzo; the other, to a woman.

Though a young man, Giuliano had known many lovers. His former mistress, Simonetta Cattaneo, wife of Marco Vespucci, had been hailed as the most beautiful woman in Florence until her death two years ago. He had chosen Simonetta for her looks: She was fine-boned and fair, with masses of curling golden hair that fell far below her waist. So lovely was she that they had carried her to her grave with her face exposed. Out of deference to the husband and family, Giuliano had watched from a distance, but he had wept with them.

Even so, he had never been faithful. He had dallied with other women and occasionally he had reveled in the talents of whores.

Now, for the first time in his life, Giuliano desired only one woman: Anna. She was handsome, to be sure, but it was her intelligence that had entrapped him, her delight in life, and the greatness of her heart. He had come to know her slowly, through conversation at banquets and parties. She had never flirted, never attempted to win him; indeed, she had done everything possible to discourage him. But none of the dozens of Florentine noblewomen who vied and simpered for his affections matched her. Simonetta had been vapid; Anna had the soul of a poet, a saint.

Her goodness made Giuliano see his former life as repugnant. He abandoned all other women and sought the company of only Anna, yearned to please only her. Just the sight of her made him want to beg her forgiveness for his past carnal indulgences. He longed for her grace more than God's.

And it seemed like a miracle when she at last confided her feelings: that God had created them for each other, and that it was His cruelest joke that she was already given to another man.

As passionate as Anna's love for him was, her love of purity and decency was even greater. She belonged to another, whom she refused to betray. She admitted her feelings for Giuliano, but when he cornered her alone during Carnival at his brother's house and begged for her, she rejected him. *Duty,* she had said. *Responsibility.* She had sounded like Lorenzo, who had always insisted his brother make an advantageous match and marry a woman who would add even more prestige to the family.

Giuliano, accustomed to having whatever he wanted, tried to bargain his way around it. He pleaded with her to at least come to him in private—simply to hear him out. She wavered, but then agreed. They had met once, in the ground-floor *appartamento* at the Medici palazzo. She had indulged in his embraces, his kiss, but would go no further. He had begged her to leave Florence, to go away with him, but she had refused.

"He knows." Her voice had been anguished. "Do you understand? He knows, and I cannot bear to hurt him any longer."

Giuliano was a determined man. Neither God nor societal convention gave him pause once he had made up his mind. For Anna, he was willing to give up the prospect of a respectable marriage; for Anna, he was willing to endure the censure of the Church, even excommunication and the prospect of damnation.

And so he had made a forceful argument: She should go with him to Rome, to stay in a family villa. The Medici had papal connections;

he would procure for her an annulment. He would marry her. He would give her children.

She had been torn, had put her hands to her lips. He looked in her eyes and saw the misery there, but he also saw a flicker of hope.

"I don't know; I don't know," she had said, and he had let her return to her husband to make her decision.

The next day, he had gone to Lorenzo.

He had wakened early and been unable to return to sleep. It was still dark—two hours before sunrise—but he was not surprised to see light emanating from his brother's antechamber. Lorenzo sat at his desk with his cheek propped against his fist, scowling down at a letter he held close to the glowing lamp.

Normally Lorenzo would have looked up, would have forced away the frown to smile, to utter a greeting; that day, however, he seemed in uncommonly ill sorts. No greeting came; Lorenzo gave him a cursory glance, then looked back at the letter. Its contents were apparently the cause of his bad humor.

Lorenzo could be maddeningly stubborn at times, overly concerned with appearances, coldly calculating when it came to politics, and at times dictatorial concerning how Giuliano should comport himself and with whom he should allow himself to be seen. But he could also be enormously indulgent, generous, and sensitive to his younger brother's wishes. Although Giuliano had never desired power, Lorenzo always shared information with him, always discussed with him the political ramifications of every civic event. It was clear that Lorenzo loved his brother deeply and would gladly have shared control of the city with him, had Giuliano ever shown an interest.

It had been hard enough for Lorenzo to lose his father and to be forced to assume power when so young. True, he had the talent for it, but Giuliano could see it wore on him. After nine years, the strain showed. Permanent creases had established themselves on his brow; shadows had formed beneath his eyes.

A part of Lorenzo reveled in the power and delighted in extending the family's influence. The Medici Bank had branches in Rome, in Bruges, in most of the greater cities of Europe. Yet Lorenzo was often exhausted by the demands of playing the *gran maestro*. At times, he complained, "Not a soul in the city will marry without my blessing." Quite true. And that very week, he had received a letter from a congregation in rural Tuscany, begging for his advice: The church fathers had approved the creation of a saint's statue; two sculptors were vying for the commission. Would the great Lorenzo be so kind as to give his opinion? Such missives piled up in great stacks each day; Lorenzo rose before dawn and answered them in his own hand. He fretted over Florence as a father would over a wayward child, and spent every waking moment dedicated to furthering her prosperity and the Medici interests.

But he was keenly aware that no one loved him, save for the favors he could bestow. Only Giuliano adored his brother truly, for himself. Only Giuliano tried to make Lorenzo forget his responsibilities; only Giuliano could make him laugh. For that, Lorenzo loved him fiercely.

And it was the repercussions of that love Giuliano feared.

Now, staring at his distracted brother, Giuliano straightened and cleared his throat. "I am going," he said, rather loudly, "to Rome."

Lorenzo lifted his brows and his gaze, but the rest of him did not stir. "On pleasure, or on some business I should acquaint myself with?"

"I am going with a woman."

Lorenzo sighed; his frown eased. "Enjoy yourself, then, and think of me suffering here."

"I am going with Madonna Anna," Giuliano said.

Lorenzo jerked his head sharply at the name. "You're joking." He said it lightly, but as he stared at Giuliano, his expression grew incredulous. "You *must* be joking." His voice fell to a whisper. "This is foolishness. . . . Giuliano, she is from a good family. And she is *married*."

Giuliano did not quail. "I love her. I won't be without her. I've asked her to go with me to Rome, to live."

Lorenzo's eyes widened; the letter slipped from his hand and fluttered to the floor, but he did not retrieve it. "Giuliano . . . Our hearts mislead us all, from time to time. You're enthralled by an emotion; believe me, I understand. But it will ease. Give yourself a fortnight to re-think this idea."

Lorenzo's paternal, dismissive tone only strengthened Giuliano's resolve. "I've already arranged the carriage and driver, and sent a mes-sage to the servants at the Roman villa to prepare for us. We must seek an annulment," he said. "I don't say this lightly. I want to marry Anna. I want her to bear my children."

Lorenzo leaned back in his chair and stared intently at his brother, as if trying to judge whether he were an impostor. When he was satis-fied that the words had been meant, Lorenzo let go a short, bitter laugh. "An annulment? Courtesy of our good friend Pope Sixtus, I suppose? He would prefer to see us banished from Italy." He pushed himself away from his desk, rose, and reached for his brother; his tone softened. "This is a fantasy, Giuliano. I understand that she is a mar-velous woman, but . . . she has been married for some years. Even if I *could* arrange for an annulment, it would create a scandal. Florence would never accept it."

Lorenzo's hand was almost on his shoulder; Giuliano shifted it back, away from the conciliatory touch. "I don't care what Florence will or won't accept. We'll remain in Rome, if we have to."

Lorenzo emitted a sharp sigh of frustration. "You'll get no annul-ment from Sixtus. So give up your romantic ideals: If you can't live without her, have her—but for God's sake, do so discreetly."

Giuliano flared. "How can you speak of her like that? You know Anna; you know she would never stoop to deception. And if I can't have her, I won't have any other woman. You can stop all your match-making efforts right now. If I can't marry her—"

Even as he spoke, he felt his argument fail. Lorenzo's eyes were filled with a peculiar light—furious and fierce, verging on madness—a light that made Giuliano think his brother was capable of malevo-lence. He had seen such a look in Lorenzo's eyes only rarely—never before had it been directed at him—and it chilled him.

"You'll do what? Refuse to marry anyone at all?" Lorenzo shook his head vehemently; his voice grew louder. "You have a duty, an obli-gation to your family. You think you can go to Rome on a whim, pass our blood on to a litter of bastards? You would stain us with excommunication? Because that's what would happen, you know—to both of you! Sixtus is in no mood to be generous to us."

Giuliano said nothing; the flesh on his cheeks and neck burned. He had expected no less, though he had hoped for more.

Lorenzo continued; the hand that had reached for his brother now became a jabbing, accusatory finger. "Do you have any idea of what will happen to *Anna*? What people will call her? She's a decent woman, a good woman. Do you really want to ruin her? You'll take her to Rome and grow tired of her. You'll want to come home to Florence. And what will she have left?"

Angry words scalded Giuliano's tongue. He wanted to say that although Lorenzo had married a harridan, he, Giuliano, would rather die than live in such loveless misery, that he would never stoop to fathering children upon a woman he despised. But he remained silent; he was unhappy enough. There was no point in making Lorenzo suffer the truth, too.

Lorenzo emitted a growl of disgust. "You'll never do it. You'll come to your senses."

Giuliano looked at him a long moment. "I love you, Lorenzo," he said quietly. "But I am going." He turned and moved to the door.

"Leave with her," his brother threatened, "and you can forget that I am your brother. Don't imagine I am joking, Giuliano. I'll have nothing more to do with you. Leave with her, and you'll never see me again."

Giuliano looked back over his shoulder at Lorenzo and was suddenly afraid. He and his older brother did not joke with each other when they discussed important matters—and neither could be swayed when he had made up his mind. "Please don't make me choose."

Lorenzo's jaw was set, his gaze cold. "You'll have to."

Later, in the evening, Giuliano had waited in Lorenzo's ground-floor apartment until it was time to meet Anna. He had spent the entire day contemplating Lorenzo's comment about how she would be ruined if she went to Rome. For the first time, he permitted himself to consider what Anna's life would be like if the Pope refused to grant an annulment.

She would know disgrace and censure; she would be forced to give up her family, her friends, her native city. Her children would be called bastards and be denied their inheritance as Medici heirs.

He had been selfish. He had been thinking only of himself when he made the offer to Anna. He had spoken too easily of the annulment, in hopes that it would sway her to go with him. And he had not, until that moment, considered that she might reject his offer; the possibility had seemed too painful to contemplate.

Now he realized that it would save him from making an agonizing choice.

But when he went to meet her at the door and saw her face in the dying light, he saw that his choice had been long ago made, at the moment when he gave his heart to Anna. Her eyes, her skin, her face and limbs exuded joy; even in the shadowy dusk, she shone. Her movements, which had once been slow, weighed down by unhappy consequence, were now agile and light. The exuberant tilt of her head as she looked up at him, the faint smile that bloomed on her lips, the swift grace with which she lifted her skirts and rushed to him, relayed her answer more clearly than words.

Her presence breathed such hope into him that he moved quickly to her and held her, and let it infuse him. In that instant, Giuliano realized that he could refuse her nothing, that neither of them could escape the turning of the wheel now set in motion. And the tears that threatened him did not spring from joy; they were tears of grief, for Lorenzo.

He and Anna remained together less than an hour; they spoke little—only enough for Giuliano to convey a time, and a place. No other exchange was needed.

And when she was gone again—taking the light and Giuliano's confidence with her—he went back to his own chamber and called for wine. He drank it sitting on his bed and recalled, with exquisite clarity, an incident from childhood.

. . .

At age six, he had gone with Lorenzo and two of his older sisters, Nannina and Bianca, for a picnic on the shores of the Arno. Attended by a Circassian slave woman, they had traveled by carriage across the Ponte Vecchio, the bridge built a millennium before by the Romans. Nannina had been captivated by the goldsmiths' shops that lined the bridge; soon to be married, she was already interested in womanly things.

Lorenzo had been restless and glum. He had just begun to take on the Medici responsibilities; the year before, he had begun receiving letters asking for his patronage, and their father, Piero, had already sent his eldest son to Milan and Rome on politically motivated trips. He was a homely boy, with wide-set slanting eyes, a jutting jaw, and soft brown hair that fell in a neatly trimmed fringe across a pale, low forehead; yet the sensitive intelligence that shone in those eyes made him oddly attractive.

They made their way to the pastoral neighborhood of Santo Spirito. Giuliano recalled tall trees, and a sweeping grass lawn that sloped down to the placid river. There, the slave woman set a linen cloth on the ground and brought out food for the children. It was late spring, warm with a few lazy clouds, though the day before it had rained. The river Arno was quicksilver when the sun struck it, leaden when it did not.

Lorenzo's sullenness that day made Giuliano sad. It seemed to him that their father was too intent on making Lorenzo an adult before his time. So, to make him laugh, Giuliano had run down to the riverbank, gleefully ignoring the slave's outraged threats, and stomped, splashing, into the water fully clothed.

His antics worked; Lorenzo followed, laughing, tunic, mantle, slippers, and all. By this time, Nannina, Bianca, and the slave were all shouting their disapproval. Lorenzo ignored them. He was a strong swimmer, and soon made his way quite a distance from the shore, then dove beneath the waters.

Giuliano followed tentatively but, being younger, fell behind. He watched as Lorenzo took a great gulp of air and disappeared beneath the gray surface. When he did not reappear immediately, Giuliano treaded water and laughed, expecting his brother to swim beneath him and grasp his foot at any moment.

Seconds passed. Giuliano's laughter turned to silence, then fear— then he began to call for his brother. On the shore, the women— unable to enter the water because of their heavy skirts—began to cry out in panic.

Giuliano was only a child. He had not yet overcome his fear of diving beneath the water, yet love for his brother drove him to suck in a deep breath and submerge himself. The silence there astonished him; he opened his eyes and peered in the direction where Lorenzo had been.

The river was muddy from the previous day's rains; Giuliano's eyes stung as he searched. He could see nothing but a large, irregular dark shape some distance away, deep beneath the waters. It was not human—not Lorenzo—but it was all that was visible, and instinct told him to approach it. He surfaced, drew in more air, then compelled himself to dive down again.

There, the length of three tall men beneath the surface, lay the craggy limbs of a fallen tree.

Giuliano's lungs burned, yet his sense that Lorenzo was nearby made him push against the quiet water. With a final, painful burst, he reached the sunken branches and pressed a palm against the slick surface of the trunk.

At once, he grew remarkably dizzy, and heard a rushing in his ears; he shut his eyes and opened his mouth, gasping for air. There was none to be had, and so he drank in the foul Arno. He retched it up at once; then reflex forced him to gulp in more.

Giuliano was drowning.

Though a child, he understood clearly that he was dying. The realization prompted him to open his eyes, to capture a last glimpse of Earth that he might take with him to Heaven.

At that instant, a cloud moved overhead, permitting a shaft of sunlight to pierce the river so thoroughly that it caused the silt suspended in the water to glitter, and illumined the area directly before Giuliano's eyes.

Staring back at him, an arm's length away, was the drowning Lorenzo. His tunic and mantle had been caught on an errant branch, and he had twisted himself about in a mad effort to be free.

Both brothers should have died then. But Giuliano prayed, with a child's guilelessness: *God, let me save my brother.*

Impossibly, he had pulled the tangled clothing loose from the branch.

Impossibly, the freed Lorenzo had seized Giuliano's hands and pulled the two of them up to the surface.

From there, Giuliano's memory became blurred. He remembered only snippets: of himself vomiting on the grassy shore while the slave woman pounded his back; of Lorenzo wet and shivering, wrapped in picnic linens; of voices calling out: *Brother, speak to me!* Of Lorenzo in the carriage on the ride home, furious, fighting tears: *Don't ever risk yourself for me! You almost died! Father would never forgive me!* . . . But the unspoken message was louder: Lorenzo would never forgive himself.

Recalling the incident, Giuliano swallowed wine without tasting it. He would have gladly surrendered his life to save Lorenzo's—just as easily and thoughtlessly as Lorenzo would have sacrificed himself to save his younger brother. It seemed to Giuliano a mockery that God had given him such a gift as Anna's love—only to require him to wound the man he loved most.

Giuliano sat for hours, watching the darkness of night deepen, then slowly fade to gray with the coming of dawn, and the day he was to leave for Rome. He sat until the arrival of his insistent visitors, Francesco de' Pazzi and Bernardo Baroncelli. He could not imagine why the visiting Cardinal should care so passionately about Giuliano's presence at Mass; but if Lorenzo had asked him to come, then that was good enough reason to do so.

He hoped, with sudden optimism, that Lorenzo might have

changed his mind, that his anger had faded and left him more receptive to discussion.

Thus Giuliano rallied himself and, like a good brother, came as he was bidden.

V

*B*aroncelli hesitated at the door of the cathedral as his objectivity briefly returned to him. Here was a chance to flee fate; a chance, before an alarm could be sounded, to run home to his estate, to mount his horse and head for any kingdom where neither the conspirators nor their victims had influence. The Pazzi were powerful and persistent, capable of mounting efforts to hunt him down—but they were neither as well connected nor as dogged as the Medici.

In the lead, Francesco had turned and goaded Baroncelli on with a murderous glance. Giuliano, still distracted by a private sorrow, was heedless and, flanked by the uncertain Baroncelli, followed Francesco inside. Baroncelli felt he had just crossed the threshold from reason into madness.

Inside, the smoke-filmed air was redolent with frankincense and sweat. The sanctuary's massive interior was dim, save for the area surrounding the altar, which was dazzling in the late morning light streaming from the long arched windows of the cupola.

Again taking the least noticeable path along the north side, Francesco headed toward the altar, followed closely by Giuliano, then Baroncelli. Baroncelli could have closed his eyes and found his way by

smell, measuring the stench of the poor and working class, the lavender scent of the merchants, and the rose of the wealthy.

Even before he caught sight of the priest, Baroncelli could hear
him delivering his homily. The realization quickened Baroncelli's
pulse; they had arrived barely in time, for the Eucharist was soon to
follow.

After the interminable walk down the aisle, Baroncelli and his
companions arrived at the front row of men. They murmured apolo-
gies as they sidled back to their original places. An instant of confusion came as Baroncelli tried to move past Giuliano, so that he could
stand on his right, the position dictated by the plan. Giuliano, not understanding Baroncelli's intent, pressed closer to Francesco—who
then whispered something in the young man's ear. Giuliano nodded,
stepped backward, and made an opening for Baroncelli; in so doing,
he grazed the shoulder of the penitent, who stood waiting behind him.

Both Francesco de' Pazzi and Baroncelli watched, breathless, to see
whether Giuliano would turn and make apology—and perhaps recognize the man. But Giuliano remained lost in his own misery.

Baroncelli craned his neck to look farther down the row, to see if
Lorenzo had noticed; fortunately, the elder Medici brother was busy
bending an ear to a whispered comment from the manager of the family bank, Francesco Nori.

Miraculously, all of the elements were now in place. Baroncelli had
nothing to do save wait—and pretend to listen to the sermon while
keeping his hand from wandering to the hilt at his hip.

The priest's words seemed nonsensical; Baroncelli strained to understand them. *Forgiveness,* the prelate intoned. *Charity. Love thine
enemies; pray for those who persecute you.*

Baroncelli's mind seized upon these phrases. Lorenzo de' Medici
had picked this Sunday's priest himself. Did Lorenzo know of the plot?
Were these seemingly innocuous words a warning not to proceed?

Baroncelli glanced over at Francesco de' Pazzi. If Francesco had detected a secret message, he gave no sign of it; he stared straight ahead
at the altar, his gaze unfocused but his eyes wide, bright with fear and
hatred. A muscle in his narrow jaw twitched madly.

The sermon ended.

The elements of the Mass proceeded with almost comical swiftness: The Creed was sung. The priest chanted the *Dominus vobiscum* and *Oremus.* The Host was consecrated with the prayer *Suscipe, sancte Pater.*

Baroncelli drew in a breath and thought he would never be able to release it. The ceremony abruptly slowed; in his ears, he could feel the desperate thrum of his heart.

The priest's assistant approached the altar to fill the golden chalice with wine; a second assistant added a small amount of water from a crystal decanter.

At last, the priest took the chalice. Carefully, he lifted it heavenward, proffering it to the large wooden carving of a dolorous, crucified Christ suspended above the altar.

Baroncelli's gaze followed the cup. A shaft of sunlight caught the gold and reflected blindingly off the metal.

Again, the priest chanted, in a wavering tenor that sounded vaguely accusatory.

Offerimus tibi, Domine . . .

Baroncelli turned to look at the younger Medici next to him. Giuliano's expression was grave, his eyes closed. His right hand was clenched in a fist; his left hand clasped it, and both were pressed tightly to his lips. His head was bowed, as if he were preparing to greet Death.

This is foolish, Baroncelli thought. He had no personal enmity toward this man; indeed, he liked Giuliano, who had never asked to be born a Medici. His quarrel with him was purely political, and certainly not great enough to warrant what he was about to do.

Francesco de' Pazzi jabbed Baroncelli fiercely in the ribs, relating the unspoken message perfectly: *The signal has been given! The signal has been given!*

Baroncelli released a reluctant, inaudible sigh and drew his great knife from its hilt.

VI

moment earlier, Lorenzo de' Medici was engaged in courteous but muted conversation with Cardinal Raffaele Riario. Although the priest was finishing up his sermon, the wealthy power brokers of Florence thought nothing of discussing matters of pleasure or business—sotto voce—during Mass. The social opportunity was simply too great to ignore, and the priests had long ago become inured to it.

A scrawny lad, Riario looked younger than his seventeen years, and though he was currently a student of law at the University of Pisa, his enrollment there was clearly due more to his kinship with Pope Sixtus than any native intelligence.

Nephew, Sixtus called him. It was the euphemism by which popes and cardinals sometimes referred to their bastard children. The Pope was an extremely clever man, but obviously had got this boy on a woman with charms other than beauty or brains.

Even so, Lorenzo was obliged to show the young Cardinal a fine time while he was visiting Florence. Riario had specifically asked to meet with the Medici brothers and to be given a tour of their property and collection of art; Lorenzo could not refuse. This was the Pope's

so-called nephew—and although Lorenzo had endured public humiliation at Sixtus' hands, even been forced to hold his tongue while the
Medici were replaced by the Pazzi as the papal bankers—perhaps this
was an overture. Perhaps Sixtus was trying to make amends, and this
gangly young creature in scarlet robes was his emissary.

Lorenzo was eager to return to the family palace to ascertain
whether this was indeed the case; otherwise, the Cardinal's visit would
irritate him greatly, if Sixtus was simply taking brazen advantage of
Lorenzo's generosity. It would be another insult.

But in case it was not, Lorenzo had called for a magnificent feast to
be served after Mass in honor of the Cardinal. And if it happened that
young Raffaele had come only out of a desire to enjoy the Medici art,
he could at least report to his uncle that Lorenzo had treated him lav-
ishly and well. It could serve as a diplomatic opening, one that
Lorenzo would use to full advantage, for he was determined to re-
claim the papal coffers from the clutches of the Pazzi Bank.

And so Lorenzo practiced his most gracious behavior, even though
Francesco Salviati, Archbishop of Pisa, stood smiling disingenuously
on Riario's other flank. Lorenzo had no personal quarrel with Salviati,
though he had fought long and bitterly against his appointment as
archbishop. As she was controlled by Florence, Pisa deserved an archbishop of Medici blood—and Salviati was related to the Pazzi, who already were gaining too much favor with the Pope. While the Medici
and the Pazzi publicly embraced one another as friends, in the arena of
business and politics, there were no fiercer adversaries. Lorenzo had
written an impassioned letter to Sixtus, explaining why appointment
of a Pazzi relative as Archbishop would be disastrous to papal and
Medici interests.

Sixtus not only failed to respond, he ultimately dismissed the
Medici as his bankers.

Most would consider the papal request that Riario and Salviati be
treated as honored guests a stinging blow to Medici dignity. But
Lorenzo, ever the diplomat, welcomed them. And he insisted that his
dear friend and senior manager of the Medici Bank, Francesco Nori,

show not the slightest sign of offense. Nori, who stood beside him now in silent support, was desperately protective of Lorenzo. When the news came from Rome that the Pazzi had been appointed the papal bankers and the Medici were ousted, Nori had raged incessantly. Lorenzo had been obliged to calm his employee, though he had held his own anger in check, and spoke little of the affair. He could not afford the energy; he was already too busy scheming how he might win Sixtus back.

So he had exchanged pleasantries with the young Cardinal throughout the service and, from a distance, smiled a greeting to the Pazzi, who were in full attendance. Most of them had gathered at the other side of the cathedral, except for Guglielmo de' Pazzi, who stuck to the Archbishop's side like a burr. Lorenzo honestly liked Guglielmo; he had known him since he, Lorenzo, was a boy of sixteen, when Guglielmo had escorted him to Naples to meet Crown Prince Federigo. The older man had treated him like a son then, and Lorenzo had never forgotten. In time, Guglielmo married Lorenzo's older sister, Bianca, strengthening his position as a friend to the Medici.

At the start of the sermon, the boy Cardinal gave a strange, sickly smile and whispered, "Your brother . . . where is your brother? I thought surely he would come to Mass. I had so hoped to meet him."

The question took Lorenzo by surprise. Although Giuliano had made polite noises about coming to the Mass in order to meet Cardinal Riario, Lorenzo felt certain no one, least of all Giuliano, had taken the promise seriously. The most famous womanizer in Florence, Giuliano was notorious for his failure to appear at formal or diplomatic functions—unless Lorenzo insisted vehemently upon it. (Certainly he had not done so here.) Giuliano had already proclaimed himself unable to attend the luncheon.

Lorenzo had been thoroughly taken aback the previous day when Giuliano had announced his desire to run off to Rome with a married woman. Up to that point, Giuliano had taken none of his lovers very seriously; he had never spouted such foolishness before and certainly had never spoken of marriage. It had always been understood that, when the time came, Lorenzo would choose his bride and Giuliano would submit.

But Giuliano had been adamant about getting the woman an annulment—an achievement which, if Cardinal Riario had *not* come as a papal overture, was well beyond Lorenzo's grasp.

Lorenzo was frightened for his younger brother. Giuliano was too trusting, too willing to see the good in others, to realize he had many enemies—enemies who hated him solely for the fact he had been born a Medici. He could not see, as Lorenzo did, that they would use this affair with Anna to tear him down.

Giuliano, the sweet soul, thought only of love. Though it had been necessary, Lorenzo had not relished being cruel to him. And he could not blame Giuliano for his noble view of the tender sex. At times, he yearned for the freedom his younger brother enjoyed. This morning Lorenzo particularly envied him; would that he could linger in the arms of a beautiful woman and let Giuliano deal with the Pope's nephew—who was still gazing politely at Lorenzo, waiting to learn the whereabouts of his wayward brother.

It would be impolitic to tell the Cardinal the truth—that Giuliano had never really intended to come to Mass, or meet Riario—and so instead Lorenzo indulged in a polite lie. "My brother must have been detained. Surely he will be here soon; I know he is eager to meet Your Holiness."

Riario blinked; his girlish lips thinned.

Ah, Lorenzo thought. Perhaps young Raffaele's interest was more than superficially diplomatic. Giuliano's handsomeness was legendary, and he had stirred the passions of at least as many men as women.

Guglielmo de' Pazzi leaned across the Archbishop and gave the Cardinal an encouraging pat on the shoulder. "Have no fear, Holiness. He will come. The Medici always treat their guests well."

Lorenzo smiled warmly at him; Guglielmo dropped his gaze without meeting Lorenzo's and gave a quick nod of acknowledgment, but did not return the smile. The gesture seemed odd, but Lorenzo was at once distracted by Francesco Nori's whisper.

"*Maestro. . . .* your brother has just arrived."

"Alone?"

Nori glanced briefly to his left, at the north side of the sacristy. "He has come with Francesco de' Pazzi and Bernardo Baroncelli. I do not like the look of it."

Lorenzo frowned; he did not care for it, either. He had already greeted Francesco and Baroncelli when he had first entered the cathedral. His diplomatic instincts took hold of him, however; he inclined his head toward Raffaele Riario and said softly, "You see, Holiness? My brother has indeed come."

Beside him, Cardinal Riario leaned forward, looked to his left, and caught sight of Giuliano. He gave Lorenzo an odd, tremulous grin, then with a snap of his head, forced his gaze back to the altar, where the priest was blessing the sacred Host.

The lad's movement was so peculiar, so nervous, that Lorenzo felt a faint stirring of anxiety. Florence was always full of rumors, most of which he ignored; but Nori had recently reported that Lorenzo was in danger, that an attack was being planned against him. As usual, Nori could offer no specifics.

Ridiculous, Lorenzo had scoffed. *There will always be whispers, but we are the Medici. The Pope himself might insult us, but even he dare not lift his hand against us.*

Now, he felt a pang of doubt. Beneath the cover of his mantle, he fingered the hilt of his short sword, then gripped it tightly.

Only seconds later, a shout came from the direction Riario had glanced—a man's voice, the words unintelligible, impassioned. Immediately after, the bells of Giotto's campanile began to toll.

Lorenzo knew at once that Nori's so-called rumors were fact.

The front two rows of men broke rank, and the scene became a clumsy dance of moving bodies. In the near distance, a woman screamed. Salviati disappeared; the young Cardinal flung himself at the altar and knelt, sobbing uncontrollably. Guglielmo de' Pazzi, clearly terrified, began wringing his hands and wailing. "I am no traitor! I knew nothing of this! Nothing! Before God, Lorenzo, I am completely innocent!"

Lorenzo did not see the hand that reached from behind him and lightly settled on his left shoulder—but he felt it as though it were a lightning bolt. With grace and strength that came from years of swordsmanship, he pushed forward out of the unseen enemy's grasp, drew his sword, and whirled about.

During the sudden movement, a keen blade grazed him just below the right ear; involuntarily, he gasped at the sensation of his tender skin parting, of warm liquid flowing down his neck onto his shoulder. But he stayed on his feet and held up his sword, ready to block further attacks.

Lorenzo faced two priests: one trembling behind a small shield, halfheartedly clutching a sword as he glanced at the crowd scrambling about him—most of them headed for the cathedral doors. But he was obliged to turn his attention to Lorenzo's personal attendant, Marco, a muscular man who, though no expert with a sword, made up for it with brute strength and enthusiasm.

The second priest—wild-eyed and intent on Lorenzo—raised his weapon for a second attempt.

Lorenzo parried once, twice. Haggard, pale-skinned, unshaven, this priest had the fiery eyes, the open, contorted mouth of a madman. He also had the strength of one, and Lorenzo came close to buckling beneath his blows. Steel clashed against steel, ringing off the high ceilings of the now mostly deserted cathedral.

The two fighters locked blades, pressing hilt against hilt with a ferocity that caused Lorenzo's hand to tremble. He stared into the eyes of his determined enemy, and drew in a breath at the emotion he saw there.

As the two stood with blades crossed, neither willing to give way, Lorenzo half shouted, "Why should you hate me so?"

He meant the question sincerely. He had always wished the best for Florence and her citizens. He did not understand the resentment others felt at the utterance of the name Medici.

"For God," the priest said. His face was a mere hand's breadth from his intended victim's. Sweat ran down his pale forehead; his breath was hot upon Lorenzo's cheek. His nose was long, narrow, aristocratic; he probably came from an old, respected family. "For the love of God!"

And he drew back his weapon so forcefully that Lorenzo staggered forward, perilously close to the blade.

VII

*E*arlier, as he drew his long knife and hefted it overhead, Baroncelli remembered all the dozens of phrases he had rehearsed for this instant; none of them came to his lips, and what he finally shouted sounded ridiculous to his own ears.

"Here, traitor!"

The church bells had just begun clanging when Giuliano looked up. At the sight of the knife, his eyes widened with mild surprise.

Yielding at last to madness, Baroncelli did not hesitate. He brought the blade down.

Lorenzo stumbled, off balance, toward his opponent—and let go a roar of self-disgust at the realization that he would never be able to lift his sword in time to fend off the coming blow.

But before the wild-eyed priest could shed any more of Lorenzo's blood, Francesco Nori stepped in front of his employer with his sword drawn. Other friends and supporters began to close in around the would-be assassins. Lorenzo became vaguely aware of the presence of Angelo Poliziano, of the aged and portly architect Michelozzo, of the family sculptor Verrocchio, of a business associate, Antonio Ridolfo, of the socialite Sigismondo della Stuffa. This crowd sealed him off from his attacker and began to press him toward the altar.

Lorenzo resisted. "Giuliano!" he cried. "Brother, where are you?"

"We will find and protect him. Now, go!" Nori ordered, gesturing with his chin toward the altar, where the priests, in their alarm, had dropped the full chalice, staining the altarcloth with wine.

Lorenzo hesitated.

"*Go!*" Nori shouted again. "They are headed here! Go past them, to the north sacristy!"

Lorenzo had no idea who *they* were, but he acted. Still clutching his sword, he hurdled over the low railing and leapt into the octagonal carved wooden structure that housed the choir. Cherubic boys shrieked as they scattered, their white robes flapping like the wings of startled birds.

Followed by his protectors, Lorenzo pushed his way through the flailing choir and staggered toward the great altar. The astringent smoke of frankincense mixed with the fragrance of spilled wine; two tall, heavy candelabra were ablaze. The priest and his assistants now encircled the blubbering Riario protectively. Lorenzo blinked at them. The afterimage from the lit tapers left him near blinded, and in an instant of dizziness, he put his free hand to his neck; it came away bloodied.

Yet he willed himself, for Giuliano's sake, not to faint. He could not permit himself a moment's weakness—not until his brother was safe.

At the same moment that Lorenzo ran north across the altar, Francesco de' Pazzi and Bernardo Baroncelli, down in the sanctuary, were pushing their way south, clearly unaware that they were passing their intended target.

Lorenzo stopped in mid-stride to gape at them, causing collisions within his trailing entourage.

Baroncelli led the way, brandishing a long knife and shouting unintelligibly. Francesco was limping badly; his thigh was bloodied, his tunic spattered with crimson.

Lorenzo strained to see past those surrounding him, to look beyond the moving bodies to the place where his brother had been standing, but his view was obstructed.

"Giuliano!" he screamed, with all the strength he possessed, praying he would be heard above the pandemonium. "Giuliano . . . ! Where are you? Brother, speak to me!"

The crowd closed around him. "It's all right," someone said, in a tone so dubious it failed to provoke the comfort it intended.

It was *not* all right that Giuliano should be missing. From the day of his father's death, Lorenzo had cared for his brother with a love both fraternal and paternal. "Giuliano!" Lorenzo screamed again. "Giuliano . . . !"

"He is not there," a muffled voice replied. Thinking it meant his brother had moved south to find him, Lorenzo turned back in that direction, where his friends still fought the assassins. The smaller priest with the shield had fled altogether, but the madman remained, though he was losing the battle with Marco. Giuliano was nowhere to be seen.

Discouraged, Lorenzo began to turn away, but the glint of swift-moving steel caught his eye and compelled him to look back.

The blade belonged to Bernardo Baroncelli. With a viciousness Lorenzo would never have dreamed him capable of, Baroncelli ran his long knife deep into the pit of Francesco Nori's stomach. Nori's eyes bulged as he stared down at the intrusion; his lips formed a small, perfect O as he fell backward, sliding off Baroncelli's sword.

Lorenzo let go a sob. Poliziano and della Stuffa took his shoulders and pushed him away, across the altar and toward the tall doors of the sacristy. "Get Francesco!" he begged them. "Someone bring Francesco. He is still alive; I know it!"

He tried again to turn, to call out for his brother, but this time his people would not let him slow their relentless march to the sacristy. Lorenzo felt a physical pain in his chest, a pressure so brutal he thought his heart would burst.

He had wounded Giuliano. He had hurt him in his most vulnerable moment, and when Giuliano had said, *I love you, Lorenzo. . . . Please don't make me choose,* Lorenzo had been cruel. Had turned him away, without help—the one thing he owed Giuliano most of all.

How could he explain to the others that he could never leave his younger brother behind? How could he explain the responsibility he felt for Giuliano, who had lost his father so young and had always looked to Lorenzo for guidance? How could he explain the promise he had made to his father on the latter's deathbed? They were all too concerned with the safety of Lorenzo *il Magnifico*, whom they considered to be the greatest man in Florence, but they were wrong, all of them.

Lorenzo was pushed behind the thick, heavy doors of the sacristy. They slammed shut after someone ventured out to fetch the wounded Nori.

Inside, the airless, windowless chamber smelled of sacrificial wine and the dust that had settled on the priests' vestments. Lorenzo grabbed each man who had pushed him to safety; he studied each face, and was each time disappointed. The greatest man in Florence was not here.

He thought of Baroncelli's great curving knife and of the bright blood on Francesco de' Pazzi's thigh and tunic. The images propelled him to move for the doors, with the intention of flinging them open and going back to rescue his brother. But della Stuffa sensed his intention, and immediately pressed his body against the exit. Old Michelozzo joined him, then Antonio Ridolfo; the weight of the three men held the doors shut fast. Lorenzo was pushed to the outer edge of the engraved brass. There was a grimness in their expressions, an unspoken, unspeakable knowledge that Lorenzo could not and would not accept.

Hysterically, he pounded on the cold brass until his fists ached— and then he continued to pound until they bled. The scholar Angelo Poliziano struggled to wrap a piece of wool, torn from his own mantle, around the bleeding cut on Lorenzo's neck. Lorenzo tried to push the distraction away, but Poliziano persisted until the wound was bound tight.

All the while, Lorenzo did not cease his frantic efforts. "My brother!" he cried shrilly, and would not be moved by those who came to comfort him, would not be stilled or quieted. "I must go and find him! My brother! Where is my brother? . . ."

. . .

Moments earlier, Giuliano had looked up in amazement as Baroncelli lifted his great knife overhead—the tip of the blade pointed directly at the younger Medici brother's heart.

It happened too quickly for Giuliano to be frightened. Instinctively, he backed away—into a body that pressed against him, so firm and so fast, there could be no doubt its owner was part of the conspiracy. Giuliano glimpsed the man behind him, dressed in the robes of a penitent—and then gasped at the cold, burning sensation of steel sliding into his back, just below his ribs.

He had been terribly wounded. He was surrounded by assassins, and about to die.

The realizations did not distress him as much as the fact that he was trapped and unable to warn Lorenzo. Surely his brother would be the next target.

"Lorenzo," he said emphatically, as Baroncelli's knife at last came flashing down, the blade reflecting a hundred tiny flames from the candles on the altar. But his utterance was drowned out by Baroncelli's panicked, nonsensical cry: "Here, traitor!"

The blow caught Giuliano between his uppermost pair of ribs. There came the dull crack of bone, and a second spasm of pain so intense, so impossible, it left him breathless.

Baroncelli's clean-shaven face, so close to Giuliano's own, gleamed with sweat. He grunted with effort as he withdrew the knife; it came out whistling. Giuliano fought to draw another breath, to call out Lorenzo's name again; it came out less audible than a whisper.

And in that instant, as he stared up at the knife, as Baroncelli prepared to deliver another blow, Giuliano was transported to another place, another time: to the river Arno, on a long-ago day in late spring.

He called out for his brother, but no answer came; Lorenzo had disappeared beneath the cloudy water. Giuliano's eyes stung. He could not find his strength or his breath, but he knew what he must do.

Dear God, he prayed, with the sincerity of a child. *Let me rescue my brother.*

With strength he did not have, he pushed backward against the penitent, causing the man to step back onto the hem of his garment and fall, tangled in his robes.

Giuliano was free to flee, to stagger away from his attackers—but he knew that their main target must be Lorenzo.

Time slowed, just as it did that day in the Arno. Despite his lethargy, Giuliano willed himself to do the impossible and create a barrier between the attackers and Lorenzo. If he could not cry out a warning to his brother, he could at least slow the murderers down.

He heard his brother's voice. *Giuliano! Brother, speak to me!*

He could not have said whether it came from within the Duomo, or whether it was an echo from childhood, the voice of an eleven-year-old boy calling from the banks of a river. He wanted to tell his brother to run, but he could not speak. He struggled to draw in a breath, and choked on warm liquid.

Baroncelli tried to edge by him, but Giuliano wobbled intentionally into his path. Francesco de' Pazzi pushed past his co-conspirator. The sight of blood had stirred him to frenzy; his small black eyes sparkled; his wiry body shook with hatred. Raising his dagger—a long blade, almost as slender and keen as a stiletto—he, too, tried to move beyond Baroncelli's victim, but Giuliano would not let him pass.

Giuliano opened his mouth. What came out was an anguished wheeze, but he meant to shout, *You will never get near my brother. I will die first, but you will never lay a hand on Lorenzo.*

Francesco snarled something unintelligible and struck. Weaponless, Giuliano raised a defensive hand; the knife pierced his palm and forearm. Compared to the agony in his chest and back, these fresh wounds were no worse than the sting of an insect. Taking a step toward Francesco, toward Baroncelli, he forced them backward, giving Lorenzo time to flee.

Francesco, vicious little man, let loose a torrent of all the rage, all the enmity, that his family had felt toward the Medici. Each phrase was punctuated by a further blow of the dagger.

Sons of whores, all of you! Your father betrayed my father's trust. . . .

Giuliano felt the piercing bite in his shoulder, in his upper arm. He could no longer keep his arm raised; it fell limply to his blood-soaked side.

Your brother has done everything possible to keep us out of the Signoria.

Harsher wounds: his chest again, his neck, a dozen blows to his torso. Francesco was a madman. His hand, his blade, pummeled Giuliano so swiftly the two were enveloped in a crimson spray. His movements were so wild and careless, he struck himself in the thigh, shrieking as his blood mingled with his enemy's. Pain fueled Francesco's fury; again and again, he struck.

Spoken ill of us to His Holiness
Insulted our family
Stolen the city

Giuliano was drowning. Such calumny against his brother would normally have incited his anger, but he had come to a place where his emotions were still.

The waters inside the cathedral were murky with blood; he could scarcely see the wavering images of his attackers against the backdrop of scrambling bodies. Baroncelli and Francesco both were shouting. Giuliano saw their mouths agape, saw the glint of wielded steel, dulled by the muddy Arno, but heard nothing. In the river, all was silent.

A shaft of sunlight streamed in from the open door leading north to the Via de' Servi. He stepped toward it, looking for Lorenzo, but the current pulled strongly on him now. It was so hard to walk through the swirling water.

Just beyond his reach, the raven-haired Anna was weeping, wringing her hands, mourning the children they might have had; her love tugged at him. But it was Lorenzo who had the final hold on his heart. Lorenzo whose heart would break when he found his younger sibling. It was Giuliano's greatest regret.

"*Brother.*" Giuliano's lips formed the word as he sank to his knees.

Lorenzo was sitting on the banks of the Arno, clutching a blanket round his shoulders. He was soaked through and shivering, but he was alive.

Relieved, Giuliano let go a shallow sigh—all the air that remained in his lungs—then sank forward and down, down to where the waters were deepest and black.

VIII

26 *April 1478*
To the Priors of Milan

My most illustrious lords,

My *brother Giuliano has been murdered and my government is in the gravest danger. It is now time, my lords,
to aid your servant Lorenzo. Send as many soldiers as you
can with all speed so that they will be the shield and safety
of my state, as always.*

Your *servant*
Lorenzo de' Medici

DECEMBER 28, 1479

IX

*B*ernardo Baroncelli rode kneeling in a small horse-drawn cart to his doom.

Before him, in the vast Piazza della Signoria, loomed the great, implacable palazzo, seat of Florence's government and the heart of her justice. Topped by battlements, the fortress was an imposing, almost windowless rectangle, with a slender campanile tower at one corner. Only an hour before he was led to the cart, Baroncelli had heard its bell tolling, low and dolorous, summoning witnesses to the spectacle.

In the morning gloom, the palazzo's stone façade appeared pale gray against the darkening clouds. Before the building, rising out of a colorful, varied assembly of Florence's rich and poor, stood a hastily built scaffolding, and the gallows.

The weather had turned bitterly cold; Baroncelli's final breaths hung before him as mist. The top of his cloak gaped open, but he could not pull it closed, for his hands were bound behind his back.

In this manner, unsteady and lurching each time the wheels encountered a stone, Baroncelli arrived in the piazza. No fewer than a thousand had gathered to witness his end.

At the crowd's edge, a small boy, a *fanciullo,* caught sight of the approaching cart and, in his childish falsetto, sang out the rallying cry of the Medici: *"Palle! Palle! Palle!"*

Hysteria rippled through the throng. Soon its collective shout thundered in Baroncelli's ears.

"Palle! Palle! Palle!"

Someone nearby threw a stone; it clattered harmlessly against the cobblestones beside the creaking cart. Only curses were hurled afterward. The Signoria had placed several policemen on horseback at strategic locations to prevent a riot; Baroncelli was flanked by mounted, armed guards.

This was to prevent him from being torn apart before he could be properly executed. He had heard the tales of his fellow conspirators' gruesome fates: how the Perugian mercenaries hired by the Pazzi had been pushed from the high tower of the Palazzo della Signoria, how they had fallen into the waiting crowd below, who had hacked them to pieces with knives and shovels.

Even old Iacopo de' Pazzi, who during his life had been respected, had not escaped Florence's wrath. Upon the sound of Giotto's chiming campanile, he had climbed upon his horse and tried to rally the citizens with the cry *Popolo e libertà!* The phrase was a rallying cry to overthrow the current government—in this case, the Medici.

But the populace had answered with the cry *Palle! Palle! Palle!*

Despite his sin, he had been granted a proper burial after his execution—with the noose still round his neck. But the city had been so filled with hatred in those wild days, he had not been at rest long before the Signoria decided it would be best to rebury his body outside the city walls, in unhallowed ground.

Francesco de' Pazzi and the rest had swiftly met justice; only Guglielmo de' Pazzi had been spared, because of Bianca de' Medici's desperate pleading with her brother Lorenzo.

Of the true conspirators, Baroncelli alone had escaped—by hiding in the Duomo's campanile, its air still aquiver from the ringing of the bell. When his way was clear, he had fled on horseback—without a word to his family—due east, to Senigallia on the coast. From there, he had sailed to exotic Constantinople. King Ferrante and Baroncelli's Neapolitan relatives had sent funds enough to sustain a dissolute life. Baroncelli made mistresses of the slave girls he had purchased, immersing himself in pleasure, trying to submerge all memory of the murders he had committed.

Yet his dreams were haunted by the image of Giuliano, frozen at the instant he had glanced up at the shining blade. The young man's dark curls were tousled, his innocent eyes wide, his expression unself-conscious and slightly dazed by the sudden appearance of Death.

Baroncelli had had more than a year to contemplate the question, Would removing the Medici and replacing them with Iacopo and Francesco de' Pazzi have bettered the city? Lorenzo was levelheaded, cautious; Francesco hot-tempered, swift to act. He would quickly have descended to the level of a tyrant. Lorenzo was wise enough to nurture the people's love, as evidenced by the size of the crowd now gathered in the plaza; Francesco would have been too arrogant to care.

Lorenzo was, most of all, persistent. In the end, even Constantinople was not beyond his reach. Once his agents had located Baroncelli, Lorenzo had sent an emissary laden with gold and jewels to the sultan. Thus was Baroncelli's fate sealed.

All criminals were hanged outside the city gates, then hastily stuffed into unhallowed ground. Baroncelli would be buried in a hole with them—but given the gravity of his misdeed, his execution was to take place in Florence's most public arena.

Now, as the little cart rattled past the crowd toward the scaffolding, Baroncelli let go a loud groan. Fear gripped him with an anguish far worse than any physical pain; he felt unbearably cold, searingly hot, felt a dizzying sense of sinking. He thought he would faint, yet unconsciousness, cruelly, would not come.

"Courage, signore," the *nero* said. "God rides with you."

His *nero,* his Comforter, walked alongside the cart. He was a

Florentine citizen named Lauro, and a lay member of the Compagnia di Santa Maria della Croce, also known as the Compagnia de' Neri— the Company of the Black Ones—because its members all wore black robes and hoods. The company's purpose was to give comfort and mercy to those in need—including those anguished souls condemned to die.

Lauro had remained with him from the moment he had arrived in Florence. He had seen to it that Baroncelli received fair treatment, was allowed proper clothing and food, that he was permitted to send letters to loved ones (Giovanna never responded to his plea to see her). Lauro had listened kindly to Baroncelli's tearful admissions of regret, and remained in the cell to pray for him. The Comforter had beseeched the Virgin, Christ, God, and Saint John, patron of Florence, to give Baroncelli comfort, to grant him forgiveness, to allow his soul into Purgatory and thence to Heaven.

Baroncelli did not join him in prayer; God, he felt, would take it as a personal affront.

Now, the black-hooded Comforter walked beside him, speaking loudly—a psalm, a hymn, or prayer, all floating on the air as white vapor—but given the noise made by the crowd, Baroncelli could not make out the words. A single phrase thrummed in his ears and pulsed to the beating of his heart.

Palle Palle Palle

The cart rolled to a stop in front of the steps leading up to the gallows. The Comforter slid an arm under Baroncelli's bound one and helped him awkwardly onto the cold flagstone. The weight of terror dropped the shivering Baroncelli to his knees; the Comforter knelt beside him and whispered in his ear.

"Do not be afraid. Your soul will ascend directly to Heaven. Of all men, you need no forgiveness; what you did was God's own work, and no crime. There are many of us who call you hero, brother. You have taken the first step in purging Florence from great evil."

Baroncelli's voice shook so he could scarce understand his own words. "From Lorenzo?"

"From debauchery. From paganism. From the pursuit of profane art."

Teeth chattering, Baroncelli glared at him. "If you—if others—believe this, then why have you not rescued me before now? Save me!"

"We dare not make ourselves known. There is much to be done before Florence, before Italy, before the world, is ready for us."

"You are mad," Baroncelli breathed.

The Comforter smiled. "We are fools for God."

He helped Baroncelli to his feet; enraged, Baroncelli pulled away from him and staggered up the wooden steps alone.

On the scaffolding, the executioner, a young, slender man whose face was hidden beneath a mask, stood between Baroncelli and the waiting noose. "Before God," the executioner said to Baroncelli, "I beg your forgiveness for the act I am sworn to commit."

The inside of Baroncelli's lips and cheeks cleaved to his teeth; his tongue was so dry, it left behind a layer of skin as he articulated the words. Yet his tone sounded astonishingly calm. "I forgive you."

The executioner released a small sound of relief; perhaps there had been other doomed men more eager to let their blood stain his hands. He caught Baroncelli's elbow and guided him to a particular spot on the platform, near the noose. "Here." His voice was oddly gentle. And he produced from within his cloak a white linen scarf.

In the instant before he was blindfolded, Baroncelli scanned the crowd. Near the front was Giovanna, with the children. She was too distant for Baroncelli to be sure, but it seemed to him that she had been weeping.

Lorenzo de' Medici was nowhere to be seen—but Baroncelli had no doubt that he was watching. Watching from a hidden balcony, or a window; perhaps from inside the Palazzo della Signoria itself.

Below, at the foot of the scaffolding, stood the Comforter, his expression serene and oddly satisfied. In an instant of epiphany, Baroncelli realized that he, Francesco de' Pazzi, Messer Iacopo, Archbishop Salviati—all of them—had been fools, their small ambitions used to serve part of a larger scheme, one that filled him with almost as much dread as the prospect of his imminent death.

The executioner tied the scarf over Baroncelli's eyes, then guided the noose over his chin and tightened it around his neck.

In the instant before the platform beneath him dropped, Baroncelli whispered two words, directed at himself.

"Here, traitor."

X

The instant that Baroncelli's body ceased its twitching, a young artist near the front of the crowd set to work. The corpse would hang in the piazza for days, until its decomposition caused it to drop from the rope. But the artist could not wait; he wanted to capture the image while it still possessed an echo of life. Besides, young hooligans, *giovani,* would soon amuse themselves by casting stones at it, and the imminent rain would cause it to bloat.

He sketched on paper pressed against a board of poplar, to give him a firm surface to work against. He had cut back the plume from his quill pen, for he used it so continually that any barbs there irritated his long fingers; he had carved the nib himself to a fine, sharp point, and he dipped it regularly, mindlessly, into a vial of brown iron gall ink securely fastened to his belt. Since one could not properly draw constrained by gloves, his bare hands ached from the cold, but he dismissed the observation as unworthy of his time. In the same manner, he dismissed the sorrow that threatened to overwhelm him— for the sight of Baroncelli evoked profoundly painful memories—and focused instead on the subject before him.

Despite all attempts to mask their true feelings, all men and women nonetheless revealed them through subtle signs in expression, posture, and voice. Baroncelli's regret was blatant. Even in death, his eyes were downcast, as if contemplating Hell. His head was bowed, and the corners of his thin lips were pulled downward by guilt. Here was a man overwhelmed by self-loathing.

The artist struggled not to yield to his hatred, though he had very personal reasons for despising Baroncelli. But hate was against his principles, so—like his aching fingers and heart—he ignored it and continued with his work. He also found killing unethical—even the execution of a murderer such as Baroncelli.

As was his habit, he jotted notes on the page to remind himself of the colors and textures involved, for there was an excellent chance the sketch might become a painting. He wrote from right to left, the letters a mirror image of conventional script. Years before, when he had been a student in Andrea Verrochio's workshop, other artists had accused him of unwarranted secrecy, for when he showed them his sketches, they could make no sense of his notes. But he wrote as he did because it came most naturally to him; the privacy conferred was a coincidental benefit.

Small tan cap. The quill scratched against the paper. *Black serge jerkin, lined woolen singlet, blue cloak lined with fox fur, velvet collar stippled red and black, Bernardo Bandino Baroncelli, black leggings.* Baroncelli had kicked off his slippers during his death throes; he was shown with bare feet.

The artist frowned at Baroncelli's patronymic. He was self-taught, still struggling to overcome his rustic Vinci dialect, and spelling bedeviled him. No matter. Lorenzo de' Medici, *il Magnifico,* was interested in the image, not the words.

He did a quick, small rendering at the bottom of the page, showing Baroncelli's head at an angle that revealed more of the gloom-stricken features. Satisfied with his work, he then set to his real task of scanning the faces in the crowd. Those near the front—the nobility and more prosperous merchants—were just beginning to leave, hushed and somber. The *populo minuto,* the poor and struggling, remained behind to entertain themselves by hurling epithets and rocks at the corpse.

The artist carefully watched as many men as possible as they left the piazza. There were two reasons for this: The ostensible one was that he was a student of faces. Those who knew of him were used to his intent stares.

The darker reason was the result of an encounter between himself and Lorenzo de' Medici. He was looking for a particular face—one he had seen twenty months earlier, for only the briefest of instants. Even with his talent for recalling physiognomies, his memory was clouded—yet his heart was equally determined to succeed. This time, he was resolved not to let emotion get the better of him.

"Leonardo!"

The sound of his own name startled the artist; he jerked involuntarily and, out of reflex, capped the vial of ink, lest it spill.

An old friend from Verrocchio's workshop had been on his way out of the piazza, and moved toward him.

"Sandro," Leonardo said, when his friend at last stood before him. "You look like a lord prior."

Sandro Botticelli grinned. At thirty-four, he was several years Leonardo's senior, in the prime of his life and career. He was indeed dressed grandly, in a scarlet fur-trimmed cloak; a black velvet cap covered most of his golden hair, cut chin-length, shorter than the current fashion. Like Leonardo, he was clean-shaven. His green eyes were heavy-lidded, filled with the insolence that had always marked his manner. Even so, Leonardo liked him; he was possessed of great talent and a good heart. Over the past year, Sandro had received several fat commissions from the Medici and Tornabuoni, including the massive painting *Primavera,* soon to be a wedding gift from Lorenzo to his cousin.

Sandro eyed Leonardo's sketch with sly humor. "So. Trying to steal my job, I see."

He was referring to the recently painted mural on a façade near the Palazzo della Signoria, partially visible behind the scaffolding now that the crowd was beginning to thin. He had received a commission from Lorenzo in those terrible days following Giuliano's death: to depict each of the executed Pazzi conspirators as they dangled from the rope. The life-sized images duly inspired the terror they were meant to provoke. There was Francesco de' Pazzi, entirely naked, his wounded thigh encrusted with blood; there, too, was Salviati in his archbishop's robes. The two dead men were shown facing the viewer—effective, though not an accurate depiction of fact. Like Botticelli, Leonardo had been in the Piazza della Signoria at the moment Francesco— dragged from his bed—had been pushed from the uppermost arched window of the palazzo, hung from the building itself for all to see. A moment later, Salviati had followed and, at the instant of his death, had turned toward his fellow conspirator and—whether in a violent, involuntary spasm or in a final moment of rage—had sunk his teeth deep into Francesco de' Pazzi's shoulder. It was a bizarre image, one so troubling that even Leonardo, overwhelmed by emotion, failed to record it in his notebook. Paintings of other executed men, including Messer Iacopo, were partially completed, but one murderer was alto- gether missing: Baroncelli. Botticelli had probably taken notes himself this morning, intending to finish the mural. But at the sight of Leonardo's sketch, he shrugged.

"No matter," he said breezily. "Being rich enough to dress like a lord prior, I can certainly let a pauper like yourself finish up the task. I have far greater things to accomplish."

Leonardo, dressed in a knee-length artisan's tunic of cheap used linen and a dull gray wool mantle, slipped his sketch under one arm and bowed, low and sweeping, in an exaggerated show of gratitude.

"You are too kind, my lord." He rose. "Now go. You are a hired hack, and I am a true artist, with much to accomplish before the rains come."

He and Sandro parted with smiles and a brief embrace, and Leonardo returned at once to studying the crowd. He was always happy to see Sandro, but the interruption annoyed him. Too much was at stake; he reached absently into the pouch on his belt and fin- gered a gold medallion the size of a large florin. On the front, in bas relief, was the title PUBLIC MOURNING. Beneath, Baroncelli raised his long knife above his head while Giuliano looked up at the blade with surprise. Behind Baroncelli stood Francesco de' Pazzi, his dagger at the ready. Leonardo had provided the sketch, rendering the scene with as much accuracy as possible, although for the viewer's sake, Giuliano was depicted as facing Baroncelli. Verrocchio had made the cast from Leonardo's drawing.

Two days after the murder, Leonardo had dispatched a letter to Lorenzo de' Medici.

My lord Lorenzo, I need to speak privately with you concerning a matter of the utmost importance.

No reply was forthcoming: Lorenzo, overcome with grief, hid in the Medici palazzo, which had become a fortress surrounded by scores of armed men. He received no visitors; letters requesting his opinion or his favor piled up unanswered.

After a week without a reply, Leonardo borrowed a gold florin and went to the door of the Medici stronghold. He bribed one of the guards there to deliver a second letter straightaway, while he stood waiting in the loggia, watching the hard rain pound the cobblestone streets.

My lord Lorenzo, I come neither seeking favor nor speaking of business. I have critical information concerning the death of your brother, for your ears alone.

Several minutes later he was admitted after being thoroughly checked for weapons—ridiculous, since he had never owned one or had any idea of how to wield one.

Pale and lifeless in an unadorned tunic of black, Lorenzo, his neck still bandaged, received Leonardo in his study, surrounded by artwork of astonishing beauty. He gazed up at Leonardo with eyes clouded by guilt and grief—yet even these could not hide his interest in hearing what the artist had to say.

On the morning of the twenty-sixth of April, Leonardo had stood several rows from the altar in the Cathedral of Santa Maria del Fiore. He'd had questions for Lorenzo about a joint commission he and his former teacher Andrea Verrocchio had received to sculpt a bust of Giuliano, and hoped to catch *il Magnifico* after the service. Leonardo attended Mass only when he had business to conduct; he found the natural world far more awe-inspiring than a man-made cathedral. He was on very good terms with the Medici. Over the past few years, he had stayed for months at a time in Lorenzo's house as one of the many artists in the family's employ.

To Leonardo's surprise that morning in the Duomo, Giuliano had arrived, late, disheveled, and escorted by Francesco de' Pazzi and his employee.

Leonardo found men and women equally beautiful, equally worthy of his love, but he lived an unrequited life by choice. An artist could not allow the storms of love to interrupt his work. He avoided women most of all, for the demands of a wife and children would make his studies—of art, of the world and its inhabitants—impossible. He did not want to become as his master Verrocchio was—wasting his talent, taking on any work, whether it be the construction of masks for Carnival or the gilding of a lady's slippers, to feed his hungry family. There was never any time to experiment, to observe, to improve his skills.

Ser Antonio, Leonardo's grandfather, had first explained this concept to him. Antonio had loved his grandson deeply, ignoring the fact that he was the illegitimate get of a servant girl. As Leonardo grew, only his grandfather noted the boy's talent, and had given him a book of paper and charcoal. When Leonardo was seven years old, he had been sitting in the cool grass with a silverpoint stylus and a rough panel of wood, studying how the wind rippled through the leaves of an olive orchard. Ser Antonio—ever busy, straight-shouldered and sharp-eyed despite his eighty-eight years—had paused to stand beside him, and look with him at the glittering trees.

Quite suddenly and unprompted, he said, *Pay no attention to custom, my boy. I had half your talent—yes, I was good at drawing and eager, like you, to understand how the natural world works—but I listened to my father. Before I came to the farm, I was apprenticed to him as a notary.*

That is what we are—a family of notaries. One sired me, and so I sired one myself—your father. What have we given the world? Contracts and bills of exchange, and signatures on documents which will turn to dust.

I did not give up my dreams altogether; even as I learned about the profession, I drew in secret. I stared at birds and rivers, and wondered how they worked. But then I met your grandmother Lucia and fell in love. It was the worst thing ever to happen, for I abandoned art and science and married her. Then there were children, and no time to look at trees. Lucia found my scribblings and cast them into the fire.

But God has given us you—you with your amazing mind and eyes and hands. You have a duty not to abandon them.

Promise me you will not make my mistake; promise me you will never let your heart carry you away.

Young Leonardo had promised.

But when he became a protégé of the Medici and a member of their inner circle, he had been drawn, physically and emotionally, to Lorenzo's younger brother. Giuliano was infinitely lovable. It was not simply the man's striking appearance—Leonardo was himself far more attractive, often called "beautiful" by his friends—but rather the pure goodness of his spirit.

This fact Leonardo kept to himself. He did not wish to make Giuliano, a lover of women, uncomfortable; nor did he care to scandalize Lorenzo, his host and patron.

When Giuliano appeared in the Duomo, Leonardo—only two rows behind him, for he had made his way as close as possible to Lorenzo, the better to intercept him—could not help but stare steadily at him. He noted Giuliano's downcast demeanor, and was filled with neither sympathy nor attraction but with a welling of bitter jealousy.

The previous evening, the artist had set out with the intention of speaking to Lorenzo about the commission.

He had made his way onto the Via de' Gori, past the church of San Lorenzo. The Palazzo Medici lay just ahead, to his left, and he stepped out into the street toward it.

It was dusk. To the west lay the high, narrow tower of the Palazzo della Signoria and the great curving cupola of the Duomo, distinct and dark against an impossible horizon of incandescent coral fading gradually to lavender, then gray. Given the hour, traffic was light, and Leonardo paused in the street, lost in the beauty of his surroundings. He watched as a carriage rolled toward him, and enjoyed the crisp silhouettes of the horses, their bodies impenetrably black, set against the backdrop of the brilliant sky with the sun behind them, so that all detail was swallowed. Sundown was his favorite hour, for the failing light infused forms and colors with a tenderness, a sense of gentle mystery, that the noon sun burned away.

He grew lost in the play of shadow on the horses' bodies, on the rippling of muscles beneath their flesh, the spirited lift of their heads— so much so that as they came rumbling down upon him, he had to collect himself and move swiftly out of their way. He crossed in front of them and found himself standing on the southern flank of the Palazzo Medici; his destination, less than a minute's walk away, was the Via Larga.

A short distance in front of him, the driver of the carriage jerked the horses to a stop; the door opened. Leonardo hung back and watched as a young woman stepped out. The twilight turned the marked whiteness of her skin into dove gray, her eyes and hair to nondescript darkness. The drabness of her gown and veil, the downward cast of her face, marked her as the servant of a wealthy family. There was purpose in her step and furtiveness in her posture as her gaze swept from side to side. She hurried to the palazzo's side entrance and knocked insistently.

A pause, and the door opened with a long, sustained creak. The servant moved back to the carriage and gestured urgently to someone inside.

A second woman emerged from the carriage and moved gracefully, swiftly, toward the open entry.

Leonardo said her name aloud without intending to. She was a friend of the Medici, a frequent visitor to the palazzo; he had talked to her on several occasions. Even before he saw her clearly, he recognized her movements, the cant of her shoulders, the way her head swiveled on her neck as she turned to look up at him.

He took a step closer, and was finally able to see her face.

Her nose was long and straight, the tip downturned, the nostrils flared; her forehead was broad and very high. Her chin was pointed, but the cheeks and jaw were gracefully rounded, like her shoulders, which inclined toward the Palazzo Medici although her face was turned toward his.

She had always been beautiful, but now the dimness softened everything, gave her features a haunting quality they had not heretofore possessed. She seemed to melt into the air; it was impossible to tell where the shadows ended and she began. Her luminous face, her décolleté, her hands, seemed to float suspended against the dark forest of her gown and hair. Her expression was one of covert joy; her eyes held sublime secrets, her lips the hint of a complicitous smile.

In that instant, she was more than human: She was divine.

He reached out with his hand, half thinking it would pass through her, as if she were a phantom.

She pulled away and he saw, even in the grayness, the bright flare of fear in her eyes, in the parting of her lips; she had not meant to be discovered. Had he possessed a feather, he would have whisked away the deep line between her brows and resurrected the look of mystery.

He murmured her name again, this time a question, but her gaze had already turned toward the open doorway. Leonardo followed it, and caught a glimpse of another familiar face: Giuliano's. His body was entirely obscured by shadow; he did not see Leonardo, only the woman.

And she saw Giuliano, and bloomed.

In that instant, Leonardo understood and turned his cheek away, overwhelmed by bitterness, as the door closed behind them.

He did not go to see Lorenzo that night. He went home to his little apartment and slept poorly. He stared up at the ceiling and saw the gently lucent features of the woman emerging from the blackness.

The following morning, gazing on Giuliano in the Duomo, Leonardo dwelled on his unhappy passion. He recalled, again and again, the painful instant when he had seen the look pass between Giuliano and the woman, when he had realized Giuliano's heart belonged to her, and hers to him; and he cursed himself for being vulnerable to such a foolish emotion as jealousy.

He had been so ensnared by his reverie that he had been startled by a sudden movement in front of him. A robed figure stepped forward an instant before Giuliano turned to look behind him, then released a sharp gasp.

There followed Baroncelli's hoarse shout. Leonardo had stared up, stricken, at the glint of the raised blade. In the space of a breath, the frightened worshipers scattered, pulling the artist backward with the tide of bodies. He had thrashed, struggling vainly to reach Giuliano with the thought of protecting him from further attack, but he could not even hold his ground.

In the wild scramble, Leonardo's view of Baroncelli's knife entering Giuliano's flesh had been blocked. But Leonardo had seen the final blows of Francesco's unspeakably brutal attack—the dagger biting, again and again, into Giuliano's flesh, just as Archbishop Salviati would, in due turn, bite into Francesco de' Pazzi's shoulder.

The instant he realized what was happening, Leonardo let go a loud shout—inarticulate, threatening, horrified—at the attackers. At last the crowd cleared; at last no one stood between him and the assassins. He had run toward them as Francesco, still shrieking, moved on. It was too late to shelter, to protect, Giuliano's good, innocent spirit.

Leonardo dropped to his knees beside the fallen man. He lay half curled on his side, his mouth still working; blood foamed at his lips and spilled from his wounds.

Leonardo pressed a hand to the worst of them, the gaping hole in Giuliano's chest. He could hear the frail, gurgling wheeze of the victim's lungs as they fought to expel blood and draw in air. But Leonardo's efforts to stanch the flow were futile.

Each wound on the front of Giuliano's pale green tunic released its own steady stream of blood. The streams forked, then rejoined, creating a latticework over the young man's body until at last they merged into the growing dark pool on the marble floor.

"Giuliano," Leonardo had gasped, tears streaming down his cheeks at the sight of such suffering, at the sight of beauty so marred.

Giuliano did not hear him. He was beyond hearing, beyond sight: His half-open eyes already stared into the next world. As Leonardo hovered over him, he retched up a volume of bright, foaming blood; his limbs twitched briefly, then his eyes widened. Thus he died.

Now, standing in front of Lorenzo, Leonardo said nothing of Giuliano's final suffering, for such details would only fuel *il Magnifico's* grief. Leonardo spoke not of Baroncelli, nor of Francesco de' Pazzi. Instead, he spoke of a third man, one who had yet to be found.

Leonardo recounted that he had seen, in the periphery of his vision, a robed figure step forward on Giuliano's right, and that he believed it was this man who had delivered the first blow. As Giuliano tried to back away from Baroncelli, the figure had stood fast, pressing hard against the victim to trap him. The crowd had obscured Leonardo's sight to a great degree at that point—the unknown figure had briefly disappeared, perhaps had fallen, but he had gotten back on his feet. He did not even recoil when Francesco struck out wildly with the dagger, but remained firmly in place until Francesco and Baroncelli had moved on.

Once Giuliano had died, Leonardo glanced up and noticed the man moving quickly toward the door that led to the piazza. He must have paused at some point to look behind him, to be sure that his victim died.

"Assassin!" the artist shouted. "Stop!"

There was such outraged authority, such pure force in his voice that, amazingly, the conspirator stopped in mid-stride and glanced swiftly over his shoulder.

Leonardo captured his image with a trained artist's eye. The man wore the robes of a penitent—crude burlap—and his clean-shaven face was half shadowed by a cowl. Only the lower half of his lip and his chin were visible.

Held close to his side, his hand gripped a bloodied stiletto.

After he had fled, Leonardo had gently rolled Giuliano's body onto its side and discovered the puncture—small but very deep—in his mid-back.

This he relayed to Lorenzo. But he did not admit what he knew in his tortured heart: that he, Leonardo, was responsible for Giuliano's death.

His guilt was not irrational. It was the product of long meditation on the events that had occurred. Had he, the artist, not been so overcome by the emotions of love and pain and jealousy, Giuliano might have lived.

It was Leonardo's habit to study crowds—faces, bodies, posture—and from this, he usually learned a great deal of information. Almost as much could be read from a man's back as from his front. If the artist had not been absorbed by thoughts of Giuliano and the woman, he would surely have noticed the exceptional tension in the penitent's stance, for the man had been almost directly in front of him. He might have noticed something peculiar in Baroncelli's or Francesco de' Pazzi's demeanor as they waited beside Giuliano. He would have sensed the anxiety of the three men and deduced that Giuliano was in great danger.

If he had only paid attention, he would have seen the penitent surreptitiously reach for the stiletto; he would have noticed Baroncelli's hand tensing on the hilt of his knife.

And there would have been time for him to take a single step forward. To reach for the penitent's hand. To move between Giuliano and Baroncelli.

Instead, his passion had reduced him to a witless bystander, rendered helpless by the panicked, fleeing crowd. And it had cost Giuliano his life.

He bowed his head at the weight of the guilt, then raised it again and looked in *il Magnifico*'s sorrowful, eager eyes.

"I am certain this man was disguised, my lord."

Lorenzo was intrigued. "How can you possibly know that?"

"His posture. Penitents indulge in self-flagellation and wear hair shirts beneath their robes. They slump, cringe, and move gingerly, because of the pain each time the shirt touches their skin. This man moved freely; his posture was straight and sure. But the muscles were tensed—from emotional distress.

"I believe, as well, that he was from the upper classes, given the dignity and gentility of his aspect."

Lorenzo's gaze was penetrating. "All this you have ascertained from a man's movements, a man who was draped in a robe?"

Leonardo stared back unflinching. He judged all men the same; the powerful did not intimidate him. "I would not have come if I had not."

"Then you shall be my agent." Lorenzo's eyes narrowed with hatred and determination. "You shall help me find this man."

So it was over the past year that Leonardo had been summoned several times to the Palazzo della Signoria's basement jail, to carefully examine the lips and chins and postures of unfortunate men. None of them matched those of the penitent in the cathedral.

The night before Baroncelli's execution, Lorenzo, now called *il Magnifico*, had sent two guards to bring Leonardo to the palazzo on the Via Larga.

Lorenzo had changed little physically—save for the pale scar on his neck. If his unseen wound had similarly healed, this day had torn it open, rendered it fresh and raw.

Leonardo, too, struggled beneath the burdens of sadness and guilt. Had he not been so stricken, he might have permitted himself to delight in *il Magnifico*'s unique features, especially his nose. The bridge rose briefly just beneath the eyebrows, then flattened and abruptly disappeared, as if God had taken his thumb and squashed it down. Yet it rose again, rebellious and astonishing in its length, and sloped precipitously to the left. Its shape rendered his voice harshly nasal and produced another odd effect as well: In the years Leonardo had known him, Lorenzo had never once stood in his famed garden and lifted a flower to inhale its scent. He had never once complimented a woman on her perfume, nor taken note of any odor, agreeable or disagreeable; indeed, he seemed caught off guard when anyone else did. Only one conclusion was possible: Lorenzo had no sense of smell.

That evening, *il Magnifico* wore a woolen tunic of deep rich blue; white ermine edged the collar and cuffs. He was an unhappy victor this night, but he seemed more troubled than gloating. "Perhaps you have already deduced why I have called for you," he said.

"Yes. I am to go to the piazza tomorrow to look for the third man." Leonardo hesitated; he, too, was troubled. "I need your assurance first."

"Ask and I will give it. I have Baroncelli now; I cannot rest until the third assassin is found."

"Baroncelli is to die, and rumor has it that he was tortured mercilessly."

Lorenzo interrupted swiftly. "And with good reason. He was my best hope to find the last conspirator. But he insisted he did not know the man; if he did, he will take the secret to Hell with him."

The bitterness in *il Magnifico*'s tone gave Leonardo pause. "Ser Lorenzo, if I find this third assassin, I cannot in good conscience turn him over to be killed."

Lorenzo recoiled as if he had been struck full in the face; his pitch rose with indignance. "You would let an accomplice to my brother's murder go free?"

"No." Leonardo's own voice trembled faintly. "I esteemed your brother more highly than any other."

"I know," Lorenzo replied softly, in a way that said he *did* know the full truth of the matter. "That is why I also know that, of all men, you are my greatest ally."

Gathering himself, Leonardo bowed his head, then lifted it again. "I would want to see such a man brought to justice—to be deprived of his freedom, condemned to work for the good of others, to be forced to spend the remainder of his life contemplating his crime."

Lorenzo's upper lip was invisible; his lower stretched so taut over his jutting lower teeth that the tips of them showed. "Such idealism is admirable." He paused. "I am a reasonable man—and like you, an honest one. If I agree that this accomplice, should you find him, will not be killed but instead imprisoned, will you go to the piazza to find him?"

"I will," Leonardo promised. "And if I fail tomorrow, I will not stop searching until he is found."

Lorenzo nodded, satisfied. He looked away, toward a Flemish painting of bewitching delicacy on his wall. "You should know that this man—" He stopped himself, then started again. "This goes far deeper than the murder of my brother, Leonardo. They mean to destroy us."

"To destroy you and your family?"

Lorenzo faced him again. "You. Me. Botticelli. Verrocchio. Perugino. Ghirlandaio. All that Florence represents." Leonardo opened his mouth to ask, *Who? Who means to do this?*, but *il Magnifico* lifted a hand to silence him. "Go to the piazza tomorrow. Find the third man. I mean to question him personally."

It was agreed that Lorenzo would pay Leonardo a token sum for a "commission"—the sketch of Bernardo Baroncelli hanged, with the possibility that such a sketch might become a portrait. Thus Leonardo could honestly answer that he was in the Piazza della Signoria because Lorenzo de' Medici wanted a drawing; he was a very bad liar, and prevarication did not suit him.

As he stood in the square on the cold December morning of Baroncelli's death, staring intently at the face of each man who passed, he puzzled over *il Magnifico*'s words.

They mean to destroy us. . . .

PART TWO

Lisa

XI

I will always remember the day my mother told me the story of Giuliano de' Medici's murder.

It was a December day thirteen and a half years after the event; I was twelve. For the first time in my life, I stood inside the great Duomo, my head thrown back as I marveled at the magnificence of Brunelleschi's cupola while my mother, her hands folded in prayer, whispered the gruesome tale to me.

Midweek after morning Mass, the cathedral was nearly deserted, save for a sobbing widow on her knees just beyond the entry, and a priest replacing the tapers on the altar's candelabra. We had stopped directly in front of the high altar, where the events of the assassination had taken place. I loved tales of adventure, and tried to picture a young Lorenzo de' Medici, his sword drawn, leaping into the choir and running past the priests to safety.

I turned to look at my mother, Lucrezia, and tugged at her embroidered brocade sleeve. She was dark-haired, dark-eyed, with skin so flawless it provoked my jealousy; she, however, seemed unaware of her amazing appearance. She complained of the adamant straightness of her locks, of the olive cast to her complexion. Never mind that she was fine-boned, with lovely hands, feet, and teeth. I was mature for my years, already larger than she, with coarse dull brown waves and troubled skin.

"What happened after Lorenzo escaped?" I hissed. "What became of Giuliano?"

My mother's eyes had filled with tears. She was, as my father often said, easily provoked to deep emotion. "He died of his terrible wounds. Florence went mad; everyone wanted blood. And the executions of the conspirators . . ." She shuddered at the memory, unable to bring herself to finish the thought.

Zalumma, who stood on her other side, leaned forward to scowl a warning at me.

"Didn't anyone try to help Giuliano?" I asked. "Or was he already dead? I would have at least gone to see if he was still alive."

"Hush," Zalumma warned me. "Can't you see she is becoming upset?"

This was indeed cause for concern. My mother was not well, and agitation worsened her condition.

"She was the one who told the story," I countered. "I did not ask for it."

"Quiet!" Zalumma ordered. I was stubborn, but she was more so. She took my mother's elbow and, in a sweeter tone, said, "Madonna, it's time to leave. We must get home before your absence is discovered."

She referred to my father, who had spent that day, like most others, tending his business. He would be aghast if he returned to find his wife gone; this was the first time in years she had dared venture out so far and so long.

We had secretly planned this outing for some time. I had never seen the Duomo, though I had grown up looking at its great brick cupola from the opposite side of the Arno, in our house on the Via Maggio. All my life, I had attended our local church of Santo Spirito and thought it grand, with its interior classical columns and arches made of *pietra serena,* a fine, pale gray stone. Our main altar was also centered beneath a cupola designed by the great Brunelleschi, his final achievement; I had thought Santo Spirito, with its thirty-eight side altars, impossibly grand, impossibly large—until I stood inside the great

Duomo. The cupola challenged the imagination. Gazing on it, I understood why, when it was first constructed, people were reluctant to stand beneath it. I understood, too, why some of those who heard the shouting on the day of Giuliano's murder had rushed outside, believing the great dome was finally collapsing.

Magic it was, for something so vast to rise into the air without visible support.

My mother had brought me to the Piazza del Duomo not just to marvel at the cupola, but to slake my yearning for art—and hers. She was wellborn and well educated; she adored poetry, which she read in Italian and Latin (both of which she had insisted on teaching to me). She had passionately acquired a wealth of knowledge about the city's cultural treasures—and had long been troubled by the fact that her illness had prevented her from sharing them with me. So when the opportunity arose on that bright December day, we took a carriage east and headed across the Ponte Vecchio into the heart of Florence.

It would have been more efficient to head straight down the Via Maggio to the nearest bridge, the Ponte Santa Trinità, but that would have denied me a visual treat. The Ponte Vecchio was lined with the *botteghe* of goldsmiths and artists. Each *bottega* opened directly onto the street, with the owner's wares prominently displayed in front of the shop. We all wore our best fur-lined capes to protect us from the chilly air, and Zalumma had tucked several thick woolen blankets around my mother. But I was too elated to feel cold; I stuck my head outside the carriage to gape at golden plaques, statuettes, belts, bracelets, and Carnival masks. I gazed on chiseled marble busts of wealthy Florentines, on portraits in progress. In the early days, my mother said, the bridge was home to tanners and fabric dyers, who used to dump their noxious-smelling chemicals directly into the Arno. The Medici had objected: The river was cleaner now than it had ever been, and the tanners and dyers worked in specified areas of the city.

On our way to the Duomo, our carriage paused in the vast piazza, in front of the imposing fortress known as the Palazzo della Signoria, where the Lord Priors of Florence met. On a prominent wall of an adjacent building was a grotesque mural: paintings of hanged men. I knew nothing of them save that they were known as the Pazzi conspirators, and that they were evil. One of the conspirators, a small naked man, stared wide-eyed and sightless back at me; the effect was unnerving. But what intrigued me most was the portrait of the last hanging body. His form differed from the others, was more delicately portrayed, more assured; its subtle shadings poignantly evoked the grief and remorse of a troubled soul. And it did not seem to float, as the others did, but possessed the shadow and the depth of reality. I felt as though I could reach into the wall and touch Baroncelli's cooling flesh.

I turned to my mother. She was watching me carefully, though she said not a word about the mural, nor the reason we had lingered there. It was the first time I had stayed for any length of time in the piazza, the first time I had been allowed such a close view of the hanged men. "This last one was done by a different artist," I said.

"Leonardo, from Vinci," she said. "He has an amazing refinement, doesn't he? He is like God, breathing life into stone." She nodded, clearly pleased by my discernment, and waved for the driver to move on.

We made our way north to the Piazza del Duomo.

Before entering the cathedral, I had examined Ghiberti's bas relief panels on the doors of the nearby octagonal Baptistery. Here, near the public entry at the southern end of the building, scenes from the life of Florence's patron saint, John the Baptist, covered the walls. But what truly tantalized me was the Door of Paradise on the northern side. There, in fine gilded bronze, the Old Testament came to life in vivid detail. I stood on tiptoe to finger the sweeping curve of an angel's wing as he announced to Abraham that God desired Isaac as a sacrifice; I bent down to marvel at Moses receiving the tablets from the divine hand. What I most yearned to touch were the delicately rendered heads and muscular shoulders of oxen, emerging from the metal of the uppermost plaque to plow a field. I knew the tips of the horns would be sharp and cold against my fingertip, but they lay too high for my reach. Instead, I contented myself with rubbing the numerous tiny heads of prophets and sibyls that lined the doors like garlands; the bronze burned like ice.

The interior of the Baptistery was for me less remarkable. Only one item caught my attention: Donatello's dark wooden carving of Mary Magdalen, larger than life. She was a ghastly, spectral version of the seductress: aged now, her hair so wild and long that she clothed herself in the tangles, just as Saint John clothed himself in the skins of animals. Her cheeks were gaunt, her features worn down by decades of guilt and regret. Something about the resignation in her aspect reminded me of my mother.

We three made our way into the Duomo proper then, and once we arrived in front of the altar, my mother immediately began speaking of the murder that had taken place there almost fourteen years earlier. I had only moments to draw in the astonishing vastness of the cupola before Zalumma grew worried and told my mother it was time to leave.

"I suppose so." My mother reluctantly agreed with Zalumma's urgings. "But first I must speak to my daughter alone."

This frustrated the slave. She scowled until her brows merged into one great black line, but her social status compelled her to say calmly, "Of course, Madonna." So she retreated, but only a short distance away.

Once my mother satisfied herself that Zalumma was not watching, she retrieved from her bosom a small, shining object. A coin, I thought, but after she had pressed it into my palm, I saw it was a gold medallion, stamped with the words PUBLIC MOURNING. Beneath the letters, two men with knives readied themselves to attack a startled victim. Despite its small size, the image was detailed and lifelike, rendered with a delicacy worthy of Ghiberti.

"Keep it," my mother said. "But let it be our secret."

I eyed her gift greedily, curiously. "Was he really so handsome?"

"He was. It is quite accurate. And quite rare. It was created by the same artist who painted Baroncelli."

I tucked it at once into my belt. My mother and I both shared a love of such trinkets, and of art, though my father disapproved of my having anything so impractical. As a merchant, he had worked hard for his wealth, and hated to see it squandered on anything useless. But I was thrilled; I hungered for such things.

"Zalumma," my mother called. "I am ready to leave."

Zalumma came to fetch us at once and took hold of my mother's arm again. But when my mother began to turn away from the altar, she paused and wrinkled her nose. "The candles . . ." she murmured. "Have the altar vestments caught fire? Something is burning. . . ."

Zalumma's expression went slack with panic, but she recovered herself immediately and said calmly, as if it were the most normal thing in the world: "Lie down, Madonna. Here, on the floor. All will be well."

"It all repeats," my mother said, with the odd catch in her voice I had come to dread.

"Lie down!" Zalumma ordered, as sternly as she would a child. My mother seemed not to hear her, and when Zalumma pressed on her limbs, trying to force her to the ground, she resisted.

"It all repeats," my mother said swiftly, frantically. "Don't you see it happening again? Here, in this sacred place."

I lent my weight to Zalumma's; together we fought to bring my mother down, but it was like trying to bring down an immovable mountain—one that trembled.

My mother's arms moved involuntarily from her sides and shot straight out, rigid. Her legs locked beneath her. "There is murder here, and thoughts of murder!" she shrieked. "Plots within plots once more!"

Her cry grew unintelligible as she went down.

Zalumma and I clung to her so that she did not land too harshly.

My mother writhed on the cold floor of the cathedral, her blue cloak gaping open, her silver skirts pooling around her. Zalumma lay across her body; I put my kerchief between her upper teeth and tongue, then held on to her head.

I was barely in time. My mother's dark eyes rolled back until only the veined whites were visible—then the rigors began. Head, torso, limbs—all began to jerk arrhythmically, rapidly.

Somehow Zalumma held on, rising and falling with the waves, whispering hoarsely in her barbarous tongue, strange words coming so fast and so practiced I knew they were part of a prayer. I, too, began to pray without thinking in a language equally old: *Ave Maria, Mater Dei, ora pro nobis pecatoribus, nunc et in hora mortis nostrae . . .*

I focused on the linen kerchief in my mother's mouth—on her champing teeth, and the small specks of blood there—and on her jerking head, which I now held fast in my lap, so I was startled into fright when a stranger beside us began praying loudly, also in Latin.

I glanced up and saw the black-frocked priest who had been tending the altar. He alternated between sprinkling my mother with liquid from a small vial and making the sign of the cross over her while he prayed.

At last the time came when my mother gave a final wrenching groan, then fell limp; her eyelids fluttered shut.

Beside me, the priest—a young red-haired man with pockmarked florid skin—rose. "She is like the woman from whom Jesus cast out nine devils," he said with authority. "She is possessed."

Sore and halting from the struggle, Zalumma nonetheless rose to her full height—a hand's breadth taller than the priest—and glared at him. "It is a sickness," she said, "of which you know nothing."

The young priest shrank, his tone now only faintly insistent. "It is the Devil."

I glanced from the priest's face to Zalumma's stern expression. I was mature for my age and knew responsibility: The increasing number of my mother's fits had caused me to act as mistress of the household many times, playing hostess to guests, and accompanying my father in her place on social occasions. For the last three years, I had gone with Zalumma to market in my mother's place. But I was young in terms of my knowledge of the world, and of God. I was still undecided as to whether God was punishing her for some early sin, and whether her fits were indeed of sinister origin. I knew only that I loved her, pitied her, and disliked the priest's condescension.

Zalumma's white cheeks turned shell pink. I knew her well: A scathing reply had formed in her mind, and teetered upon her rouged lips, but she checked it. She had need of the priest.

Her manner turned abruptly unctuous. "I am a poor slave, with no right to contradict a learned man, Father. Here, we must get my mistress to the carriage. Will you help us?"

The priest looked on her with justifiable suspicion, but he could not refuse. And so I ran to find our driver; when he had brought the carriage round to the front of the cathedral, he and the priest carried my mother to it.

Exhausted, she slept with her head cradled in Zalumma's lap; I held her legs. We rode home directly back over the Ponte Santa Trinità, a homely stone bridge which housed no shops.

Our palazzo on the Via Maggio was neither large nor ostentatious, though my father could have afforded to adorn the house more. It had been built a century before by his great-great-grandfather from plain *pietra serena*, the expensive subtle gray stone. My father had made no additions, added no statuary nor replaced the plain, worn floors or the scarred doors; he eschewed unnecessary adornment. We rode inside the gate; then Zalumma and the driver lifted my mother from the carriage.

To our horror, my father, Antonio, stood watching in the loggia.

XII

$\mathcal{M}$y father had returned early. Dressed in his usual dark *farsetto*, crimson mantle, and black leggings, he stood with his arms crossed at the entry to the loggia so that he would not miss us. He was a sharp-featured man, with golden-brown hair that grew in darker at the crown, a narrow hooked nose, and thunderous thick eyebrows above pale amber eyes. His disregard for fashion showed in his face; he wore a full beard and mustache at a time when it was common for men to be clean-shaven or wear a neat goatee.

Yet, ironically, no one knew more about Florence's current styles and cravings. My father owned a *bottega* in the Santa Croce district, near the ancient Wool Guild, the Arte de Lana. He specialized in providing the very finest wools to the city's wealthiest families. He often went to the Medici palazzo on the Via Larga, his carriage heavy with fabrics colored with *chermisi,* the most expensive of dyes made from the dried carcasses of lice, which produced the most exquisite crimson, and *alessandrino,* a costly and beautiful deep blue.

Sometimes I rode with my father and waited in the carriage while he met with his most important clients at their palazzi. I enjoyed the

rides, and he seemed to enjoy sharing with me the details of his business, speaking to me as if I were his equal; at times, I felt guilty because I was not a son who could take over the family trade. I was his
sole heir, and a girl. God had frowned upon my parents, and it was
taken for granted that my mother and her fits were to blame.

And now there was no hiding the fact that our secret escapade had
just caused her to suffer another one.

My father was, for the most part, a self-possessed man. But certain
things goaded him—my mother's condition was one of them—and
could induce an uncontrollable rage. As I crawled from the carriage to
walk behind Zalumma and the others, I saw the danger in his eye and
looked guiltily away.

For the moment, love of my mother took precedence over my father's anger. He ran to us and took Zalumma's place, catching hold of
my mother tenderly. Together, he and the driver carried her toward the
house; as they did, he glanced over his shoulder at Zalumma and me.
He kept his tone low so it would not distress my semiconscious
mother, but I could hear the anger coiled in it, waiting to lash out.

"You women will see her to bed; then I will have words with you."

This was the worst possible outcome. Had my mother not suc-
cumbed to a fit, we could have argued that she had been too long
housebound and deserved the outing. But I was overwhelmed by a
sense of responsibility for all that had happened, and ready to submit
to a well-deserved tirade. My mother had taken me into the city because she delighted in me and wished to please me by showing me the
city's treasures. My father could never be bothered; he scorned the
Duomo, calling it "ill-conceived," and said that our church at Santo
Spirito was good enough for us.

So my father carried Mother up to her bed. I closed the shutters to
block out the sun, then helped Zalumma undress her down to her
camicia of embroidered white silk so fine and thin it could scarce be
called cloth. Once that was done, and Zalumma was certain my
mother was sleeping comfortably, we stepped quietly out into her
antechamber and closed the door behind us.

My father was waiting for us. His arms were again folded against his chest, his lightly freckled cheeks flushed; his gaze could have withered the freshest rose.

Zalumma did not cower. She faced him directly, her manner courteous but not servile, and waited for him to speak first.

His tone was low but faintly atremble. "You knew of the danger to her. You knew, and yet you let her leave the house. What kind of loyalty is this? What shall we do if she dies?"

Zalumma's tone was perfectly calm, her manner respectful. "She will not die, Ser Antonio; the fit has passed and she is sleeping. But you are right; I am at fault. Without my help, she could not have gone."

"I shall sell you!" My father's tone slowly rose. "Sell you, and buy a more responsible slave!"

Zalumma lowered her eyelids; the muscles in her jaw clenched with the effort of holding words back. I could imagine what they were. *I am the lady's slave, from her father's household; I was hers before we ever set eyes on you, and hers alone to sell.* But she said nothing. We all knew that my father loved my mother, and my mother loved Zalumma. He would never sell her.

"Go," my father said. "Get downstairs."

Zalumma hesitated an instant; she did not want to leave my mother alone, but the master had spoken. She passed by us, her skirts sweeping against the stone floor. My father and I were alone.

I lifted my chin, instinctively defiant. I had been born so; my father and I were evenly matched in terms of temper.

"*You* were behind this," he said; his cheeks grew even more crimson. "You, with your notions. Your mother did this to please you."

"Yes, I was behind it." My own voice trembled, which annoyed me; I fought to steady it. "Mother did this just to please me. Do you think I am happy that she had a spell? She has gone out before without incident. Do you think I meant for this to happen?"

He shook his head. "A girl so young, so full of such brazen disrespect. Listen to me: You will stay at home, by your mother's side, all week. You are not to go to Mass or market. Do you not *know* how serious this offense is? Do you not *know* how terrified I was, to come home and find her gone? Do you not feel at all ashamed that your self-ishness has hurt your mother so? Or do you care nothing for her life?"

His tone steadily rose throughout his discourse, so that by its end, he was shouting.

"Of *course*—" I began, but broke off as my mother's door opened, and she appeared in the doorway.

Both my father and I were startled and turned to look at her. She looked like a wraith, clutching the doorjamb to keep her balance; her eyes were heavy-lidded with exhaustion. Zalumma had taken down her hair, and it spilled darkly over her shoulders, her bosom, and down to her waist; she wore nothing but the billowing *camicia,* with its long, puffed sleeves.

She spoke in nothing more than a whisper, but the emotion in it could be clearly heard. "Leave her be. This was my idea, all of it. If you must shout, shout at me."

"You mustn't be up," I said, but my words were drowned out by my father's angry voice.

"How could you do such a thing when you know it is dangerous? Why must you frighten me so, Lucrezia? You might have died!"

My mother gazed on him with haggard eyes. "I am tired. Tired of this house, of this life. I don't care if I die. I want to go out, as normal folk do. I want to live as any normal woman does."

She would have said more, but my father interrupted. "God forgive you for speaking so lightly of death. It is His will that you live so, His judgment. You should accept it meekly."

I had never heard venom in my gentle mother's tone, had never seen her sneer. But that day, I heard and saw both.

Her lip tugged at one corner. "Do not mock God, Antonio, when we both know the truth of it."

He moved swiftly, blindingly, to strike her; she shrank backward.

I moved just as quickly to intervene. I pummeled my father's shoulders, forcing him away from her. "How dare you!" I cried. "How *dare* you! She is kind and good—everything you are not!"

His pale golden eyes were wide, bright with rage. He struck out with the back of his hand; I fell back, startled to find myself sitting on the floor.

He swept from the room. As he did, I looked frantically about for something to hurl after him; but all I had was the cape still about my shoulders, a gift from him of heavy *alessandrino* blue wool.

I bunched it in my hands and threw it, but it went scarcely farther than an arm's length before dropping silently to the floor—a vain gesture.

And then I came to myself and ran into my mother's room to find her on her knees beside the bed. I helped her up into it, covered her with a blanket, and held her hand while she—once again half asleep— wept softly.

"Hush," I told her. "We didn't mean it. And we will make amends."

She reached up blindly, looking for my hand; I clasped hers. "It all repeats," she moaned, and her eyes at last closed. "It all repeats. . . ."

"Hush now," I said, "and sleep."

XIII

I sat at my mother's bedside the rest of the day. When the sun began to set, I lit a taper and remained. A servant came bearing my father's request that I come down and sup with him; I refused. I did not want to be reconciled yet.

But as I sat in the darkness watching my mother's profile in the candleglow, I felt a stirring of regret. I was no better than my father; out of love and a desire to protect her, I had permitted my rage to overtake me. When my father had lifted his hand, threatening her—though I did not believe he would actually strike her—I had struck him, and not once, but several times. This, even though I knew our fighting broke my mother's heart.

I was a bad daughter. One of the worst, for I was vengeful and plotting against those who harmed the people I loved. When I was ten, we had a new servant, Evangelia, a stocky woman with black hairs on her chin and a broad red face. When she first witnessed one of my mother's fits, she proclaimed—like the priest in the Duomo—that my mother was possessed of the Devil and needed prayer.

That claim alone would not have provoked my hatred, only my dislike: As I said, I was still undecided as to whether it was true, but I knew such statements embarrassed and hurt my mother. But Evangelia would not let the matter rest. Whenever she was in the same room as my mother, she crossed herself and made the sign to avert the evil eye—two fingers pointing outward in a vee at the level of her own eyes. She began to wear a charm in a pouch hung round her neck, then at last did the unforgivable: She left a second charm hanging from my mother's door. It was supposedly to keep my mother confined to her room; when other servants confessed the truth of it, my mother wept. But she was too kind and ashamed to say anything to Evangelia.

I took matters into my own hands; I would not tolerate anyone who made my mother cry. I stole into my mother's room and took her finest ring, a large ruby set in delicately crafted gold, a wedding gift from my father.

I hid it within Evangelia's belongings, then waited. The predictable occurred: The ring was found, to everyone's horror—especially Evangelia's. My father dismissed her at once.

At first I felt a sense of satisfaction: Justice had been served, and my mother would no longer weep with shame. But after a few days, my conscience began to pain me. Most of Florence knew of Evangelia's supposed crime, and she was widowed with a small daughter. No family would hire her. How would she survive?

I confessed my sin to the priest and to God. Neither brought relief. At last I went to my mother and tearfully told her the truth. She was stern and told me outright what I already knew—that I had ruined a woman's life. To my relief, she did not tell the full truth to my father, only that a terrible mistake had been made. She begged him to find Evangelia and bring her back, that her name might be cleared.

But my father's efforts were futile. Evangelia had already left Florence, unable to find employment.

I lived from then on with the guilt. And as I sat watching my sleeping mother that night, I remembered all the angry outbursts of my youth, every vengeful act I had ever committed. There were many; and I prayed to God, the God Who loved my mother and did not want her stricken with fits, to relieve me of my dreadful temper. My eyes filled; I knew my father and I added to my mother's suffering every time we fought.

As the first tear spilled onto my cheek, my mother stirred in her sleep and murmured something unintelligible. I put a gentle hand on her arm. "It's all right. I am here."

The instant I uttered the words, the door opened softly. I glanced up to see Zalumma, a goblet in her hand. She had removed her cap and scarf, and plaited her wild hair, but a halo of untamed curls framed her white face.

"I brought a draught," she said quietly. "When your mother wakes, this will let her sleep through the night."

I nodded and tried to wipe my damp cheek casually, hoping Zalumma would not notice as she set the goblet beside my mother's bed.

Of course she noticed everything, even though her back was to me at the instant I accomplished the act. She turned to me, and with her voice still low, she said, "You mustn't cry."

"But it's my fault."

Zalumma flared. "It's not your fault. It's never been your fault." She sighed bitterly as she looked down on her sleeping mistress. "What the priest in the Duomo said—"

I leaned forward, eager to hear her opinion. "Yes?"

"It is vileness. It is ignorance, you understand? Your mother is the truest Christian I know." She paused. "When I was a very young girl . . ."

"When you lived in the mountains?"

"Yes, when I lived in the mountains. I had a brother. Closer to me than a brother; he was a twin." She smiled with faint affection at the memory. "Headstrong and full of mischief he was, always making our mother wring her hands. And I was always helping him." The faint, wry smile faded at once. "One day he climbed a very tall tree. He wanted to reach the sky, he said. I followed him up as far as I could, but he climbed so high that I grew frightened, and stopped. He crawled out onto a limb . . ." There was the slightest catch in her voice; she paused, then resumed calmly. "Too far. And he fell."

I straightened in my chair, aghast. "Did he die?"

"We thought he would; he had cracked his head and it bled terribly, all over my apron. When he was better and could walk, we went outside to play. Before we went too far, he fell and began to shake, just as your mother does. Afterward, he could not speak for a while, and slept. Then he was better again until the next time."

"Just like Mother." I paused. "Did the fits . . . did they ever . . . did he . . . ?"

"Did the fits kill him? No. I don't know what became of him after we were separated." Zalumma eyed me, trying to judge whether I had grasped the point of her tale. "My brother never had fits before he hurt his head. His fits came after his injury. His fits came because of his injury."

"So . . . Mother has struck her head?"

Zalumma averted her gaze a bit—perhaps she was only telling a story, calculated to soothe me—but she nodded. "I believe so. Now . . . do you think God pushed a little boy from a tree to punish him for his sins? Or do you think he was so craven that the Devil possessed him and caused him to leap?"

"No, of course not."

"There are people who would disagree with you. But I knew my brother's heart, and I know your mother's; and I know that God would never be so cruel, nor allow the Devil to rest in such sweet souls."

The instant Zalumma said it, my doubts about the matter vanished. Despite what Evangelia or the priest said, my mother was not host to demons. She attended Mass daily at our private chapel; she prayed constantly and had a shrine to the Virgin of the Flower—the lily, symbol of resurrection and of Florence—in her room. She was generous to the poor and never spoke ill of anyone. To my mind, she was as holy as any saint. The revelation gave me great relief.

But one thing still troubled me.

There is murder here, and thoughts of murder. Plots within plots once more.

I could not forget what the astrologer had told me two years earlier: that I was surrounded by deceit, doomed to finish a bloody deed others had begun.

It all repeats.

"The strange things Mother cries out," I said. "Did your brother do that, too?"

Zalumma's fine porcelain features reflected hesitation; at last she yielded to the truth. "No. She spoke of such things before the fits came, since she was a girl. She . . . she sees and knows things that are hidden from the rest of us. Many of the things she has said have come to pass. I think God has touched her, given her a gift."

Murder, and thoughts of murder. This time, I did not want to believe what Zalumma said, and so I chose to believe that, in this case, she was being superstitious. "Thank you," I told her. "I will remember what you have said."

She smiled and leaned down to put an arm around my shoulder. "No more vigil; it's my turn now. Go and get something to eat."

I looked past her at my mother, uncertain. I still felt responsible for what had happened that morning.

"Go," Zalumma said, in a tone that allowed no argument. "I'll sit with her now."

So I rose and left them—but I did not go in search of the cook. Instead, I went downstairs with the intent of going to pray. I wandered outside into the rear courtyard and garden. Just beyond, in a small separate structure, was our chapel. The night was bitter cold, the sky clouded and moonless, but I carried a lamp that I might not stumble over my skirts or a stepping-stone.

I opened the chapel's heavy wooden door and slipped inside. The interior was dark and gloomy, lit only by the votives flickering in front of small paintings of our family's patron saints: the woolly John the Baptist in honor of Florence; the Virgin of the Lily—Santa Maria del Fiore—my mother's favorite, for which the Duomo was named; and my father's namesake, Saint Anthony, who bore the Christ child in his arms.

Most private Florentine families' chapels were decorated with large murals, often portraying members as saints or Madonnas. Ours lacked such embellishment, save for the paintings of the three saints. Our grandest adornment was suspended over the altar: a large wooden statue of the crucified Christ, his expression as haunted and mournful as that of the aged, repentant Magdalen in the Duomo's Baptistery.

As I entered, I heard a soft, low moaning. And as I lifted the lamp toward the direction of the noise, I saw a dark figure kneeling at the altar railing. My father was praying earnestly, his forehead pressed hard against the knuckles of his tightly folded hands.

I knelt beside him. He turned toward me; the lamplight glittered off the unshed tears in his amber eyes.

"Daughter, forgive me," he said.

"No," I countered. "It is you who must forgive me. I hit you—a horrible thing for a child to do to her father."

"And I struck you, without cause. You were only thinking to protect your mother. And that was my intent, yet I find myself doing the opposite. I am older, and should be wiser." He looked up at the image of the suffering Christ. "After all these years, I should have learned to control myself. . . ."

I wished to coax him from his mood of self-reproach. I rested a hand on his arm and said lightly, "So, I inherited my ill temper from you, then."

He sighed and ran the pad of his thumb tenderly over the contours of my cheek. "Poor child. This is no fault of yours."

Still kneeling, we embraced. At that instant, the forgotten medallion chose to slip from my belt. It struck the inlaid marble flooring, rolled in a perfect circle, then fell flat on its side.

Its appearance embarrassed me. Curious, my father reached for the coin, lifted it, and examined it—then narrowed his eyes and drew back his head slightly, as if threatened by a slap. After a long pause, he spoke.

"You see," he said, his voice low and soft. "This is what comes of anger. Dreadful acts of violence."

"Yes," I echoed, eager to end the conversation, to return to the warmer feeling of conciliation. "Mother told me about the killing in the Duomo. It was a terrible thing."

"It was. There is no excuse for murder, regardless of the provocation. Such violence is heinous, an abomination before God." The piece of gold, still held aloft, caught the feeble light and glinted. "Did she tell you the other side of it?"

I tried and failed to understand; I thought at first he referred to the coin. "The other side?"

"Lorenzo. His love for his murdered brother drove him to madness in the days after." He closed his eyes, remembering. "Eighty men in five days. A few of them were guilty, but most were simply unfortunate enough to have the wrong relatives. They were tortured mercilessly, drawn and quartered, their hacked, bloodied bodies heaved out the windows of the Palazzo della Signoria. And what they did to poor Messer Iacopo's corpse. . . ." He shuddered, too horrified by the thought to pursue it further. "All in vain, for even a river of blood could not revive Giuliano." He opened his eyes and stared hard at me. "There is a vengeful streak in you, child. Mark my words: No good can come of revenge. Pray God delivers you of it." He pressed the cold coin into my palm. "Remember what I have said each time you look on this."

I lowered my gaze and accepted the chastisement meekly, even as my hand closed swiftly over my treasure. "I will."

To my relief, he at last rose; I followed suit.

"Have you eaten?" I asked.

He shook his head.

"Then let us find Cook."

On the way out, my father picked up my lamp and sighed. "God help us, daughter. God help us not to give in to our anger again."

"Amen," I said.

XIV

*B*efore Zalumma retired that night, I sought her out and coaxed her into my little room. I closed the door behind us, then jumped upon my cot and wrapped my arms around my knees.

More of Zalumma's wild, wiry tendrils had escaped from her braids, and they glinted in the light of the single candle in her hand, which lit her face with a delightfully eerie, wavering glow—perfect for the gruesome tale I wished to hear.

"Tell me about Messer Iacopo," I coaxed. "Father said they desecrated his body. I know they executed him, but I want to hear the details."

Zalumma resisted. Normally, she enjoyed sharing such things, but this was one subject that clearly disturbed her. "It's a terrible story to tell a child."

"All the adults know about it; and if you won't tell me, I'll just ask Mother."

"No," she said, so sharply her breath nearly extinguished the flame. "Don't you dare bother her with that." Scowling, she set the candle down on my night table. "What do you want to know?"

"What they did to Messer Iacopo's body . . . and why. He didn't stab Giuliano . . . so why did they kill him?"

She sat on the edge of my bed and sighed. "There's more than one answer to those questions. Old Iacopo de' Pazzi was the patriarch of the Pazzi clan. He was a learned man, very esteemed by everyone. He was a knight, you know, which is why they called him 'Messer.' He didn't start the plot to kill the Medici brothers; I think he got talked into it once it was clear the others were going to go ahead with or without him.

"Your mother has told you that when they murdered Giuliano, they rang the bells in the campanile next to the Duomo?"

"Yes."

"Well, that was the signal for Messer Iacopo to ride his horse into the Piazza della Signoria and shout, *'Popolo e libertà!,'* rallying the people to rise up against the Medici. He had hired almost a hundred Perugian soldiers to help him storm the Palazzo della Signoria; he thought the citizens would help him. But it didn't go as he planned. The Lord Priors dropped stones on him and his army from the palazzo windows, and the people turned on him, crying, *'Palle! Palle!'*

"So when he was captured, they hung him from a window of the palazzo—the same one as Francesco de' Pazzi and Salviati. Because of his noble rank and the people's respect for him, he was first allowed to confess his sins and receive the final sacrament. Later, he was buried in his family tomb at Santa Croce.

"But a rumor started, that before he died, Iacopo had commended his soul to the Devil. The monks at Santa Croce grew frightened and exhumed the body to rebury it outside the city walls, in unconsecrated ground. Then some *giovani* dug up the body when Messer Iacopo was three weeks dead.

"He had been buried with the noose still round his neck, and so the *giovani* dragged his corpse by its rope all over the city." She closed her eyes and shook her head, remembering. "They mocked him for days as if his body were a puppet. They took him to his palazzo and banged his head against the door, pretending that he was demanding entry. I . . ." She faltered and opened her eyes, but did not see me.

"I saw him, and the *giovani*, as I was walking back from market one day. They had propped the corpse against a fountain and were speaking to it. 'Good day, Messer Iacopo!' 'Please pass, Messer Iacopo.' 'And how is your family today, Messer Iacopo?'

"And then they pelted the cadaver with stones. It made an awful sound—dull thuds; it had been raining for four days while he was buried in the earth, and he was very bloated. He had been wearing a beautiful purple tunic the day he was hung—I had been in the crowd. That tunic had rotted, covered now with a greenish-black slime, and his face and hands were white as the belly of a fish. His mouth gaped open, and his tongue, all swollen, thrust outward. He had one eye shut and one open, covered with a gray film, and that one eye seemed to look right at me. He seemed to be pleading for help from beyond the grave.

"I prayed for his soul, then, even though everyone was afraid of saying a kind word about the Pazzi. The *giovani* played with his body for a few more days; then they grew tired of it and threw it in the Arno. It was seen floating to the sea as far away as Pisa." She paused, then looked directly at me. "You must understand: Lorenzo has done many good things for the city. But he kept the people's hatred of the Pazzi alive. I have no doubt at least one of the *giovani* pocketed a florin or two, dropped into his palm by Lorenzo himself. His vengeance knew no bounds, and for that, God will someday make him pay."

The next day, by way of apology, my father took me with him in his carriage to deliver his very best wools to the Medici palazzo on the Via Larga. We rode inside the great iron gates. As always, I remained in the carriage while servants tethered the horses and my father went in the side entry, accompanied by Medici servants laden down with his wares.

He was inside longer than usual—almost three quarters of an hour. I grew restless, having memorized the building's façade and exhausted my imagination as to what lay behind it.

At last the guards at the side entry parted and my father emerged. But instead of returning to our coach, he stepped to one side and waited. A cadre of guards sporting long swords followed him out the door. An instant later, a single man emerged, leaning heavily on the muscular arm of another; one of his feet was unslippered, wrapped to just above the ankle in the softest combed wool used for newborns' blankets.

He was sallow and slightly stooped, blinking in the bright sun. He looked to my father, who directed his attention to our carriage.

I leaned forward on the seat, mesmerized. The man—homely, with a huge crooked nose and badly misaligned lower jaw—squinted in my direction. After a word to his companion, he drew closer, wincing with each agonizing step, scarcely able to bear any weight on the stricken foot. Yet he persisted until he stood no more than the length of two men from me. Even then, he had to crane his neck forward to see me.

We stared unabashed at each other for a long moment. He appraised me intently, his eyes filled with a cloaked emotion I could not interpret. The air between us seemed atremble, as though lightning had just struck: He *knew* me, though we had never met.

Then the man gave my father a nod, and retreated back inside his fortress. My father entered the carriage and sat beside me without a word, as if nothing unusual had just taken place. As for me, I uttered not a word; I was stricken speechless.

I had just had my first encounter with Lorenzo de' Medici.

XV

*T*he New Year brought ice-covered streets and bitter cold. Despite the weather, my father abandoned our parish of Santo Spirito and began crossing the Arno to attend Mass daily at the cathedral of San Marco, known as the church of the Medici. Old Cosimo had lavished money on its reconstruction and maintained a private cell there, which he had visited more frequently as he neared death.

The new prior, one Fra Girolamo Savonarola, had taken to preaching there. Fra Girolamo, as the people called him, had come to Florence from Ferrara less than two years earlier. An intimate of Lorenzo de'Medici, Count Giovanni Pico, had been much impressed by Savonarola's teachings, and so had begged Lorenzo, as the unofficial head of San Marco, to send for the friar. Lorenzo complied.

But once Fra Girolamo gained control of the Dominican monastery, he turned on his host. No matter that Medici money had rescued San Marco from oblivion; Fra Girolamo railed against Lorenzo—not by name, but by implication. The parades organized by the Medici were pronounced sinful; the pagan antiquities assiduously collected by Lorenzo, blasphemous; the wealth and political control enjoyed by him and his family, an affront to God, the only rightful wielder of temporal power. For those reasons, Fra Girolamo broke with the custom followed by all of San Marco's new priors: He refused to pay his respects to the convent's benefactor, Lorenzo.

Such behavior appealed to the enemies of the Medici and to the envious poor. But my father was entranced by Savonarola's prophecies of the soon-to-come Apocalypse.

Like many in Florence, my father was a sincere man who strove to understand and appease God. Being an educated man, he was also aware of an important astrological event that had occurred several years earlier: the conjunction of Jupiter and Saturn. All agreed this marked a monumental event. Some said it augured the arrival of the Antichrist (widely believed to be the Turkish sultan Mehmet, who had stolen Constantinople and now threatened all Christendom), others that it predicted a spiritual cleansing within the Church.

Savonarola believed it foretold both. My father returned one morning breathless after Mass; Fra Girolamo had admitted during the sermon that God had spoken directly to him. "And he said that the Church would first be scourged, then purified and revived," my father said, his face aglow with a peculiar light. "We are living at the end of time."

He was determined to take me with him the following Sunday to hear the friar speak. And he begged my mother to accompany us. "He is touched by God, Lucrezia. I swear to you, if only you would listen to him with your own ears, your life would be forever changed. He is a holy man, and if we convinced him to pray for you . . ."

Normally my mother would have refused her husband nothing, but in this case, she held firm. It was too cold for her to venture out, and crowds tended to excite her overmuch. If she went out for Mass, it would be to our own church of Santo Spirito, only a short walk away—where God would hear her prayers just as surely as He heard Fra Girolamo's. "Besides," she pointed out, "you can always listen to him, then come and tell me directly what he has said."

My father was disappointed and, I think, irritated, though he kept it from my mother. And he was convinced that, if my mother would only go and listen to Fra Girolamo, her condition would improve magically.

The day after my parents' disagreement on this subject, a visitor came to our palazzo: Count Giovanni Pico of Mirandolo, the very man who had convinced Lorenzo de' Medici to bring Savonarola to Florence.

Count Pico was an intelligent, sensitive man, a scholar of the classics and the Hebrew Kabbalah. He was handsome as well, with golden hair and clear gray eyes. My parents received him cordially—he was, after all, part of the Medici's inner circle . . . and knew Savonarola. I was allowed to sit in on the adults' conversation while Zalumma hovered, directing other servants and making sure Count Pico's goblet was full of our best wine. We gathered in the great chamber where my mother had met with the astrologer; Pico sat beside my father, directly across from my mother and me. Outside, the sky was obscured by lead-colored clouds that threatened rain; the air was cold and bone-achingly damp—a typical Florentine winter's day. But the fire in the hearth filled the room with heat and an orange light that painted my mother's pale face with a becoming glow, and glinted off the gold of Pico's hair.

What struck me most about Ser Giovanni, as he wished to be called, was his warmth and utter lack of pretension. He spoke to my parents—and most strikingly, to me—as if we were all his equals, as if he were beholden to us for our kindness in welcoming him.

I assumed he had come for purely social reasons. As an intimate of Lorenzo de' Medici, Ser Giovanni had encountered my father several times when he had come to sell his wools. Fittingly, the conversation began in earnest with a discussion of *il Magnifico*'s health. It had been poor of late; like his father, Piero *il Gottoso*, Lorenzo suffered terribly from gout. His pain had recently become so extreme that he had been unable to leave his bed or receive visitors.

"I pray for him." Ser Giovanni sighed. "It is hard to witness his agony. But I believe he will rally. He takes strength from his three sons, especially the youngest, Giuliano, who spends what time he can spare from his studies to be at his father's side. It is inspiring to see such devotion in one so young."

"I hear Lorenzo is still determined to win a cardinal's hat for his second boy," my father said, with the faintest hint of disapproval. He kept stroking his bearded chin with the pad of his thumb and his knuckle, a habit he usually indulged only when nervous.

"Giovanni, yes." Pico flashed a brief, wan smile. "My namesake."

I had seen both boys. Giuliano was fair of face and form, but Giovanni looked like an overstuffed sausage with spindly legs. The eldest brother, Piero, took after his mother, and was being groomed as his father's successor—though rumor said he was a dullard, entirely unfit.

Pico hesitated before continuing; his mien was that of a man being pulled in two directions. "Yes, Lorenzo is quite attached to the idea . . . though, of course, Giovanni is far too young to be considered. It would require a . . . bending of canon law."

"Lorenzo is quite talented at bending things," my father said offhandedly. Even I had overheard enough of this particular topic to know the outrage it had incited in most Florentines; Lorenzo had lobbied to raise taxes in order to pay for Giovanni's cardinalship. My father's mood grew abruptly jocular. "Tell Madonna Lucrezia what he said about his boys."

"Ah." Pico lowered his face slightly as his lips curved gently upward. "You must understand that he does not say it to them directly, of course. He dotes on them too much to show them any unkindness." At last, he gazed straight into my mother's eyes. "Just as you so obviously do on your daughter, Madonna."

I did not understand why my mother flushed. She had been uncharacteristically quiet up to this point, though she was clearly taken, as we all were, with the charming Count.

Pico appeared to take no note of her discomfort. "Lorenzo always says: 'My eldest is foolish, the next clever, and the youngest, good.'"

My mother's smile was taut; she gave a nod, then said, "I am glad young Giuliano is a comfort to his father. I am sorry to hear of Ser Lorenzo's illness."

Pico sighed again, this time in mild frustration. "It is hard to witness, Madonna. Especially since—I am sure your husband has spoken of this—I am a follower of the teachings of Fra Girolamo."

"Savonarola," my mother said softly, her posture stiffening at the mention of the name. Suddenly, I understood her reticence.

Messer Giovanni continued speaking as if he had not heard. "I have begged Lorenzo several times to send for Fra Girolamo—but *il Magnifico* still rankles at having been rebuffed by San Marco's new prior. I truly believe, Madonna Lucrezia, that were Fra Girolamo permitted to lay hands upon Lorenzo and pray for him, he would be healed at once."

My mother averted her face; Pico's tone grew more impassioned.

"Oh, sweet Madonna, do not turn from the truth. I have seen Fra Girolamo work miracles. In my life, I have met no man more devoted to God or more sincere. Forgive me for being so blunt in your presence, but we have all seen priests who consort with women, who overindulge in food and wine and all manner of worldly corruption. But Fra Girolamo's prayers are powerful because his ways are pure. He lives in poverty; he fasts; he expiates his sin with the whip. When he is not preaching or ministering to the poor, he is on his knees in prayer. And God speaks to him, Madonna. God gives him visions."

As he spoke, Ser Giovanni's countenance grew incandescent; his eyes seemed brighter than the fire. He leaned forward and took my mother's hand in his with great tenderness and a concern that held no trace of impropriety. My father moved toward her as well, until he was balanced precariously on the edge of his chair. Clearly, he had brought Pico here expressly for this purpose.

"Forgive my boldness, but your husband has told me of your suffering, Madonna Lucrezia. I cannot bear to think of one so young and fair being denied a normal life—especially when I know, with infinite certainty, that Fra Girolamo's prayers can cure you."

My mother was mortified, furious; she could not meet Pico's gaze. Yet despite the intensity of her emotions, her tone was controlled as she replied, "Other holy men have prayed to God on my behalf. I and my husband have prayed, and we are good Christians, yet God has not seen fit to heal me." At last, she brought herself to face Pico. "Yet, if you are so convinced of the efficacy of Fra Girolamo's prayers, why do you not ask him to pray for me from afar?"

In his urgency, Messer Giovanni vacated his chair to bend on one knee before my mother in a posture of outright supplication; he lowered his voice so that I had to lean forward myself in order to hear it over the crackling of the fire.

"Madonna . . . you have certainly heard of the prophecy of the *papa angelico?*"

Everyone in France and Italy knew of the ages-old prophecy of the angelic Pope—one elected not by cardinals but by God, who would come to cleanse the Church of its corruption and unite it shortly before Christ's return.

My mother gave the most cursory of nods.

"He is Fra Girolamo; in my heart, I am convinced. He is no ordinary man. Madonna, what harm can it do for you to come hear him once? I will arrange for him to meet you privately after Mass, this very Sunday if you are willing. Think of it: Through Fra Girolamo's hands, God will heal you. You need be a prisoner in this house no longer. Only come, Madonna . . ."

She glanced over at my father. There was reproach in her gaze at first, for he had put her in the most awkward possible situation; yet that reproach melted away as she caught sight of his face.

There was nothing conniving in my father's expression, nothing that smacked of satisfaction or victory. Like Pico's, his face was aglow—not with reflected firelight or godly inspiration, but with the purest, most desperate love I had ever seen.

It was that, more than Pico's persuasive charm, which made her yield; and when at last she answered the Count, she was gazing upon my father, with all the pain and love that had been hidden in her heart now visible in her expression. Her eyes shone with tears, which spilled onto her cheeks when she spoke.

"Only once," she said—to my father, not to the kneeling Pico. "Only once."

XVI

That Sunday the sky was blue, lit by a sun too feeble to soften the gripping cold. My thickest cloak, of scarlet wool lined with rabbit fur, was not enough to warm me; the air stung my eyes and made them water. In the carriage, my mother sat rigid and expressionless between me and Zalumma, her black hair and eyes in striking contrast to the white ermine cape wrapped about her emerald velvet gown. Across from us, my father glanced solicitously at his wife, eager to obtain a sign of encouragement or affection, but she gazed past him as if he were not present. Zalumma glanced directly at my father and did not bother to hide the outrage she felt on behalf of her mistress.

Count Pico rode with us and did his best to distract my father and me with pleasant comments, but there was no ignoring my mother's humiliation, icy and bitter as the weather. Arrangements had been made for us to meet privately with Fra Girolamo directly after the service, so that he could lay hands upon my mother and pray for her.

I gasped as we rolled up to the entrance of the church at San Marco. My awe was not generated by the building—a plain structure of unadorned stone, of the same style as our parish at Santo Spirito—

but rather by the number of people who, being unable to find room inside the sanctuary, pressed tightly against one another in the doorway, on the steps, all the way out into the piazza.

Had Count Pico not been with us, we would never have gained entry. He called out as he stepped from the carriage, and at once, three generously sized Dominican monks came forward and escorted us inside. Their effect on the the crowd was magical; it melted away like wax before a flame. In a moment, I found myself standing between my mother and father not far from the pulpit and the main altar, beneath which Cosimo de' Medici lay entombed.

Compared to the grand Duomo, San Marco's interior was sedate and unremarkable, with its pale stone colonnades and its simple altar. Yet the mood inside the sanctuary was feverish; despite the numbing chill, women fanned themselves and whispered, agitated. Men stamped their feet—not against the cold, but out of impatience—and monks groaned as they prayed aloud. I felt as though I were at Carnival, awaiting a much-anticipated joust.

The choir began to sing, and the processional began.

With rapt expressions, worshipers turned eagerly toward the parade. First came the young acolytes, one holding the great cross, another swinging a thurible which perfumed the air with frankincense. Next came the deacon, and then the priest himself.

Last of all came Fra Girolamo, in the place of highest honor. At the sight of him, people cried out: "Fra Girolamo! Pray for me!" "God bless you, Brother!" Loudest of all was the cry "Babbo! Babbo!" that sweet term only the youngest children use to address their fathers.

I stood on tiptoe and craned my neck trying to get a glimpse of him. I caught only the impression of a frayed brown friar's robe poorly filled by a thin figure; the hood was up, and his head was bowed. Pride was not among his sins, I decided.

He sat, huddled and intimidated, with the acolytes; only then did the people grow calmer. Yet as the Mass progressed, their restlessness again increased. When the choir sang the *Gloria in excelsis,* the crowd began to fidget. The Epistle was chanted, the Gradual sung; when the priest read the Gospel, people were murmuring continuously—to themselves, to each other, to God.

And to Fra Girolamo. It was like listening to the thrum of insects and nocturnal creatures on a summer's night—a sound loud and unintelligible.

The instant he ascended the pulpit, the sanctuary fell profoundly silent, so silent that I could hear a carriage's wooden wheels rattling on the cobblestones of the Via Larga.

Above us, above Cosimo's bones, stood a small gaunt man with sunken cheeks and great, protruding dark eyes; his hood was pushed back, revealing a head crowned by coarse black curls.

He was even homelier than his nemesis, Lorenzo de' Medici. His brow was low and sloping. His nose looked as if someone had taken a great axe-shaped square of flesh and pressed it to his face; the bridge jutted straight out from his brow in a perpendicular line, then dropped down at an abrupt right angle. His lower teeth were crooked and protruded so that his full lower lip pushed outward.

No messiah was ever more unseemly. Yet the timid man I had seen in the procession and the one who ascended the pulpit could not have differed more. This new Savonarola, this touted *papa angelico,* had increased magically in stature; his eyes blazed with certainty, and his bony hands gripped the sides of the pulpit with divine authority. This was a man transformed by a power greater than himself, a power that radiated from his frail body and permeated the chill air surrounding us. For the first time since entering the church, I forgot the cold. Even my mother, who had remained subdued, beaten, and silent throughout the ritual, let go a soft sound of amazement.

On the other side of my father, the Count clasped his hands in a gesture of supplication. "Fra Girolamo," he cried, "give us your blessing and we will be healed!" I glanced at his upturned face, radiant with devotion, at the sudden tears filling his eyes. At once I understood why Zalumma had once derided Savonarola and his followers as *piagnoni*—"wailers."

But the emotion swirling about us was infinite, wild, genuine. Men and women stretched forth their arms, palms open, pleading.

And Fra Girolamo responded. His gaze swept over us; he seemed to see us, each one, and to acknowledge the love directed at him. He made the sign of the cross over the crowd with hands that trembled faintly from contained emotion—and when he did, contented sighs rose heavenward, and at last the sanctuary again was still.

Savonarola closed his eyes, summoning an internal force, and then he spoke.

"Our sermon comes today from the twentieth chapter of Jeremiah." His voice, loud and ringing against the vaulted ceiling, was surprisingly high-pitched and nasal.

He shook his head sorrowfully and lowered his face as if shamed. "I am in derision daily, everyone mocketh me . . . because the word of the Lord was made a reproach unto me. . . ." He raised his face skyward, as if looking straight at God. "But His word was in mine heart as a burning fire shut up in my bones, and I was weary with forbearing. . . ."

Now he looked on us. "People of Florence! Though others mock me, I can no longer hold back the word of the Lord. He has spoken unto me, and it burns in me so bright I must speak or be consumed by its flame.

"Hear the word of God: Think you well, O you wealthy, for affliction shall strike you! This city shall no longer be called Florence, but Den of Thieves, Immorality, Bloodshed. Then you will all be poor, all wretched. . . . Unheard-of times are at hand."

As he spoke, his voice deepened and grew stronger. The air vibrated with his booming assertions; it trembled with a presence that might well have been God.

"O you fornicators, you sodomites, you lovers of filth! Your children shall be brutalized, dragged into the streets and mangled. Their blood will fill the Arno, yet God will not heed their piteous cries!"

I started as a woman close behind us let out an anguished howl; the church walls echoed with racking sobs. Overwhelmed by remorse, my own father buried his face in his hands and wept along with Count Pico.

But my mother stiffened; she seized my arm protectively and, blinking rapidly from anger, tilted her chin defiantly at Fra Girolamo. "How dare he!" she said, her gaze fixed on the monk, who had paused to give his words time to take effect. Her voice was raised, loud enough to be heard over the wailing crowd. "God hears the cries of innocent children! How can he say such horrid things?"

Just as my mother had clutched my arm protectively, so Zalumma quickly took my mother's. "Hush, Madonna. You must calm yourself. . . ." She leaned closer to whisper directly into my mother's ear. My mother gave an indignant shake of her head and wound her arm about my shoulders. She pressed me tightly to her side as though I were a small child. Zalumma ignored the preacher and his *piagnoni* and kept her keen gaze focused on her mistress. I, too, grew worried; I could feel the rapid rise and fall of my mother's bosom, feel the tension in her grip.

"This is not right," she whispered hoarsely. "This is not right. . . ."

So many in the church were crying and moaning, murmuring to Fra Girolamo and God, that not even my father noticed her; he and Pico were far too captivated by the preacher.

"Oh Lord!" Fra Girolamo cried sharply. The monk pressed his forehead to his folded hands; he released a bitter sob, then raised his tear-streaked face toward Heaven. "Lord, I am only a humble monk. I have not asked for Your visitation; I do not crave to speak for You, or to receive visions. Yet I humbly submit to Your will. In Your name, I am willing, as Jeremiah was, to endure the sufferings inflicted by the unholy on Your prophets."

He gazed down at us, his eyes and voice suddenly tender. "I weep . . . I weep as you do, for the children. I weep for Florence, and the scourge that awaits her. Yet how long can we sin? How long offend God, before He is compelled to unleash His righteous wrath? Like a loving father, He has stayed His hand. But when His children continue to err grievously, when they mock Him, He must, for *their* good, mete out harsh punishment.

"Look at you women: you, with sparkling jewels hanging heavy round your necks, from your ears. If one of you—only *one* of you— repented of the sin of vanity, how many of the poor might be fed?

Look at the swaths of silk, of brocade, of velvet, of priceless gold thread that adorn your earthly bodies. If but *one* of you dressed plainly to please God, how many would be saved from starvation?

"And you men, with your whoring, your sodomy, your gluttony and drunkenness: Were you to turn instead to the arms of your wife alone, the Kingdom of God would have more children. Were you to give half your plate to the poor, none in Florence would go hungry; were you to forswear wine, there would be no brawling, no bloodshed in the city.

"You wealthy, you lovers of art, you collectors of vain things: How you offend, with your glorification of man instead of the Divine, with your vile and useless displays of wealth, while others die for want of bread and warmth! Cast off your earthly riches and look instead for that treasure which is eternal.

"Almighty God! Turn our hearts from sin toward You. Spare us the torment that is surely coming to those who flout Your laws."

I looked to my mother. She was staring with a gaze fixed and furious, not at Savonarola but at a point far beyond him, beyond the stone walls of San Marco.

"Mother," I said, but she could not hear me. I tried to slip from her embrace, but her grip only tightened until I yelped. She had turned stone rigid, with me caught in her grasp. Zalumma recognized the signs at once and was speaking gently, rapidly to her, urging her to free me, to lie down here, to know that all would be well.

"*This* is the judgment from God!" my mother shouted, with such force that I struggled in vain to lift my hands to my ears.

Fra Girolamo heard. The congregation near us heard. They looked to my mother and me, expectant. My father and Pico regarded us with pure horror.

Zalumma put her arms about my mother's shoulders and tried to bring her down, but she was planted firm as rock. Her voice deepened and changed timbre until I no longer knew it.

"Hear me!" Her words rang with such authority that it silenced the whimpering. "Flames shall consume him until his limbs drop, one by one, into Hell! Five headless men shall cast him down!"

XVII

*M*y mother fell heavily against me. I crumpled beneath her, colliding with my father as I did. I snatched a fleeting impression of Pico pulling him back before I reached the cold, unforgiving marble. I landed on my side, simultaneously striking my head, my shoulder, and my hip.

There came flashes of green velvet and white ermine, the hems of women's skirts and the boots of men. I heard whispers, exclamations, and Zalumma's shouts.

My mother lay atop me, her side pressed to mine. Her limbs thrashed; her elbow spasmed and dug into my ribs. At the same time, my mother's teeth champed; the air released each time she opened her mouth whistled in my ear. The sound terrified me. I should have been holding her head, making sure she did not bite her tongue or otherwise harm herself.

Zalumma's loud commands suddenly became intelligible. "Grab her arms! Pull her out!"

Strong hands seized my wrists, lifted my arms above my head. I was rolled onto my back. My mother's head fell onto my breast; her teeth whistled through the air, then snapped fiercely together. All the while, her arms and legs pummeled me; her hand swiped beneath my chin, and drew away a piece of flesh beneath her fingernail.

Near my feet, invisible, Zalumma bellowed: "Pull her *out!*"

My father at once came to himself. With uncanny force, he clasped my upraised arms and dragged me out from under my mother's writhing body. The movement caused an excruciating surge of pain in my ribs.

But the instant I was free, it was forgotten. I did not acknowledge my father's aid; instead, I clambered to my knees and turned toward my struggling mother. Zalumma had already crawled forward and used her body to weigh down her mistress's kicking legs.

I found the furred edge of my mother's cape and jammed it between her gnashing teeth. My intervention came late: She had bitten through her tongue, with frightening result. Blood stained her lips and teeth, cheek and chin; the white ermine round her face was spattered with crimson. Though I held her head fast, it jerked so violently in my hands that her cap fell back beneath her. My fingers soon were interlaced in her soft dark hair; the careful coils arranged earlier that morning by Zalumma frayed into tangles.

"It is the Devil!" A man stepped forward—young, red-haired, with pockmarked skin; I recognized him as the priest from Santa Maria del Fiore. "I saw her do this before, in the Duomo. She is possessed; the evil inside her cannot bear to stand upright in the house of God."

Murmurs surrounded us and increased to a rumble until, above us, Savonarola cried out, "Silence!"

All looked to him. His eyebrows were knit in a thunderous scowl of indignation at such an offensive display. The red-haired priest stepped back and disappeared into the crowd; the others, silent and docile, went rustling back to their places.

"The Evil One desires nothing more than to interrupt the word of the Lord," Fra Girolamo intoned. "We must not let ourselves be distracted. God will prevail."

He would have said more, but my father moved toward the pulpit. His gaze fastened on the monk, he gestured with his arm toward his afflicted wife and called desperately, plaintively, "Fra Girolamo, help her! Heal her now!"

I still held my mother's head, but like the others, I watched San Marco's prior closely, breathlessly.

His frown eased; his eyes flickered briefly with uncertainty before his sense of complete authority returned. "God will help her, not I. The sermon will continue; Mass will be celebrated." As my father bowed his head, downcast, Fra Girolamo signaled to Count Pico and two Dominican monks in the congregation. "Attend to her," he told them softly. "Take her to the sacristy to await me."

Then in a loud voice, he began again to preach. "Children of God! Such evil portents will only increase, until all in our city repent and turn their hearts to the Lord; otherwise, a scourge will come, such as the Earth has never seen. . . ."

From that moment, I heard the cadence and pitch of his sermon, but not the sense of it, for two brown-robed monks had appeared at my mother's side. Pico took charge.

"Fra Domenico," he said, to the larger one, who possessed a great square head and a dullard's eyes. "I will have the women move away. Then you lift Madonna Lucrezia"—he gestured at my mother, still in the throes of her fit—"and carry her off. Fra Marciano, help him if he needs it."

Neither Zalumma nor I budged. "My mother cannot be moved— it might injure her," I insisted, indignant.

Fra Domenico listened silently; then, with movements calm and deliberate, he parted Zalumma's protective arms and grasped my mother's waist.

He lifted her with ease, forcing Zalumma to fall back. I reached vainly for my mother as her head, with its chaotic tangles of hair swinging, rose from my lap. Flinching only slightly at her flailing limbs, Domenico slung her over one shoulder, as a baker might a sack of flour. My mother's legs beat against his chest and torso, her arms against his back, yet he seemed not to feel it.

"Stop!" Zalumma cried out at the monk. She was almost as terrifying a sight as her mistress: The scarf beneath her cap was askew, permitting some of her billowing curls to escape; worse, she had been struck in the eye, which was already swollen half shut; the cheekbone beneath was dull red and shiny, promising to become a magnificent bruise.

"Leave her be!" I shouted at Fra Domenico. I struggled to stand, but bystanders stood on my skirts, and I fell again.

"Let her rise!" a male voice commanded above me. People made room where there was none. A strong arm reached down to grasp mine and pulled me to my feet; I rose, gasping, to stare up into the eyes of a stranger—a tall, thin man wearing the distinguished dress of a *Buonomi,* a Goodman, one of the twelve elected every two months to counsel the eight Lord Priors. He met my gaze with an odd, intense recognition, though we had never met before.

I pulled away from him immediately and followed the implacable Domenico, who was already making his way through the crowd. Forgetting he was in God's house, my father hurried after Domenico, demanding he be gentler with my mother.

Domenico's companion, Fra Marciano, offered Zalumma and me an arm for support. Furious, silent, Zalumma refused it, though she limped noticeably. I, too, waved his arm away. But Fra Marciano's demeanor remained concerned and kindly. He was frail and older, with thinning hair; his eyes revealed a gentle goodness.

"Be reassured," he told me. "The lady is in God's own hands; He will let no harm come to her."

I did not answer. Instead I walked, wordless as the others, behind Fra Domenico and his burden until we arrived at the sacristy.

It was a small room, far colder than the sanctuary, which was warmed by hundreds of bodies; I could see my own breath. Fra Domenico carried my mother to the only place possible: a narrow wooden table, which my father first covered with her soft fur cape. Once the monk set her down, my father pushed him away with a vehemence that startled me. The two men, breathing hard, shared a look of pure loathing; I thought they would come to blows.

Domenico's gaze flickered. At last he looked down, then turned and lumbered away. Fra Marciano remained with us, apparently hoping to lend what comfort or aid he could.

At some point during her journey, my mother's fit had passed. Now, as she lay stuporous and limp, my father removed his crimson mantle and covered her with it. Count Pico laid a hand upon his shoulder.

My father tried to shrug it off. "How could God permit such a thing?" His tone was bitter. "And why did Fra Girolamo permit her to be handled by that beast?"

Pico spoke softly, though his tone was oddly hard. "Fra Domenico is always by Fra Girolamo's side; you know that, Antonio. Perhaps God has let Madonna Lucrezia suffer this indignity just so that He might raise her up all the more greatly. Her healing will be a marvelous testament to all. Have faith. Believe in God's greatness. He has not brought us this far to disappoint us."

"I pray not," my father said. He cupped his hands over his eyes. "I cannot bear to see her so. When she learns what has happened . . . the shame will be more than she can bear."

He parted his hands and gazed down at my sleeping mother, so sallow and pale her features seemed cast from wax—wax smeared and flecked with darkening blood. Gently, he brushed a disheveled lock of hair from her brow; as he did, I chanced to glimpse Zalumma, who stood opposite him.

The frank hatred in her expression astonished me. It was well outside the behavior appropriate to a slave, yet I understood. She loved my mother as a sister and despised my father with equal fervor. Until this moment, however, she had kept her feelings toward him concealed.

I was simply troubled. Some time ago, I had laid my worries about the source of my mother's fits to rest. Zalumma's tale about her brother and the injury to his head had convinced me that the cause of my mother's malady was natural. Now, after her terrifying utterance before Savonarola, I was no longer certain. Could a soul as gentle and pious as my mother's be a tool of the Evil One?

For a quarter of an hour, our unhappy group waited in the unheated sacristy. I wrapped my mantle tightly about me to no avail. The perspiration from my earlier exertion chilled me through; my breath condensed and turned icy on the wool. My poor mother, in her stupor, shivered despite my father's mantle and the fur cloak on which she lay.

At last, the heavy door opened with a creak; we turned. Savonarola appeared in the doorway, standing next to the burly Fra Domenico and looking far smaller than he had in the pulpit.

My father stepped next to my mother and rested a hand on her arm. His expression was hard; he stared at Fra Domenico even as he spoke to Savonarola. "We have no need of *him.*" He inclined his chin at Domenico.

"He is my right hand," Fra Girolamo said. "If he does not enter, *I* do not enter."

My father blinked and lowered his gaze, defeated. The two monks stepped inside; Domenico's expression was guarded.

Just behind them in the open doorway, the red-haired, pockmarked priest from the Duomo appeared.

"Surely God has sent you to Florence, Fra Girolamo!" he exclaimed, his face florid with adulation. "You bring countless sinners to repentance each day. You are this city's salvation!"

Fra Girolamo struggled not to be swayed by such flattery. His face and gaze were slightly averted in a sincere effort to remain humble, yet the words clearly pleased him. In his high nasal voice, he countered, "It is the Lord Who shall save Florence, not I. Keep your devotion focused on God, not on any man." He paused, then said, his tone firm, "I have other business now."

His latter words were meant to dismiss the priest, who now stood blocking the entry to the sacristy, as if unwilling to let the friar pass until he granted a boon. But instead of leaving, the young man looked into the sacristy. "Ah! This is the woman possessed of many devils!"

Fra Girolamo gave him a sharp look. "We will let God be the judge of her affliction." He glanced pointedly at Fra Domenico, who had been sympathetically inclined to the priest; the towering monk took a reluctant step toward the door.

The priest sidled gracefully past the larger monk and stepped inside the chamber before he could be barred. "But Fra Girolamo, you said it yourself: The Evil One tried to stop the people from hearing the message God has given you. No one would ever have uttered such words as she did if the Devil himself had not authored them." His pale eyes brightened with unsettling conviction. "She did the very same thing in the Duomo—cried out words which the Devil forced from her."

Fra Domenico listened, spellbound; even the gentle Fra Marciano stepped forward from our group to hear the charismatic young priest.

"It's true, Babbo," Domenico said to his master. "Your presence would provoke devils. How angry you must make them! How frightened! Here is a chance to show the true power of the Lord."

Uncomfortable with the direction of the conversation, yet unable to ignore it, Savonarola moved past Domenico and the priest until he stood at my mother's side, directly across from my father and Pico.

"Is this true?" Fra Girolamo quietly asked my father. "Did she utter strange words in the Duomo before a fit?"

Silent, cautious, my father looked to me and Zalumma. She was brazen, challenging, her cap now removed, her wild blue-black hair as intimidating as Medusa's serpentine crown.

"No," she lied. "She has suffered from fits after an injury to her head, but there is naught of the Devil in it."

Savonarola moved to my mother's head and gently laid his hands upon her shoulders; his timidity evaporated, and he said with confidence, "Let us pray silently."

We all obeyed, bowing our heads; I dared to peer from beneath half-closed lids. The priest and Domenico entered, the latter closing the large brass door behind him. Both hurried over to stand by Fra Girolamo. They pushed their way to stand on my mother's right side, as close to the object of their adoration as possible; the act displaced Zalumma and me, forcing us down toward my mother's legs.

My father—his eyes red-rimmed—lowered his head, but his eyes were open, his gaze vigilant and fierce. He stood on my mother's left, with Pico beside him.

After a long pause, Savonarola's eyebrows knit together. "God has spoken to me. Unexpiated sin has led to this woman's malady—a sin too long secret and buried; it has tainted her soul. I shall pray for God to open her heart and remove her burden, that she may be freed from any influence of the Evil One." He lifted his face and, in a lower tone, asked my father, "Do you know, sir, of a grievous sin she may have been unwilling to confess?"

My father glanced up at him with unalloyed surprise; sudden emotion so overwhelmed him that he could not speak, could only let go an anguished sob.

Pico faced him. "Antonio, my friend, you must trust in Fra Girolamo. God has brought us all here for a purpose. This is all for Madonna Lucrezia's good."

"Does anyone lack faith? Does anyone wish to leave?" Fra Girolamo stared at us each in turn.

"I shall pray with you!" said the priest, excited.

Savonarola gave him a look of warning. "Those who wish may lay hands upon her with me and follow silently with my prayer."

"Only pray no harm comes to her," my father said urgently. "Only pray that God heals her!"

Savonarola answered with a stare that quieted him at once. The priest and Fra Domenico quickly laid their palms upon my mother's upper arms and waist; my father put a hand upon her right arm, along with Pico. Zalumma and I could do no more than rest our hands upon my mother's ankles.

The little monk lifted his hands, pressed them more firmly against my mother's shoulders, then squeezed his eyes shut. "O Lord!" he exclaimed, in the thunderous tone he had used when preaching. "You see before you a woman, a miserable sinner. . . ."

Beneath his hands, my mother stirred. Her eyelids fluttered. Hoarsely, she whispered, "Antonio?"

He took her hand and spoke softly. "Lucrezia, I am here. All will be well. Fra Girolamo is praying for your healing. Rest, and have faith."

During their gentle exchange, the friar continued his prayer.

"There is darkness buried here, an opening for Satan. Lord! It has left her body stolen, wrenched from her. . . ."

My mother's eyes widened from fright. Though drowsy, she sensed Savonarola's grip tightening on her shoulders; she moved weakly as if to shake off all the hands holding her down. "Antonio! What is he saying? What has happened?"

At that very moment, the priest—who had begun to tremble with righteous fervor—cried out: "Devils possess her, O Lord!"

"Yes!" Domenico rumbled, in a great, deep voice. "Devils, Lord!"

"Stop," my mother whispered.

Zalumma interrupted, her words swift and sharp, directed mostly at the priest, but also at Savonarola. She pressed against Domenico's great, broad back, trying to reach her mistress. "Stop! You are frightening her! She must stay calm!"

"All will be well, Lucrezia," my father said. "All will be well. . . ."

Savonarola paid no one heed; his earnest conversation was between himself and God. "O Lord! None can save her but You. I am not worthy to face You myself, but I beg most humbly: Save her from her sins. Heal her. . . ."

The pockmarked priest, lost in his own frenzy, continued the prayer as if it were his own. "Free her from Satan's grip! Hear me, Devil! It is not I but God Who commands you—leave this woman! In the name of Christ Jesus, leave her body and set her free!"

Fra Domenico, prompted to righteous zeal by the priest's words, leaned down and seized both my mother's arms with undue force. Spraying spittle, he shouted directly into her face: "Go, Devil, in the name of Christ!"

"Help me," my mother called out weakly. "Antonio, in the name of God . . ."

At the same time, my father gripped Fra Domenico's thick wrists, shouting, "Unhand her! Let her go!"

Savonarola's tone rose sharply, a rebuke to the priest, to Domenico, to my father. "We ask for healing here, for forgiveness of sin. Only then, Lord, will the Evil One loosen his hold upon her—"

"Stop this!" Zalumma commanded, at the cacophony of prayer. "Can't you see what you are doing to her?"

My mother's body went rigid. Her jaw began to work, her limbs to pound against the wooden table. Her head jerked from side to side; blood from her injured tongue sprayed the men.

Zalumma and I tried to move to our positions of emergency, but the monks and priests would not let me near my mother's head. With Zalumma, I lay down across my mother's legs—but Fra Domenico pushed us away with one great backward sweep of his arm, without looking at us. My father bent over my mother and put an arm beneath her shoulder.

"You see, Babbo, the Devil shows himself!" Domenico crowed in triumph, and laughed. "Begone! You have no power here!"

"Let us pray to God," Fra Girolamo thundered. "O Lord, we beg you for this woman's freedom from sin, from the influence of the Evil One; we ask for her healing. If there be any obstacle, reveal it now, Lord!"

"Satan begone," the priest countered, with equal volume and fervor. "Leave, in the name of the Father!"

Fra Domenico, his dull features alight with frightening conviction, was caught between the prayers of prior and priest. Echoing his master's words, he cried out, "Reveal it now, O Lord! Leave, Satan, in the name of the Son!"

As he uttered the words, my mother's body heaved upward in spasm, so violently that the men lost their hold upon her. An odd silence ensued; the priest and Savonarola, startled, ceased praying. In response, Domenico brought the heels of his massive hands downward, with full force, upon my mother's heart.

"Leave, in the name of the Spirit!"

In the unexpected quiet, I heard a soft but horrible noise: a snap dulled by the cover of flesh, the sound of my mother's breastbone breaking. I screamed, scarcely aware of Zalumma's own shrieks, of my father's furious roar.

My mother's eyes bulged. Blood welled up from deep within her and spilled from the corners of her mouth down the sides of her cheeks, into her ears. She tried to cough and instead inhaled blood; there followed the wrenching sound of gurgling, of one desperately seeking air and finding only liquid. She was drowning.

My father wrested Domenico away from my mother, then returned to her side. Without thought, I threw myself against the stolid monk and pummeled him with my fists, vaguely aware that Zalumma, too, was striking him.

Coming to myself, I moved to my mother's side. There I bent low, my elbows resting on the table, my face close to my mother's, near my father's. Zalumma was beside me, her shoulder pressed against mine.

The monks had altogether abandoned her. Fra Girolamo had removed his hands and was staring down at her with an expression of frank confusion and dismay; the priest had withdrawn in fear and was crossing himself repeatedly. Pico, too, stood at a distance, trying to make sense of the dreadful turn of events.

Only my father remained at my mother's side. "Lucrezia!" he cried. "Oh God, Lucrezia, speak!"

But my mother could not. The movement of her limbs grew weaker and weaker until at last they stilled. Her face had taken on the color of a dove's breast; blood bubbled from her lips as she fought to draw air. I tried to help in the only way I knew: I pressed my face close to hers and said that I loved her, and all would be well.

I watched as the light of terror faded from her eyes along with life itself, and I saw the instant her stare grew dull and fixed.

XVIII

*U*nmindful of the blood, I laid my head upon my mother's breast. Zalumma took her hand and pressed it to her lips; my father pressed his cheek against hers. We three mourned over her a time; and then rage swept over me. I raised my damp face and turned to face Domenico. But before I could open my mouth to accuse him, my father screamed, his voice wrenching and raw.

"You have murdered her!" He flung himself at Domenico; his hands were claws, reaching for the big man's throat. "You have murdered her, and I will see you hang for it!"

The monk's face darkened; he lifted an arm to protect himself. Pico and the red-haired priest both threw themselves on my father and barely managed to hold him back.

I screamed along with Zalumma, as we gave vent to our outrage.

"Murderer!"

"Assassin!"

Savonarola stayed well clear of the fray. Once Pico and the priest had subdued my father, Fra Girolamo stepped in front of Domenico, who cringed. "God forgive me," he whimpered. "I am incapable of intentional harm; this was an accident, a dreadful accident. . . . Oh, please believe me, Babbo!"

There came my father's voice behind me, soft and deadly. "This was no accident. You meant to kill her. . . ."

"Here now," Pico stated firmly. "This *was* an accident, and no more. Fra Girolamo and Fra Domenico both came here with the godly intent of healing her."

Savonarola stepped forward, once again the confident man who had ascended the pulpit. "These are the words the Lord has given me: Madonna Lucrezia is free of her affliction. In the hour of her death, she repented of her sin, and dwells now in Purgatory. Be joyful in the knowledge that her soul will soon be with God."

His words tore my father's heart in two. "That is true," he whispered. "But it is no less true that Domenico murdered her."

Fra Girolamo was unrelenting. "What happened here was an act of God. Fra Domenico was merely an instrument. Women!" He turned to exhort the two of us. "Dry your tears! Rejoice that your mistress shall soon be in Heaven."

With a baleful glance, Zalumma spat in his direction, then turned back to her grieving.

"God sees the guilty," I said to him. "God knows the crime that was committed here, and none of your pretty words can ever hide it from His view. He will see justice done to you and to Fra Domenico in His own time." Then, with an abrupt practicality that amazed me, I added, "If you wish to make any effort toward recompense, you can see her brought to our carriage."

"That can be done," Savonarola said. "Afterward, I will pray that God might forgive your hateful words. In time, you will come to accept what has happened. But first, we shall pray for Madonna Lucrezia, that her time in Purgatory might be short. And then I will fetch a priest"—this I took as a deliberate snub to the one in our midst—"to give her Holy Unction." He spoke to all of us, but his gaze was directed at my father, who still stood, defiant, resisting all of Pico's attempts to comfort him. "Let us kneel," Savonarola said. Pico, the priest, and the two monks all obeyed. Zalumma and I remained with my mother.

My father stood, heavy, solid, raw. "He killed her."

"He was the Hand of God," Savonarola countered fiercely. "God responded to our prayers by taking your Lucrezia; soon she will be with Him, free of all suffering. This is a blessing compared to the life she led . . . an outcome to be desired even more than that of a healing here on Earth. You should be thankful." He paused, then again demanded, "Kneel. Kneel, and pray with us for your wife's soul to enter Paradise."

My father let go a sob that was also a roar. He stayed on his feet and stared at Domenico with hell in his eyes.

Domenico knelt behind his master, then opened his eyes and met my father's gaze. His features radiated unmistakable victory. It was a gloating expression, with nothing of God or righteousness in it; in his eyes came a flash of calculating intelligence—so infinitely wicked and cold I could not find my breath.

Then Fra Domenico, looking fast at my father, inclined his head ever so slightly at the table, where my mother lay; and then he slowly, deliberately, inclined his head at me.

My father saw it and recoiled.

"Kneel," Domenico echoed softly.

My father's chest rose and fell so hard, I thought it might burst. And then, covering his face with his hands, he sank to his knees beside Pico.

Domenico smiled and closed his eyes.

But I would not bow. Zalumma would not bow. I did not understand what had transpired between the big monk and my father; I only knew that my father had let himself be broken.

Clinging to my mother's body, I had never despised him so much as I did that moment. Indeed, I could not say whom I most hated at that instant: God, Savonarola, Fra Domenico, or my father, and so I decided to hate them all.

XIX

*A*fter she received Last Rites from San Marco's priest, my mother was taken to our carriage. Most of the crowd had dispersed by then—but even in my grief, I noticed that the sharp-featured stranger who had helped me to my feet stood on the church steps, watching.

We rode back over the Ponte Santa Trinità. Swaddled in bloodied ermine and emerald velvet, my mother lay limp in my father's arms during the ride. He would let no one else touch her. Pico insisted on accompanying us. The Count's presence offended me, but Ser Giovanni's distress was unfeigned. The turn of events had sincerely devastated him.

But my father would not look at Pico, and sat rigidly beside him so that their legs, their elbows, did not accidentally touch. He prayed softly, rapidly, for my mother's soul, alternating between the *Ave Maria* and the Lord's Prayer. When Pico joined in, he hesitated—as if reluctant to accept his friend's prayers—but then he relented and continued.

Unable to bear the sights inside the carriage, I looked out the window. It was an insult that the exterior of San Marco, that the Via

Larga, looked the same. People walked gingerly down the icy streets, their faces wrapped against the cold, but there was no sign of mourning, no respect for the omnipotence of Death.

I felt both pity and anger toward my father. At the same time, I was overcome by a sense of responsibility, and it was that which directed my actions when we at last arrived home. When the carriage rolled to a stop behind our house, I was the first to rise.

"Ser Giovanni." I addressed Count Pico as if we were both adults and I his peer. "Arrangements must be made for a gravedigger today, and a priest for the morrow; she would want to be buried at Santo Spirito. Could you be so kind—"

Before I could finish, Pico answered solemnly. "It would be my honor, Madonna Lisa. In the meantime . . ." He turned to my father, who still cradled my mother's body. "Let us carry her inside."

"Up to her chambers," I said. "Zalumma, go before them and cover her bed so that it is not soiled, and have servants fetch towels and water."

My father pressed his dead wife tightly against his breast. "I will carry her myself."

"Come now," Pico soothed. "You will need help, at least, getting out of the carriage."

My father remained distant toward Pico, refusing to meet his eyes, but he at last nodded. The men lifted my mother from the carriage; but the instant she was free, my father seized her from Pico. "I have her now." He would not be cajoled, so Pico left for Santo Spirito. Zalumma hurried ahead of us into the house.

I walked a few steps ahead of my father, who muttered frantically: "*Ave Maria, gratia plena Dominus tecum, benedicta tu . . .* Almighty God, let her soul rise swiftly to you. Such hell, and all my doing, from the start . . ."

Madness gave him strength. He entered the house without breaking stride and negotiated the high, narrow stairs.

At my mother's chambers, Zalumma, red-eyed but tentatively composed, waited at the open door. "The water to bathe her is coming," she said, "but I have readied the bed."

With infinite care, my father laid my mother down on the bed, covered with many old linens.

"Here," I said. "Let us take this away." I reached for the beautiful emerald velvet cape, its ermine trim stiff with darkening blood. Zalumma helped me pull it from beneath my mother. When we were done, my father dropped to his knees, clasped his wife's hand, and kissed it.

Wails emanated from downstairs as the driver began to tell the other servants. The water and towels soon arrived. "You must go now," I told my kneeling father. "We must wash her."

He shook his head, clinging firmly to my mother. "We must pray for her. Pray until we receive a sign from God that she is in Heaven and suffers no more. *Adveniat regnum tuum.* Thy kingdom come."

"Enough has come of praying today! Leave!" Zalumma's eyes were stark with fury.

I moved between them. "Father, if you want, you can continue in another room." I gently pried his hand from my mother's, then gripped it firmly and helped him rise to his feet.

"We will not be long," I told him. I led him to the door, and firmly shut it behind him.

Then I turned back to face the bed. As I did, I caught sight of Zalumma, looking down at her mistress with a grief mixed with the purest love. In an instant we were both clinging to each other, sobbing.

"How can this be?" I gasped. My chin pressed into her shoulder. "How could God author such a terrible thing?"

"God gives the power of choice to men to do good or ill," Zalumma murmured. "All too often, they accomplish the latter."

I had loved my mother more than anything in all the world; as for my father, whatever love I possessed for him was now tainted. There was Zalumma now, only Zalumma. My mother and her need for care had always united us; now we would have to find a new purpose.

Zalumma patted my back as gently as she might an infant's. "Enough, enough," she said, sighing. I withdrew and calmed myself.

"Look at you," I said, with an incongruous surge of humor, looking at her wild halo of hair, at the brown-red smears on her face. "You could frighten the most stalwart hero."

"I could say as much for you," Zalumma said, with a weak smile. "We had best wash our hands first, but then we must hurry." Her expression darkened as she fought tears. "She will grow stiff quickly now."

We moved to opposite sides of the bed and set to work. The unlacing of the extravagant brocade sleeves, with their gold embroidery, came first; then my mother's heavy overgown, also of green velvet. The close-fitting dress, the *gamurra,* was next, and last was the spattered, stained *camicia,* the undergown of ivory silk. We removed it all from her, until she lay naked; then Zalumma removed her emerald ring and presented it solemnly to me. Earrings and necklace, all had to be removed; no adornment was permitted.

Out of respect, Zalumma handed me one of the towels and let me have the task of cleaning the blood from my mother's battered face. I dipped the towel into the basin again and again, until the water turned cloudy.

Zalumma noticed. "I will fetch more water," she said, for though I had almost finished my mother's face and Zalumma her hands, there was still more blood on her neck and breast.

After she had left, I took my mother's best white woolen *camicia* from the cupboard, and a white linen veil—for the laws were such that she could wear only a simple white garment, and plain wool and linen only were permitted. Then I found her comb and did the best I could to unfasten her hair. It was pitifully tangled, but I was as gentle as possible, drawing the comb first through the ends, then carefully working up toward the scalp. Her hair smelled of rosewater and iron.

As I combed her tangles, I cradled her head in one hand in order to reach those locks at the back of her neck. As I proceeded, gently shifting the position of her head, I felt the teeth of the comb dip, then rise slightly as they ran over her scalp.

The sensation was odd enough that I stopped, set down the comb, and, with unsteady fingers, found the indentation in my mother's skull, between her temple and left ear. I parted the hair there, and found the depression and the scar.

My mother had always insisted that Zalumma, and none of the

other servants, be allowed to arrange her hair. Even I had never been permitted to touch it.

At that instant Zalumma returned, walking circumspectly so as not to spill the fresh water. At the sight of my stricken expression, her own eyes widened; she set down the basin on my mother's night table and closed the door.

"There is a wound on her head," I said, my tone rising with emotion. "A wound, and a scar."

I followed her with my gaze as she deliberately wrung two towels out in the water, then walked over to hand me one.

"You knew," I said. "You always knew. Why didn't you simply tell me? You only hinted at it—but you knew it for a fact."

The towel hung limp in her hands; she lowered her face, overwhelmed. When she raised it at last, it wore a look of bitter resolve. She opened her mouth to speak, but before she could utter the first word, a pounding came at the door.

My father opened it without being bidden; at the sight of his dead wife upon her bed, he winced and averted his eyes. "Please," he said, "let me pray for her in here. I want to be with her now, before she is gone forever."

Zalumma turned on him, her fists balled as if ready to strike. "How dare you!" she seethed. "How dare you, when you are the one responsible for this!"

"Zalumma," I warned. My father had been foolish and wrong to take her to Savonarola, but his intention had been for a happy outcome.

"It's true!" she hissed. "You have finally finished what you started so long ago. So leave—leave now, and let us care for her!"

My father withdrew and closed the door behind him without a word.

Zalumma still stood facing the door, her entire body taut and trembling. I put a hand on her shoulder, but she shrugged it away, then wheeled on me. Years of repressed loathing tumbled from her:

"He struck her! Do you understand? He struck her, and I was bound so long as she lived not to tell!"

XX

I felt like Saint Sebastian—pierced by a hundred arrows, wounded beyond surviving. I could not respond.

Instead, I moved heavily, silently, as Zalumma and I finished cleaning my mother's body, then dressed her in the woolen *camicia*, and affixed to her loose, unplaited hair the linen veil.

We left, and I called for the servants to come for her with words I do not remember.

During her burial in the churchyard, my father proclaimed loudly that Savonarola was right, *Adveniat regnum tuum,* the end of the world was coming; a good thing, for that meant he and his beloved Lucrezia would soon be reunited.

Afterward, when evening had fallen, my father came to call on me.

I was alone in my mother's chamber—prompted by an odd determination to sleep in her bed—when a knock came on the door. "Enter," I said. I expected Zalumma to entreat me again to have something to eat.

Instead, my father stood in the doorway still dressed in the loose-fitting black robe, the *mantello,* of mourning. "Zalumma," he said, his tone timid, unsure. "She was quite angry. . . . Did she say anything more to you? About me and your mother?"

I stared at him with contempt. "She said enough."

"Enough?" The anxiety in his eyes made me hate him all the more.

"Enough," I said, "to make me wish I had never been born your child."

He lifted his chin and blinked swiftly. "You are all I have now," he said, his voice a hoarse whisper. "The only reason I draw breath."

My cruel reply had apparently given him the answer he sought, for he turned and went quickly away.

I slept fitfully that night, awakened by dreams of my mother—that we had made a mistake, that she had never died at all, that Fra Domenico had not killed her. During one dream I was wakened not by emotion, but by the sound of stirring in the room. I lifted my head and made out Zalumma's tall, familiar form in the darkness. She was moving toward the mattress on the floor, where she had always slept beside my mother. At last she realized I was awake, staring at her.

"I am your slave now," she said, and with that she took her place on the floor by my side and settled down to sleep.

XXI

*O*urs was an unhappy home. While Zalumma and I became inseparable, our time was taken up with domestic chores, empty of meaning. I continued my routine: going to market on gray winter days in my mother's stead, buying meat from the butcher, and doing other errands necessary to maintain the smooth running of the household, accompanied always by Zalumma and the driver. But this time, I had no one to instruct me; the decisions were now mine.

I avoided my father as much as possible. We ate uncomfortably when we supped together; many nights he lingered late in the city under the pretense of work, and so I dined alone. Despite my desire to be loving and forgiving, like my mother, I could not hide my resentment; I could not be kind. Not once did it occur to me to ask forgiveness for my vicious remark, for it remained the truth.

In his misery, he clutched at the teachings of Savonarola: He often repeated the friar's contention that the end of the world was nigh, for only this—or death—would bring him closer to his beloved Lucrezia. I suppose he had no choice but to believe that God had taken his wife in order to spare her suffering; otherwise, he would have to accept a large measure of guilt for her death. Otherwise, he would have to deem Savonarola and the dullard Domenico murderers. Twice a day, he attended Mass at San Marco, with Giovanni Pico always at his side.

Pico became a frequent visitor to our home. My father and he began to dress alike—in simple black clothing which could have been taken for priestly garb were it not for the fine tailoring and the exquisiteness of the cloth. Although my father treated the Count with the greatest hospitality—making sure he received the finest morsels from our kitchen and the very best wine—there was a reticence in him, a coolness toward Pico that had not been there before my mother's death.

At supper, my father would repeat what Fra Girolamo had said. He yearned to find the right turn of phrase, to evoke the precise emotion that would procure my forgiveness and inspire me to go to San Marco with him. I never responded to his assertions, but addressed myself strictly to the food before me.

I walked with Zalumma twice a day, in sun and rain, to our nearby church of Santo Spirito. I did so not because I wished to be pious—I still possessed a good deal of rancor toward God—but because I wanted to be close to my mother. Santo Spirito had been her favorite refuge. I knelt in the cold church and stared at the graceful wooden carving of Christ, expired upon the cross. On His face was a look not of suffering, but of deep repose. I hoped my mother shared a similar peace.

Three miserable weeks passed in this fashion. Then, one evening, after I had supped alone because my father was late, a knock came at my chamber door.

I had been reading my mother's precious copy of Dante, trying to decide in which circle of Heaven Fra Girolamo might place himself; trying to decide to which circle of Hell I would confine him.

Zalumma was with me. She had grieved in private as best she could, hiding her tears, but she had known my mother far longer than I had. I would wake at night after disturbing dreams to find her sitting up, motionless in the dark. During the day, she devoted herself to me with a passion. When the knock came that evening, she was squinting next to the oil lamp we shared, decorating one of the handkerchiefs for my *cassone,* my wedding chest, with fine embroidery.

"Come," I said reluctantly. I recognized the knock and had no desire for conversation.

My father opened the door halfway. He still wore his heavy black mantle and his cap. He slumped against the jamb and said, in a tired voice:

"There is cloth downstairs, in the great chamber. I had the servants spread it out for you. There was too much to bring up here." He moved as if those words alone were explanation enough.

"Cloth?"

My question made him pause. "Choose what you wish, and I will bring a tailor for you. You are to have a new gown. Have no concern regarding the expense: It must be as becoming as possible."

Beside me, Zalumma—who had also done her best to ignore my father since my mother's death—glanced up sharply from her sewing.

"Why?" I could not imagine what had prompted this in him, other than a sudden desire to win back my affections. But such behavior was at total odds with the teachings of Savonarola: The friar frowned on sartorial display.

He sighed. The question vexed him; he answered grudgingly. "You are to attend a function at the house of Lorenzo de' Medici."

Il Magnifico—the very target of Savonarola's preaching against wealth and excess. I was too stunned for an instant to reply.

He turned and left then, heading quickly down the stairs, and none of my calls after him would bring him back.

Zalumma and I went down that night, but in order to better see my father's gift, we returned in the morning so that we had the light.

In the reception chamber, measures of Florence's most breathtaking fabrics—in my father's puzzling defiance of the city's sumptuary laws—had been neatly folded and arranged in a dazzling display. These were not the somber colors suitable for a child of one of Savonarola's *piagnoni*. There were peacock blues, turquoise, blue-violets and bright saffron, vivid greens and roses; there were delicate shades known as "peach blossom," "Apollo's hair," and "pink sapphire." For the *camicia,* there were fine white silks, as light as air and embroidered in silver thread, others in gold; there was a dish set nearby of seed pearls, which could be added to the finished product. There were shiny damasks, rich brocades, voided velvets, multiple-pile velvets, and thinner silk velvets threaded with gold and silver. What caught my eye was the *cangiante,* shot silk with a stiff taffeta weave. When held to the light, it reflected at first a deep scarlet; yet when the fabric was slowly moved, the color changed to emerald.

Zalumma and I were like children presented with a plate of sweets: We indulged ourselves, unwinding the fabrics, placing some together to better imagine the finished product. I draped them over my shoulder, across my body, then stared into my mother's hand mirror to see which color most suited me; Zalumma gave her blunt opinion on each. For the first time in weeks, we laughed softly.

And then a thought struck me, abruptly darkening my mood. I had not been able to fathom why my pious father would permit me to attend a party at the Medici palazzo. First, it was too soon after my mother's death for me to be seen dressed in a party gown; second, he was, by virtue of his devotion to Savonarola, an enemy of the Medici now (business matters, of course, had nothing to do with those of the soul, and so he continued to sell his wares to them). There was only one explanation for his desire to send his daughter in magnificent attire to see *il Magnifico:* Lorenzo was the unofficial marriage broker for all of moneyed Florence. No child of the upper classes dared wed without his approval, and most families preferred that Lorenzo choose the spouse. I was to be scrutinized, judged like a calf before slaughter. But almost every bride had seen fifteen summers.

My presence in the household was a reproach to my father, a constant reminder of how he had ruined my mother's life. "I am not quite thirteen," I said, carelessly dropping the bewitching *cangiante* into a pile on my lap. "Yet he cannot wait to be rid of me."

Zalumma set down a fine measure of voided velvet and smoothed it with her hand, then gazed steadily at me. "You *are* too young," she said. "But Ser Lorenzo has been very ill. Perhaps your father merely wishes to have his counsel while he is still among us."

"Why would my father consult him at all, unless he saw a way to marry me off quickly now?" I countered. "Why else take the advice of a Medici? Why not wait and see me married off to one of the *piagnoni*?"

Zalumma moved to a sumptuous piece of celery-colored damask and lifted it. Sunlight reflected off its shiny, polished surface, revealing a pattern of garlands woven into the cloth. "You could refuse," she said. "And, as you say, wait a few more years and then be married off to one of Savonarola's weepers. Or . . ." She tilted her lovely face to study me. "You could let *il Magnifico* make the choice. Were I the bride, I would certainly prefer the latter."

I considered this, then set the *cangiante* aside. While the interplay of hues was intriguing, the fabric was too stiff, the red and green too intense for my coloring. I rose, took the celery damask from Zalumma's hand, and set it down beside a deep blue-green voided velvet, a pattern of satin vines running through the thick plush. "This," I said, resting a finger on the velvet, "for the bodice and skirt, edged with the damask. And the brocade with greens and violets, for the sleeves."

The dress was assembled within a week, after which I was called upon to wait. *Il Magnifico*'s health had been steadily declining, and it was uncertain when or even whether the affair would take place. I was strangely relieved. Though I did not relish living under my father's roof, I relished even less the thought of going to live so soon under a stranger's. And while taking up residence in my mother's quarters brought painful memories, it also brought an odd comfort.

A second week passed; then, at supper, my father was uncharacteristically silent. Though he often repeated the friar's assertion that God had taken my mother to Heaven out of kindness, his eyes betrayed uncertainty and guilt, as they did that night.

I could not bear to look at him for long; I finished my meal swiftly. When I excused myself from the table, he interrupted.

"*Il Magnifico* has summoned you." His tone was curt. "Tomorrow, in the late afternoon, I am to take you to the palazzo on the Via Larga."

XXII

I was not, my father iterated firmly, to speak of this with any of the servants save Zalumma. Not even our driver was to know; my father would take me himself, in the carriage he reserved for business.

The next day found me overcome by anxiety. I was to be on display, my good attributes and bad noted and used to determine my future. I would be studied and critiqued by Lorenzo and, I expected, a group of carefully chosen highborn women. My nerves were further undermined by the revelation that Zalumma would not be allowed to accompany me.

The gown, cunningly fitted to suggest a woman's shape where there was none, was far grander than anything I had worn. The full skirts, with a short train, were of the deep blue-green velvet with its pattern of satin vines; the bodice was of the same velvet with insets of Zalumma's pale green damask. At the high waist was a belt of delicately wrought silver. The sleeves were slashed and fitted, made from a brocade woven from turquoise, green, and purple threads interlaced with those of pure silver. Zalumma pulled my *camicia* through the slits, and puffed it according to the fashion; I had chosen the gossamer white silk, shot through with silver thread.

With my hair there was nothing but frustration. I wore a cap made from the brocade, trimmed with seed pearls, and since I was an unmarried girl, my hair was allowed to fall free onto my shoulders. But the coarse waves were irregular, in need of taming; Zalumma struggled with a hot poker to create fetching ringlets. But my locks would not hold them, and the effort created only more chaos.

As it was late February, I put on the sleeveless overdress—the brocade, trimmed with a thick stripe of the damask, then by white ermine. It was open at the center to reveal the full glory of the gown. Round my neck I wore my mother's necklace of seed pearls, with a large pendant of aquamarine; it had been sized to fall just above the bodice, so that it rested cold against my skin.

At the last, Zalumma drew me to stand before a full-length mirror. I drew in a breath. I had never seen myself look so comely; I had never looked so much like my mother.

When she led me down to my waiting father, I thought that he would weep.

I sat beside my father in the carriage, as I often had when I used to accompany him on business to homes of the nobility. I wore a dark blue wool cape to hide my finery, in compliance with the sumptuary laws.

As he drove, my father was gloomy and reticent; he stared at the late winter landscape, his eyes haggard, squinting at the bright afternoon sun. He wore his usual attire of a plain black wool tunic and worn leggings with a black mantle—not at all appropriate for the function we were about to attend.

The afternoon air was pleasantly brisk, scented with the smoke from countless hearths. We rode alongside the Arno, then crossed the Ponte Vecchio, where most of the shops were still open. I remembered my exuberance the last time I had crossed the old bridge with Zalumma and my mother, how I had taken delight in the magnificent fabrications of the artists and goldsmiths; now, sitting beside my father, I was unable to summon a scrap of joy.

When we crossed the bridge onto the broad Via Larga, I realized that, should I want to voice the question that had been gnawing at me, I had to do so quickly, as we would soon be at our destination.

"Fra Girolamo does not approve of the Medici," I said. "Why do you take me to Lorenzo?"

My father gazed out at the landscape and rubbed his beard. "Because of a promise. One that I made long ago."

So, perhaps Zalumma had been right. Perhaps my mother had asked that her daughter's husband be chosen by the wisest marriage broker in town, and my father, when he was still besotted with his wife instead of Savonarola, had agreed. And knowing that Lorenzo's health was failing, my father was being cautious and choosing the groom well ahead of time.

Shortly thereafter, my father pulled the carriage up to the gated entry of Lorenzo's palazzo. An armed man opened the iron gate and we rolled inside, near the stables. I waited for my father to rise and help me down, then escort me on his arm into the palazzo. For the first time in years, I was grateful for his presence.

But he surprised me. "Wait," he said, extending a warning arm when I moved to rise. "Just wait."

I sat in a torment of anticipation until, minutes later, the side doors to the palazzo swung open, and a man—followed by a pair of guards—walked out slowly, gingerly, with the help of an exquisitely carved wood-and-gold cane.

In the months since I had seen him, Lorenzo had aged; though he was only a few years past forty, he looked decades older. His skin was sagging, jaundiced. Only one thing pointed to his relative youth: his hair, pure black without a single lock of gray.

But even leaning on the cane, he walked with grace and dignity, and the self-possessed air of a man who had never once questioned his own importance. He glanced over his shoulder at one of the guards and gave a nod; the summoned man hurried forward and offered me his arm. I took it and let him help me down.

My father followed and bowed to our approaching host.

"God be with you, Ser Antonio," *il Magnifico* said as he stepped up to us.

"And with you, Ser Lorenzo," my father replied.

"So this is our Lisa?"

"This is she."

"Madonna Lisa." Lorenzo bowed stiffly, cautiously, from the shoulders. "Forgive me if I cannot make proper genuflection to such a beautiful young woman."

"Ser Lorenzo." I made a full proper curtsy, though I was undone.

"Lisa." My father spoke softly, swiftly. "I leave you to Ser Lorenzo's care. I will be in the chapel here, attending vespers. When you are ready, I will fetch you."

"But Father—" I began; before I could say more, he had bowed again to Ser Lorenzo, then followed one of the guards into the palazzo.

I was abandoned. I understood my father's intention then: No one but the parties directly involved would ever know he had brought me here. Even those who saw us come in the gate would think that he was simply conducting business, delivering wools to Ser Lorenzo as he always had, with his daughter to accompany him.

Panicked, I looked back at *il Magnifico.*

He was smiling sympathetically. His eyes were amazing; kind now, and reassuring for my sake, but beneath that was a brilliance, breathtakingly shrewd and sensitive. "Don't be afraid, young Madonna," he said, in a weak, nasal voice. "Your father has personal and religious reasons for being uncomfortable at our gathering; it is kinder to release him from such an obligation, don't you think?"

He held out his free arm to me and I took it, winding mine around his so that my hand lightly clasped his wrist. His own hands were gnarled, the fingers so misshapen and overlapping he could scarcely grip his cane. I suspected it had been some years since he held a pen.

We began to stroll together. I could sense that he used the walking stick to bear a great deal of his weight, so I tried to be more of a support to him than a hindrance.

"Yes," I said, dully, for all my wit had fled. "He has always disliked social functions; in fact, I cannot remember when he last attended one."

"I am afraid that you are burdened with me for an escort this evening," he said, as we made our way to the entry. "And I am sorry for it. Every marriageable young woman who has entered my household has been nervous enough, but at least the others have been comforted by the presence of family."

"Their mothers and sisters," I added, thinking how I had none.

He nodded, then said softly, "I hope, dear Lisa, that you are not too dreadfully uncomfortable."

"I am terrified," I answered quite earnestly, then blushed at my own unintended candor.

He lifted his face to the waning sun and laughed. "I like that you are honest and given to frank speech, Madonna. You will fare better than most."

We made our way past armed guards into a wide hallway with polished marble flooring and displays of centuries-old armor and weapons; from there, we passed into another corridor, its walls adorned with paintings hung in gilded frames.

"I gave my condolences regarding your mother's death to your father," Ser Lorenzo said. "I should like now to give them to you. Madonna Lucrezia was a fine woman, of great beauty and intelligence; none had a nobler soul."

I studied him askance. "You knew her?"

He smiled wanly. "When she was younger, and well." He said no further, for we had arrived at the hall's conclusion, and tall arching doors; a pair of servants, one on either side, threw them open.

I expected a chamber of moderate size, filled with at most a dozen Florentine noblewomen. I encountered something quite different.

The room could easily have held more than a hundred people; it was high ceilinged and as vast as a sanctuary. Though the sun still hung low in the sky, torches and candelabra of every description blazed. Despite its size, the room was quite warm, given the presence of three large hearths, well fed and blazing. Here again were displays of ancient armor and weaponry, marble busts on pedestals, breathtaking tapestries—one of them, the Medici crest with the *palle,* in Florence's colors of blue and gold. Pagan-themed paintings covered the walls; what was not obscured was festooned in beribboned garlands, decorated by ornate masks, a salute to Carnival.

Banquet tables—laden with roast lamb and pig and every type of fowl imaginable, as well as nuts, fruits, bread, cheese, and sweets—had been pushed against the walls. But there was to be no formal dining; the vast display of food was available to any guest at any moment they wished. There were servants to provide plates and knives, servants with empty goblets and flagons of wine. The guests helped themselves to refreshment, then stood talking, or seated themselves upon convenient groupings of chairs.

I was last to arrive: The wine had apparently been flowing for some time, for the conversation was convivial and quite loud, competing with the musicians. I was too overwhelmed to actually count, but my impression was that there were at least thirty persons in the room.

And I the only female.

As was the custom for girls being considered for marriage, I expected for all talking to cease; I expected each man to turn around, and for Lorenzo to make an announcement that I had arrived. I expected to be eyed carefully.

But Lorenzo said nothing, and as we entered the room, the men—divided into several small groups, some laughing, some arguing, some telling tales—did not so much as look up at us.

I kept staring into the crowd, thinking I would at least find one feminine face—perhaps that belonging to Lorenzo's daughter-in-law, Madonna Alfonsina—but she was nowhere to be seen. This was strictly a gathering of gentlemen, and I could not help but wonder whether my future husband stood among them.

"These are my friends." Lorenzo raised his reedy voice above the noise. "I have been unable to enjoy their company for some time. As it is Carnival, I thought they would enjoy some small entertainment." He inclined his head to smile at me. "As I hope you will."

I did not refuse when he summoned a servant, who brought a goblet—of exquisite gold, adorned with the darkest blue lapis lazuli I had ever seen. It contained watered wine, the most delicious I had ever tasted. The goblet was embarrassingly full.

"This is quite a lot of wine," I remarked, then silently cursed myself. His expression turned sly and playful. "Perhaps you shall need it." Of that, I had no doubt. "Will you not have some?"

He shook his head, his smile grown sheepish. "My time for indulgence is long past, I fear. Here"—he glanced up, and with his sharp chin indicated a small group of men sitting in the center of the room— "I should like to introduce you to some of my dearest friends."

I took a swift sip of wine. So, I was to be judged after all—and by the closest of Medici associates. I firmly fixed a small, demure smile upon my lips, and walked arm in arm with my host.

Il Magnifico steered us toward a group of four men, three sitting and one standing beside a table, where plates of food and goblets of wine rested. The man on his feet, the speaker of the moment, was approaching the half-century mark in age. His blond hair was streaked with gray, his body fleshy, his clean-shaven face puffy from drink; even so, one could see he had been quite handsome as a youth, for he had full, sensual lips and great, heavy-lidded eyes. Obviously wealthy, he wore a sapphire velvet *farsetto* beneath a skillfully draped sky-blue mantle. In one hand was a small plate, heaped with food; in the other, the tiny leg of a roasted quail, which he held up and addressed as if it could hear him.

"Alas, sweet bird," he intoned mockingly, "how tragic for you that you were never rescued by our friend here—and how fortuitous for me that you have instead made my acquaintance first!"

Off to the side sat a dark-haired, dark-eyed lad of perhaps eighteen, whose great high brow seemed precariously balanced atop a jaw so foreshortened it looked as though he had lost all his teeth; his appearance was not helped by the fact that his eyes bulged, or that his demeanor was withdrawn and sullen. He clutched his wine, sipping it while the others enjoyed amicable conversation. The second was an old man, wizened and bald save for a few wisps of hair at the temples. And the third . . .

Ah, the third. The third, the "friend" to whom the speaker referred, I judged to be between the ages of thirty and forty—or perhaps ageless, for his dress and grooming were quite out of fashion, more appropriate to that of ancient Greece or Rome. He wore a tunic so long it reached his knees, of rose-colored, unadorned fabric and untailored construction. His hair, pale brown streaked with gold and silver, fell in perfect waves past his shoulders, almost to his waist, and his beard, also waving, matched it in length. Despite the oddity of his attire, he was, quite simply, the most beautiful thing in the room. His teeth were white and even, his nose straight and narrow, and his eyes . . . If Lorenzo was brilliant, this man was the sun. In his eyes was a remarkable sensitivity, a razor-keen perceptiveness.

I prayed silently: *Dear God, if I must have one man in Florence— one man out of thousands—let it be he.*

Lorenzo lingered just far enough back so that the four need not interrupt their conversation to acknowledge him. Just as the first man finished speaking, the old one, sitting in the chair next to my beautiful philosopher, frowned at him and asked, "Is it true, then, what they say? That you go to market to buy caged birds and set them free?"

My philosopher grinned charmingly; the standing man with the quail answered for him. "I have accompanied him several times on such missions," he said, then popped the roasted leg into his mouth and drew out the bone, stripped of flesh. Chewing, he added, his voice muffled: "He has done so since he was a stripling."

The old man stared in disbelief at the philosopher. "So you eat *no* meat?"

My man said simply, with neither judgment nor apology, "I do not, sir. Have not, for the course of my adulthood."

The old man recoiled. "Outrageous notion! How is it, then, that you have survived?"

"Through wit alone, and barely then, dear Marsilo. That, and soup, bread, cheese, fruits, and fine wine." He raised his goblet and took a sip.

"But surely this will shorten your life!" Marsilo persisted, truly alarmed. "Man must have meat to be strong!"

My philosopher set his goblet upon the table and leaned forward engagingly. "Shall we wrestle to determine the truth of the matter? Perhaps not you, Marsilo, given your venerable condition, but our

Sandro here will gladly take your place." He glanced up at the quail-eater's ample belly. "He has clearly eaten the lion's portion of Florence's meat—indeed, he has taken a portion just now. Sandro! Off with your mantle! Let us set to it and decide this empirically!"

The old man laughed at such foolishness; Sandro said, with mock boredom, "It would be an unfair contest. You have ridden all night from Milan to come see Lorenzo, and are tired. I have too much pity to take advantage of an old friend—who would lose the fight even were he well rested."

There came a pause; Lorenzo stepped into it, with me on his arm. "Gentlemen."

They turned. All but the beautiful philosopher seemed startled to find me, a mere girl, in their company.

"Here is a young lady you must meet." Lorenzo took a step back from me, breaking our link, and gestured at me as though I were a prize. "This is Madonna Lisa di Antonio Gherardini, daughter of the wool merchant."

The consumer of quail set down his plate, put a hand to his breast, and bowed grandly. "Sandro Botticelli, a humble painter. I am pleased to make your acquaintance, Madonna."

"And this is my dear friend Marsilo Ficino," Lorenzo said, gesturing at the elderly gentleman, who by virtue of his age and infirmity did not rise; Ficino greeted me with a disinterested nod. "Our Marsilo is head of the Florentine Academy as well as the famed translator of the *Corpus Hermeticum,* and so is greatly respected by us all."

"An honor, sirs," I said to both men, and curtsied, hoping that the great Botticelli would not detect the quaver in my voice. He had created his greatest masterpieces by then: *Primavera,* of course, and *The Birth of Venus,* both of which graced the walls of Lorenzo's villa at Castello.

"This young lad"—Lorenzo lowered his voice and smiled faintly at the dark-haired, scowling youth who could scarcely bring himself to look at us—"is the talented Michelangelo, who resides with us. Perhaps you have heard of him."

"I have," I said, emboldened perhaps by the young man's extreme shyness. "I attend the church of Santo Spirito, where his handsome wooden crucifix is displayed. I have always admired it."

Michelangelo lowered his face and blinked—perhaps a response, perhaps not, but I took it as one, and the others seemed to judge it normal.

My philosopher rose. He was slender, straight, and tall—his body, like his face, was perfectly proportioned. At first sight of me, he had recoiled slightly, as if troubled; as his unease faded, it was replaced by an odd and tender melancholy. "I am called Leonardo," he said softly, "from the little town of Vinci."

XXIII

I stifled a surprised gasp. I remembered when my mother and I had stared together at the last portrait on the wall in the Piazza della Signoria, that of the murderer Bernardo Baroncelli—the painting done with a surer, more elegant hand. Here was its creator.

"Sir," I said, my voice catching, "I am honored to meet such a great artist." In the corner of my eye, I saw Botticelli jab Leonardo with an elbow in a display of mock jealousy.

He took my hand and studied me so intently that I flushed; there was more than an artist's admiration in his gaze. I saw deep appreciation, mixed with an affection I had not earned. "And I am honored, Madonna, to meet a living work of art." He bent down and brushed the back of my hand with his lips; his beard was as soft as child's hair.

Please, I repeated silently. *Let him be the one.*

"I thought you were bound to Milan now," I said, wondering why he was present.

"It is true, the Duke of Milan is my patron," he replied amiably as he let go my hand. "Though I owe my career entirely to the graciousness of *il Magnifico.*"

"Quite the genius, our Leonardo," Botticelli interjected dryly. "In Milan, he paints, he sculpts, he sketches plans for magnificent palazzi, he directs the construction of dams, he plays the lute and sings. . . ." He faced his old friend. "Tell me, is there anything you do *not* do for the Duke?"

The tone of the question was markedly sly; old Ficino let go the beginnings of a snigger, then drew himself up short as if suddenly remembering Lorenzo's and my presence. Lorenzo directed a veiled warning glance at the two men.

"That is the extent of it," Leonardo responded mildly. "Although I do have plans for altering the course of the sun."

Laughter followed—issuing from all save Michelangelo, who huddled more closely to his goblet, as though frightened by the noise.

"If anyone could do it, you could," Ficino quipped.

"Good Leonardo," Lorenzo said, with an abrupt switch to seriousness. "It is my wish to give Madonna Lisa a tour of the courtyard—but I require a moment of rest, and the time has come for me to partake of one of the noxious potions my physician has prescribed. Would you be so kind?"

"I can think of nothing more delightful." The artist proffered me his arm.

I took it, unnerved but not about to show it. Was this a sign that *il Magnifico* considered him a likely candidate for my husband? The prospect of life with this charming, talented, famed stranger—even in faraway Milan, in the court of Duke Ludovico Sforza—seemed agreeable, even if I was too young.

"I shall retire for a moment, then." Lorenzo took his leave with a short, stiff bow.

"It is most unfair," Botticelli said, watching him go, "that only one of us should have the pleasure of accompanying you."

Leonardo and I took our leave. He directed me toward a pair of far doors; servants on either side opened them as we approached.

As we passed over the threshold, Leonardo said, "You must not be nervous, Lisa. I perceive you are a woman of intelligence and sensitivity; you are among your peers, not your betters."

"You are kind to say so, sir, but I have no talent. I can only admire the beauty others create."

"An eye for beauty is itself a gift. Ser Lorenzo possesses such talent."

The air outside was chill, but there were several large torches and a small bonfire contained by a circle of heaped stones.

"Madonna, may I offer you my mantle?" He turned his perfect face toward mine; the light from the setting sun imbued his skin with a coral hue.

I looked at the proffered piece of cloth; it was of thin dark wool, worn and patched. I smiled. "I am quite warm, thank you."

"Let me give you a brief tour, then." He steered me toward the bonfire. Beside it, on a high pedestal, was the bronze statue of a naked young man, his hair long and curling beneath a straw shepherd's hat, his body soft and rounded as a woman's. He stood with a fist braced coquettishly against one hip; the other hand grasped the hilt of a sword, its sharp tip resting on the ground. At his feet lay the grotesque, severed head of a giant.

I walked up to it; the firelight gleamed on the dark metal. "Is this David?" I asked. "He looks like a girl!" I put my hand to my mouth, immediately embarrassed by my thoughtless remark. Who was I to so rudely judge a masterpiece?

"Yes," my guide murmured, a bit distracted. I glanced at him to find he had been scrutinizing me the entire while, as if he had never before set eyes upon a woman. "David, by the great Donatello." After a long and unself-conscious pause, he came to himself and said, "He is always here; in fact, he has guarded this courtyard since Lorenzo was a boy. But other things have been brought here for your enjoyment."

For my *enjoyment?* I pondered this, then decided Leonardo was indulging in flattery.

We moved next to a pair of busts, each set upon its own pedestal, and each so worn that I could not determine the stone. "These look quite old."

"They are indeed, Madonna. These are the heads of Caesar Augustus and the general Agrippa, created in the times of ancient Rome."

I reached out a finger to touch the one called *Augustus*. It was commonplace to cross the Ponte Vecchio, created so long ago by Roman laborers—but to see a work of art, created from the face of a man more than a thousand years dead, filled me with awe. My guide let go of my arm and let me inspect the works.

"Lorenzo is fond of antiquities," he said. "This house contains the greatest collection of art, both modern and ancient, in the world."

I moved to another bust, this one also of white stone, of an older man with a round, bulbous nose and a full beard, though not so impressive as Leonardo's. "And who is this?"

"Plato."

This, too, I had to touch gently, to feel the cold stone beneath my fingertips and imagine the living, breathing man it represented. There was another statue, as well—a contemporary one—of Hercules, muscular and robust, the purported founder of Florence. At some point, I was so distracted I set down my goblet and forgot it altogether.

Despite my excitement, I was growing chilled and on the verge of asking that we go back inside, when my gaze lit upon another bust—life-sized, of terra-cotta—in a corner of the courtyard. This was a modern man, handsome and strong-featured, in the prime of life. His eyes were large and open wide, and the hint of a smile played on his lips, as if he had just caught sight of a dear friend. I liked him immediately.

"He looks familiar." I frowned with the effort to recall precisely where I had seen him.

"You have never met," Leonardo countered; though he tried to keep his tone light, I detected a hint of dark emotion. "He died before you were born. This is Giuliano de' Medici, Lorenzo's murdered brother."

"He looks so alive."

"He was," my guide answered, and at last I heard grief.

"You knew him, then."

"I did. I came to know him well during the time I was a familiar of the Medici household. A more good-hearted soul was never born."

"I can see it, in the statue." I turned to face Leonardo. "Who was the artist?"

"My master Verrocchio began the piece when Giuliano was still alive. I completed it—after his death." He paused to reflect on a distant sorrow, then forced it away. With practiced movements, he reached for a pad and quill, both attached to the belt hidden beneath his mantle; his tone became animated. "Madonna, will you do me a kindness? Will you permit me to do a quick sketch of you, here, looking at the bust?"

I was taken aback, overwhelmed by the notion that the great artist from Vinci would deign to sketch *me,* the insignificant daughter of a wool merchant; I could find no words. Leonardo did not notice.

"Stand there, Lisa. Could you move to your right? Just . . . there. Yes. Now, look up at me, and relax your face. Think of Augustus and Agrippa, and how you felt when you touched them. Here, close your eyes, take a breath, and let it go slowly. Now, don't see me at all. See, instead, Giuliano, and remember how you felt when you first laid eyes on him."

I tried to do as instructed, though my nerves would not let me forget the face of Leonardo—his eyes passionate and intense as they glanced swiftly up and down, from me to the sketchpad. The quill scratched loudly against paper.

At one moment, he hesitated, the pen poised in his hand: No longer the artist, but only the man, he looked on me with yearning tinged with sadness. Then he gathered himself firmly and grew businesslike once more; the scratching grew more rapid.

The sun had finally set, leaving everything gray and fading swiftly to dark; the torches glowed brighter.

"*Breathe,*" the artist urged, and I realized with a start that I had not been doing so.

It was difficult, but I found within myself the strength to relax, to soften, to let go of the fear. I thought of Giuliano's smile and how he had no doubt looked so kindly upon the artist who had asked him to sit.

And when I had at last forgotten myself, my gaze wandered beyond Leonardo's shoulder, to the window of the great chamber where the festivities awaited us. The heavy tapestry covering it had been pulled aside, and a man stood staring at us, backlit by the room's brilliance.

Though his face was in shadow, I recognized the watcher from his stooped posture and pained demeanor: It was Lorenzo de' Medici.

XXIV

*T*he artist and I returned shortly afterward to the party. Leonardo only had time to create what he called a cartoon—a quick rendering in ink of my basic features. I felt somewhat disappointed; in my naïveté, I had expected him to present me with a completed portrait in a matter of minutes. Yet it unquestionably resembled me, though it failed to capture the grandeur of my gown, or my fine cap.

Il Magnifico now approached us from the opposite side of the room, accompanied by a boy perhaps a year or two my senior, and a young man of perhaps twenty. Despite his frailty and his cane, Lorenzo moved with sudden speed, and when he met me, he took my hand in his and squeezed it with a warmth that startled me.

"Lisa, my dear," he said. "I trust you enjoyed the few displays out on the courtyard?"

"Very much, yes."

"They are nothing compared to what you shall now see." He turned to the youths beside him. "But first, let me introduce you to my sons. This is my eldest, Piero."

With an insolent boredom that far outweighed Botticelli's, Piero sighed slightly as he bowed. Tall and broad shouldered, he had inherited his late mother's arrogance and ill temper, and none of his father's wit or charm. Everyone in Florence knew that he was Lorenzo's chosen successor, and everyone rued it.

"And this is my youngest, Giuliano." His tone warmed subtly.

The lad was well named. He favored his father little, for he had even features, a straight nose and teeth, and the same sort of wide, inquisitive eyes as his deceased uncle. Yet like his father, he had a gracious poise. "Madonna Lisa," he said. "An uncommon pleasure." Like Leonardo, he bowed low and kissed my hand. When he straightened, he held my gaze and my hand so long that I lowered my face and looked away, embarrassed.

I fancied Lorenzo shot his youngest a warning glance before continuing. "My middle boy, Giovanni, was unable to attend the celebration." He paused. "Boys, go and see that our dear Leonardo is well fed and cared for after his long journey. As for you, young Madonna . . ." He waited until the others had wandered away before continuing. "I should be most honored if you would consent to an examination of the art in my personal chambers."

There was no suggestion of lechery in his tone; it was a chivalrous offer. Yet I was thoroughly perplexed. I was not well-bred enough to be marriageable to his youngest son (Piero was already married to an Orsini, Madonna Alfonsina), and so did not understand the purpose of the introduction, other than satisfying a sense of courtesy. And if I were here to be sized up by potential grooms—especially, as I hoped, Leonardo—why was I to be led away from the group?

Perhaps the shrewd *il Magnifico* wished to examine my faults and assets more closely. Despite my confusion, I was also ecstatic. I had never dreamt that I would live to see the famed Medici collection.

"Sir, I should be thrilled," I answered honestly. He clasped my hands firmly in his crippled ones, as though I were his own daughter; whatever had happened during his absence from the group had stirred his emotions, and he was trying mightily to hide them from me.

I took his arm again and we walked from the chamber, back through the corridors lined with paintings and sculpture, then up a flight of stairs. This pained and winded him, but he set his jaw and kept a slow, measured pace; he tucked his cane beneath his arm and leaned heavily upon the railing while I clutched his opposite arm tightly, offering what support I could.

At last we arrived at the top, and he let go a long sigh and stood a moment, gathering his strength. "You must indulge me." His words came out as soft gasps. "I have had little opportunity of late to exercise my limbs. But with each effort, they become stronger."

"Of course," I murmured, and so we waited until his breath came more easily. He led me then to a great wooden door—guarded, as always, by a servant who opened it when we approached.

"This is my study," he said as we entered.

How shall I describe such a room? It was not remarkable in construction; it was of modest size, with four walls and a low ceiling—certainly not as impressive in scope as my own family's great chamber. Yet no matter where my focus settled—on a wall, on the inlaid marble floor, on shelves and pedestals—it lit upon a gem, a glittering antiquity, an exquisite creation by one of the world's great artists.

I was dizzy at the sight of so much beauty gathered in a single place. We moved past a pair of earthenware vases the height of my shoulders, painted with beautiful Eastern designs. Lorenzo acknowledged them with a casual nod. "A gift," he said, "from the Sultan Qa'it-Baj." He pointed to the wall. "A portrait of my old friend Galeazzo Maria Sforza—Duke of Milan—before he died and Ludovico assumed his place. And there, a painting by Uccello, and del Pollaiuolo, one of my favorites." These were names known to every educated Florentine, though few had the good fortune to set eyes upon their works. "And there is a nice one by Fra Angelico."

Fra Angelico: This was the famed Dominican monk who had painted glorious murals on the walls of San Marco's convent—even in the brothers' cells—at the behest of Cosimo de' Medici. As I gazed upon the painting, I could not help but wonder whether Savonarola approved of such unnecessary adornment. Saint Sebastian, our protector from plague, was shown in his death agony; his placid eyes gazed heavenward even as he slumped, bound to a tree, his body and even his brow cruelly pierced by arrows.

Before I could begin to absorb such wonders, Lorenzo called for my attention again. He led me to a long table which contained "a fraction of my collection of coins and stones." A wall lamp had been hung just above it, so that the light glinted off the shining metal and gems and rendered them dazzling. There were perhaps two hundred items displayed. I had never imagined there was such wealth in all the world, much less in Florence alone.

"These are from the times of the Caesars." He gestured at a row of dull, worn coins, many of which were irregular in shape. "Others come from Constantinople and the Orient. Here." He clumsily lifted a ruby half the size of his fist and proffered it to me, then laughed at my unwillingness to take it. "It's all right, child; it has no teeth. Hold it to the light, like so, and look for irregularities—cracks or tiny bubbles in the stone. You will find none."

I did as instructed—trying not to tremble at the fact that I held in my fingers more wealth than my family possessed—and gazed through it at the lamp, now bathed in crimson. "It's beautiful."

He nodded, pleased, as I returned it to him. "We have many medallions, too, designed by our best artists. Here is one made many years ago by our own Leonardo. It is quite rare; few were cast." He replaced the ruby almost carelessly, then reached with greater reverence for a gold coin; a faint melancholy settled over him.

I took the medallion and read the inscription: PUBLIC MOURNING. There was Giuliano, vainly lifting his hands against the blades wielded by his assassins. At the same time I appreciated its beauty, I inwardly shuddered at Zalumma's tale of Messer Iacopo's corpse. *Eighty men in five days,* my father had said. Could this gentle man have been capable of such crimes?

"Please," he said. "Take it, as a gift."

"I have one," I said—and was immediately embarrassed by my thoughtless response to such an unthinkably generous offer. "My mother gave it to me."

He had been studying me quite intently; at my words, his gaze sharpened further, then gradually softened. "Of course," he said. "I had forgotten that I presented some of these to friends."

Instead, he gave me a different medallion, one which featured a picture of his grandfather Cosimo and the Medici crest. This was by a different artist, one skilled though lacking the delicacy of Leonardo's hand; even so, I was simply amazed and perplexed by *il Magnifico*'s generosity.

He seemed to grow tired after that, but he persisted in showing me another collection, one of cameos of chalcedony ranging from the palest white to the darkest gray, and another of brilliant red and orange carnelians. Most of those were intaglios, beautifully carved into the stone, some inlaid with gold by the famous Ghiberti.

There was also a display of goblets carved from precious stones, set with gems, and adorned with silver and gold; but he was near the end of his strength by then, and so he singled nothing out from among them. Instead, he led me to a pedestal where a single shallow dish—slightly larger than the one from which I took my supper—was displayed.

"This also is chalcedony, though the cup itself is reddish brown," he said, his voice a hoarse whisper. On top of the darker background was a milky cameo of several figures from ancient times. "It is my single greatest treasure. This is Osiris, holding the cornucopia, and here is his wife, Isis, seated. Their son Horus plows the Earth." He paused, and pride crept into his tone. "This cup was used by the kings and queens of Egypt in their rituals. Cleopatra herself drank from it. When Octavian defeated her, it was lost for a time, then it resurfaced in Constantinople. From there, it traveled to the court of King Alfonso of Naples. At last it came to Rome, where I acquired it." He read my poorly restrained eagerness and smiled. "Go ahead. Touch it."

I did so, marveling at its perfection despite its age; its condition was so pristine that I had assumed, before Lorenzo's comments, that it was another Florentine creation. The edges were cold and perfectly smooth. I glanced back at Ser Lorenzo with a smile and realized that he was studying, with great fondness and enjoyment, not the cup, but me.

My rapture was interrupted by the sound of footfall. I turned and saw Giovanni Pico, bearing in his hand a goblet filled with dark liquid. He was as surprised to see me as I him. Caught off guard, I recoiled. He smiled politely; I could not.

"Why, it is Antonio Gherardini's daughter," he remarked. I doubt he remembered my name. "How are you, my dear?"

Lorenzo faced him with great weariness. "So, Giovanni, you know our Madonna Lisa."

"I am a close friend of Antonio's." Pico acknowledged me with a nod. It was impolite, but I said nothing; I had not seen Count Pico since the day of my mother's funeral. While he had come often to visit my father afterward, I had refused to receive him and stayed in my room. Despite his courteous demeanor now, he surely knew I hated him.

Pico's expression was studied, but he could not entirely hide his curiosity as to my presence; although he was part of the Medici household, he was apparently neither a part of this evening's celebration nor privy to its cause. "I have been looking for you, Lorenzo," he scolded amiably. "You are late in taking the physician's draught." He smiled knowingly at me. "Our host is often too busy attending to the needs of others to give enough thought to his own care."

Lorenzo grimaced mildly. "Ser Giovanni has been one of our most cherished household guests for many years. We do not agree on certain subjects . . . but we remain friends."

"I shall convert you yet," Pico replied with good humor. Yet there was a sense of unease in the air, as if their alliance were forged now of convenience and a desire to keep an eye on what the other was doing. "Forgive me for interrupting your conversation. Please, Madonna Lisa, Ser Lorenzo, continue. I shall wait patiently until you are finished. But mind, dear Lorenzo, that you do not forget your health."

Lorenzo noted my curious glance regarding the draught; after all, he had left Leonardo and me alone in the courtyard with the comment that he was going inside to take it. "I was . . . detained by other business," he murmured, for my ears alone.

"You have been most gracious, Ser Lorenzo," I said, thinking only of escape, for the proximity of Pico left me unnerved; the memory of my mother's death was still too fresh. "But I believe you would benefit by a period of rest. With your permission, I should like to take my leave."

Perhaps he heard the distress in my voice—or perhaps he was exhausted—for he did not protest. "Leave the draught," he told Pico. "Go and see that Ser Antonio's carriage is ready, and tell him his daughter will meet him there. You will find him in the chapel. Then go see Piero and send him to me."

I felt great relief the instant Pico left. Once he did, *il Magnifico* said, "The presence of Ser Giovanni upsets you."

I stared down at the gleaming marble floor. "He was present when my mother died."

"Yes. I recall him mentioning it." He gathered his thoughts. "There is nothing more bitter than losing those we most love. An early death, a wrongful one, provokes the worst sort of grief. It turns the heart easily toward hatred." He lowered his gaze. "I lashed out vengefully when my brother died. It has come to haunt me now." He paused to stare at the place where Pico had stood. "Ser Giovanni is a man given to great extremes. A more educated man does not exist, yet his heart belongs to the friar Girolamo now. The world has lost one of its greatest philosophers. Have you heard of his theory of syncretism?"

I shook my head.

"It proposes that all philosophies and religions hold the kernel of truth—and all contain errors. Our Giovanni said that each should be examined, to determine common truths and dismiss the fallacies." He smiled wryly. "For that, the Pope suggested he be burned. He came here two years ago, to enjoy my protection. And now he supports a man who would see me brought down."

His face clouded suddenly; he let go a sigh that seemed to issue from his very bones. "Child, I must be discourteous and ask to sit in your presence. This evening has drained me more than I expected."

I helped him to a chair. This time he relied heavily upon my arm, no longer able to maintain the pretense that he was mostly recovered. He sat down with a small groan beneath the picture of the dying Saint Sebastian and leaned against the wall. He closed his eyes; in the shadow of the torchlight, he looked twice his age. Frightened, I asked, "Shall I bring you the draught?"

He smiled thinly, then opened his eyes and gazed on me with affection. "No. But will you hold an old man's hand, my dear, to comfort me until Piero comes?"

"Of course." I moved to stand beside him and bent down a bit to clasp his hand; it was cold and so thin one could easily feel the twisted bones.

We remained this way in easy silence until *il Magnifico* asked softly, "If I summon you, Lisa, will you come again?"

"Of course," I repeated, though I could not imagine what might provoke him to do so.

"Our Leonardo was quite taken with you," he said. "I confess, I saw him sketch you in the courtyard. I shall commission him to paint your portrait when he is able to leave his duties in Milan for a time. Would that be agreeable to you?"

I was stunned beyond speech. My first thought was of my father: Such an honor would greatly increase his prestige and enhance his business, yet I doubted that would outweigh his fanatical devotion to Savonarola's teachings. It would solidify his relationship to the Medici in a way that was sure to garner the disapproval of his new associates.

But now was not the time to voice such doubts. When I could speak, I said, "It would be more than agreeable, *maestro*. I am thrilled by the thought."

"Good," he replied, and gave a short, determined nod. "It is done."

We spoke no further until the door opened again, and Lorenzo's son entered.

"Giuliano," he said. His tone betrayed his irritation. "I sent for your brother. Where is Piero?"

"Indisposed," Giuliano answered swiftly. His face was flushed, as though he had run in response to the summons; at the sight of me, his expression brightened slightly. "Are you feeling unwell, Father?" He glanced about the room and caught sight of the untouched draught. "You are late in taking the physician's prescription. Let me bring it to you."

Lorenzo let go my hand and waved his son's words away. "My

youngest," he said to me with unmistakable fondness, "is as quick to indulge my wishes as my eldest is to ignore them."

Giuliano smiled; something in the gesture reminded me of the terra-cotta bust in the courtyard.

"I regret that I cannot accompany you back to your father," Lorenzo continued, "but Giuliano is a responsible young man. I give you my guarantee that he will see you safely there." He reached for my hand once more and squeezed it with remarkable force for one so infirm. "God be with you, my dear."

"And with you, sir. Thank you for your kindness in inviting me to your home. And for the commission of the portrait . . ." We released our grip upon each other reluctantly. I felt an odd sadness as I took young Giuliano's arm and left his father, a frail and ugly man surrounded by the wealth and beauty of the centuries.

XXV

*I*n the corridor, Giuliano and I walked past more sculptures and portraits and delicate porcelain vases half my height, all lit by tapers held in elegantly wrought candelabra of bronze, silver, and gold. We did so in awkward silence; I rested my hand stiffly upon his forearm, while he stared straight ahead and moved with a natural dignity more suited to one a decade his senior. Like his sire, he was dressed in dark, somber colors and a simple fitted tunic of my father's finest wool.

"I am sorry, Madonna Lisa, that my father's illness interrupted your visit with him."

"Please don't apologize," I answered. "I'm sorry that Ser Lorenzo is still unwell."

In the wavering light, Giuliano's shadowed expression grew solemn. "Father makes light of it to his visitors, but he has been so sick the past few months we all thought he would die. He is still very weak; the doctors told him not to invite any guests, but he was determined to see his friends again. He especially wanted to see Leonardo. And—he did not tell me, but I assume that he wished to meet you for the purpose of a future marriage arrangement?"

"Yes," I said. The mention of the artist from Vinci—who had

made special effort to come for this gathering—stirred my hopes. "But it is terrible about your father. What ails him?"

"His heart." Giuliano gave a frustrated shrug. "At least, that is what the doctors say, but I think they know far less than they admit. He has always suffered from gout—sometimes so bad that he shrieks in agony if even bed linen brushes his skin. And his bones ache. But lately, he has been plagued by a dozen different complaints, none of which his physician seems able to relieve. He is weak; he cannot eat; he is restless and in pain. . . ." He shook his head and stopped in mid-stride. "I have been so worried for him. He is forty-three, but he seems like an old man. When I was little, he was so strong, running with us children, playing as if he were one of us. He used to lift me up on his horse and I would ride with him . . ." His voice broke; he fell silent in order to gather himself.

"I am so sorry." I had just lost my mother; I understood well the fear that now gripped this boy. "But he *is* improved from before, is he not?"

"Yes . . ." He nodded rapidly without meeting my gaze.

"Then certainly he will continue to get better. You must have hope."

He came to himself suddenly. "Forgive me, Madonna! You are our guest, and here am I complaining to you. I should not trouble you with such concerns. . . ."

"But I wish to know such things. Ser Lorenzo was so kind to me; he was showing me his collection, even though he was so tired."

Giuliano smiled wistfully. "That is like my father. He loves to collect beautiful things, but they bring him no real pleasure unless he can share them with others and watch them take delight in them. I have heard people say that he can be cruel when it comes to business or politics, but I have seen only good in him." He paused; his tone lightened. "Did you enjoy the tour, Madonna?"

"Very much."

"I know my father would want to finish sharing his collection with you. May I ask him whether you could return to view more of it? Perhaps we could arrange for you to visit our villa at Castello; there are many amazing paintings there and beautiful gardens."

"I would like that." Though I reeled happily at the thought, my answer was hesitant. I doubted my father would ever allow me a second chance to visit the Medici. I was still worrying whether he would ever consider letting an artist—even one as renowned as Leonardo—enter our home.

Giuliano smiled at my response. "That would be wonderful, Madonna Lisa! As my father is unwell, perhaps he would permit me to serve as your guide."

I was suddenly unsettled by the realization that he was taken with me. Surely Lorenzo had not invited me here as a potential bride for his son—Giuliano was still a few years away from the marriageable age for men. And when he did wed, his bride would come from one of the noblest houses in Italy. She would certainly not be the daughter of a wool merchant.

A proper reply escaped me. Fortunately, we had arrived by that time at the side entry to the palazzo. There were no servants here; I remembered dimly that guards stood on the other side, out in the cold. Giuliano halted.

"I leave you here only an instant, Madonna, to make sure your father is waiting for you. I shall return to escort you to him."

He leaned forward impulsively, unexpectedly, and kissed my cheek. Just as swiftly, he was gone.

I was glad for his disappearance and the absence of witnesses. Judging from the heat on my face and neck, I must have blushed deep as *chermisi* crimson.

I was torn. This was a kind, likable lad, and handsome—a catch certainly beyond my hopes—yet I could not help but respond to his kiss with a rush of giddiness. At the same time I reminded myself that I was smitten with Leonardo da Vinci. I was safest resting my hopes for wedlock there. Even though he was the result of an illicit union with a servant girl, Leonardo's father was one of the best-known notaries in Florence. He came from a good family, of roughly the same wealth and prestige as my father's.

By the time Giuliano returned, I was still too abashed to meet his gaze. He led me out into the chill night, past the guards with swords prominent on their hips, and helped me into the carriage without any acknowledgment of the illicit kiss. And when I settled beside my father, he said simply, "Good night, Madonna. Good night, Ser Antonio. May God be with you both."

"And with you," I replied.

As we rode out onto the Via Larga my father was distant, troubled; prayer and contemplation had apparently done little to soothe him or ease the sting of delivering his only child into the hands of Savonarola's enemy. He spoke without meeting my eyes.

"How was it?" he asked curtly. "What did they do, put you on display for the women?"

"There were no women there. Only men."

"Men?" He turned his head to glance at me.

"Friends of *il Magnifico*." Leery of my father's disapproval, I did not want to reveal too much, but my curiosity would not let me rest. "Many artists. Leonardo da Vinci was there." I knew better than to mention Lorenzo's commission of my portrait; I would leave such negotiations to better diplomats than I. I paused, suddenly timid. "Does he have a wife?"

"Leonardo?" Distracted, my father frowned in the failing light at the road ahead. "No. He is one of our most famous sodomites. Years ago, he was brought up on charges; they were dropped, but he has lived for years with his 'apprentice,' young Salai, who is surely his lover." His voice was without inflection—odd, considering his normally pious disapproval of such men.

With apparently great effort, he asked me the appropriate questions: Who else had been there? Had Ser Lorenzo given any indication as to what man he thought might be suitable? What had I done while there?

I answered curtly, with fewer and fewer words; he did not seem to notice that his offhanded words about Leonardo had stung me. At last he fell quiet, lost in some unhappy reverie, and we rode without speaking through the cold dark city. I hugged the fur-lined overdress tightly to my body as we crossed over the deserted Ponte Santa Trinità, toward home.

XXVI

I spent the next week newly eager to meet my father for supper, in case he had received word from Lorenzo. I still ached over the news about Leonardo's preference for men. A part of me hoped my father was wrong, or perhaps lying in order to dissuade me from marrying an artist, since such men were generally judged to make unreliable husbands. But I knew I had seen the light of attraction in the artist's eye.

During this time, I received a brief letter from the so-called sodomite, smuggled to me without my father's knowledge. When I broke the seal, two more pieces of paper fell out, and slipped to the floor.

Greetings, Madonna Lisa, from Milan.

Our good Lorenzo has commissioned me to paint your portrait. I can think of nothing more agreeable; your beauty begs to be recorded for all time. As soon as I fulfill certain obligations for the venerable Duke Ludovico, I will come to Florence for an extended stay.

*I enclose some rough sketches I have made, for your
enjoyment. One is a more careful rendering, based on the
cartoon I made that evening in the Medici palazzo. The
other is copied from my own notebook, and is of special
interest to those in the Medici inner circle.*

*I am eager to begin work on the painting, and look for-
ward to seeing you more than I can say.*

Your good friend,
Leonardo

I retrieved the papers from the floor and studied them with reverence. I understood completely now why Leonardo had been called
upon to finish the sculpture of Giuliano de' Medici after his death:
His recall of my features was astonishing. From the sparsely rendered
ink drawing made in the courtyard, he had produced, in crisp and delicate silverpoint on cream paper, a remarkable rendering of my face,
neck, shoulders—truer, it seemed, and more sacred, more profound
than any image rendered by my mirror. He had caught me not in the
pose he had requested, but rather the instant before, when I had been
staring at Giuliano's terra-cotta bust, then turned to look over my
shoulder at the artist. Only my face, in three-quarter profile, was de-
veloped and carefully shaded; my hair and shoulders were intimated
by a few quick lines. At the back of my head was a vague structure
that might have been a hairnet or a halo. My eyelids, the prominence
of my chin, the area of my cheeks just beneath my eyes, had been
highlighted by the careful application of white lead.

The corners of my lips curled ever so slightly: not a smile, but the
promise of one. It was a reflection of the goodness I had seen in the
dead Giuliano's eyes; I might have been an angel.

Dazzled, I stared at the drawing for some time before I finally directed my attention to the other page.

This was a swifter, cruder rendering, and one which provoked my
memory; I had seen the image somewhere before, and it took me some

time before I recalled that I had seen it together with my mother, on a wall near the Palazzo della Signoria.

It was that of a man dangling from a noose, his face downcast, his hands bound behind his back. Beneath it, the artist had written: *"The execution of Bernardo Baroncelli."*

It was a gruesome image, inappropriate to send to a young girl; I could not imagine what had prompted Leonardo to do so. What had Baroncelli to do with me?

The letter itself also renewed my confusion. *I look forward to seeing you more than I can say. . . .* Was this an allusion to love? But he had signed the letter, with unusual casualness, *your good friend.* Friend, and nothing more. At the same time, the letter thrilled me: Lorenzo's commission, then, was a reality, and not just idle speech intended to flatter.

So I waited each night for my father, desperate for word of the portrait or, more important, mention of an invitation to visit Castello.

Each night I was disappointed. My father offered nothing on the matter and grunted a negative reply each time I dared ask whether he had heard anything from Ser Lorenzo about a possible match.

Yet after one such discouraging supper, as I retired to my bedroom, Zalumma met me, lamp in hand, and closed the door behind us.

"Do not ask how I acquired this; the less you know, the better," she said, and withdrew from her bodice a sealed letter. I seized it, thinking it would be from Lorenzo. The wax bore the imprint of the *palle* crest, but the content was far from expected. By the light of Zalumma's lamp, I read:

My esteemed Madonna Lisa,

Forgive the liberty I took when you came to my father's palazzo recently; and forgive the one I take now by writing you this letter. I am too bold, I know, but my courage springs from a desire to see you again.

Father is very ill. Even so, he has given leave for me to

take you, with an escort of his choosing and one chosen by your father, to our villa at Castello for a tour. This very day, my brother Piero is writing a letter to Ser Antonio asking permission for you to accompany us.

I am filled with anticipation at the prospect of meeting you once more. Until then, I remain

> *Your humble servant,*
> *Giuliano de' Medici*

XXVII

or the next few days, I forced all thoughts of Leonardo da Vinci away—though in private I puzzled over the drawing of Bernardo Baroncelli. Foolish girl that I was, I focused instead on the moment Giuliano had leaned forward to place a kiss upon my cheek. I dreamed of Botticelli's *Venus* and *Primavera*. I had only heard them described; now I tried to imagine how they looked on the walls at Castello. I even imagined what my own portrait might look like hanging next to them. I yearned to immerse myself once more in beauty, as I had under Ser Lorenzo's gentle guidance. At night, I lay in bed and, for the first time since my mother's death, had thoughts that took me outside myself, outside my father's house and all the sorrow.

Recently, my father's business had increased, requiring him to return even later than usual; I had taken to giving up and retiring without speaking to him until morning. He often came home with Giovanni Pico, drinking wine and talking, ignoring the dinner table.

But now I was filled with special determination: I waited steadfastly, ignoring the grumbling of my stomach, sitting for hours at the supper table until he came. I asked no questions of him; I merely sat and ate, certain each night that he would at last mention Lorenzo's invitation. This I did for four nights, until I could suffer my impatience no longer.

I bade Cook keep supper warm, then seated myself at the readied table. There I sat three hours, perhaps more, until the burning tapers were almost spent and my hunger had grown so strong I contemplated telling Cook to bring me food.

At last my father entered—blessedly, without Count Pico. In the candles' glow, he appeared haggard and disheveled; he had not taken the time to trim his gold-tinged beard since his wife's death. Here and there, hairs curled, unruly and out of place, and his mustache, too long, touched his lower lip.

He seemed disappointed, though not surprised, to see me.

"Come sit," I said, gesturing, then went to tell Cook to bring the meal. When I returned, he was seated but had not bothered to remove his mantle, though the fire in the hearth was quite warm.

We remained silent as Cook brought first the *minestra,* the soup, and set it before us. When she had gone, I let a moment pass while my father addressed himself to his supper, then asked—trying, and failing altogether, to hide the nervousness I felt:

"Have you received a letter of late on my behalf?"

Slowly he set down his spoon and gazed across the table at me, his amber eyes unreadable. He did not answer.

"From Lorenzo de' Medici?" I pressed. "Or perhaps Piero?"

"Yes, I received a letter," he said, then lowered his face and took another spoonful of soup.

Did he enjoy tormenting me? I was forced to ask, "And your reply?"

He paused over his bowl, then—with a contained ferocity that made me start—slammed his spoon down against the table. "There will be no reply," he said. "I kept my promise to your mother: I will let Lorenzo serve as your marriage broker. But he had best choose a godly man—if he lives long enough to make a decision."

His anger aroused my own. "Why can I not go? What harm is there in it? I have been so unhappy! This is the only thing that can ease it."

"You will never again set foot in the house of the Medici." His eyes were lit with fury. "Their time is about to end. God will cast them down; their fall shall be great. Relish the memory of all the beautiful treasures you were shown, for they will all soon be gone, reduced to ash."

I judged him to be parroting the words of his new savior and so ignored this. But I demanded hotly, "How do you know I was shown treasures? How do you know?"

He ignored the question. "I have been patient with you, out of tenderness and respect for your sorrow. But I fear for your soul. You will come with me tomorrow to hear Savonarola preach. And you will ask God to turn your thoughts away from worldly things and toward the heavenly. And you will pray, too, for forgiveness for your anger at Fra Girolamo."

My fists clenched; I set them upon the table, bitter at the realization that a bright and beautiful world—one filled with art and the Medici, with Leonardo and the rendering of my own image by delicate, skilled hands—was going to be denied me. "It is *you* who should pray to God for forgiveness. You are the one who caused your wife's malady; you are the one who led her to her death. You are the one who camps now with her murderers, and remains blind to their guilt in order to ease your own."

He stood so rapidly the chair behind him screeched against the stone. His eyes filled with angry tears; his right hand trembled as he struggled to keep it by his side, to keep it from rising and striking out at the one who provoked his rage. "You know nothing. . . . You know nothing. I ask you this only because I love you! May God forgive you."

"May God forgive *you*," I retorted. I abandoned my chair and turned, skirts whirling; it gave me some small satisfaction that I left the room before he could.

Later that night, lying abed listening to Zalumma's soft, regular breath and my own growling stomach, I reveled in my disappointment. The inability to see Giuliano made me yearn all the more to set eyes upon him again.

During those brief moments when I did not stew in self-pity, I contemplated what my father had said. Had he merely assumed that *il Magnifico* would not be able to resist showing a new visitor—be she only a most insignificant girl—the glories contained in his study? Or was there more behind his words?

I slept fitfully, waking several times. It was not until the sky outside began to lighten that I woke again, my mind clear and focused on a singular image.

It was that of Giovanni Pico clad all in black, the physician's draught nestled carefully in his hands.

XXVIII

*T*he following morning, as Zalumma helped me dress for market, a knock came at my door.

"Lisa," my father called. "Hurry and finish. The driver is ready to take us to Mass."

So, he intended to make good on the previous evening's threat. My heart began to pound. Curious, Zalumma frowned at me.

"He intends to take me to hear Savonarola," I hissed at her. "Before God, I will not go!"

Zalumma, unshakably on my side, ceased lacing my sleeves and called out, "She was slow to wake and will be ready in a few moments, Ser Antonio. Can you return then?"

"I cannot," my father answered, his tone unyielding, determined. "I will stand here until she comes out. Tell her to hurry; we must leave soon."

Zalumma looked at me and lifted a finger to her lips—then she crept to a chair and gestured for me to help. Together, we lifted it quietly from the floor and took it to the door. She propped it so that it barred entry, then silently slid the bolt to lock us in.

Then, as if we had committed no crime, I stood while Zalumma returned to lacing my sleeves.

After a long pause, my father again pounded the wood. "Lisa? I can't wait longer. Zalumma, send her out."

Zalumma and I faced each other, our eyes wide and solemn. The long silence that followed was interrupted by the sound of the door being tried, then muttering, then renewed pounding.

"Do you dare defy me! How shall you face God, disobeying your father so when all he has at heart is your well-being?"

Angry words came to my lips. I pressed them tightly together and held my tongue.

"Lisa, answer me!" When none came, he called, "What shall I do? Bring an axe, then?"

Still I would not speak, though my temper vexed me. After a lull, I heard him weeping. "Do you not see?" he moaned. "Child, I'm not doing this to be cruel. I do this for love of you. For love of you! Is it so horrible going to listen to Fra Girolamo, knowing that it will please me?"

His tone was so pitiful that I was almost moved, but I held my silence.

"It is the End of Days, child," my father said mournfully. "The End of Days, and God comes to pass judgment." He paused, then let go a heartfelt sob. "I feel as though it is the end. . . . Lisa, please, I cannot lose you, too. . . ."

I bowed my head and held my breath. At last I heard him move away; there followed the sound of his tread upon the stairs. We waited some time, fearful of a trick. Finally, I motioned for Zalumma to unbar the entry. She did so, and after a quick glance outside to confirm my father's absence, she gestured for me to come to the window.

Below us, my father was walking alone to the carriage, where the driver waited.

My sense of jubilation was temporary; I knew I could not elude him forever.

That evening, I did not go down for supper. Zalumma smuggled me a plate, but I had little appetite and ate sparingly.

The knock came later, as I expected; once again, my father tested the door, which I had bolted. This time he did not call out, only stood quietly for a time, then let go a deep sigh of surrender and retreated.

This continued for more than two weeks. I began to take all my meals in my chamber and ventured out only when I knew my father was absent; often, I sent Zalumma alone to market in my place. After a time, he ceased coming to my door, but filled with mistrust, I continued to avoid him and kept myself locked in my room. When he was at Mass, I slipped away to Santo Spirito, arriving late and worshiping briefly, then leaving before the service had ended.

I had, like my mother, become a captive in my own home.

Three weeks passed. Lent came, and with it, my father's zeal increased. He frequently stood outside my door and preached of the dangers of vanity, gluttony, and wealth, of the evils of Carnival and celebration while the poor starved. He begged me to attend Mass with him. So great were the crowds who came to listen to Florence's fiery Savonarola—some journeying from the surrounding countryside as his fame spread—that he had moved from the smaller church at San Marco to the massive sanctuary at San Lorenzo, the church which housed the bones of the murdered Giuliano. Even then, my father said, the building could not house all the faithful; they swelled out onto the steps and into the street. The hearts of Florentines were turning to God.

I remained silent, protected by the thick wood that stood between us. At times I lifted my hands to my ears in an effort to blot out the sound of his earnest voice.

Life grew so unpleasant I began to despair. My only escape was marriage, yet I had given up hope on the artist from Vinci, and Giuliano, owing to his high position, was unattainable. In the meantime, Lorenzo—who alone was capable of uttering the name of an appropriate groom—was too ill to speak.

Yet my spirits were lifted when Zalumma, smiling, returned from market one day and slipped another letter, stamped with the Medici seal, into my hands.

My dearest Madonna Lisa,

I am truly disappointed that your father has yet to respond to our letter requesting that you be permitted to visit Castello with us. I can only assume that this is no oversight, but a tacit refusal.

Forgive me for not writing you sooner. Father has been so desperately ill that I am beginning to give up hope. The gemstones suspended in wine, administered by the doctors, have proven useless. Because of his poor health, I have not troubled him; however, I have spoken to my eldest brother, Piero, who has agreed to write a second letter on my behalf to Ser Antonio. He will suggest to your father whether, should he deem a visit to Castello inappropriate, he might entertain the possibility of my visiting you at your palazzo—with your father and my brother present, of course.

Should that be refused as well, I must ask: Is there perhaps a public place where we might accidentally encounter one another in the city?

I apologize for my brazenness. It is desperation to see you again that makes me so. I remain

Your humble servant,
Giuliano de' Medici

The letter remained in my lap for some time as I sat, thinking.

The marketplace was the obvious choice. I went there often, so no one would think it odd. Yet it was likely that I would encounter a neighbor there, or a family friend, or the wife or servant of a man who knew my father. It was a crowded public place—but not crowded enough to elude our driver's keen eye and too full of familiar faces. A tryst between a young girl and a Medici son would be noticed. There was no other place the driver regularly took me. If I went anywhere out of the ordinary, he would certainly report it to my father.

Zalumma stood beside me, consumed by curiosity. Courtesy, however, kept her silent, waiting for me to share what I wished of the missive's contents.

"How long," I finally asked her, "would it take for Ser Giuliano to receive a reply?"

"It would be in his hands by the morrow." She favored me with a collusive smile. I had told her everything of the tour in the Medici palazzo: of Ser Lorenzo's kindness and frailty, of young Giuliano's boldness, of Leonardo's graciousness and beauty. She knew, as I did, the impossibility of a match with Giuliano, yet I think a part of her reveled in flouting convention. Perhaps she, too, was possessed of a wild hope that the impossible might somehow occur.

"Bring me quill and paper," I said, and when they came, I scratched out a reply. Once it was folded and sealed, I handed it to her.

Then I rose, unbolted my door, and went downstairs to seek my father.

XXIX

My father embraced me when I told him I would attend Mass with him. "Two days," I told him. "Give me but two days to pray and ready my heart; then I will go with you." He granted it happily.

The next day, as Zalumma had promised, the letter was delivered into Giuliano's hands; Giuliano made my unknown messenger wait, and penned a reply that very hour. By evening, shuttered in the safety of my bedchamber, I read and reread his answer until Zalumma finally insisted I blow out the candle.

Though it had rained steadily the day before, the evening of the second day was as beautiful as one could hope for in early April. As we rode up to the church of San Lorenzo, the sun hung low in the sky, its warmth offset by a cool breeze.

My father had not exaggerated concerning the size of the crowd that came to hear the friar preach. The throng covered the church steps and spilled out into the piazza; yet despite the size of the gathering, there was no sense of excitement, no liveliness or joy here. It was as hushed as a funeral, the quiet broken only by sighs and softly murmured prayers. Every form was draped in somber colors. There were no women dressed brightly for display, no flash of jewels or gold. It was as though a great flock of chastened ravens had gathered.

There was no possible way for us to push through the crowd to hear. For a moment, I grew sick with fear: Did my father intend for us to stand outside in the piazza? If so, all was lost. . . .

Yet as my father helped me climb from the carriage, Giovanni Pico appeared; he had been awaiting us. The act of setting eyes upon him still made me flinch.

My father embraced Pico, but I knew him well enough to notice his enthusiasm was feigned. There was just a hint of coolness in his smile, which faded almost instantly when he drew away—a little too swiftly.

His arm upon my father's shoulder, the Count turned and led us toward the church. The crowd parted for him; most recognized him and bowed, acknowledging his close tie to Fra Girolamo. He sidled easily into the sanctuary, guiding my father as he held my arm and pulled me along; Zalumma followed closely.

San Marco had been filled to capacity when I had last heard Savonarola preach, but here in San Lorenzo people eschewed all social niceties and sat pressed against one another, shoulder to shoulder, barely able to raise their arms to cross themselves. Though it was a cool night, the church was heated by the great number of bodies; the air was close, redolent of perspiration, filled with the sound of breathing, sighing, praying.

Pico led us to the front of the church, where the bulky monk Domenico held our place. I turned my face away lest he or the others see my hatred.

He lumbered past us, speaking briefly only to Pico, and disappeared into the throng. Only then did I look about me—and notice the distinctive and familiar face of a gangly, taciturn youth. It took me a moment to recall where I had seen him: in the Palazzo Medici, sitting silently with Botticelli and Leonardo da Vinci. It was the sculptor Michelangelo.

Service began. The ritual of Mass was brief, pared to its bones in acknowledgment that the people had not come to partake of the Eucharist; they had come to hear Savonarola speak.

And so he did. The sight of the homely little monk gripping the edges of the pulpit pierced me far more painfully than the presence of Pico, or even the murderer Domenico.

When the preacher opened his mouth and the sound of his rasping voice filled the cathedral, I could not prevent a tear from spilling onto my cheek. Zalumma saw and gripped my hand tightly. My father saw, too; perhaps he thought my sadness sprang from repentance. After all, many listeners—mostly women but some men, too—had begun to weep as soon as Savonarola uttered his first sentence.

I could focus little on his words; I caught only snatches of the sermon:

> The Holy Mother Herself appeared unto me and spoke. . . .
>
> The scourge of the Lord approaches. . . . Cling you unto sodomy, O Florence, to the filth of men loving men, and the Lord will strike you down. Cling you unto the love of riches, of jewels and vain treasures, while the poor cry out for want of bread, and the Lord will strike you down. Cling you unto art and adornment which celebrates the pagan and fails to glorify Christ, and the Lord will strike you down. Cling you unto earthly power, and the Lord will strike you down.

I thought of Leonardo, who by then had surely, wisely, returned to Milan. I thought of Lorenzo, who was bound to remain, though his own people's hearts were being poisoned against him. I thought of Giuliano the elder, whose earthly remains rested here, and wondered if he listened with horror from Heaven.

> Disaster shall befall you, Florence; retribution is at hand.
>
> The time is here. The time is here.

I turned and whispered to Zalumma. I put my hand to my forehead and swayed as if dizzied. My actions were not entirely feigned.

She reacted with concern. She leaned past me, toward my father, and said, "Ser Antonio, she is ill; I fear she will faint. It is the crowd. With your leave, I will take her outside briefly for some air."

My father nodded and made a quick, impatient gesture for us to go; his eyes were wide and shining, directed not at us, but at the man in the pulpit.

Pico, too, was so captivated by the words of Fra Girolamo that he paid us no mind. I turned—to find standing directly behind me a man, tall and thin, with a long, sharp chin, whose face provoked an elusive and unpleasant recognition. He nodded in acknowledgment; startled, I nodded in return, though I could not place him.

Zalumma and I forced our way through the barrier of contrite flesh—first to the great open doors, then down the stairs, then through the throng in the piazza, who pressed as closely as possible toward the church, hoping to catch a word, a glimpse, of the great prophet.

Once we were free, I craned my neck in search of the driver. He was nowhere to be found—a relief. I nodded to Zalumma and we hurried to the church garden, walled in and hidden behind a gate.

Inside, beyond the stony memorials to the dead and a path lined with bloomless, spiny rosebushes, two cloaked men—one tall and one of average height—stood beneath the branches of a budding tree. The light was fading, but when the shorter pulled back his hood, I recognized him at once.

"Giuliano!" I half ran to him, and he to me. Our respective escorts—his scowling and sporting a long sword—remained two paces behind us.

He took my hand—this time with some awkwardness—and bent to kiss it. His fingers were long and slender, as his father's must have been before they grew twisted from age and disease. We stared at each other and lost our tongues. His cheeks were flushed and streaked with tears.

After a struggle to regain composure, he said, "Father is so sick he can barely speak; today he did not recognize me. The doctors are worried. I was afraid to leave him."

I squeezed his hand. "I am sorry. So sorry . . . but he has been very sick and recovered before. I will pray for him, for God to heal him."

He gestured with his chin at the sanctuary. "Is it true, what they say? That Savonarola preaches against him? That he says unkind things?"

I answered reluctantly. "He has not spoken of him by name. But he condemns those with wealth and art and power."

Giuliano lowered his face; his curling brown hair, chin length, spilled forward. "Why does he hate Father? He is in such pain now. . . . I can't bear to hear his groaning. Why would anyone want to destroy everything my family has done to help Florence? All the beauty, the philosophy, the paintings and sculptures . . . My father is a kind man. He has always given freely to the poor. . . ." He lifted his face again and eyed me. "You don't believe such things, do you, Madonna? Are you one of the *piagnoni* now?"

"Of course not!" I was so offended by the statement that my ire convinced him at once. "I would not be here at all, were it not for the chance of seeing you. I despise Fra Girolamo."

His shoulders slumped slightly, relaxed by my words. "For that I am glad. . . . Lisa—may I address you so?" At my nod, he continued. "Lisa, I regret that my sorrow intrudes on us at this meeting. For I have come to speak of a matter you might find preposterous . . ."

I drew in a breath and held it.

"The evening you came to visit us—I have thought of nothing else. I think of nothing but you, Lisa. And though I am too young, and though my father might have objections, I want nothing more. . . ." He grew embarrassed and dropped his gaze as he fumbled for words. For my part, I could scarce believe what I was hearing, though I had dreamed of it often enough.

He still held my hand; his grip tightened, and his fingers began to worry my flesh. At last he looked up at me and said, his words rushing together: "I love you—it is awful; I cannot sleep at night. I want no life without you. I wish to marry you. I am young, but mature enough to know my own mind; I have borne more responsibility than most my age. Father would want a more strategic match, I am sure, but when he is better, I have no doubt that I could make my case to him. We would have to wait a year, perhaps two, but . . ." At last he ran out of breath, then took in a great gulp of air and said, his eyes shining not with tears now, but pure fear, "Well, first I must know how you feel."

I answered without pause or thought. "I want nothing more fervently."

His smile dazzled. "And your feelings? . . ."

"Are the same as yours. But," I added softly, "my father would never permit it. He *is* one of the *piagnoni.*"

His enthusiasm was limitless. "We could negotiate with him. If we required no dowry . . . If we paid him sufficiently so that he need not work . . . I have met Ser Antonio. He has always been most respectful, and seems to be a reasonable man." He fell silent, reflecting. "Father is too ill to consider this . . . but I will take this up with my elder brother, Piero. I can reason with him. By the time Father recovers, the engagement will have been announced. He has always indulged me, and this time will be no different."

He spoke with such wild optimism that I found myself convinced. "Is it possible?"

"More than possible," he said. "It is done: I shall see to it. I will not be dissuaded. I will speak to Piero tonight, and hound him in the morning, if need be. And I will bring a report of my success to you tomorrow. Where shall we meet, and when?"

"Here." I could think of no better place for subterfuge. "And at the same time."

"Tomorrow evening, then." Abruptly, he leaned forward and kissed me full on the lips; startled, I recoiled slightly—but I would be a liar if I did not admit that I quickly returned his ardor.

That was, of course, the impetus for our respective escorts to pounce and separate us. Giuliano was herded toward a waiting carriage, while Zalumma led me back to the church.

I whispered to Zalumma. "Am I foolish, or is it possible?"

Her hand was on my shoulder, guiding me; her gaze was focused on the near-distant crowd. "Nothing is impossible," she said.

This time, I did not have to feign my unsteady step.

XXX

I slept not at all that night—knowing that Giuliano, too, probably lay awake in his bed on the other side of the Arno. I surrendered all heartbreak over learning that Leonardo favored men; I told myself that his admiring gaze had been that of an artist assessing a potential subject, and nothing more. *Friend,* he had written, and that was precisely what he had meant.

But Giuliano . . . handsome, intelligent, appreciative of the arts, and young, like me . . . I could dream of no better husband. And the love he bore for me provoked my own. Yet I could imagine no earthly bribe—gold, jewels, property—that would convince my father to give me to a Medici.

I prayed that night to God for Ser Lorenzo to recover and give Giuliano permission to marry me, for Him to soften my father's heart and make such a union possible. I prayed, too, that the portrait *il Magnifico* had commissioned would become reality.

Just before dawn, when the darkness was barely beginning to ease to gray, I was seized by an unpleasant revelation: The stranger who had nodded at me in the sanctuary was the same man who had been standing behind me, and helped me to my feet, at San Marco the day my mother had died.

. . .

That morning, my father was pleased to hear that I would again attend Mass at San Lorenzo. I was tired from want of sleep, and my nerves allowed me to eat little that day; my obvious pallor would, I hoped, provide me with the excuse I needed to again slip outside the sanctuary, to the garden.

It was the sixth of April. I remember the date clearly, given what was to follow.

The morning had been clear, but sunset found the sky eclipsed by blackening clouds; the wind bore the smell of coming rain. Had I not been so desperate to see Giuliano, or my father so desperate to hear the teachings of the prophet, we might well have stayed at home to avoid the imminent deluge.

Outside San Lorenzo, the ranks of the faithful had swelled to a number even greater than that of the previous evening; the prospect of ill weather had done nothing to discourage them.

Once again, I was forced to set eyes upon Count Pico, who greeted us with his usual unctuous courtesy, and upon Fra Domenico, who held our place near the pulpit, then disappeared. Given my nerves, I remember little of the ceremony or the sermon; but Fra Girolamo's opening words were delivered so forcefully I will never forget them.

"Ecco gladius Domine super terram cito et velociter!" he shouted, with such vehemence that many of his listeners gasped. "Behold the sword of the Lord, sure and swift over the Earth!"

The worshipers fell abruptly silent. The only sound in the great cathedral was that of Savonarola's hoarse, ecstatic proclamations.

God had spoken to him, Fra Girolamo claimed. He had attempted the previous night to pen a sermon about Lazarus the risen, but the proper words eluded him—until God Himself spoke them aloud to his prophet.

God's patience had been tried; no more would He hold back His hand. Judgment was coming, judgment was *here,* and nothing now could stop it. Only the faithful would be spared. He spoke so convincingly that I had to struggle not to be frightened.

The air was warm and close. I closed my eyes and swayed, then felt the sudden conviction that I had to break free of the crowd or else be violently sick, there in the sanctuary. I caught Zalumma's arm with fierce desperation. She had been waiting for my signal, but at the sight of my honest distress grew alarmed.

"She is sick," she told my father, but he was once again utterly beguiled by the prophet and did not hear. And so Zalumma pushed me through the barricade of bodies outside, into the cool air.

The words of Savonarola's sermon were whispered from person to person until they found their way outside, onto the church steps, where a peasant shouted them for those gathered there.

Repent ye, O Florence! Mothers, wail for your children!

The black, roiling clouds made early evening as dark as night. A cold wind off the Arno brought with it a brackish smell. The freedom and air revived me somewhat, though I was still anxious to hear Giuliano's report.

We made our way to the church garden; I pushed open the gate. Inside, there was darkness, and against it the blacker shapes of trees whose branches writhed with each fresh gust of wind, setting blossoms asail.

But Giuliano was not there.

Not *yet* there, I told myself firmly and, raising my voice above the wind, said to Zalumma, "We will wait."

I stood, my gaze fixed firmly on the open gate as I tried to conjure Giuliano and his guard from the shadows. Zalumma shared no such hope; her face was turned toward the starless sky, her attention on the coming storm. In the distance, a man's voice floated on the breeze.

These are the words of God Himself. I am an unworthy messenger; I know not why God has chosen me. Ignore my frailties, O Florence, and focus your hearts instead on the voice of He Who warns you now.

We waited as long as we dared. I would have stayed longer, but Zalumma patted my shoulder. "It's time. Your father will become suspicious."

I silently resisted until she took my elbow and propelled me toward the gate. I walked back toward the church, my throat and chest aching with contained emotion. Despite the ominous weather, the crowd on the steps and in the piazza had not thinned; many had lit torches, their winding ranks a great, glittering snake.

Neither Zalumma nor I had the strength to push our way back inside; her insistence that they should let a noblewoman pass was greeted with scornful laughter.

I turned, thinking to go back to the garden, but Zalumma gripped my arm. "Stay," she urged. "Do you hear? They have stopped repeating his sermon. Mass is almost over; your father will be out soon." She added, in a lower voice, "If he had been able to come, he would have been waiting for you."

I turned my face away, then started at the nearby rumble of thunder. Murmurs came from the crowd; an old man shouted, "He speaks the truth. The judgment of God *is* upon us!"

An inexplicable fear seized me.

When my father emerged from the church, trailed by Count Pico, he did not scold me, as I expected. To the contrary: He was kind. As he helped me up into the carriage, he said, "I know you have not been well of late. And I know how difficult it is for you to see Fra Girolamo. . . . But in time, your heart will heal. I tell you," he said, his voice wavering with emotion. "Your mother is smiling sweetly down on you from Heaven this night."

We arrived home only moments before the storm.

That night, I awoke to crashing thunder and lightning so bright that I saw the first flash through closed eyes. The storm was too powerful to allow us to sleep, and so Zalumma and I went to the window and stared out across the Arno, watching the dazzling bolts illuminate the sky.

When it was at last over and we returned to bed, I fell into a sleep filled with evil dreams.

XXXI

*T*he next morning we went to the market. I was distracted, downcast over the possibility that Giuliano had experienced a change of heart, that his father or Piero had finally convinced him of the foolishness of marrying beneath his station.

Yet even riding in the carriage, I sensed that something of import had happened in the city. In the *botteghe*, most artisans' wares had not yet been put out for display; in those shops that were open, the owners huddled with their clients in serious conversation. In the thoroughfares, people stood in clusters, whispering.

Our first stop was the butcher. He was an older man, thick of girth and bone, and so bald that his pink scalp glistened in the sun; he had dealt with my grandmother, and my mother after her. He worked beside his youngest son, a lad whose brilliant golden hair had already thinned to reveal a bare crown.

Today, the butcher's easy smile and good humor were missing. He leaned forward, his demeanor grim; I thought at once that someone had died.

"Did you hear, Monna Lisa?" he asked, before I could inquire after the matter. "Did you hear about Santa Maria del Fiore?"

I shook my head. "The Duomo?"

"Collapsed," he said gravely. "God hurled a thunderbolt, and the great dome has finally come down." He crossed himself.

I gasped. Such horror, to imagine the beautiful Duomo reduced to rubble . . .

"But I could see it, crossing the bridge," Zalumma said scornfully. "It still stands. If it had collapsed, we both would have noticed its absence. Look!" She pointed. "You can even catch a glimpse of it from here!"

The butcher was vehement. "The center. The very center has fallen. What you see is the outer shell. If you do not believe me, go and look for yourself. I have the report of witnesses."

His son, who was cleaving a lamb's skull for the brains inside, caught our conversation and called over his shoulder. "Some say it was Lorenzo de' Medici's doing. That he had a magical ring with a genie trapped inside, and that it escaped last night and caused the havoc."

His father snorted and shook his head. "Superstition! But . . . I must confess, this incident gives credence to Fra Girolamo's teachings. I was not a follower, but perhaps I will go to San Lorenzo this evening to hear what he has to say about the matter."

Shaken to the core, I left with the lamb's shoulder and kidneys, leaving the brains for another. Our next stop would have been the baker's, but I told our driver of the catastrophe. Though he was loyal to my father and forsworn to deliver me only to those places I was permitted, he was easily convinced to take us to the Piazza del Duomo to see the devastation for ourselves.

The roads leading to Santa Maria del Fiore were crowded, but the closer we drew to the cathedral, the more we were reassured: The red brick dome still rose against the Florentine sky.

"Foolish gossip!" Zalumma muttered. "Wild imaginings, fomented by that madman."

Madman, I thought. The perfect term for Fra Girolamo, but one I dared not use in my own home . . . and given the maniacal devotion of his followers, one that was not safe to utter on the streets.

The piazza was filled with carriages and people on foot who had come to see the destruction. It was not of the scale alleged by the butcher, but lightning had struck the brass lantern that topped the great cupola, leaving it scorched. And there was damage to the structure: Two niches had hurtled to Earth, one splitting the cupola, the other leaving a gaping hole in the roof of a nearby house. Chunks of marble had fallen as well and rolled to the west side of the sanctuary, where they rested in the piazza. Pedestrians had congregated around each one, standing at a respectful distance; a child reached forth to touch one of the stones, and his mother swiftly snatched him away, as if the marble itself were somehow cursed.

A white-haired elder pointed west, toward the Via Larga. "You see?" he cried, apparently addressing the entire crowd. "They have rolled toward the Medici palazzo. God has warned *il Magnifico* to repent his wicked ways, but He can hold back His anger no more!"

I walked back to our driver, who still sat on top of the carriage, marveling at the sights.

"I have seen enough," I said. "Take us back home, and quickly."

I took to my bed and told my father that I was ill and could not attend the evening Mass with him. I spent that day and the next waiting for a letter from Giuliano which never came.

I did come down for a late supper at my father's special request. I thought at first that he intended to make a special appeal for me to attend Mass with him the following morning and so was reluctant, and did my best to appear as miserable as possible. But he had come, instead, to share perplexing news.

"The lions in the Palazzo della Signoria," he began. I knew of them, of course; they had been gifts from Lorenzo. The two lions were kept in cages and displayed as symbols of Florence's power. "After all this time, one has killed the other. These are signs, Lisa. Signs and portents."

It was the evening of the eighth of April. I undressed for bed and lay down, but my eyes would not close; I tossed until I annoyed Zalumma, who murmured a drowsy complaint.

When I heard the sound of a carriage rumbling to a stop behind our palazzo, I pulled on my *camicia* and hurried out to the corridor to peer out the window. The driver was climbing down by that time; I could make out little else but the outline of horses and a man moving beneath the glow of the torch he held aloft. The cant of the driver's shoulders, his rapid pace, spoke of unhappy urgency.

He was headed for the loggia. I turned and moved swiftly to the top of the stairs, listening carefully. He pounded the door and cried out my father's name. Some confusion ensued, with the scuffling sounds of sleepy servants, until at last the driver was admitted.

After a time, I heard my father's stern voice, and the driver's unintelligibly soft reply.

By the time my father's footfall—the hurried steps of a man startled into wakefulness—rang on the stairs, I had already wrapped myself in my *mantello*. I held no candle, and so he started at the sight of me. His face was ghoulishly illuminated by the candle in his hand.

"So, you are awake then. Did you hear?"

"No."

"Get dressed, and quickly. Bring your cloak, the one with the hood."

Utterly confused, I returned to my chamber and roused Zalumma. She was sleepy and could make no sense of my uncertain explanation, but she helped me tug on a gown.

I went downstairs, where my father waited with his lamp. "No matter what he says to you," he began, then was seized by an unidentifiable emotion. When he recovered, he repeated, "No matter what he says to you, you are my daughter and I love you."

XXXII

I did not reply, for I had no idea how to respond. He led me outside, through the loggia, to a waiting carriage and driver. I stopped in mid-stride at the sight of the *palle* crest upon the door. Giuliano? But that was impossible—my father would never happily surrender me to him.

My father helped me inside, then closed the door and reached through the window for my hand. He seemed uncertain whether to accompany me. At last, he said, "Be careful. Try not to be seen or to speak to others. Tell no one of what you see or hear." And with that, he stepped back and motioned for the driver to move on.

The hour had dulled my ability to think clearly—but by the time the carriage rattled over the flagstones on the Ponte Vecchio, I realized I had been summoned.

The trip took longer than I had expected. We headed not to the Palazzo Medici, but out of the city, a good hour into the countryside. At last we rolled past the black shapes of trees onto a gravel driveway. We traveled some way before the driver brought the horses to a stop between a square formal garden and the front of the house.

Though the hour was late, every window was golden with light; here was a house where no one slept.

The men who stood guard at the entrance to the villa had abandoned their posts and sat nearby, next to lit torches in the open air, talking softly. As the driver helped me from the carriage, one of them pinched the bridge of his nose just beneath his brow and began to sob loudly. The others hushed him, and one of them hurried over to admit me.

Inside, a young servant girl was waiting in the grand, breathtakingly adorned hall.

"How is he?" I asked, as she led me at a swift pace down the corridor.

"Dying, Madonna. The doctors do not expect him to survive this night."

I felt pierced by this news, heartsick for Giuliano and his family. The works of art I moved past—the paintings alive with riotous colors, the sculptures delicate and gilded—seemed cruel.

We arrived at Lorenzo's bedchamber door to find it shut. The antechamber, like the one in the Via Larga palazzo, was filled with carefully arranged jewels, goblets, and gold intaglios. Piero's wife, Madonna Alfonsina, sat in the room, slumped, pregnant and ungainly despite her beautiful coppery gold curls. She wore a simple *camicia* with a shawl thrown over her shoulders. Beside her sat Michelangelo, who held his great head in his hands and did not look up as I entered.

Alfonsina, however, shot me the most baleful of glances when I curtsied and introduced myself. She turned her face scornfully away. She had clearly assumed the role of family matriarch and seemed more agitated than mournful. Her eyes were dry and angry, giving the impression that she was deeply annoyed with her father-in-law for inconveniencing her so.

The old philosopher Marsilo Ficino stood at the door, apparently the go-between. "Madonna Lisa," he said kindly, though he struggled to contain his tears. "I am glad to see you again, and sad that it must be under such circumstances."

He reached for my arm to take me inside the inner sanctum—but our progress was halted by shouts echoing down the corridor, moving toward us with the sound of rapid footsteps. I turned to see Giovanni

Pico leading Savonarola in our direction; behind them, Piero and Giovanni de' Medici followed.

Piero's face was red and streaked with tears. "You have betrayed us, bringing him here!" he shouted. "Why do you not simply strike us, spit on us at the time of our worst grief? Such acts would be far kinder than this!"

At the same time, his brother Giovanni thundered: "Do not disregard us! Come away from him, or I shall fetch the guards!"

As Pico and Savonarola neared Ser Marsilo and the closed door, Alfonsina rose, unmindful that her shawl slipped from her shoulders, and slapped Pico with such force that he took a faltering step back.

"Traitor!" she screeched. "You would mock us by bringing this ape under our roof at such a time? Get out! Get out, both of you!"

Michelangelo watched the scene with the helpless eyes of a child; he neither rushed to Alfonsina's defense nor spoke up on behalf of his prophet. Marsilo wrung his hands and murmured, "Madonna, you must not agitate yourself so. . . ."

Pico was stymied in the face of such hostile resistance; apparently he had expected a more gracious welcome. "Madonna Alfonsina, I wish to cause your family no pain—but I must do as God directs me."

Savonarola remained silent, his gaze directed inward, his stiff posture betraying his discomfort.

The door to the inner chamber opened; everyone turned as if awaiting word from an oracle.

My Giuliano stood in the doorway, his brow furrowed in disapproval. "Hush, all of you!" He seemed older than when we had last met. He was not even fifteen, and while his skin and hair bore the luster of youth, his eyes and posture were those of a man worn down by many cares. "What is this?"

Even as he asked the question, his gaze lit upon Savonarola. There was a swift, subtle flash of contempt in his eyes, immediately replaced by uncommon, careful poise. His tone turned gentle and concerned.

"Please, all of you. Remember that Father can still hear us. We have a responsibility toward him—he who has always been responsible for all of us—to make his last moments as calm and serene as possible. Let us cause him no more dismay."

Still glaring at Pico and his companion, Alfonsina picked up her shawl and flung it over her shoulders.

Giuliano took note. "Piero," he called to his brother in a light tone. "Your wife has not eaten all day. Could you take her and see that she gets some food? It would make Father happy to know that she is seen to. . . ."

Piero visibly surrendered his anger. He nodded and put his arm around Alfonsina's shoulders. She looked up at her husband with affection; clearly, she loved him, and he her. I saw the subtle shift in Giuliano's expression at the sight: He was moved, pleased, and deeply relieved that these two should now take care of each other.

He then addressed his brother, the Cardinal: "Dear brother, have you finished the arrangements?"

Portly and rumpled, Giovanni shook his head. Like Giuliano, he had not wept; his composure seemed to spring from a natural reserve rather than from a desire to spare others pain. He spoke in a practical tone, free from the emotion that had taken hold of the others. "Not all the details of the service. The opening hymn eludes me. . . ." A slight exasperation entered his tone. "Father did a poor job, choosing only the Gospel and one hymn. Such things need to be given a great deal of forethought, as they will make a lasting impression on the crowd."

Giuliano's speech was uncontrived and sincere. "Of any person, we trust you to choose rightly, even though the time is short. Perhaps prayer will help." He sighed. "Brothers, go and do what you can. You know we will send for you the very instant Father worsens. Now let me deal with our unexpected guest."

Alfonsina and the two brothers swept past Pico and Savonarola with disdain. When they were out of earshot, Giuliano said gently, as if speaking to a much-loved child, "Michelangelo, brother. Have you eaten?"

The great head lifted; dark, tormented eyes beheld his questioner. "I will not. I cannot. Not so long as he suffers."

"Would it ease your heart to pray?"

The young sculptor shook his head. "I am where I wish to be. I am not like the others, Giuliano. You need not worry yourself with me." As if to give proof of that, he sat up and clasped his hands upon his lap, struggling to display composure; the corner of Giuliano's mouth quirked with affection and skepticism, but he let the young man be.

Next he turned and addressed Pico and the friar: "Gentlemen, please seat yourselves. I will consult with my father as to whether he is strong enough to receive you. But first, I must speak to a friend." He paused. "Kind Marsilo, will you see to Ser Giovanni and Fra Girolamo's needs? They have come a long way and might require food or drink."

At last he took my arm and led me over the threshold, then closed the door behind us. There was an instant, before he led me into the room, when we looked at each other and it felt as though we two were alone—yet there was no joy between us. His expression was numb, his eyes filled with strain.

"It was kind of you to come when Father called for you," he said, as though kindly addressing a stranger. "I must apologize for not being able to go to the garden—"

"Do not even speak of that," I said. "I am so sorry, so sorry. Your father is a good man, and you are, too." I moved to take his hand.

He drew back; emotion welled up in him. "I can't . . ." His voice broke. "Nothing has changed for us, Lisa. Surely you understand that. But I must be strong, and any show of gentleness makes it difficult. . . . It's for Father, do you understand?"

"I understand. But why did he send for *me*?"

Giuliano seemed perplexed by the question. "He likes you. It's his way. And . . . you know that he has raised Michelangelo as his son, yes? He saw him one day on our property, sketching a faun. He saw the talent. And he must see something in you worth nurturing."

He led me back to where Lorenzo sat propped up by several pillows on a large bed covered with fur and velvet throws. His eyes were dazed, distant; they gazed up dully as I neared the bed. In the room was a fetid smell.

In a chair a short distance away sat another man, next to a small table on which a goblet, gems, and a mortar and pestle were set.

"My father's physician." Giuliano gestured. "Pier Leone, Madonna Lisa Gherardini."

The physician nodded curtly, without speaking. His face was slack, as was his entire body—weighed down by the helplessness reflected in his eyes.

"The others . . ." Lorenzo rasped. I realized then that he could not see well enough to know me. Giuliano moved swiftly to take the chair placed bedside.

"They are all well cared for, Father," Giuliano said, in a clear, cheerful voice. "You must not worry about them. Piero has taken Alfonsina to get something to eat, Giovanni is preoccupied with arrangements for your service, and Michelangelo . . ." He paused to concoct a kind lie. "He is praying in the chapel."

Lorenzo murmured a few words.

"Yes, I just saw him," Giuliano said. "Prayer has comforted him greatly. You need not be concerned."

"Good boy," Lorenzo croaked. Blindly, with great effort, he lifted a hand a few inches into the air; his son caught it and leaned down, so close that their shoulders almost touched. "My good boy . . . and who comforts you?"

"I am like you, Father," Giuliano countered, with humor. "I was born without need of comfort." He raised his voice slightly. "But here, you have a visitor. It is Lisa di Antonio Gherardini. You sent for her."

I moved closer until my hip pressed against the edge of the bed. "The dowry," the older man whispered; his breath smelled of the grave.

"Yes, Father." Giuliano's face was barely a finger's breadth from his father's. He smiled, and Lorenzo, just able to discern the sight, smiled faintly back.

"The only one," he breathed. "Like my brother. So good."

"Not so much as you, Father. Not ever so much as you." Giuliano paused, then turned his face toward me and said, again very clearly so that Lorenzo might understand, "My father wishes to let you know that he has made arrangements for your dowry."

Lorenzo wheezed, struggling for air; Giuliano and the doctor both moved quickly to lean him forward, which seemed to ease his discomfort. When he was recovered, he beckoned for his son and whispered a word I could not decipher; Giuliano gave a little laugh.

"Prince," he said. And despite his feigned lightheartedness, his voice caught as he looked at me and said, "Enough money so that you might marry a prince if you wish."

I smiled in case Lorenzo could see, but my gaze was on Giuliano. "Then you have not chosen the man?"

Lorenzo did not hear; but his son already had the answer. "He has not chosen the man. He has bequeathed that task to me."

I pressed against the bed and leaned closer to the dying man. "Ser Lorenzo." I raised my voice. "Can you hear me?"

His eyelids fluttered; he whispered a rapid response, his tongue thick, cleaving to the inside of his dry mouth so that I could not divine his meaning. Giuliano glanced up. "He hears you."

Boldly, I reached for his hand. It was limp and hideously gnarled, a talon, yet I pressed it to my lips with sincere affection and reverence. He was aware of the gesture; his eyes, shot through with blood, softened with great warmth and tenderness.

"You have been so kind to me, a wool merchant's daughter; you have been so generous to so many people. The beauty, the art, that you have given us all, Ser Lorenzo—it is a debt we can never repay."

His eyes filled with tears; a small moan escaped him.

I knew not whether it was a sign of pain or emotion, and looked to Giuliano in case there was need of the doctor; he shook his head.

"What can I do to show my gratitude?" I pressed. "In what small way can I ease your suffering?"

Lorenzo whispered again; this time, I divined the words from the movement of his lips before his son echoed them. "Pray . . ."

"I will. I will pray for you each day I live." I paused and squeezed Lorenzo's hand before letting go of it. "Only tell me why you have shown me such favor."

He struggled very hard to enunciate the words clearly, so that I heard them directly from his lips and not those of an intermediary. "I love you, child."

The words startled me; perhaps, I thought, Ser Lorenzo in his death throes was delirious, overly given to emotion, or not quite aware of what he was saying. At the same time, I acknowledged their truth. I had been drawn to Ser Lorenzo from the first moment I saw him; I had recognized at once a dear friend. So I answered, most honestly, "And I love you."

At that, Giuliano turned his head, that his father might not see his struggle to contain himself. Lorenzo, a look of the purest adoration on his face, moved feebly to pat his arm. "Comfort him . . ."

"I will," I said loudly.

Then he uttered something that made no sense. "Ask Leonardo . . ."

He gave a small gasp and dropped his hand, as if the effort had exhausted him. He stared beyond me, at something or someone invisible to the rest of us; he squeezed his eyes shut and grimaced with sorrow. His voice was still a whisper, yet agitation strengthened it so that I could understand every word.

"The third man. I failed you. . . . How can I go? Leonardo now, he and the girl . . ."

The ravings of a dying man, I thought, but Giuliano turned back toward his father at once, eyes narrowed. He understood Lorenzo's meaning very well, and it troubled him. He put a comforting hand on his father's shoulder.

"Don't worry about that, Father." He chose his words carefully. "Don't worry. I'll take care of everything."

Lorenzo mumbled a partly inaudible response; I decided he had said, *How can I go to him when I have failed?* His limbs moved weakly beneath the covers.

Giuliano looked up at me. "It is best he rest for a moment now."

"Good-bye, Ser Lorenzo," I said loudly.

He seemed not to hear. His head lolled on the pillow; his eyes were still fixed on the past.

I straightened and stepped back from the bed. Giuliano accompanied me, and we went together toward the door and the small foyer that gave us a measure of privacy.

I did not know how to rightly take my leave of him. I wanted to tell him that until that moment, I had been a silly girl with a foolish infatuation based upon his social charms and letters, a girl who had thought she was in love because she yearned for a life filled with beauty and art, free of the misery beneath her father's roof.

I wanted to tell him how he now truly had my love—a love as real as if he were my brother, my kin. And I was amazed and humbled that one so compassionate and strong should have chosen me.

I did not tell him these things for fear of making him cry. But I could not resist the impulse to embrace him before leaving; with honest affection and grief, we pressed against each other tightly without saying a word.

He opened the door and handed me to Marsilo Ficino, then closed it again. I was escorted to the carriage. It was a clear night, and cool. I leaned out of the window and stared up at the stars, too saddened to weep.

When I returned home, my father was sitting in the great hall staring into the hearth, the tormented expression on his face painted coral by the fire. As I passed by, he leapt to his feet and came to me, his entire face a question.

"He has bequeathed me a large dowry," I said shortly.

He looked at me, his gaze keen, searching. "What else did he say?"

I hesitated, then decided to be honest. "That he loved me. And that Giuliano was good. His mind was failing him, and he said a few things that made no sense. That's all."

His eyes held unspeakable misery. He bowed his head. *He is honestly sad,* I realized. *He is grieving. . . .*

Then he lifted his head abruptly. "Who was there? Did anyone see you?"

"Lorenzo, of course. Giuliano. Piero, his wife, and Giovanni . . . and Michelangelo." I took a step away from him. I was in no mood to recount the events of that evening. As an afterthought, I added, "Pico brought Savonarola. The family was very upset."

"Pico!" he said, and before he could stop himself, added, "Was Domenico with him?"

"No. I'll talk about it another time, please." I was profoundly exhausted. I lifted my skirts and went up the stairs, not caring that he stood behind me, watching my every step.

In my room, Zalumma was asleep. Rather than wake her, I remained dressed and leaned upon the windowsill, still watching the stars. I knew they shone down on the villa at Careggi, and I felt that by gazing on them, I remained connected to those who held vigil there.

I had been there perhaps an hour when a light flared high in the heavens, then streaked across the dark sky, leaving a trail of swift-fading brilliance in its wake.

Signs, I heard my father say. *Signs and portents.*

Still dressed, I lay on the bed but did not sleep. The sky had barely begun to lighten when I heard the tolling bells.

XXXIII

*L*orenzo lay in state in the church where his brother was buried. All of Florence turned out to mourn him, even those who had so recently agreed with Savonarola that *il Magnifico* was a pagan and a sinner, and that God would strike him down.

Even my father wept. "Lorenzo was violent in his youth," he said, "and did many bad things. But he grew kinder in his old age."

Giovanni Pico came to our house to discuss the loss, as if whatever news I had borne home to my father was of little consequence. I was not the only one to have seen the comet that night; servants at Careggi had witnessed it as well. "On his deathbed, Ser Lorenzo received Savonarola and was greatly comforted by him," Pico reported, dabbing his eyes and slurring after many glasses of the wine my father served him. It surprised me to see him so bitterly torn by Lorenzo's passing. "I believe that he, indeed, repented his sins, for he kissed a jeweled cross several times and prayed with Fra Girolamo."

Savonarola did not preach that day. Instead, the citizens who had so recently swarmed upon the steps of San Lorenzo to listen to Florence's prophet now waited patiently to catch a final glimpse of her greatest patron. All of Pico's influence could not spare us hours of standing along with the others.

We entered the church sometime after noon. Near the altar lay
Lorenzo, in a simple wooden box atop a pedestal. He had been
dressed in a plain white linen robe, and his hands—the fingers pulled
and carefully arranged so they no longer appeared so contorted—had
been folded over his heart. His eyes were closed, his lips smoothed
into a slight smile. He was no longer in pain, no longer weighed down
by crippling responsibilities.

I glanced up from his body to see Giuliano, standing a short distance from the casket between his brother Piero and a bodyguard. Behind them stood a haggard Michelangelo and the artist from Vinci,
uncommonly stern and solemn.

The sight of Leonardo brought me no hope, no joy: My thought
was only of Giuliano, and I stared steadily at him until our gazes met.
He was worn from crying, and now too exhausted for tears. His expression was composed, but his misery showed in his stance, even the
cant of his shoulders.

At the sight of me, a light flickered in his eyes. It was inappropriate
for us to speak, for us even to acknowledge each other—but in that instant, I learned all I wanted to know. It was as I had thought: We had
not spoken of the fact that his father had given him the task of choosing my husband, but he had not forgotten.

I had only to be patient.

The next morning I walked, as usual, with Zalumma to Mass at Santo
Spirito. When the service was over and we stepped outside into the
pleasant spring sun, Zalumma lingered behind the departing crowd.

"I wonder," she said, "if I might be permitted to see your mother."

I did not answer immediately. My grief was still too raw to go to
the place where my mother had been buried.

"Do what you wish," I said. "I'll stay here, on the steps."

"Won't you come?" Zalumma said, with uncharacteristic wistfulness; I turned away and stared determinedly up at the swaying limbs
of alder trees against the sky. Only after I heard her steps recede did I
relax.

I had stood only a moment, warming myself in the sun, trying not to think about my mother, when I heard earnest voices in the near distance. One was Zalumma's; the other, a man's, somewhat familiar.

I turned. Less than a minute's stride away, amid the crypts and headstones, statues and rose brambles, Zalumma stood talking to Leonardo. He stood in profile, a wooden slate in one hand. Beneath a red skullcap, his hair fell in waves just past his shoulders; his beard had been shortened and trimmed. He seemed to sense me watching, for he turned and smiled broadly, then bowed from the shoulders.

I gave a slight curtsy and held my ground as he approached. Zalumma flanked him, with an air of furtive complicity. She had known he would be waiting.

"Madonna Lisa," he said at last. Although he smiled, his air was grave, given that Florence was still in a state of mourning. "Forgive me for intruding on your privacy."

"It's no intrusion," I said. "I'm glad to see you."

"And I you. I left Milan at once when I heard *il Magnifico* was failing, but sadly, I arrived too late. I have been staying at the Palazzo Medici. I heard you might be here today. I hope it is not too thoughtless of me, given the unhappy circumstances. . . . I wonder if I might convince you to sit for me."

I spoke without thinking. "But Ser Lorenzo is gone. So there is no longer any commission."

His answer was swift and firm. "I have already been paid."

I sighed. "I don't think my father would permit it. He thinks art is foolishness. He is a follower of Savonarola."

Leonardo paused. "Is he with you?"

I looked at the slate in his hand. Fresh paper had been attached to it; he wore a very large pouch on his belt. I put a hand to my hair, my skirts. "You intend to draw me *now?*"

The corners of his eyes crinkled with amusement. "You are perfection, just as you are."

I felt mildly panicked. "I can't stay long. I am only supposed to attend Mass, then return home. If I'm late, the servants will wonder where I've been and might say something to my father when he comes home."

"We were paying our respects to your mother," Zalumma said loudly. I shot her a glance.

Leonardo, by that time, had pulled something from his pouch: a piece of burned charcoal tied to a small, sanded stick. "I know I sent you a copy, based on the sketch I made that night in the Medici court-yard. But I am displeased with it."

"Displeased!"

"It resembles you, certainly, but I want . . . something more. I am not good at expressing myself in words, but if you would simply trust me . . . and sit only for a few minutes, no longer. I have no desire to cause any problems with your father. Your servant here will keep watch over the time."

I relented. He led me a short ways from the churchyard, where a great boulder rested beneath an oak. There I sat; and he encouraged me to turn gently, again looking over my shoulder at him, so that my face was in three-quarter view.

He took the charcoal—made, he explained, from a stick of willow that had been scorched in an oven until it turned black—and began to draw with impressive speed. The broad outlines came first and quickest.

After a minute or two of silence, I asked, "So, how is it that you re-membered all my features so easily—after seeing me only once? The cartoon you made of me was very crude. Yet the drawing you sent me . . . you remembered every detail."

He kept his focus on his work and answered distractedly, "The memory can be trained. If I want to remember a face, I study it very closely. Then, at night, when I lie awake, I recall every feature, one by one."

"I could never remember them so clearly!"

"It's quite simple, really. Consider noses: There are only ten types of profiles."

"Ten types!" I gave a short laugh. He lifted an eyebrow at that, and I immediately stifled my smile and did my best to relax my face into its original pose.

"Ten types of profiles: straight, sharp, aquiline, flat, round, bunched, some with a hump or curve above the middle, some with the same below. If you commit those types to memory, then you have a storehouse to draw on, which will aid your recall."

"Amazing."

"Then there are, of course, *eleven* different sorts of noses when one looks at them from the front. Even, or thick in the middle, or thick at the beginning, or thick at the tip . . . but I am boring you."

"Not at all. And the nostrils?"

"They are a separate category, Madonna."

I fought to suppress a grin. After a while, I changed the subject to one I was more keenly interested in. "You are staying at the Palazzo Medici. You are very close to the family, then."

"As close as an outsider can be."

"How are . . . how are the sons faring?"

A faint crease appeared above his nose. "Giovanni is fine, as always. The world could end and it would not affect him. Piero . . . I think Piero finally realizes the gravity of his situation. Everyone had been speaking to him for years about the responsibility he would take on when his father died. It's just now become real to him."

"And Giuliano?" I pressed, a little too quickly. He saw, lowered his gaze a bit, and gave a faint, sad smile.

"Giuliano is grieving. No one was dearer to Lorenzo than he."

"He is a very good person."

The artist's expression softened; he paused, the charcoal in his hand hovering just above the paper. "He is." His tone lightened. "He was quite pleased to hear I intended to honor the commission."

"He was?"

He smiled in the face of my poorly hid excitement. "Yes. I think he appreciates your friendship greatly."

I flushed, unable to speak.

"Perfect!" he said; the charcoal flew over the page. "Continue thinking of that. Just that . . ."

I sat in flustered silence. He stared at me and drew, then stared at me again, for a long moment. . . . And some troubling thought made him flush and look down. He stared at the drawing, but he did not see it.

But he had seen something. Something in me, something he had recognized. It tugged at him, and he averted his eyes from me, lest they reveal a secret. At last, he regained control of himself, and continued to draw until Zalumma finally said, "It's time."

I rose and dusted off my skirts. "When will I see you again?"

"I don't know," he said. "I must return to Milan tomorrow. Perhaps, by the next time we meet, I will have produced a sketch that satisfies me. If so, I will transfer it to a panel so the painting can begin." His tone grew dark. "With Lorenzo gone . . . difficult times are coming for his sons. If things deteriorate, it might no longer be an advantage to be friends with the Medici. If you are thinking of making a match . . ." He had embarrassed himself by saying too much; he fell silent.

I drew back and frowned; my cheeks began to burn. Why was he saying such a thing? Did he think I was interested in Giuliano for personal gain, for the prestige? "I must leave now," I said, and began to turn away.

A thought stopped me. I turned back and demanded, "Why do you wish to paint me?"

He was the one now flustered. "I thought I had answered that question."

"It's not because of the money. What is it?"

He opened his mouth to speak, then closed it again. When he finally did answer, he said, "Perhaps I do it for Giuliano. Perhaps I do it for me."

My beloved Lisa,

    I write to you for two reasons: first, to let you know that I intend to beseech my brother Piero for leave to ask your father for your hand. An appropriate period of mourning must first pass, of course.

*And now I can formally ask you to forgive me for fail-
ing to appear at the scheduled place and time. I know how
it must have hurt you, and perhaps made you think that I
no longer cared for you. Quite the opposite is true.*

*Second, I must thank you. Your words to Father—
about all the good he has done for Florence and the
people—were compassionate and wise, and they touched
him greatly. No daughter could have been sweeter or offered greater comfort.*

*So few have taken Father's true feelings into considera-
tion, even though he, in his final moments, thought only of
others. When he knew he was dying, he summoned his
dearest friends and did his best to comfort them, instead
of permitting them to comfort him.*

*He was even gracious enough to allow Giovanni Pico
to bring the monk Savonarola into his bedchamber. God
forgive me, but I cannot help but hate the friar, who ma-
ligned my father for his good works. Serving as patron to
so many artists, supporting the Platonic Academy, entertaining the poor with circuses and parades—these were
pagan things, Savonarola said, and for that, my father
would burn in Hell unless he repented. Had I known he
intended to say such things, I would never have allowed
him audience.*

*The ugly little monk repeated his horrible accusations,
beseeching him to "Repent, for all the blood you have
shed!"*

*In reply, my father turned his face to the wall. Only at
my urging and that of several guards were we able to succeed in removing the friar from his presence. How could
he have been so cruel as to call my father a murderer—
my father, who never lifted a weapon unless it was in
self-defense?*

*Fra Girolamo then turned to me and said, "You would
be wise to repent and fall to your knees, for your*

arrogance—and that of your brothers—will soon bring you there anyway."

My father called for me then, so I hurried to his side. He had begun to grow incoherent. He asked the same question, over and over: "Please!" he said. "Please, please tell me—where is he?" I told him I did not understand who he was talking about, but if he said the name, I would bring the man at once to his bedside, but he only groaned and said, "Ah, Giuliano, after all these years, I fail you!"

He worsened soon after, and the doctors tried to give him another potion, which he was unable to swallow. He dozed restlessly, and woke, disoriented and much weaker. He called for me many times, but would not be comforted by my presence as I held his hand and tried to soothe him. And then he grew very still, until all one could hear in the room was his struggle to draw breath; he seemed to be listening for something.

After a time, he seemed to hear it, for he smiled, and with great joy whispered: "Giuliano . . . it is you. Thank God, you have made it to shore."

Soon after, he expired.

I am now troubled by a suspicion that allows me no rest. I have come to believe that the draughts prescribed by the physician during the last several months of my father's life made his condition much worse.

Trust that my thoughts are not simply fueled by my grief; I suspect a conspiracy to hasten my father's death— perhaps even to induce it. My beliefs have been reinforced by the fact that my father's personal physician, Pier Leone, was found drowned in a well two days after my father died. A suicide, they say, owing to his dismay over his patient's death.

The Signoria has taken a special vote allowing my brother Piero to take over our father's role even though he is only twenty. He is terribly distraught and uncertain at this

*time, hence I cannot trouble him with matters of marriage
yet. I must be a support to him now, not a distraction.*

*My grief is heightened by the fact that I could not
speak to you at my father's funeral, and that I was never
able to meet you that evening at San Lorenzo.*

*It would be wise to destroy this letter; if we have ene-
mies, I would not want you ever to become their target.*

*Know that I love you always. Know that I will ap-
proach Piero at the first opportune moment.*

Yours forever,
Giuliano

XXXIV

*O*ver the next few months, as spring turned to summer, my life became an agony of waiting. I heard nothing from Leonardo, received no letters or striking sketches from Milan. Even worse, I heard no more from Giuliano.

His elder brother, however, fueled much gossip all over the city. Piero directed his attention more to sports and women than to diplomacy and politics. It had long been said that his father had often despaired because of Piero's lack of acumen and his arrogance.

Especially his arrogance, and Lorenzo proved right. Only months after *il Magnifico*'s death, Piero managed to alienate two of his father's closest advisors, and most of the Lord Priors. It did not help matters that his mother, Clarice, had been from the noble and powerful Orsini clan, who considered themselves princes; nor did it help that Piero had married Alfonsina Orsini from Naples. For this reason he was considered an outsider—only one-third Florentine and two-thirds self-proclaimed royalty.

Savonarola astutely used this in his sermons, rallying the poor against their oppressors, though he took care not to mention Piero by name. Anti-Medici sentiment began to grow; for the first time, people

against the family, in the streets and even in grand

misery, no longer had excuses to avoid Fra Girolamo's sermons. I tolerated them, hoping that my obedience as a daughter would soften my father's heart and keep him from rejecting Giuliano as a suitor. So I found myself twice daily in San Lorenzo, listening to the fiery little Dominican preach. In late July, when Pope Innocent died, Savonarola proclaimed it another sign of God's wrath; in mid-August, when a new pope ascended St. Peter's throne, Savonarola grew red-faced with rage. Cardinal Rodrigo Borgia, now Pope Alexander VI, dared to take up residence in the Vatican with his three illegitimate children: Cesare, Lucrezia, and Jofre. And he did not, as most cardinals and popes had in the past, refer to them as niece and nephews; he blatantly insisted that his children be recognized as his own. There were rumors, as well, of whores in the papal palace, of orgies and drunkenness. Here was proof that God's wrath was imminent.

Zalumma sat beside me in church with lowered lids and a distant expression. Clearly she was not contemplating the prophet's words, as one might believe; I knew she was somewhere else in her imagination, perhaps in the beloved mountains she had left as a girl. I was elsewhere, too. In my imagination, I conjured the villa at Castello, and the glories housed there, or resorted to the memory of my tour in *il Magnifico*'s study, recalling the brilliance of a great ruby or the smoothness of Cleopatra's chalcedony cup.

Those memories sustained me as I listened to Savonarola's words; they sustained me as I dined each evening with my father and Giovanni Pico, who drank far too much wine and often wound up weeping. My father would take him to his study, and they would talk quietly late into the night.

Fall came, then winter, and the new year. At last, Zalumma smuggled me a letter bearing the Medici seal, and I tore it open with a mixture of desperation and wild joy.

"Madonna Lisa," it began, and with those two distant words, my hope was crushed.

I am at wit's end. Piero has steadfastly denied me permission to wed you; he seeks for me a bride who increases the family's standing and better secures his position as Father's successor. He thinks only of politics, not of love. My brother Cardinal Giovanni is determined that I should wed an Orsini, and will hear of nothing else.

I will not have it. I tell you such things not to discourage you, but rather to explain my long silence and assure you of my frustration and my determination. I will be matched to no one else. My inability to see you has not cooled my desire; indeed, it has fanned it. I think day and night of nothing but you, and of a way for us to be together. I am committed to designing that way.

I will be with you soon, my love. Have faith in that.

Giuliano

I let the letter fall to my lap and wept inconsolably. I had no faith—in God's kindness, in Savonarola's merciless teachings, in Giuliano's ability to escape the demands of duty and station. I was only a wool merchant's daughter that Lorenzo had taken a foolish interest in, that Giuliano had been silly enough to develop feelings for—feelings that certainly would pass with time.

I wanted to feed the letter to the lamp, to shred it into a thousand pieces, throw them into the air, and watch them settle like dust.

Fool that I was, I folded the letter carefully and put it away with other keepsakes: Giuliano's medallion, and that of Cosimo and the Medici crest; the drawing of me by Leonardo, and his letter; and Giuliano's letters, including the one he had expressly asked me to burn.

XXXV

The year 1493—the year after Lorenzo's death, the first full year of Piero's reign—passed grimly for me. I began my monthly bloods and did everything possible to hide the fact from my father, bribing the laundress not to mention the stained linens. Even so, Father began to speak of potential husbands. He had kept his promise to my mother, he said; it was not his fault that Lorenzo had died before giving his opinion on a match. And my fate could certainly not be trusted to that dolt, Piero, who had already proved useless as Florence's marriage broker—he had allowed several pairings that provoked the disapproval of old noble families. No, my father had in mind a distinguished man, well placed in Florentine society but nonetheless godly, and when the time was right, he would receive him as my suitor.

Fortunately, I was still young, and my father's talk of a husband remained simply that. Despite our uneasy relationship, I knew my father loved me, and that he missed my mother terribly. I was his one connection to her, and so I believed he was reluctant to part company with me.

That same year, the legend of the *papa angelico*—that unworldly pope who would be chosen by God, not man—merged with a second old story, that of the coming of a second Charlemagne, who would cleanse the Church. This Charlemagne would then unite Christendom under the spiritual rule of the *papa angelico*.

It did not help matters that the French king was named Charles, or that he listened to such legends and took them to heart. Nor did it help that he set his sights on Naples, deciding that the southern principality by the sea rightly belonged to him. After all, it had been wrested from French control only a generation earlier by old King Ferrante's father, Alfonso the Magnanimous. Barons with French loyalties still dwelled within the city and would gladly raise their swords in support of their true ruler, Charles.

Savonarola seized on these ideas, merging them with his holy vision. He was shrewd enough never to suggest directly that he was that angelic pope, but he began to preach that Charles would wield the Lord's avenging sword. Charles would scourge Italy and bring her to penitent knees, and the faithful should welcome him with open arms.

Perhaps Fra Girolamo and his most devoted followers were eager to see a foreign king invade Italy, but everyone I knew was unnerved by the thought. A sense of gathering doom hung over us all. By the end of the year, everyone in Florence was aware that Charles was making plans to invade Naples the following June.

"O Lord," the prophet cried, during one of his Advent sermons, "You have dealt with us as an angry father; You have cast us from Your presence. Hasten the punishment, and the scourge, that we may more quickly be united with You!" He spoke of an ark that the penitent could enter to be protected from the fury that was coming. And he ended each speech with the phrase *"Cito! Cito!* Quickly! Quickly!" urging the faithful to seek refuge before it was too late.

But with the passing of another year, the spring of 1494 brought—for me, at least—new hope. Long after I had surrendered my dream of seeing Giuliano again, Zalumma dropped another letter bearing the waxen Medici seal into my lap.

My most beloved Lisa,

Perhaps now you will believe that I am a man of my word. I did not give up, and here is the result: My brother Piero has at last given me permission to ask for your hand. My heart rejoices; this Earth has become for me no less than Heaven.

I hope that my long silence did not make you doubt the depth of my feelings for you, and I pray God that your own feelings have not changed toward me. I must in good faith warn you: We Medici have heard the grumblings against us, and the unfair accusations against Piero. Public sentiment has turned; and if your father and you accept my proposal, be aware that you might well be marrying into a family whose influence is waning. Piero remains confident that all will be well, but I fear a different outcome. He has received a letter from Charles's ambassadors demanding that the French army be given free passage through Tuscany, as well as arms and soldiers. Piero feels he can give no clear answer; he is bound through family ties to support Naples, and Pope Alexander has issued a bull proclaiming Alfonso of Calabria king of that southern realm. His Holiness has also threatened to withhold our brother Giovanni's benefices as Cardinal should Piero fail to protect Naples from Charles's advance.

Yet every member of the Signoria is required by law to take an oath never to raise arms against France, and Florence has always relied heavily on her trade. And so my eldest brother finds himself in an impossible situation. It does not help matters that his advisors give him conflicting advice. Show the people that all is well, one man tells him, and so my brother kicks a football in the public streets, plays a game in full view of the citizens, to give the impression that life goes on as normal. What is the result? Ne'er-do-well, the people call him, and Zuccone, pumpkin-head.

I cannot help but think that he is the victim of a concerted effort to discredit and bring down our house.

Ponder this before you write me, love, and give me your answer. Let me know whether your feelings toward me have changed. And if you give me word: I shall come! Once I have received permission to call on your father, I will inform you of the day and hour.

I count the moments until I see you again. My happiness now resides in your hands.

Whether yea or nay, I remain

Yours forever,
Giuliano

I dropped the letter into my lap and raised my hands to my burning cheeks. Zalumma was, of course, standing over me, eager to learn what the letter contained.

I stared up at her, my face slack, my tone dull with the deepest amazement. "He is coming here to ask for my hand," I said.

We looked, both wide-eyed, upon each other for one long moment, then seized each other's shoulders and giggled like children.

XXXVI

$\mathcal{J}$responded immediately to Giuliano. So great was my hope that I refused to remember my father's railing against the Medici, or his threat to marry me to a godlier man. Instead, I clung to Giuliano's promise that he would find a way to strike an agreement. He was after all *il Magnifico*'s son, skilled at diplomacy and the art of compromise. I trusted him to achieve the impossible. And because I was dangerously unskilled at diplomacy—especially when it came to my father—I held my tongue and said nothing to him of Giuliano's intent.

Lent arrived. On the first Friday of the season, Savonarola took the pulpit. He preached that a "new Cyrus" was preparing to cross the Alps—not the Persian king of ancient times, but obviously Charles, who would be forced to do so on his southern march into Italy.

If the people had watched Fra Girolamo with awe before, they now looked upon him as a demigod, for he had—in their minds—predicted two years earlier what came to be known as "the trouble with France."

"God is his guide," Savonarola proclaimed of this new Cyrus. "Fortresses will fall before him, and no army will be able to resist him. And he who leads Florence will behave as a drunken man, doing the opposite of what should be done." Having criticized Piero, the preacher targeted the Borgia pope: "Because of you, O Church, this storm has arisen!" Again, he spoke of the Ark, where the righteous could take refuge from the coming deluge ending his sermon again with the cry "*Cito! Cito!* Quickly! Quickly!"

During this time, King Charles moved his court from Paris southward to Lyons—uncomfortably close to Tuscany. Every Florentine citizen grew anxious; those who had formerly scoffed at Fra Girolamo now began to listen.

A few weeks before Easter, upon a morning gray and overcast with clouds, Zalumma and I arrived home quite early from market; a light drizzle hung in the air and had settled on my face and hair. My father had announced earlier that he would forgo not only meat for Lent but fish as well, and since we were all obliged to join him in his piety, I had no need to stop at either the butcher's or the fishmonger's.

As our carriage pulled round to the back of our palazzo, I spied there a second vehicle—one bearing the Medici coat of arms on its door. It had not been there long; the handsome white horses were still breathing heavily from their trip across the Arno. The driver, sitting at his post, smiled amiably in greeting.

"God have mercy on us!" Zalumma uttered.

I climbed down and gave our own driver instructions to take the food round to the kitchen. I was at once furious at my father; he had obviously arranged a meeting with my suitor at a time when I would be absent. At the same time, I was surprised that he had even agreed to speak with Giuliano. It rekindled my hope that my intended could convince not only his brother, but my father as well.

My anger turned to terror as I took stock of my appearance. To quiet my father, I had taken to wearing very plain, dark clothes, and even maintained the outdated tradition of wearing topaz, a gem reputed to cool the flames of Eros and help virgins keep their chastity.

That day, I had chosen a high-necked gown of dark brown wool, which went nicely with the topaz necklace: I looked the part of a devoted *piagnona*. My veil of black gossamer had failed to protect my hair from the dampness, and a mutiny of frizzy locks peeked out from beneath.

I seized Zalumma's hand. "You must find a way to hear their conversation! Go!"

She needed no further prompting, but set off almost running, while I walked more slowly, with what little decorum I could muster, into the house.

The door to the great room stood open, further proof that my arrival had not been expected.

I heard my father's calm and earnest tone, which relieved me at once; I had expected it to be hostile. As I passed by the open door, he glanced up.

Had I been gifted with more self-control, I might have continued on, but I stopped to gaze at Giuliano. Out of respect for my father, he had dressed conservatively in unadorned blue wool, and a mantle of a blue so dark it was almost black. I had not set eyes on him for months, since the morning of his father's funeral. He had grown and matured a great deal since then. He was taller, his face leaner and more angular, his shoulders and back broader. I was relieved to see that my father had received him properly, summoning wine and food for his guest.

Giuliano in turn studied me, and his radiance stole my breath.

"Lisa," my father called. For one giddy instant, I thought he might invite me in, but he said, "Go to your chambers."

I moved numbly up the stairs. Behind me, Zalumma's voice inquired whether Ser Antonio wanted more wine. She would serve as my eyes and ears, but this comforted me little. I went to my room but could not rest, so I ventured out into the corridor. I could not hear what was happening below me—the voices were too soft to distinguish—and so, helpless, I stared out the window at the driver and the fine horses.

The quiet voices were a good omen, I told myself. Giuliano, a gifted diplomat, had found a way to reason with my father.

I suffered for several minutes before I at last saw Giuliano emerge from our loggia and cross the courtyard toward his carriage.

I flung open the window and cried out his name.

He turned and looked up at me. The distance was enough to hinder speech, but I learned all I needed in a glimpse.

He was downcast. Yet he raised a hand in the air as if reaching for me; and he took that hand and pressed the palm against his heart.

I did an outrageous thing, an unspeakable thing: I lifted my skirts high and ran down the stairs at breakneck speed, determined to stop Giuliano in his carriage, to join him, to ride away from the house where I was born.

I might have made it—but my father had just stepped outside of the chamber where he had entertained his guest and, realizing where I was headed, stepped in front of the door and barred my path.

I raised both hands to strike him—or perhaps just to push him out of the way. He seized my wrists.

"Lisa, are you mad?" He was honestly amazed.

"Let me go!" I shouted, my tone anguished, for I could hear Giuliano's carriage already rumbling toward the gate.

"How do you know?" His tone turned from one of amazement to one of accusation. "How do you know why he came? What made you think this was anything other than business? And how did you come to be so infatuated with him? You have been lying to me, hiding things from me! Do you have any idea how dangerous that is?"

"How could you turn him away, seeing how we love each other so? You loved Mother—how would you have felt if you had been refused her? If her father had turned you away? You care nothing for my happiness!"

Instead of raising his voice to match mine, he lowered his. "To the contrary," he said. "I care everything for your happiness—which is why I turned him away." Then in an impatient burst, he demanded, "Do you not hear the discontent in the streets? The Medici have attracted God's wrath and that of the people. For me to give my daughter over to them would be to put her directly in harm's way. It is only a matter of time before the French king comes, bearing the scourge of God in his hand; what then will become of Piero and his brothers? You attend Mass twice daily with me. How is it you have not heard all that Savonarola has said?"

"Fra Girolamo knows nothing," I replied heatedly. "Giuliano is a good man, from a family of good men, and I will marry him someday!"

He reached forth to slap me so swiftly that I never saw the gesture; in the next instant, I was holding my hand to my stinging cheek.

"God forgive me," he said, as surprised as I by his action. "God forgive me, but you provoke me. How can you speak of marrying one of the Medici? Have you not heard what the prophet has said of them? Have you not heard the people's talk?"

"I've heard." My tone was ugly. "I don't care what you, or Fra Girolamo, or the people think."

"You terrify me." He shook his head. "I am frightened for your sake. Frightened for you. How many times must I repeat myself? You are following a dangerous path, Lisa. Safety lies only with Fra Girolamo. Safety lies with the Church." He drew in a shuddering sigh, his expression tortured. "I will pray for you, child. What else can I do?"

"Pray for us both," I countered, as unkindly as possible, then turned imperiously and ran up the stairs to my chamber.

XXXVII

*Z*alumma had not managed to hear all of the conversation between my father and Giuliano, but she heard enough to know that an offer of land and ten thousand florins had been refused. When Giuliano finally asked what offer would be acceptable, and what he could possibly do to prove the sincerity of his intent, my father had finally replied, "You know, Ser Giuliano, that I am a disciple of Fra Girolamo."

"Yes," Giuliano admitted.

"Then you understand my reasons for refusing you, and why I will never yield on this subject." Then my father had risen and proclaimed the discussion at an end.

"But," Zalumma confided in me, "I saw Ser Giuliano's eyes, and the set of his jaw. He is just like his uncle; he will never give up. Never."

During that spring and summer, I refused to abandon hope. I was convinced I would hear from Giuliano again.

Indeed, when Piero's third cousins, eager for recompense from

France, concocted a plot against him, I told myself that this was the
worst that could possibly happen. And when Piero—avoiding his father's mistake with the Pazzi—put the conspirators under house arrest, in a generous gesture designed to quiet his detractors, I felt great
relief. A crisis had been averted; surely the people would quit criticiz-
ing Piero's every move.

But Florence was cruelly fickle. She had, after all, exiled both Petrarch and Dante, those whom she now hailed as her greatest sons.
Piero was deemed weak, ineffective.

With my father and Count Pico—who was growing wan and
sickly—I listened to Savonarola's Easter sermon. He had delivered the
Lord's message as best he could, he said, and this sermon was the last
he would deliver until God summoned him to the pulpit again. It took
all my resolve not to smile with relief.

Let everyone hurry to enter the refuge of God's Ark, he said.
"Noah invites you today; the door stands open, but the time will come
when it shall close, and many will regret not having entered."

I had no intention of either entering or entertaining regret. Indeed,
I was jubilant to be spared Fra Girolamo's frantic proclamations. I
still attended Mass twice daily—accompanied by Zalumma and my
father but, blessedly, not by the unctuous Pico—at the church of Santo
Spirito, where my mother was buried, where her memory gave me
peace, where God was a just and loving deity, more interested in res-
cuing souls and comforting the sick than in tormenting sinners.

I needed no God to provide torment; my own heart provided it easily. One evening after supper, in the privacy of my chamber, I penned
a single line with my mother's quill. After signing it, I carefully folded
the paper twice and sealed it with red wax.

I proffered it then to Zalumma.

She stood with arms folded over her breast. She looked formidable
with her curling black hair brushed out, creating a voluminous, unruly frame for her face, which in the candle's glow had taken on the
color of the moon. "It is no longer so easy," she said. "Your father
watches me closely."

"Then someone else can go to the Palazzo Medici. I don't care how you do it; just get it done."

"First you must tell me what it says."

Had it been anyone other than Zalumma, who had cared so attentively for my mother in her illness and stood beside me at her death, I would have reminded her at once that she was exhibiting dangerous impertinence for a slave. I sighed, dropped my shoulders in surrender, then uttered the words that had stolen my sleep for so many nights.

"Give me a sign and an opportunity, and I will come to you."

This was monstrous, beyond scandal; a proper marriage could never be obtained without the father's consent. I risked disapproval not only from society but from Giuliano himself.

I sat and waited wearily for Zalumma's tirade.

It did not come. She studied me for a long, silent moment. And then she said, softly but most deliberately: "I will go with you, of course."

She took the letter and slipped it in her bosom. I reached forth and squeezed her hand. We did not smile; our conspiracy was far too grave a matter. If my father refused, ex post facto, to give his consent to my marriage, I would have no more status than a mistress.

My dearest Lisa,

Your letter touches me so that I weep. That you should be so willing, for my sake, to risk censure for me humbles me, moves me to become a man worthy of you.

But I cannot permit you to come to me now.

Do not think for an instant that I will ever abandon you, or our love; you remain foremost in my thoughts. But you must realize that the simple act of communicating with me has opened you to danger. And that troubles my heart even more than the separation we must endure.

No doubt you have heard of the attempted overthrow of Piero by our cousins Lorenzo and Giovanni. And our

situation has grown even worse. Only today, Piero re-
ceived a letter from our ambassadors in Lyons. Charles has
dismissed them; at this moment, they are making their way
back to Tuscany. Our bankers, too, have been expelled.

Has my love waned? Never! But I cannot bear to see
you put yourself in harm's way. Be patient, beloved; let
time pass, let the matter with King Charles resolve itself.
Give me time, too, to think of a way to appease your fa-
ther, for I cannot ask you to come to me under such un-
happy circumstances—though at the same time, I am
deeply moved by your willingness to do so. You are a
strong woman; my father would be very proud.

When I am certain of your safety, I will send for you.
Until then, I remain

> *Yours forever,*
> *Giuliano*

I did not, could not, reply. What did it serve to express my hurt,
my frustration, even my anger at him for not inviting me to come to
him at once? What had politics to do with our love?

Late summer passed miserably. The weather grew sultry. Scores of
fish died and floated on the waters of the Arno, their rotting flesh glis-
tening silver in the sun; the stench permeated the city. It was the smell,
the faithful said, of Death marching southward over the Alps. Despite
the prophet's silence, more and more citizens, even those of the nobility, yielded to his teachings and gave up their fine dress. Black, deep
grays, dark blues, and browns colored the streets; gone were the brilliant peacock hues of blues, greens, and purples, the cheerful saffrons
and rich scarlets.

Come into the Ark . . . cito, cito!

Fear had gripped the public mind. Lost without Savonarola to tell
them what God was thinking, people spoke in awestruck murmurs of
signs and portents: of clouds in the sky near Arezzo forming into soldiers on horseback, swords hefted above their heads; of a nun at Santa

Maria Novella, overcome during Mass by a vision of a fiery red bull ramming the church with its horns; of a terrible storm in Puglia, its darkness interrupted by a dazzling thunderbolt which revealed not one, but three suns hung in the sky.

My father apparently forgot about Giuliano's proposal and about arranging my marriage to a *piagnone*. He grew more troubled and distracted than usual. According to Zalumma, the Medici now refused to buy their woolen goods from him, severing a business relationship that had endured since the time of Cosimo de' Medici and my great-grandfather. Business was bad: While wool was the fabric of choice for the nobler *piagnoni,* my father could no longer sell his brightly colored weaves, and it was proving difficult even to sell the dull ones, as people were reluctant to spend money on wardrobes during such uncertain times.

But there were other things perturbing him that I could not divine. He went early to Mass at Santo Spirito, then went to his shop directly afterward and did not return home until evening; I was certain he attended vespers in the Duomo, or San Marco, most likely meeting his friend Pico there. He never spoke of it, though, and he returned home late and dined with Ser Giovanni, no longer caring whether I was there to greet them at the supper table.

By August, King Charles had mobilized his troops and crossed the Alps; the conquering Cyrus had begun his inexorable march toward Tuscany. *What does Piero de' Medici plan to do to help us?* people demanded. My father snorted in disapproval. "He entertains himself with sports and women; like Nero, he plays while Rome burns."

Public hysteria increased throughout September: The eastern coastal town of Rapallo, south of Turin and Milan, was ravaged by the mercenaries who marched alongside the French. These soldiers were nothing like our Italian *condottieri,* who looted freely and trampled crops, but spared lives. No, these purchased swords belonged to the fierce Swiss, for whom treasures were not enough: They craved blood. And they spilled it generously, killing every single living soul they encountered. Infants suckling at their mothers' breasts were speared through; women whose bellies were swollen from pregnancy

were flayed alive. Limbs and heads were hacked off. Rapallo had become a gruesome graveyard of unburied, festering flesh piled high in
the sun.

And all of us in Florence were mad with terror; even my father, formerly so eager to greet the End of Days, was afraid. The public sought
reassurance, not from Piero de' Medici, not from our Lord Priors, but
from the one man who now held the city's heart in his hands: the prior
of San Marco, Savonarola. Such was the public clamor that he abandoned his self-imposed silence and agreed to preach on the Feast of
Saint Matthew in the great Duomo.

Knowing the crowds would be great, we arrived at the outskirts of
the Piazza del Duomo at dawn, when the sun was low and the light
still gray. The sky was filled with red-tinged clouds that promised rain.

We found the church steps, the garden, the square itself overflow-
ing with so many people that our driver could not pull the carriage
into the piazza proper. Zalumma, my father, and I were required to
climb down and struggle on foot toward the cathedral.

There was no Christian charity to be found. A physically strong
man, my father pushed unapologetically, even brutally, through the
crowds, creating just enough space for Zalumma and me to follow by
pressing close behind him.

It took us the better part of an hour to make it into the church.
Once my father was recognized, we were treated like dignitaries: Dominican monks escorted us the rest of the way, to the front of the
sanctuary directly facing the pulpit. Despite the size of the crowd, the
pews had been left inside the church, and seats had been reserved for
each of us.

And there, waiting for us, was Count Giovanni Pico. His appearance shocked me. He had come almost every night to my house for the
past several months, but I had not come down to catch so much as a
glimpse of him. Now I saw that he had aged beyond his years, grown
gray-skinned and gaunt. Leaning heavily upon a cane, he attempted to
rise when he saw us, but his limbs trembled so badly that he abandoned the effort. My father sat beside him, and the two conferred urgently, quietly. As I watched them, I caught a glimpse of a familiar

form behind them: Michelangelo. Wearing tailored black, he had clearly entered the ranks of the *piagnoni:* The severity of his dress served to accentuate the darkness of his eyes, his hair, the pronounced height of his pale brow, and the shortness of his jaw. At the sight of me, he lowered his face as if embarrassed.

I cannot say how long we waited for Mass to begin; I know only that a great deal of time passed, during which I said many prayers on Giuliano's behalf. I was far more frightened for his life than for my own.

At last, the processional began. The smoke of incense wafted on the air. The congregation, the choir, even the priest seemed dazed. We went through the motions of ritual halfheartedly, murmuring responses without hearing them, without considering their meaning. Our minds were focused on one thing: the appearance of the prophet.

Even I—sinner, skeptic, lover of the Medici and their pagan art— found it impossible to resist the agony of anticipation. When the prophet at last ascended the steps to the podium, I—and Pico, and my father, and Zalumma—and every other person in the cathedral, including the priest, held our breaths. The silence at that moment felt impossible, given that over a thousand souls sat shoulder to shoulder within the sanctuary, and several thousand more stood on the steps and in the piazza outside; the only sound, as Savonarola surveyed the assembly, was the distant rumble of thunder.

After his months of solitude and fasting, Fra Girolamo was ghastly pale, his cheekbones shockingly prominent. On this day, there was no confidence in his wide eyes, no righteousness, only agitation and sorrow; his jutting lower lip trembled as if he struggled to hold back tears. His shoulders slumped, and his hands gripped the edges of the lectern desperately, as though he labored beneath an unbearable weight.

Whatever words he was about to pronounce were, for him, a dreadful burden. He ran bony fingers through his unkempt black curls, then clutched them tightly and released a groan.

The long silence afterward was piercing. The prophet had last told us the story of Noah, had last urged us to enter God's Ark to find protection against the coming deluge. What would he say now?

Finally he opened his mouth, and cried, in a voice as heartrending as it was shrill: *"Ecce ego adducam aquas super terram.* Behold, I bring a flood of waters upon the Earth!"

Screams echoed through the vast sanctuary. In front of us, at our sides, men and women swooned and slid from their seats to the floor. Zalumma reached for my hand and squeezed it hard, hurting me, as if to shock me back to myself, as if to say, *Do not become caught up in this. Do not become part of this madness.*

To my right, my father and Pico began to weep—my father silently, Pico in great, wrenching sobs. They were not alone; soon the air was filled with wailing and piteous cries to God.

Even the prophet could no longer contain himself. He covered his homely face with his hands and wept, his body convulsed by grief.

Several moments passed before Fra Girolamo and his listeners were able to compose themselves; what he said afterward I do not recall. I only know that, for the first time, I considered that Florence as I knew it might disappear—and with it, Giuliano.

XXXVIII

*T*hat night, when I at last could sleep, I dreamed that I stood in the basilica of San Marco, near the altar where Cosimo was buried. The building was so crowded, the people so frenzied to hear the prophet, that bodies pressed, hot and sweating, against me—hard, harder, until I could scarcely draw a single breath.

In the midst of this desperate unpleasantness, I became aware that the great bulk leaning against my left side belonged to Fra Domenico. I tried to recoil with disgust and hatred, but faceless forms pushed against me, pinned my limbs, held me fast.

"Let him go!" I cried, without realizing I was going to cry out, nor understanding my own words until after they were uttered—for it was then that I caught sight of my Giuliano, slung over the portly monk's wide back, his head hanging halfway to Domenico's knees, his face hidden.

Overwhelmed by the crush of bodies, by terror, I shouted again at Fra Domenico: "Let him go!"

But the portly monk seemed deaf as well as mute. He stared straight ahead, toward the pulpit, while Giuliano—still suspended upside down, his hair hanging down, his cheeks flushed—turned his face toward me.

"It all repeats, Lisa, don't you see?" He smiled reassuringly. "It all repeats."

I woke, panicked, with Zalumma standing over me making clucking sounds. Apparently, I had cried out in my sleep.

From that moment on, I felt like Paul of Damascus: The scales had fallen from my eyes, and I could no longer pretend that I did not see. The situation with Giuliano and his family was highly precarious. Florence teetered on the precipice of change, and I could not wait for safer circumstances to present themselves. They might never come.

The instant dawn presented me with sufficient light, I wrote another letter, this one consisting of two sentences.

> *Give me a place and a time—or not, if you will not have me. Either way, I am coming to you soon.*

This time I would tell not even Zalumma what it said.

A week passed. My father, who delighted in telling me about Piero de' Medici's failures, had fresh news to relay: One of Charles's envoys had arrived in our city, and had demanded of the Signoria that the French king be given free passage through Florence. He required an answer at once, as the King would soon be arriving.

The Signoria had none, as the members were obliged first to obtain Piero's *sì* or *no;* and Piero, still caught between conflicting advice, could not give an immediate reply.

The outraged envoy left—and within a day, all Florentine merchants were banished from France. Shops on the Via Maggio, which relied heavily on French business, shut down at once.

"People cannot feed their families," my father said. Indeed, since his own business had suffered, we were obliged to live on more meager rations; we had long since given up meat. His workers—the shearers, the combers and carders, the spinners and dyers—were going hungry.

And it was all Piero de' Medici's fault. To prevent a rebellion, he had doubled the number of guards who stood watch over the seat of the government, the Palazzo della Signoria, as well as those who protected his own house.

I listened patiently to my father's railing; I heard the grumbling of the household servants and remained unmoved.

Even Zalumma looked pointedly at me and said, "It is not safe, these days, to be friends with the Medici."

I did not care. My plan was in place, and the time to implement it would soon arrive.

XXXIX

*N*ear October's end, Piero—at last ignoring his advisors—
rode north for three days, accompanied by only a few
friends. His destination was the fortress of Sarzana,
where King Charles camped with his army. Inspired by the late
Lorenzo, who had once gone alone to King Ferrante and with his singular charm averted war with Naples, Piero hoped his brave gesture
would similarly save Florence from Rapallo's fate.

With Piero gone, the Signoria felt free to voice its opposition even
more openly. Seven emissaries followed Piero north, with the idea of
overtaking him and eyeing his every move. They had been instructed
to tell King Charles that, no matter what Piero might say, Florence
welcomed the French.

By the fourth of November, every citizen knew that Piero had,
without coaxing, handed over the fortresses of Sarzana, Pietrasanta,
and Sarzanella to Charles. My father was furious. "A hundred years!"
he stormed, and struck the supper table with his fist, making the
dishes clatter. "A hundred years it took us to conquer those lands, and
he has lost them in a day!"

The Signoria was just as angry. At the same meal, I learned that the
priors had decided to send a small group of envoys to Pisa, to meet

Charles there. Piero would not be among them—but Fra Girolamo Savonarola would.

Such news left me dizzy with anxiety, but my determination never wavered, nor did my plans change.

On the eighth of November, I set off alone in the carriage, leaving Zalumma behind on the agreed-upon pretext that she was unwell. My father, like all good Florentine men on a Saturday morning, had gone to the public baths.

The driver took me over the Arno on the ancient Ponte Vecchio. Some of the *botteghe* were closed because of the French embargo, but some shops still proudly displayed their wares despite the prospect of imminent invasion, and the bridge was crowded with riders on horseback, pedestrians, and carriages like mine.

At last we arrived at the market—not as crowded as it might have been, but still bustling, each of its four corners marked by a church. Brunelleschi's orange brick dome hovered on the skyline near the tower of the Signoria's palace. Milling about were housewives and their servants, men in need of a shave. I was dressed in my plain dark gown, the topaz at my throat. Hidden in my bodice, for luck, were the gold medallions. I bore the basket Zalumma always carried over her arm—although on this day, I had lined it with a cloth.

There were the barbers, with their gleaming razors and bowls of leeches, the apothecaries with their powders and ointments, the greengrocers singing their luscious wares, the baker with his bins of warm, fragrant bread . . .

And, in the distance, there was the butcher's stall, with skinned hares and plucked chickens hanging overhead by their feet.

Never did a place so familiar seem so utterly strange.

Before departing, I had mentioned to the driver that I would be visiting the butcher's today, even though we had not been there in some weeks. Bones for soup, I said.

I told him to wait for me by the greengrocers' stalls. The driver pulled the horses to a stop and did not even watch as I climbed out and headed for the butcher's—which just happened to be out of his line of sight.

It was such a simple matter, really—so swift, so easy, so terrifying. The butcher was a good man, a godly man, but times were hard and uncertain. He had his price, even if he suspected the source of the bag of gold florins.

As I neared, he was laughing with a young woman I had often encountered on market day, though we had never formally met. She was sweet-faced and blushing as she raised a hand to her mouth in an effort to hide a missing front tooth.

At the sight of me, the butcher's smile faded; he quickly wrapped a thick red oxtail in a cloth. "*Buon appetito,* Monna Beatrice; may this meat keep your husband in fine form. God keep you!" He turned to the other woman waiting. "Monna Cecelia, forgive me, I have urgent business, but Raffaele will attend to you. . . ." As his son put down the cleaver and stepped forward to wait on the customer, the butcher said, far more loudly than needed, "Monna Lisa. I have in the back some excellent roasts from which you might choose. Come with me. . . ."

He led me behind a makeshift curtain, stained with brown handprints, to the back of the stall. Fortunately, the light was dim so I could not see the carcasses hung there, but I could hear the clucking of the caged chickens; the smell of blood and offal was so strong I covered my nose.

It was a short walk to the exit. In the sunlight, the warm flagstones were slick with blood draining from the stall; the hem of my skirts was soaked. But my dismay was short-lived, for only steps away waited another carriage—this one black and carefully devoid of any family crest announcing its owner. Even so, I recognized the driver— who smiled at me again in greeting.

Those few strides—given the gravity and significance they bore— seemed impossible, interminable; I was certain I would lose my balance and fall. Yet I made it to the carriage. The door opened and through magic, through miracle, I found myself inside, sitting next to Giuliano, the basket by my feet on the floor.

The driver called out to the horses. The wheels creaked and we began to rumble along at a good pace, away from the butcher, away from the waiting driver, away from my father and my home.

Giuliano was glorious, as unreal and perfect as a painting. He wore a bridegroom's *farsetto* of crimson voided velvet embroidered with gold thread, with a large ruby pinned to his throat. He stared at me with wide-eyed amazement—me, with my plain hair and translucent black veil, with my drab brown dress, the hem sodden with blood—as if I were exotic and startling.

I spoke in a swift, breathless rush; my voice shook uncontrollably. "I have the dress, of course. I will send for my slave when the thing is done. She is packing my belongings now. . . ." All the while I was thinking: *Lisa, you are mad. Your father will come and put a stop to all this. Piero will return and throw you from the palazzo.*

I might have prattled on out of sheer nerves, but he seized my hands and kissed me.

A novel sensation took hold of me, melting warmth in the area of my navel. The topaz, at last put to the test, faltered. I returned his kiss with equal fervor, and by the time we arrived at the palazzo, our hair and clothing were in disarray.

XL

*H*ad my life been like that of other girls, my marriage would have been arranged by a *sensale,* an intermediary, most likely Lorenzo himself. My father would have paid at least five thousand florins and had the amount recorded in the city ledger, else the union could not have taken place.

After the engagement was announced, my groom would have hosted a luncheon at which, before friends and family, he would have presented me with a ring.

On my wedding day, I would have worn a dazzling gown designed, as custom demanded, by Giuliano himself. Followed by my kinswomen on foot, I would have ridden a white horse across the Ponte Santa Trinità to the Via Larga and the home of the Medici. A garland of flowers would have been stretched across the street in front of my new home, which I would dare not cross until my future husband broke the chain.

From there, we would have gone to the church. After the ceremony, I would have returned on foot to my father's house and slept alone. Only the next day, after a great feast, would the marriage be consummated.

But for me, there was no *sensale;* Lorenzo was dead, and I would never know his opinion concerning the man most suited to me. There was only Giuliano's determination and yearning, and mine.

As for the dowry, Lorenzo, not my father, had paid it long ago—although Giuliano, through his government connections, had the amount recorded as coming from Antonio di Gherardini. I had no doubt that when my father learned of the deception, he would have the amount stricken from the ledger.

My dress was of my own design, worn by me three years earlier to the Palazzo Medici: a gown with skirts of deep blue-green voided velvet, with a pattern of satin vines, and a bodice of the same with insets of pale green damask. I had grown since then, and Zalumma and I had made frantic alterations in secret, lengthening the skirt and sleeves, letting out the bodice to accommodate a woman's body, not a girl's.

I rode no white horse, was accompanied by no kinswoman—not even Zalumma, who would have known best how to soothe my nerves. A house servant of Giuliano's named Laura, a kind woman perhaps two years my senior, helped me dress in an unoccupied bedchamber—beneath the portrait of a sour-faced young Clarice de' Medici, dressed in an apron and drab gown that made me look grand in comparison. I insisted on keeping Lorenzo's gold medallions next to my heart.

As the servant was pulling my *camicia* through my sleeves, and examining it so that either side was equally puffed, I stared up at Clarice's intimidating image. "Were these her rooms?"

Laura glanced up, with a glimmer of knowing humor, at the portrait. "Yes, Madonna. They belong to Madonna Alfonsina now. She has been at Poggio a Caiano for several days. I suspect Ser Giuliano will not share news of you with her until she returns."

My stomach fluttered; I could imagine her reaction. "And the others?"

"You know that Ser Piero has gone to Sarzana. . . ." When I nodded, she continued. "You need have no worry there; he is sympathetic. But there is His Holiness, Ser Giovanni, the Cardinal. He has gone to Mass and business meetings. He is not privy to anything; I do not think Ser Giuliano intends to tell him unless it is necessary."

She lifted a fine hairbrush—one that I assumed belonged to my soon-to-be sister-in-law. "Shall we just brush it out, then?"

I nodded. Had I attempted any elaborate style that morning, my father or the servants would have noticed—and so I wore it as I always did, falling loose onto my shoulders, as befitted an unmarried girl. She then fastened in place the brocade cap I had brought. For a final touch, I donned my mother's necklace of seed pearls, with a large aquamarine pendant.

It was difficult, touching it, not to think of my mother, of how she had married foolishly, how unhappily she had lived and died.

"Ah!" Laura put a gentle hand upon my elbow. "You should not be sad at such a time! Madonna, you are marrying a man with the noblest heart and the best brain in all Tuscany. These are difficult times, but so long as you are with Ser Giuliano, you need never fear.

"Here. This is what your husband will see, when you go to him. A more beautiful sight cannot be found." She handed me an exquisite mirror of heavy engraved gold inset with diamonds.

I handed the mirror back after a swift, unsatisfied glimpse, and the ridiculous thought that the colors of my gown clashed with Giuliano's gold and crimson.

Thinking we were finished, I made a move for the door. At once Laura said, "Ah, but you are not complete!" And she went to a closet and drew forth a long veil—gossamer white, embroidered with unicorns and mythical gardens in thread of gold. She placed it reverently upon my head, covering my face; the world grew indistinct and glittering.

"Madonna Clarice wore it when she married Ser Lorenzo," she said, "and Alfonsina when she married Piero. Giuliano made sure that the priest blessed it again, just for you." She smiled. "Now you are ready."

She led me down to the ground floor, to the Medici's private chapel. I had expected someone to be waiting there, in front of the door, but the corridor was empty. At the sight, I grew sick with worry.

Panicked, I turned to Laura. "Zalumma," I said. "My slave . . .

she should have arrived by now with my things. Giuliano was to have sent a carriage for her."

"Shall I inquire after her for you, Madonna?"

"Please," I said. I had made my decision, and would follow through. But Zalumma's absence troubled me deeply; I had counted on her to attend me at my wedding, just as she had attended my mother at hers.

Laura left to investigate the matter. When she returned a few moments later, I knew from her expression that the news was not what I wanted to hear. "There is no word, Madonna. The carriage has not returned."

I put fingertips to my temple, bracing it. "I cannot wait for her."

"Then let me serve as your attendant," Laura said, her tone soothing and reasonable. "No one in the household is kinder to me than Ser Giuliano; it would be a great honor to assist his bride."

I drew a breath and nodded. The situation demanded that the wedding take place as swiftly as possible, before we were discovered.

Laura opened the door to the chapel to reveal Giuliano, waiting with the priest in front of the altar. Next to them both stood the sculptor Michelangelo—a surprise, since rumor had it that he had fallen out with Piero and had left for Venice the previous month. His presence filled me with trepidation. Bad enough that Pico should be accepted into the bosom of the Medici. Now there was yet another of Savonarola's chosen, here at my own wedding.

My unease disappeared with a single glance at my waiting bridegroom. Giuliano glanced up at me with joy, longing, and fright. Even the priest's hands, which bore a small book, trembled. Faced by their terror, my own faded.

In the wake of this perverse calm, I walked toward the three men—with Laura holding my train—and allowed myself to drink in the glory of the chapel. In the chancel, above the altar, was a fresco of the Christ child being adored by the Madonna and angels, most delicately wrought. On the perpendicular wall, to my left, was a fresco rendered in a more colorful and robust style, of the Magi processing toward the Child.

The magus nearest me was young, dressed in Florentine fashion and borne by a white horse caparisoned in red and gold. Following him on horseback were faces I recognized: the old Piero de' Medici and his young sons Lorenzo—distinctly homely, even in his idealized youth—and the handsome Giuliano. Lorenzo gazed in the direction of the Holy Child, but his brother faced the viewer, staring at an indistinct point in the far distance, his expression uncharacteristically solemn.

It gave me no comfort to recognize, in a corner of the wall, the fetching visage of Giovanni Pico.

Although it was almost noon, the interior of the chapel was gloomy. Several candles burned, their light flickering off the prodigious amount of pure gold leaf applied to the walls, and highlighting the amazing colors: the pinks and corals, turquoises and greens of angels' wings and birds, the reds and golds of raiment, the dazzling whites and blues of sky, the deep greens of hills and trees.

"Madonna, stop!" The servant Laura paused; drawn away from the fresco, I glanced about, confused. Not until the priest gestured did I look down at my feet and see the garland of dried roses and wildflowers strewn across the chapel floor.

Giuliano knelt and broke the garland in two with a deliberate gesture.

I could not have been more thoroughly won. He rose, took my hand, and drew me to stand beside him at the altar.

Despite his nerves and youth, Giuliano was in command of himself; he turned to Michelangelo with the assuredness of a man who has borne much responsibility in his life. "The ring," he said. He might not have been able to provide the gown, a great cathedral filled with people, or my father's blessing, but he had endeavored to give me those things he could.

Michelangelo palmed the item to Giuliano. There was an easiness between those two conspirators that made me think they had been close friends, almost brothers, for some time, devoted to the same causes, holding the same secrets. And that, again, troubled me.

Giuliano took my hand and slipped the ring onto my finger. The band adhered to the city ordinance governing wedding rings, being of unadorned gold, and thin. It was also perilously loose, so he closed my fist over it to hold it in place, then whispered into my ear, "Your hands are even finer than I thought; we shall have it properly fitted."

He nodded to the priest, and the ceremony commenced.

I remember nothing of the words, save that Giuliano gave the priest his answer in a strong voice, while I had to clear my throat and repeat myself in order to be heard. We knelt at the wooden altar where Cosimo, Piero, Lorenzo, and the elder Giuliano had prayed. I prayed, too, not just for happiness with my new husband, but for his safety and that of his family.

Then it was over, and I was wed—under strange and uncertain circumstances, married in the eyes of God, at least, if not in those of my father or Florence.

XLI

*O*ur small wedding party moved to the antechamber of
Lorenzo's apartments where, three years earlier, *il Magnifico* had encouraged me to touch Cleopatra's cup. That
jewel of antiquity was gone now, as were almost all of the displays of
coins, gems, and golden statuettes. Only one case of cameos and intaglios remained; paintings still covered the walls, and wine had been
poured for us into goblets carved from semiprecious stones inlaid with
gold.

In a corner of the room, two musicians played lutes; a table, festooned with flowers, held platters of figs and cheeses, almonds and
pretty pastries. Though Laura prepared me a plate, I could not eat, but
I drank wine undiluted for the first time in my life.

I asked Laura again to find out whether Zalumma had come. She
left me at a most subdued celebration, which consisted of my husband, Michelangelo, and me; the priest had already left.

Awkwardly, after a prompting elbow administered by Giuliano,
Michelangelo raised his goblet—from which he had not yet drunk—
and said, "To the bride and groom; may God grant you a hundred
healthy sons."

For a fleeting moment, the sculptor smiled shyly at me. He drank a small sip and set his goblet down. I drank, too—a great swallow. The wine, astringent on my tongue, warmed me as it went down.

"I take my leave of the happy couple," Michelangelo said, then bowed and made his exit, clearly eager to be free of his social obligation.

The instant he was gone, I turned to Giuliano. "I am fearful of him."

"Of Micheletto? You are joking!" My new husband smiled; he had regained control of his nerves and was doing his best to appear relaxed. "We were raised as brothers!"

"That is precisely why I am worried," I said. "It increases the danger to you. You know my father makes—has made—me attend Fra Girolamo's sermons. And I have seen the sculptor present at almost every one. He is one of the *piagnoni*."

Giuliano lowered his gaze; his expression became thoughtful. "One of the *piagnoni*," he said, in an inscrutable tone. "Let me ask you this: If you were threatened by the *piagnoni*, how could you best protect yourself from them?"

"With guards," I answered. I had drunk more wine than was my custom, and anxiety had rendered me incapable of clear thought.

The corner of Giuliano's mouth quirked. "Well, yes, there are always guards. But isn't it better to know what your enemies are planning? And perhaps to find ways to sway them in your favor?"

"So, then," I began, with the intention of saying carelessly, *Michelangelo is your spy.* But a knock came at the door before I could utter the words.

I had hoped it was Laura, with news that Zalumma had come— but instead it was a manservant, his brow furrowed.

"Forgive the intrusion, Ser Giuliano." His well-modulated, polished voice was just loud enough to be audible. "There is a visitor. Your presence is required at once. . . ."

My husband frowned. "Who? I gave instructions that we—"

"The lady's father, sir."

"My father?" I barely got the words out before terror rendered me speechless.

Giuliano gave the servant a nod and put a comforting arm around my shoulder. "It's all right, Lisa. I expected this, and am ready to speak with him. I'll reassure him, and when he is calm, I will send for you." And he quietly ordered the servant to stay with me until Laura reappeared, and to inform her to wait with me. Then he kissed me gently upon the cheek and left.

There was nothing to do but pace nervously inside the strange but familiar chamber; I took a final sip of wine from my beautiful chalcedony goblet, then set it down. No measure of spirits could ease my fear. I felt anger, too—anger that my fate was not my own to declare, but rather something to be discussed and decided by men.

I walked back and forth, my hem whispering against the inlaid marble floor. I cannot say how many times I had crossed back and forth inside the long chamber by the time the door opened again.

Laura stepped over the threshold. Her expression was guarded— and after the manservant relayed Giuliano's command to her, it became even more so. The manservant left, and Laura stayed; the instant we were alone, I demanded of her: "Zalumma has not come, has she?"

She gazed up at me with reluctance. "No. Our driver was sent back without her. Forgive me for not telling you sooner, Madonna. I learned this before the ceremony—but it would have been cruel to have upset you beforehand."

The news struck me with force. I loved Giuliano and would not leave him—but I could not imagine what life would be like if my father forbade Zalumma to come to me. She had attended my birth, and was my truest link to my mother.

The better part of an hour passed. I refused offers of food and drink as I sat on a chair with Laura standing over me, murmuring comforting words.

I did not hear them: I was addressing myself silently, sternly. I had my husband's feelings to think of now. For Giuliano's sake, I would be poised and calm and gracious, no matter what followed.

My determined thoughts were interrupted by a loud clattering sound; something had struck the window's wooden shutters, which were closed, although the slats were open. Laura rushed over and opened the shutters, then recoiled at another loud thud—the sound of something striking the outside wall just below us.

I rose and sidled next to her in order to peer down.

His hair still damp from the baths, my father bent down in the middle of the Via Larga, ready to grasp another stone. He had climbed out of his wagon and dropped the reins. The horse, confused, took a few paces forward, then a few back; the driver of the carriage behind his cursed loudly.

"Here, you! Make way! Make way! You can't just leave your wagon there!"

My father seemed neither to see nor hear him. As he reached for the stone, one of the palazzo guards shouted, "Move on! Move on, or I shall have to arrest you!"

Several passersby—a Lord Prior on horseback, a servant with a basket full of bread, a filthy woman in tattered clothes, herding equally filthy, barefoot children—had already stopped to gape at the scene. It was midday Saturday, and the broad street was filled with carriages, pedestrians, and riders.

"Then arrest me," my father cried, "and let the world know that the Medici think they can steal anything they want—even a poor man's daughter!" Even at this distance, I could see his utter hysteria on his face, in his posture; he had rushed here without his mantle or cap. He clutched the rock and rose, ready to hurl it. The guard advanced and menacingly raised his sword.

Two floors above them, I leaned out of the window. "Stop, both of you!"

The guard and my father froze and stared up at me; so, too, did the gathering crowd. My father lowered his arm; the guard, his weapon.

I had absolutely no idea what to say. "I am well," I shouted. It was horrible, having to communicate such private matters in this way. The noise in the street forced me to call out as loudly as my lungs permitted. "If you love me, Father, grant me this."

My father dropped the stone and hugged himself fiercely, as if trying to contain the agony inside him; then he raised his arms and
waved them at me. "They have taken everything, don't you see?" His
voice was ragged, a madman's. "They have taken everything, and now
they want you, too. I will not—I cannot!—let them have you."

"Please." I leaned out the window, so precariously far that Laura
caught me by my waist. "Please . . . can't you let me be happy?"

"Stay with *him*," my father cried, "and it will be only the beginning of sorrow for you!" This was no threat; his tone held only grief.
He stretched out a hand toward me and caressed the air, gently, as if
stroking my cheek.

"Lisa," he called. "My Lisa! What can I say to make you hear me?"

That morning when I had left the house, I had summoned all of my
hatred of him so that I would have the strength to leave. I reminded
myself of how, long ago, he had struck my mother and caused her illness; how he had forced her to see Savonarola, which resulted in her
death; how, worst of all, he had betrayed her memory by allying himself with her murderers.

But now I saw only a pitiful man who, out of frantic concern for
me, had just publicly shouted himself hoarse without embarrassment.
Against my will, I remembered the unquestionable love in his eyes
when he had begged my mother to see Fra Girolamo, out of hope that
she might be cured. Against my will, I thought of the monstrous suffering he must have endured when he realized his urging had led to
her death.

"Please," he called, still reaching as if he could somehow touch me.
"I can't protect you here! You are not safe; you are not safe." He let go
a little moan. "Please, come home with me."

"I can't," I replied. Tears dripped from my eyes onto the street below. "You know that I can't. Give me your blessing; then we can receive you, and you can rejoice with us. It is so simple." And it *seemed*
to me so simple: My father only needed to rise, to enter the palazzo, to
accept and embrace us, and my life would be complete. "Father,
please. Come inside and speak to my husband."

He dropped his arm, beaten. "Child . . . come home."

"I can't," I repeated, my voice so hoarse, so faint that this time he could not hear me clearly. But he understood from my tone what had been said. He stood for a moment, silent and downcast, then climbed back onto his wagon. His teeth bared from the pain of raw emotion, he urged the horses on and drove furiously away.

XLII

*L*aura closed the shutters as I wiped my eyes on my fine brocade sleeve.

I sat down, overwhelmed. I had focused so thoroughly on my joy at going to see Giuliano, on my fear as to whether my escape would succeed, that I had forgotten I loved my father. And despite the public's dissatisfaction with Piero, despite the teachings of Savonarola, he still loved me. Somehow I had failed to realize that hurting him would feel like rending my own flesh.

Laura appeared at my elbow with a goblet of wine; I waved it away and rose. Poor Giuliano would be coming from a thoroughly upsetting encounter with my outraged father. It had been hard enough for him to get Piero's permission to marry me, and he still did not have his brother Giovanni's approval. But the deed had been done, and I could think of only one way to cheer my new husband: to focus on our joy at being together.

I looked at Laura's worried face. "Where is the bridal chamber?"

She seemed slightly taken aback. It was still daylight, after all. "Here, Madonna." She gestured at the door that led to the inner chamber.

"Lorenzo's bedroom?" I was somewhat aghast.

"Ser Piero was too uneasy to sleep there. Your husband was his father's favorite, you know, and I think it gave him comfort to take over his father's rooms. He has slept here ever since Ser Lorenzo died."

I let Laura lead me into the chamber. The room was spacious, with a floor of pale, exquisite marble and walls covered with brilliant paintings. Yet compared to the rest of the palazzo, it possessed a slightly Spartan air. I got the impression that, like the antechamber, many valuable items had been removed and stored elsewhere.

Lorenzo's ghost was absent this day. Dried rose petals had been strewn over the bed, filling the room with a lovely fragrance. On a desk nearby was a flagon of garnet-colored wine, and two goblets fashioned of gold, intricately engraved, as well as a plate of almonds and candied fruit.

"Help me undress," I told Laura. If she was surprised by this request, she hid it well. She removed my cap and sleeves, then unfastened my gown; I stepped out of the heavy garment, and watched as she folded and put it away with my other things in the polished dark wardrobe that held Giuliano's clothes.

I wore nothing now except my *camicia,* delicate and sheer as spider's silk. Zalumma had done her best to prepare me for my wedding night, but I still struggled not to let my nerves get the better of me. "I would like to be alone now," I said. "Will you tell my husband that I am waiting for him here?"

She closed the door quietly behind her as she left.

I moved to the desk and poured some of the wine into a goblet, then took a small sip. I savored it carefully, attempting to relish its deliciousness in an effort to summon the sense of pleasure and joy with which I might greet Giuliano. Beside the flagon was a small velvet pouch; I lifted it and could feel within something hard—jewelry, I guessed, a present from a groom to his bride—and I smiled.

Yet as I stood in front of the desk, I could not help noticing that one item upon it was out of place, as if the reader had been called suddenly away. The green wax seal had been broken so that the letter lay half unfolded. I might have ignored it, but the merest glimpse of a fa-

miliar script caught my eye, and I could not resist setting down my
goblet and picking the letter up.

It bore neither a signature nor any indication of its intended recip-
ient.

> *I appreciate your willingness to release me from any*
> *formal obligation to locate the penitent—the one your fa-*
> *ther referred to as the third man. But I am morally bound*
> *to continue the search, despite the dwindling possibility*
> *that this man still lives.*
>
> *All my efforts to sway Milan to your side have failed.*
> *Here is the truth about Duke Gian Galeazzo's death: The*
> *assassins acted at the behest of his uncle Ludovico Sforza*
> *who, without pausing to mourn his brother's passing, has*
> *already proclaimed himself Duke, despite the existence of*
> *Gian Galeazzo's young son, the rightful heir. With Lu-*
> *dovico in power, Milan is no longer your friend; this I*
> *learned from the new duke himself, who has come to trust*
> *me fully. He has turned the minds of Charles and his am-*
> *bassadors against you, and now prepares to betray you*
> *with hopes of stealing even more power.*
>
> *His distrust of Florence is the result of years of patient*
> *work by his advisors and certain associates. This, along*
> *with my investigation, has led me to the irrefutable con-*
> *clusion that our Ludovico is influenced by those in league*
> *with the* piagnoni.

I was startled and confused by the last sentence. The *piagnoni*
were sincere, if overly zealous, Christians. It was true that
Savonarola believed King Charles had been chosen by God to punish
Italy for her wickedness—but why would they want to influence the
Duke of Milan? And how could an advisor influencing Ludovico
against Florence possibly bring the author to the conclusion that the
piagnoni were responsible?

But I was even more intrigued by the handwriting—distinctive, strikingly vertical and slantless, the *f*'s and *l*'s long and flourished, the *n*'s squat and fat. The spelling was uncertain. A moment passed before I at last recalled where I had seen it.

Greetings, Madonna Lisa, from Milan.

Our good Lorenzo has commissioned me to paint your portrait. . . .

XLIII

I glanced up at the sound of the door opening, and did not quite manage to set the letter back down before Giuliano entered.

In one guilty glimpse, I noticed three things about him: first, that he came in with a forced smile, though he had clearly suffered an unnerving exchange with my father; second, that the forced smile faded as his lips parted in awe and his eyes widened at the sight of me in my sheer gown; and third, that he noticed the letter in my hand, and his sharp concern and irritation with himself took precedence over the other two emotions.

He took the letter from me at once. His voice filled not with accusation, but with worry. "Did you read it?"

"Why would the *piagnoni* want to influence Ludovico Sforza? I thought they were more interested in God than politics."

A frown tugged at the corners of his mouth as he folded the letter and put it in the desk. "I was a fool not to have concealed this. A fool. But I was called away quickly, and I thought I would have time before you came in here. . . ."

"I know Leonardo's hand." I did not believe in hiding anything from him. "I am your wife now, and you mustn't worry about what I know or don't know. I can hold my tongue."

"It's not that," he began. "The Duke of Milan was always a help to our family, always our greatest ally. We could rely on him for troops. When my uncle Giuliano was killed, my father wrote to the Duke for help, and received it immediately. And now . . ." He looked away, frowning, his tone dark. "Now that support has been taken from us, at a time when we need it most." He sighed. "And I have brought you into the midst of all this."

"You didn't bring me. I would have come whether you had said yes or not." With my chin, I nodded at the desk which held the letter. "If I'm in danger, it's because of who I am now, not what facts are stored in my head. This will make no difference."

"I know," he admitted, with faint misery. "I came to realize that if I truly wanted you safe, I might as well put you under my protection." He managed a smile. "You're even more headstrong than I am. At least I know where you are. Do you realize . . . Certainly you realize . . . things might get much worse. We might have to leave Florence for a time. I don't just mean going to one of our villas in the countryside. I've sent a number of priceless objects out of the city to protect them . . . and I've even packed away my things, just in case. . . ." He drew back to gaze at me with Lorenzo's brilliant eyes, yet his held a certain openness his father's had lacked. "We would go to Rome, where Giovanni has good friends, and we would have the protection of the Pope. It is terribly different from Florence—hotter, and more crowded. . . ."

"It doesn't matter," I said, my voice soft. I took a step closer to him. He stood half a head taller than I, and his chest was broader than I was from shoulder to shoulder. He was still dressed in the fitted red velvet *farsetto* and wore it with the casual poise of a prince. He was not classically handsome like his agent Leonardo. His upper lip was thin and bore a small diagonal scar from some childhood injury, and his chin jutted ever so slightly forward, a whisper of Lorenzo's deformity. The bridge of his nose was broad and the end of it upturned; his eyebrows were very thick and dark. When he smiled, a dimple formed in his left cheek. I touched it with my fingertip, and he let go a long sigh.

"You are incredibly beautiful," he said. "Even more so because you apparently don't know it."

I put my hands on his shoulders. "We have everything in the world to worry about: your family, my father, King Charles, the Signoria, the Duke of Milan, Florence herself. There's nothing we can do about it right now, this moment. We can only rejoice that you and I are standing here to face it together."

He had no choice but to lean down and kiss me. This time, we did not writhe, panting, in each other's arms, as we had in the carriage. We were man and wife now and approached each other with a sense of seriousness, of gravity. He settled me carefully on the bed and lay beside me to reach beneath my silk gown and run his palms slowly over my collarbone, my breast, my abdomen. I trembled, and not entirely from nerves.

Brazenly, I reached up and ran my hands over his velvet-covered shoulders, his muscular chest, and the hollow in its center. And then, wanting more, I fumbled, looking to free him from the *farsetto*.

He half sat. "Here," he said, and proffered me the high neck of his garment.

Without thinking, I clicked my tongue. "What makes you think I know how to unfasten a man's garment?"

"You have a father . . ."

"And his servant dresses him, not I."

He looked suddenly, charmingly, sheepish. "As mine does me."

We both burst out laughing.

He glanced toward the door. "Oh no," I said. "You've said I am headstrong: Let me prove it again."

It was a hard-fought battle, but in the end, the *farsetto* yielded. And so did Giuliano.

.   .   .

During my childhood, I had an experience of pure warmth, of opening, of unconditional union. I had been desperately sick, so sick that
the adults surrounding me spoke in muted voices about my death. I remember a terrifying weight on my chest, the sensation of drowning in
my own fluids, of not being able to breathe.

They brought up kettles and a wooden trough. They filled it with
near-scalding water, and my mother lowered me into it.

Once I was immersed to my neck in the water, its steam settled tenderly on my face; its generous heat permeated my bones. I looked down
at my reddening flesh and—thinking the way a child does—thought
that it would melt, yield, and merge with the warmth. I closed my eyes,
blissful, and felt my skin dissolve until there was nothing but my beating heart and the water. All weight, all heaviness, dispersed into the air.

I was alive. I could breathe.

Being with Giuliano was the same. There was heat; there was opening. There was union. I could breathe.

"Is Leonardo still going to paint my portrait?" I asked drowsily, after
we had worn ourselves out. We were lying naked beneath fine linens
and a crimson throw. By then, it was late afternoon and the light from
the waning sun poured bittersweet through the shutters.

The naturalness of the deed had surprised me. I had expected to
need careful instruction, had expected to fumble, but Giuliano's confidence and my own instincts had guided me surely. After our exertion, I had grown chilled, and to my embarrassment, Giuliano had
summoned a servant to build a fire in the hearth. I sat swaddled and
still until the servant departed; only then could I be coaxed to forget
myself and lie in Giuliano's arms.

"Your portrait?" Giuliano let go a long, relaxed sigh. "Yes, of
course. Father had asked for it. Leonardo is terrible about such things,
you know. Most of the commissions Father paid him for, he never finished. But . . ." He directed a wicked little smile at me. "I shall demand it. I shall hold his feet to the fire. I shall chain him in his studio,

and never let him free until it is done! But I must have your image with me forever."

I giggled.

Giuliano took advantage of the levity to broach a difficult subject. "I have assigned one of our best agents to visit Ser Antonio."

I tensed at once. "There is no reasoning with my father."

Giuliano lightly touched the tip of my nose, as if trying to distract me from the hurt. "I know; I've met the man. He is far too distraught today to be approached; he's been shocked and hurt. Give him time. My man will wait for a few days. Until then, we will watch your father to be sure he does nothing rash."

Spies, I realized, with unease. Someone was going to sit outside my father's house, watching him, and report his movements to Giuliano. At the same time that this disturbed me, it also brought relief. At least my father could not fling himself into the Arno without someone intervening.

"My man is elderly, a good Christian, and will treat Ser Antonio with a great deal of respect. I was unwise to think your father could be tempted to let you go for money or land; he is a man of character. While I don't share his love for Fra Girolamo, I understand that he needs to be reassured that you have married an honorable, pious man, and that you will not live a life of corrupt luxury, but will instead devote yourself to God and your husband.

"And Lisa," Giuliano said very earnestly, turning his face to mine; my head rested upon his shoulder and outstretched arm. "I believe in God and the need for integrity, and if your father requires that we go and listen to Fra Girolamo's sermons, I will do it."

His sincerity touched me, but I let go a snort at his last words. "Then you'll go alone," I murmured, though his words gave me hope. If Giuliano humbled himself to suffer through the preaching of the Medici's mortal enemy, it would certainly impress my father . . . and all of Florence.

My gaze wandered to three painted panels that covered the entire wall opposite us. Earlier, my nerves had allowed me to notice only blurs of red, yellow, black: Now I realized they depicted a fierce battle in progress. A wickedly sharp lance impaled a rider through his chest, lifting him from his saddle; fallen men and horses lay dead and dying amid empty helmets and dropped shields. It was a dreadful, chaotic evocation of confusion and rage. I lifted my head from Giuliano's shoulder and frowned.

"Ah," Giuliano said, and smiled. "You've noticed the paintings. This is Uccello's *Battle of San Romano,* where Florence defeated Siena a century ago."

"But it's so violent. . . . It must have been the first thing Lorenzo saw in the morning, and the last thing at night. Why would anyone want such a disturbing sight in his bedroom?"

Bright with enthusiasm, Giuliano rose naked from the bed and moved to the central panel. "Father liked it not for its violence, but for the spirit shown by the captain, Niccolò da Tolentino. He was a great hero. See? He's in the center, leading the charge." He pointed to a rider—the only one without a helmet—on the front lines, his lance aimed at the heart of his opponent. "He is unafraid. Despite the great army he faces, he is confident of success. And this is a great example of the new perspective. Look here"—with thumb and forefinger, he measured one of the fallen soldiers—"and see how the length of this man compares with that of the captain."

I stared. The fallen man was a fraction of da Tolentino's size. "He is so small!" I laughed. "But it only makes sense; if you face someone lying down, their body looks shorter than it is. And—look there. See how the men here are small, to make them look far away?"

Pleased, Giuliano smiled. "If you weren't a woman, I'd say you should be an artist! I didn't know you were so clever. Yes, that's the magic of perspective. And Uccello was one of the very first to use it. Father had a wonderful eye. Piero and Giovanni haven't a clue about the amazing art that surrounds them. It's a shame, really."

I shared Giuliano's smile. "Ser Lorenzo must have loved you greatly to have taught you such things." I thought of Lorenzo, sick and beset by enemies, taking courage from the image of the long-dead warrior.

Giuliano nodded, a bit more serious. "Of his family, I understood him best. And he understood me. Piero, he is more like Mother, and Giovanni—" He gave another short laugh. "I'm not sure who he resembles in the family. Perhaps our great-grandfather Cosimo. He is very shrewd at promoting himself."

Dusk had brought its gloom; he lit a pair of candles using the fire in the hearth, then returned to the bed and settled beside me with a sigh of pleasant exhaustion.

"Why would the *piagnoni* want to work with the Duke of Milan to oust Piero from power?" I asked softly.

His good humor fell away. He propped himself on his elbow and rolled toward me, his face in shadow. "I'm not sure exactly," he said. "But I know they want our family's downfall. Father did many unwise—even illegal—things. He stole from the city's dowry fund to buy Giovanni's cardinalship. And, in his younger years, he treated his enemies without mercy. He was willing to do anything to shield the family. There are many people, many families and groups, who had reason to hate him.

"But he had an uncanny knack for protecting himself, for making allies, for knowing—especially in his later years—when to yield, and ignore those who threatened him or spoke ill of him." He paused. "Piero and Giovanni . . . they're intelligent in their own ways, but they aren't Father. They don't understand the importance of how the public perceives them. They don't know how to be . . . humble about their position. And Piero . . . he gets conflicting advice from his counselors, and becomes so confused that he does nothing at all.

"I told him to go to Sarzana—the way Father went to King Ferrante in the hope of preventing a war. But I wanted to go with him. 'Don't listen to your advisors,' I told him. 'Let me guide you.' But he wanted to prove he could do it himself, without my help. It's—well, Father never kept it secret that I was his favorite. He always told Piero that when he finally became the leader of the family, he shouldn't do anything without consulting me. And Piero's always been jealous of that. I don't blame him, but . . ." He shook his head. "It was a mistake, handing over Sarzana and the other two citadels. I know Piero;

he doesn't know who to listen to, so he listened to no one and acted out of sheer nerves. So now the Signoria is furious, and they're sending Fra Girolamo to talk to the French king. It's all a mess. I just hope Piero will listen to me about how best to straighten it out."

His frustration was clear; he had Lorenzo's quick mind combined with his namesake uncle's sweetness. An accident of birth had stolen from him the position for which he was naturally gifted—and because of it, everything might be lost. "So the *piagnoni*," I said, trying to lead him back. "Does Savonarola have political aims? Does he want Florence for himself . . . and maybe Milan, too?"

He frowned at me. "It's more complicated than that. I have agents working on it. . . ."

Of which Leonardo was one. "How complicated? I have time—"

We were interrupted by a knock at the bedchamber door, and a male voice. "Ser Giuliano?"

"Yes?"

"Your brother has returned from Sarzana. He is waiting for you in the dining hall."

"Tell him I'll be there shortly."

I had already leapt from the bed and was pulling on my *camicia*. Giuliano looked at me, then at his leggings and *farsetto,* lying in a heap near the hearth, then at me again. "Send Laura and my valet," he called. "We need help dressing."

XLIV

*O*nce we were dressed, Giuliano led me downstairs through the vast, quiet palazzo; our steps echoed against the shining marble. The corridors seemed emptier than I remembered: Much of the art had been spirited away.

"Perhaps I shouldn't go," I hissed, my arm linked with his. "Piero will want to discuss political matters." In fact, I was nervous about the prospect of meeting him. Despite Giuliano's reassurances, I was not at all certain that the eldest Medici brother had agreed to our marriage with enthusiasm. I had already had a painful encounter with my father and was in no mood for another with Piero.

Giuliano seemed to read my thoughts. "It's true, my brother would not hear of my marrying you—at first. But I persisted. I convinced him it made great political sense. After all, the people were grumbling about the fact that Piero was the son of an Orsini woman, and had also married one. I told him, 'You've already made a strong alliance with the noble Orsinis—and Giovanni is a cardinal, which makes the Pope and Church our allies. It's time for us now to tie ourselves to the people, to show that we don't consider ourselves royalty, as they say.' He finally listened. And while Alfonsina and Giovanni disagree—well, I have no doubt your charm will win them over."

We stopped at last in front of a tall door of carved and polished dark wood. Giuliano pushed it open, then gestured for me to enter.

Warmth and light greeted me. On the opposite wall, a huge fire blazed in a massive hearth; on the long dining table, a candelabrum bearing more than a dozen burning tapers exuded the smell of heated wax. Every wall was frescoed with pastoral scenes—of Bacchus and his grapes, of nymphs and satyrs cavorting while Pan played his pipes.

Two men occupied the room. The first paced in front of the fire, arms gesticulating wildly. He was dressed like a prince, in a tunic of sapphire velvet with purple satin trim. A great amethyst hung from his thick gold necklace, and the diamonds on his fingers glittered with reflected firelight. His shoulders were broad, his waist narrow, and his leggings revealed powerful thighs and well-muscled calves. One could easily imagine him out in Florence's streets, kicking a ball.

"How dare they insult me so!" he raved bitterly. "How dare they, when I have just saved the city! I deserve a hero's welcome, and instead—" He glanced up, scowling, at our interruption.

The second man sat at the table. His manner was impassive as he meticulously carved the meat from the bones of a roasted pheasant. He wore a scarlet cardinal's gown, a red silk cap, and a ruby ring; as we entered, he half turned in his chair to get a better look at us. He was thick fingered, thick lipped, with a large, broad head and an even broader chest. He set down his fork and knife and rose. "Giuliano! Who is this?" He was surprised but not impolite. His voice was deep and arrestingly handsome, despite his plain face and small, suspicious eyes. At the sight of me, he rose.

"Who is this?" Piero demanded, echoing his brother. He stepped into the candelabrum's light, revealing a face very like his mother's, his lips thin, his chin weak.

"Piero, you remember. This is my wife, Madonna Lisa di Antonio Gherardini. Lisa, this is my brother Piero di Lorenzo de' Medici."

My husband's answer left Giovanni aghast. "Antonio the wool merchant? Is this your idea of a joke?"

"Do not insult my wife," Giuliano replied, his tone menacing.

"The Gherardini are a good family. Piero gave us permission to marry some time ago."

Piero dismissively waved a hand. "I gave you permission. But now is hardly the time to meet the young lady, when we are set upon from all sides. . . ." He bowed cursorily to me. "Forgive us, Madonna; we have urgent and private matters to discuss. Giuliano, you can introduce us to your intended later."

"She's not going anywhere, brother. She is family. The priest married us this morning."

Piero let go a faint gasp. Giovanni dropped back into his seat and put a hand upon his barrel of a chest. The latter was first to speak, in that melodious voice which, despite its owner's agitation, was pleasurable to hear. "You'll have to get it annulled. You can't waste Medici seed on a commoner."

I flushed, angry enough to forget my nervousness.

Giuliano spoke, his tone heated. "She is no commoner. She is my wife and she is staying here, under her husband's roof. The marriage has been consummated, and I will not tolerate talk of an annulment again." He turned to Piero. "As for our conversation—she already knows everything, so she will stay. You are both going to give her a kiss and welcome her into the family."

Giovanni rose and gave me a curious look as he stepped toward me and took my hands; his own were soft and fleshy. With abrupt offhanded charm, he smiled and said, "I will give you a kiss because you are so beautiful, Lisa." Then he lifted a brow and, with a swift glance at Giuliano, added, "But I can easily make arrangements. . . ."

"I will *not* hear it," Giuliano warned.

"Well, then," Giovanni said, with resigned diplomacy. "Sit beside me, Madonna Lisa. You sit, too, Giuliano. This is your wedding feast, then, is it? After so much consummation, a feast is in order. Let me ring for the servants." He rose and pulled on a nearby chain that hung from an opening in the wall, then returned to his chair and gestured for us to take ours.

Piero was too agitated to offer his hands or a kiss. He remained on the opposite side of the table as Giuliano and I sat beside the Cardinal.

"Greetings will have to wait. I've just come from the Signoria." Piero spread his hands in exasperation, as if to say, *I have given them everything . . . what more do they want?* "I have saved Florence— saved her at the small cost of a few fortresses and some ducats—"

"How many?" Giovanni demanded.

Piero's voice lowered abruptly. "Two hundred thousand."

Giuliano did not react but merely gazed steadily at his eldest brother; clearly, he already knew this fact.

Giovanni set down his goblet with such force that wine spilled over the rim onto the table. "Christ in Heaven!" Giovanni swore. "What were you thinking? No wonder the Signoria won't talk to you! No wonder they've sent this fellow full of Doomsday nonsense—this Savonarola—to Pisa."

Piero turned on him defensively. "Savonarola? To Pisa? Now they mock me openly!"

Giuliano sounded weary, frustrated. "Didn't you read the letter I sent you?"

Once again, Piero's eyes darted to the side. "You have no idea how busy I was, how beset. . . . I can't be blamed for missing a detail."

"You never read it at all," Giuliano said calmly. "If you had, you would have known that the Signoria was upset about the fortresses and the money. The French are laughing at us, brother. They hardly expected to gain Sarzana, much less Sarzanella and Pietrasanta and a mountain of gold. The Signoria is rightly furious. My letter asked you to come here directly so that we might plan a strategy to approach them."

Piero sagged, deflated; the nuances of diplomacy and negotiation were beyond him, yet he maintained a weak defiance. "Little brother," he said, in a low tone, "I had to go by myself. I have to do this by my-self; otherwise, who would respect me? I am not Father. . . ."

"None of us are," Giuliano answered gently. "But the three of us together can equal him." This he said out of apparent generosity, for Giovanni had returned to dismantling his pheasant and listened with an observer's detachment.

The speakers paused then as a servant entered. Giovanni directed him to bring wine, and food "for our two lovers here." Once the man departed, the conversation resumed.

By that time, Piero had reclaimed his indignation. "I *did* stop in front of our palazzo when I first came into town—I'm not a total idiot. There was a crowd waiting outside in the loggia, eager to hear my report. I told them the good news, that everything had been made right with Charles. I did exactly what you had suggested: I ordered sweetmeats thrown to the people and wine served, just as Father did when he returned from negotiating with King Ferrante. But no one was in the mood to celebrate, apparently. They drank my wine and ate my food, all the while staring silently at me, as if I'd done something wrong.

"So I went on to the Palazzo della Signoria." It was the custom for the highest members of Florence's government to inhabit the palazzo during their tenure; they took their meals there and even slept there. "Do you know what they did? They turned me away! Sent a servant to the door to say, 'Come back tomorrow—they are eating supper.' I showed him with a gesture what I thought of that!" He snorted. "I'm not a complete fool. I know about the people's grumbling. I've taken no chances. I made arrangements with Paolo. Eight hundred Orsini soldiers—five hundred on horseback, three on foot—are camped at the San Gallo gate right now awaiting my signal, in case there's trouble."

"Who told you to do that?" Giuliano pressed his hands to his face in disbelief and aggravation, then just as swiftly removed them.

"Dovizi."

Ser Piero Dovizi was Piero's closest advisor.

"I'm going to repeat this again: You can't trust Dovizi! I don't think he has our best interests at heart anymore." Giuliano made a noise of frustration. "Don't you see how it appears? The Signoria and the people are already angry that you acted without approval. Now you've brought an army with you. What's to keep them from thinking that you intend to seize complete power?"

"I would never do such a thing!"

"*They* don't know that. Our enemies take every opportunity to fuel rumor. We have to be extremely cautious, to think of the repercussions our actions might have. Any peasant, any citizen, who lives near the Porta San Gallo is going to see an army there. They know the French are coming—and here are Orsini soldiers waiting. What will they think?" Giuliano shook his head. "Do you know what Savonarola preached? Last week, after everyone learned that the French had sacked Fivizzano and spilled much innocent blood there?"

I thought immediately of Michelangelo sitting quietly in the great crowd at San Lorenzo, listening and remembering carefully all that was said.

"He told the crowd he had predicted Charles's coming two years ago, when he said that the sword of God would swoop down from the heavens and smite all of Florence's sinners. Smite *us*, in other words, and anyone who doesn't agree with Fra Girolamo. Don't you see that Savonarola is playing to their fears, making them worry that Florence and France will go to war? And that's precisely what they'll think when they see the Orsini camped at the gate. Why won't you consult with me before you do these things?"

Piero bowed his head, then looked toward the fire; his face relaxed and drained of arrogance and outrage. "I've tried to be what Father wanted me to be. But no matter how hard I try, I fail. I did as you said: I tried to negotiate free passage with King Charles—and now Alfonsina is furious with me, won't even speak to me. I have the feeling she's going to stay at Poggio a Caiano forever. I had to lie to Paolo Orsini to get his troops; he doesn't know of my intention to let Charles pass. And the Pope will hate us when he learns of it. What must I do?"

"Control your temper, for one thing," Giuliano said matter-of-factly. "No more obscene gestures. Let's talk tonight about a plan for approaching the Lord Priors tomorrow, and then we'll go together to the Palazzo della Signoria. As for Alfonsina, the Orsini, and the Pope—we will seek their forgiveness later. Florence must come first."

"At least you can keep a cool head," Piero said wistfully, by way of capitulation.

By then a maidservant appeared with wine and goblets, leading a parade of servants with platters of fowl, hare and venison, cheeses and sweetmeats, and every delicacy imaginable. Piero finally sat and ate with us, but he remained troubled, and made no attempt to join our more lighthearted conversation. I ate, too, but like Piero, I was filled with worry, and my gaze remained fastened on Giuliano.

That night, I waited alone in Lorenzo's bedchamber while my husband conferred with his brothers on how to approach the Signoria. I was exhausted beyond words, having lain awake the previous night, but I still could not sleep. Added to my sorrow over my father was the fact that I missed Zalumma terribly, and was half mad trying to figure out what punishment he would inflict on her for conspiring with me. I was worried, too, about what would happen when Giuliano went with his brother to the Signoria; I had already decided to convince him not to go—Florence be damned—or to let me go with him. I was childishly frightened that once I let him go, I might never see him again.

I lay tucked in bed, wide-eyed. The lamp was still lit, as well as the hearth, and the light cast wavering shadows on the walls and the painting of the Battle of San Romano. I stared for a long time at the besieged captain, just as Lorenzo certainly must have for many years.

The fire was warm—the Medici servants did not skimp on wood—and I began to perspire beneath the velvet and fur covers. I rose and went over to open the window.

Outside, the sky was clouded, hiding every star; the cold air smelled of rain. I put out my hand, and when I brought it back, it was damp with drizzle.

"Ecce ego adducam aquas super terram," I whispered, without realizing I was going to do so. *Behold, I bring a flood of waters upon the Earth.*

XLV

*G*iuliano came to me in the hours before dawn. The lamp still burned, and its light revealed the fine lines about his eyes— eyes which might have belonged to a man ten years his senior. I did not speak to him then of politics, or his plans for speaking to the Signoria, or my desire that he not go. Instead, I took him in my arms and made love to him. He deserved and needed no less.

It was the ninth of November. Morning brought with it such gloom that Giuliano and I slept quite late. I woke with the voice of the dying Lorenzo in my mind:

Ask Leonardo . . . The third man . . . I failed you . . . Leonardo, now, he and the girl . . .

And then I experienced a spasm of fear, remembering what had passed with my father; and worse, remembering that Giuliano had promised to accompany his brother to meet with the Signoria that day. After a disoriented instant, I realized I had been roused by the tolling of church bells calling the faithful to Sunday Mass. I had never heard such a loud chorus: I was accustomed to the bells at Santo Spirito, but now, in the midst of the city, I heard the songs of San Marco, San Lorenzo, Santa Maria del Fiore, all of them close by.

Beside me, sprawled on his stomach, with one arm flung above his head, the other tucked by his side, Giuliano slept, deaf to the chimes outside his window.

I slipped quietly from the bed and retrieved my silvery *camicia,* this time folded and placed carefully on a chair. I shivered as I donned it. The fire had subsided into warm ash. Careful not to wake Giuliano, I lifted a fur throw from the bed and wrapped it around me.

I opened the door leading to the antechamber, thinking to go out into the corridor beyond to call for a servant; a rush of warmth greeted me. A healthy blaze crackled in the hearth, and just outside the door, sprawled in a chair, sat a man of about thirty years. He was the tallest man I had ever seen—almost a giant, muscular and thick of bone. A sheathed sword, its hilt gleaming with orange light, hung on his hip. A large leather shield lay propped against the wall beside him.

His massive hands held a compact book, open at its center, and as I opened the door he snapped it shut guiltily. Like most merchant's daughters in Florence, I knew my letters well enough to recognize Dante's *Paradiso.* He put the book beside him on the floor and rose to direct a disarming smile at me. I had to tilt my head back to look up at him.

"Good morning, Madonna Lisa." He spoke in the deepest bass. "I trust you slept well. Shall I call for a servant? Someone to freshen the fire?"

"I just need Laura, please, and a basin of hot water. My husband is still sleeping, so if you could do this as quietly as possible. . . ."

"Of course." He bowed and I watched a moment as he went to the door leading out to the corridor. Outside, two more armed men rose as he instructed them in a low voice.

I went back to the bedchamber to find that Giuliano had already awakened. I greeted him happily, with enthusiastic kisses, as if I had never been frightened witless by the presence of the guards.

.   .   .

We attended Mass in the family chapel with Michelangelo and a few close Medici associates. Afterward we ate a late, leisurely lunch with Piero, Giovanni, and Michelangelo—again, with armed men posted just outside the door. On our way to the family dining hall, Giuliano explained that normally, the brothers took their meals with friends and advisors, but today they preferred privacy. I couldn't help thinking that *safety* was a more appropriate word than *privacy,* since the corridors were filled with guards.

Giovanni was politely distant and seemingly unconcerned about his elder brother's upcoming encounter with the Signoria; if he still nursed plans for annulling Giuliano's marriage, he kept them to himself. Michelangelo directed his gaze at his food, only occasionally lifting it to glance shyly at me or the others. I had not realized before how literal Giuliano had been when he said Lorenzo had raised Michelangelo as his own son. Indeed, the brothers treated him as an equal.

Piero wore a constant frown and kept rubbing his neck as if it ached; he radiated extreme tension. Giuliano was controlled and pleasant, his focus on calming both me and Piero. The conversation was cursory until Giuliano cheerfully said:

"Fortune is with us. Antonio Loreno is *proposto* today." I gathered Loreno was a friend—a good thing, since the *proposto* was the only Lord Prior who could propose a measure for discussion. For a day, he held the keys to the Signoria's bell tower, which summoned all Florence to the piazza.

"Loreno?" Piero glanced up from his plate with faint hope.

Giuliano nodded. "He'll make sure we get in so the Lord Priors can hear you out." He paused. "What do you think is the best time to go? Late afternoon, perhaps? Vespers? At least then they won't have the excuse of being absorbed with business or eating supper."

Piero considered this, then seized upon the notion as if it were his own. "Yes." He gave a firm nod. "We'll go at vespers. I want you with me. And about twenty armed men. And . . . Dovizi."

Giuliano rolled his eyes and sighed in frustration. "Whom do you intend to listen to? Me or him? Have you forgotten everything I told you last night? Everything he's advised has made you look bad in the eyes of the people. I tell you, he is no longer our friend."

"I'm listening to you," Piero answered flatly. "But I want Dovizi there. For appearances' sake."

Giuliano said nothing, but I could tell from his suddenly unreadable expression that he was displeased.

Unprompted, Michelangelo broke the uncomfortable silence with a most inappropriate, timidly uttered announcement. "I am leaving for Venice tomorrow."

None of the brothers had any response to this news.

The day passed too swiftly. Giuliano had business matters to attend to and a meeting with a bank agent—although I suspected the agent informed him more of political matters than financial. Laura brushed out my hair, then coiled it at the nape of my neck and tucked it in one of Madonna Alfonsina's fine gold hairnets. "After all," she said, "you are a married woman, and it would not do to let your hair hang down like a maiden's."

She then led me on a tour of the kitchens and the interior of the house, including the living quarters of Piero's wife, Alfonsina, and their children. Afterward, she showed me the library, with its tall shelves of beautifully carved wood that held countless leather-bound tomes and parchment scrolls.

I chose a copy of Petrarch—his *Canzoniere,* containing more than three hundred sonnets. Most of the other volumes were in Greek (of which I knew nothing) or Latin (in which I possessed uncertain skill). I took the little book back to Lorenzo's bedchamber and—smiling kindly at the Goliath of a guard who attended me—settled in the chair beside the freshly fed fire to read.

I had thought Petrarch a safe choice. He wrote in Tuscan, which would require little of my wavering concentration, and his love poetry would remind me of my reason for joy: Giuliano. Yet as I carefully turned the pages, I found nothing but torment. Poem after poem contained not the beauty of passion, but only the sorrow and torment it caused. Here was poor Petrarch, mourning the death of Laura, the object of his never-requited love:

> *. . . the lightning of her angelic smile, whose ray*
> *To Earth could all of paradise convey*
> *A little dust is now.*
> *And yet I live—and that I live, bewail . . .*

I scoffed at the tears that welled in my eyes and wiped them away, scolding myself; I had never been one to weep at poetry. Yet another sentence left me troubled:

> *But then my spirits are chilled, when at your departure*
> *I see my fatal stars turn their sweet aspect from me.*

My fatal stars. I remembered something I hadn't thought about for a long time: the encounter with the astrologer and my stinging words to my mother, who had only been trying to spare me worry. In my mind, I could hear the astrologer's voice: *In your stars I saw an act of violence, one which is your past and your future.*

I thought of my mother dying at Savonarola's hands and was seized by the abrupt, unreasoning fear that Giuliano—my future—was to be his next victim.

"Stop," I told myself aloud, then looked guiltily toward the door to see if my giant on the other side had heard me. There came no voice, no movement; I gave my head a little shake to clear it, then frowned and continued reading. I was determined to find something happy, something bright—a good omen to counter the ill.

I flipped through the pages again, and found, in Petrarch's fluid Tuscan, the verse

> *Il successor di Karlo che la chioma*
> *Co la corona del suo antiquo adorna*
> *Prese a gia l'arme per fiacchar la corna*
> *A Babilonia, et chi da lei si noma*

The heir of Charlemagne, whose brow
The crown of ancient times adorns
Now wields his sword against the horns
Of Babylon, and those who to her bow.

I shut the book, set it down, and went over to the fire. The heat was fierce; I crossed my arms over my chest, tightly, as if to hold in the fear. They were all connected somehow: Leonardo, the third man, Lorenzo's death, the *piagnoni* . . . and me.

When I looked up, I saw Uccello's *Battle of San Romano*, with its bright banners flying in an imaginary wind. Captain Tolentino still appeared brave and determined, but this time he seemed very alone, soon to be overwhelmed by the enemy.

Giuliano did not return until late afternoon—so close to the hour he was scheduled to leave that I summoned Laura and sent her after him to be sure he came to see me before he left.

He no longer wore his false cheerfulness; his eyes were serious, his brow faintly lined. He brought with him a valet who dressed him in a severe tunic of dark gray, untrimmed.

When the valet was gone, I said lightly, "You look like a *piagnone.*"

He did not smile. "I have to leave soon. Did Laura show you where Giovanni's suite is?"

"Yes."

"Good." He paused; I knew he was choosing his words carefully. "If for any reason Piero and I are detained . . . if we're late, or if anything happens to worry you, go to Giovanni at once. He'll know what to do."

I scowled, using displeasure and disapproval to mask my unease. "What could possibly worry me? Why would I want to go to Giovanni?"

My husband's lips twitched slightly as he made the decision to be candid. "Our things are packed. Giovanni knows where they are, and he knows where to take you. We've agreed on a place where we can meet. So if we're detained . . ."

"I want to go with you. I can't stay here."

He gave a short, soft laugh devoid of humor. My suggestion was outrageous, of course: I was a woman, and women would not be welcome at the Palazzo della Signoria. And I already knew Giuliano well enough to know he would never let me accompany him on such a dangerous outing.

"Lisa." He took my shoulders tenderly. "We've come to an agreement with King Charles; the Signoria may not like it. I was a fool to let Piero continue to listen to Dovizi—everything he's encouraged my brother to do has made our family look bad. I should never have let things get to this stage; I was too busy looking after our banking interests, left too much of the politics in Piero's hands. Piero won't like it, but from this day forth, I'll insist on being more involved. Dovizi will not be sleeping under our roof tonight. Piero will listen only to my counsel from now on."

He paused then, and looked toward the window. I knew he was listening for the bells.

"You have to go now, don't you?"

In reply, he took my face in his hands. "I love you." He gave me a small, sweet kiss. "And I'll be back soon, I promise you. Don't worry."

"All right," I said. Somehow, I managed to speak and behave very calmly. "I'll let you go without me on one condition."

"What?" He tried to sound playful.

The connection between Leonardo's letter and Lorenzo's dying words still gnawed at me, and I feared that my opportunity to learn the truth was fast escaping. "Answer this question. Who is the third man? The penitent?"

His hands dropped to his sides. His lips parted, and he frowned at me, dumbstruck. "After all this time . . . you remember my father saying that?" And then he collected himself. "He was dying. He didn't know what he was saying."

"You're a terrible liar. Who did he mean?"

Giuliano's shoulders slumped slightly in defeat. "He was the one man who escaped," he said, and at that instant the bells began to ring.

We both started, but I persisted. Time was slipping away, and I had a sudden keen desire to know, as if both our fates depended on it. "Escaped what?"

"They caught everyone involved in the conspiracy to kill my uncle. But one man escaped."

"Your father saw him?"

He shook his head, visibly anxious now, his body turning toward the door. "Leonardo," he said. "Leonardo saw him; my uncle died in his arms. Lisa, I have to go. Kiss me again."

I wanted to cry from sheer worry, but instead I kissed him.

"The guards are just outside," he said quickly, "and they will tell you if you need to go to Giovanni. Stay here. Laura will bring you something to eat." He opened the door, then turned his head to look at me one last time. His face was young, painted with fireglow; his eyes were shining and anxious. "I love you."

"I love you," I said.

He closed the door. I went over to the window and opened it, unmindful of the chill. There was finally a break in the clouds, and I caught a glimpse of the low sun, coral orange. I leaned out for a while, listening to the bells; then I watched as finally Piero and Giuliano set out on horseback, accompanied by some thirty men.

"Leonardo," I said, with no one there to hear me. Somehow we were connected to each other and the trouble that was surely coming now.

XLVI

I listened to the cascading harmony of the church bells until the very last note faded into the vibrating air. I felt I ought to go downstairs to the chapel, where Giovanni and Michelangelo were no doubt at vespers; I felt I should pray to my mother's benevolent God to protect my husband. But I was too agitated at that point to converse with God or anyone else. I was too agitated, in fact, to obey Giuliano and sit patiently in the bedchamber.

I was dressed in my wedding gown, since Zalumma had never arrived with my other clothes; because it was chilly, I put on the lovely brocade overdress with its fur lining. Something made me pause and retrieve my two gold medallions from the desk, where Laura had put them when she had undressed me the night before. I slipped them into the inside pocket of the overdress, and stepped out into the antechamber.

My giant rose to his feet. "Is there anything you need, Madonna Lisa?"

"No. I'm just going to the kitchen to get something to eat," I lied cheerily, and graced him with my best smile.

His expression grew troubled. "But Ser Giuliano gave orders—"

My smile broadened. "That I was to stay in my room. I know. But

he said if I got hungry, there was no harm in going to the kitchen. Besides, I'm bored of Petrarch. I wanted to borrow another book from
the library."

"We can fetch you food—whatever you like. And if you tell us the
book—"

"Ah, but I'm not familiar with the library, so I wouldn't know what
book to ask for." My tone grew pleading. "Please. I'll only be a minute."

"Very well," he said, reluctant. "But I must respectfully ask that
you don't dawdle. Ser Giuliano would never forgive me if he returned
and I could not account for your whereabouts." He led the way to the
antechamber door and paused to instruct the two guards there in a
low voice. As I made my way down the corridor, I could hear one of
them following me at a discreet distance.

I went downstairs, passing more armed guards. I had no desire to
go to the kitchen, of course; I only wanted to distract myself. And so I
wandered out into the courtyard.

It was almost as I remembered: There, in the center, was Donatello's sleek, girlish bronze David, and nearby a stone bust of Plato.
But many of the ancient pieces were gone, and, most notably, so was
the terra-cotta sculpture of the elder Giuliano.

I had heard of the famed Medici gardens and knew that they lay
beyond the courtyard. I passed between a pair of columns connected
by an arch of *pietra serena,* crossing through a loggia until the building opened up again.

Here I found the formal garden, a third the size of the vast palazzo.
At the center of a bright green lawn, two flagstone paths, lined by pot-
ted fruit trees, intersected. Between the trees stood thickets of rosebushes, thorny and starkly pruned for the coming winter. Behind the
bushes, at carefully placed intervals, stood life-sized statues on high
pedestals. The one that most caught my eye portrayed the Hebrew, Ju-
dith, her fist clutching the hair of her fallen enemy, Holofernes. Her
other hand bore a large sword, hefted above her head, ready to render
the blow that would finish the gory task of hacking Holofernes' head
from his body.

And stacked neatly upon the flagstone, next to the walls, were piles and piles of weapons and armor: shields, helmets, maces, long swords, daggers, and lances reminiscent of Uccello's masterpiece.

The sight evoked a thrill: All this time, the Medici had been preparing for a war.

I lifted my gaze to a small group of soldiers who stood nearby, conversing idly with one another; they stopped to stare back at me with curious, unfriendly expressions.

Perhaps, I told myself, this was simply Piero's doing—the result of his unease and mistrust, like the Orsini troops who awaited him by the San Gallo city gate. Perhaps Giuliano had never approved this, or thought it necessary.

Nevertheless, I went over to one of the mounds of knives and carefully teased out a sheathed dagger—the smallest one there. The men did not like it; one of them made a move as if to come over and stop me, but the others held him back. I was now, after all, one of the Medici.

I unsheathed the dagger and held it to the fading sunlight. It was pure steel, double-edged, with a razor-sharp tip. My breath was coming hard as I slid it back into the leather, then nestled it into the inside pocket of my overdress.

The guard who had followed me from the house was waiting beneath the archway. I gave him a challenging stare, knowing that he had watched me take the weapon; he said nothing.

I let him follow me to the library. No more Petrarch; I wanted something unemotional, dry and demanding, to force my thoughts away from all unpleasantness. This time I chose a Latin primer. If everything went as planned—if the Signoria and Piero could be reconciled—I wanted to improve my education in the classics, as I would be entertaining many scholars. I wanted never to cause my husband any embarrassment by seeming like an unlettered peasant, and I was already worrying about how to impress my new sister-in-law.

I returned to my room and closed the door, which greatly relieved my guardians. I slipped my overdress off and laid it over the chair, then sat down by the fire. The book was meant as a child's introduction to Latin; I opened the book and read:

Video, vides, videt, videmus, videtis, vident . . .

I see, you see, he sees, and so on. Had I been calm, I would have flown through the pages, but my thoughts were so scattered that I stared at the words stupidly. In order to concentrate at all, I read them aloud.

I droned on for only a few minutes when I was interrupted by a sound outside my window—the low, melancholy tolling of a bell, the one popularly known as the "cow" because it struck the same pitch as cattle lowing.

It was the bell that summoned all Florentine citizens to the Piazza della Signoria.

XLVII

I dropped the book, ran to the window, and flung open the
shutters. It was still light outside and I peered down the street,
straining toward the Piazza della Signoria. The clanging increased in tempo; I watched as servants wandered out of the grand
palazzi down the street to stare, as pedestrians below stopped and
turned their faces in the direction of the piazza, transfixed. Beneath
me, a small army of men hurried out of the main and side entrances of
our building, shields held at chest level, unsheathed swords clenched
in their fists.

I clung fiercely to reason. The citizens had been summoned; I could
not assume it was to cheer Piero's downfall. It might well be to cheer
his triumph.

I leaned out of my window for an eternity—like my neighbors,
awaiting a sign. Painful moments passed before it came: softly, from
the east and south, a distant, unintelligible rumble at first. Then a
single voice, high and clear, rode upon the wind.

Popolo e libertà! Popolo e libertà!

I thought at once of Messer Iacopo astride his horse in the great piazza, trying in vain to rally the people to his cause. Only now it was

my husband and his brother in that same piazza—and their efforts had been just as vain.

I thought of Messer Iacopo's corpse, bloated and blue-white, exhumed from its grave and dragged through the city streets.

Beyond my window, servants ran back into palazzi, slamming doors; pedestrians scattered, running toward the sound or fleeing it.

I pushed myself away and quickly donned my overdress. I had brought nothing else with me, and so had nothing else to take—but instinct stopped me at the door. I pulled open the drawer to the desk, found Leonardo's folded letter, and cast it upon the fire.

Go to Giovanni, my husband had said.

I rushed out into the antechamber to find the guards had gone. I ran into the corridor and there saw Michelangelo running toward me. His shyness was gone, replaced by urgency; this time, he met my gaze directly. We stopped just short of colliding; his breath came ragged, like mine.

"Where is Giuliano? Has he returned?" I asked.

He spoke at the same instant I did. "Madonna, you must flee! Go quickly to Giovanni!"

"Giuliano—"

"I have not seen him. I don't think he has returned. But I know he would want you to go with his brother."

He took my elbow and steered me down the stairs, across the courtyard, up another flight of stairs. He pushed me faster than I could run; twice, I stumbled over my skirts.

When we reached our destination, Michelangelo flung open the door. Giovanni, his movements deliberate and calm, was instructing a pair of servants on where his packed trunks should be taken. Only when he glanced up did I see the nervousness in his eyes, but his voice was steady.

"What is it?" He seemed irritated, almost hostile, at the interruption.

"You must take care of Madonna Lisa," Michelangelo answered brusquely, with clear dislike. "You promised your brother. My destination will not be a safe one for her."

"Oh. Yes." With a flick of his fingers, Giovanni dismissed the servants, red-faced beneath the weight of their burdens. "Of course."

Michelangelo turned to me. "I pray God we meet again, under better circumstances." Then he was gone, his rapid steps ringing in the corridor.

Giovanni's scarlet robe and red velvet cap were immaculate; he was freshly shaven and groomed, as though he had prepared himself for a high-ranking visitor. He was too distracted, perhaps too frightened, to dissemble. He stared at me without kindness. I was a nuisance, a mistake.

"Go and ready yourself for travel," he said. "I will send Laura to help you."

I did not believe him for an instant. I motioned to my clothing. "I have nothing to take. This is all I brought with me." Which was true, except for the mousy brown dress my father had insisted I wear; I was all too glad to leave that behind.

"Then go to your quarters." The Cardinal studied me, then said, "Look, this is nothing more than a few Lord Priors trying to incite a riot. With luck, my brothers"—he hesitated just before he said the last two words; I knew he had almost said *Giuliano*—"will be able to calm everyone down. In the meantime, I'm riding out to help them." He let go a sigh, as if resigned to showing mercy. "Don't worry; I won't leave you here."

"Thank you," I said.

"Go. I'll call for Laura to sit with you."

I crossed the palazzo and returned to Lorenzo's bedchamber. I could not resist staring out the open window, which had filled the room with cold air, despite the fire. Outside, dusk had fallen; in its failing light, torches flickered in the distance. They came from the west, the direction of San Marco, down the Via Larga. Those holding them aloft cried out, again and again:

Palle! Palle! Palle!

I stared at the shadowy forms materializing from the gloom. Most were on horseback, a few on foot; these were the wealthy, with their servants, probably friends and family from the palazzi lining the Via Larga, a Medici enclave. The light they bore glanced off fine unsheathed swords, off necklaces of gold, off gems. They took their places alongside the men guarding the front of the Medici palace.

Palle! Palle!

Converging from the opposite direction, from the Piazza della Signoria, the cry *Popolo e libertà!* began to take physical form: Dark figures approached, ill-lit by flaming rags lashed to long sticks or the handles of brooms.

Abaso le palle! Down with the balls!

The sharp tines of pitchforks, the points of dented, crooked lances, the smoothed tips of wooden clubs, reared against a deepening sky.

Just before the two forces met, a new contingent emerged from the ranks of Medici supporters. From my distant perch, I could not make out faces—not even that of the rider on horseback who held a lamp illuminating his features. But I recognized the scarlet of his cape, the broadness of his shoulders, his dignified carriage: Giovanni rode out slowly, surrounded by a swarm of armed soldiers.

"*Palle!*" he cried at the approaching threat, in a beautiful, thunderous voice. "Good citizens of Florence, hear me out!"

But the good citizens of Florence would not listen. A stone flew through the air, striking the shoulder of Giovanni's black mount, causing it to rear. Giovanni managed to calm it, but a decision was made: Rather than tackle their opponents head-on, the Cardinal and his group elected to gallop north, down an alleyway.

I could only pray he still intended to head for the piazza.

As Giovanni and his men receded from my view, the angry citizens advanced. Their number seemed infinite, stretching into the dim light as far as I could see. Bodies on foot were joined by wealthier Medici enemies on horseback, bearing maces, sturdy lances, swords, Turkish scimitars.

Realizing they were overwhelmed, many Medici supporters rode off, abandoning the palazzo guards to do battle alone.

I saw ghastly silhouettes, heard ghastly sounds:

A peasant was speared through his stomach and lifted off his feet by a soldier's lance; a merchant dropped to his knees as a mace shattered his skull. A fallen guard screamed hoarsely as a farmer skewered him with a pitchfork. Another rioter stooped down to seize his dropped torch and set the body ablaze.

Uccello's painting could never capture the smells, the noise, the swiftness and confusion. He had shown war as pageantry; I witnessed it as madness.

Beneath me—echoing through the house—came furious banging, the sound of metal and flesh hammering wood. Some of the rioters had made it to the door.

Laura had not come; I knew then that she never would. I made the decision to leave, but as I began to turn from the window, frantic motion in the nearest alleyway captured my attention.

The fast-moving riders held torches and lamps to light their way in the gathering dark. On their heels followed a furious, roaring crowd. I was seized by the hope that this was Giuliano. I leaned farther out the window. As the group neared the battle in front of the palazzo, I recognized Giovanni. Not until he was almost directly beneath me could I make out his desperate cries.

"Renounce . . . Piero . . . *Popolo e libertà!*"

And the angry citizens who had chased him thus far, the citizens who pelted him and his guards with stones, shouted quite rightfully: *Traitor! Traitor!*

I ran from the window. I lifted my skirts high and ran down the stairs, through the corridors, into the courtyard, through the loggia, and out into the garden. There were no weapons to be found there now—only Giovanni, exhausted, gasping, striding in the direction of the palazzo with two soldiers in tow.

"Did you see him?" I called. The noise outside the walls was dreadful.

Giovanni was all business; the earlier kindness I had seen in him had vanished, replaced by a cold determination. He passed me without a glance, without slowing, and when I ran after him, he offered up curtly: "I couldn't get to the piazza."

"You didn't see him, then? See Giuliano?"

"Piero is here." He gestured behind us.

I rushed to the wooden fence and opened a latched gate; I stepped through and found myself in the large unpaved area just outside the stables. It smelled of dung and hay and hot, lathered horses. Perhaps thirty or forty mounts, reined in by their riders, stamped nervously in place; men called to each other, discussing strategies for venturing out again while incurring the fewest casualties. I scanned their faces, but did not see the one I wanted.

"Giuliano!" I demanded. "Where is Giuliano?"

Most of the men, caught up in the turmoil of war, ignored me; a few eyed me curiously, but did not reply.

A firm hand clamped itself on my shoulder. I whirled about to see Piero, sweating and grim-faced, his eyes a bit wild.

"Where is Giuliano?" I repeated.

"It didn't go well," he said, numb of failure. "Damn Loreno—he betrayed us; he wouldn't let me enter through the main gate. I couldn't accept such an insult: 'Enter alone, through the side, and put down your arms.' What am I, a servant? I lost my temper, told them all to go to Hell, and Loreno, that son of a whore, surrendered the key to the bell tower to my enemies—"

I seized his arms. *"Where is Giuliano!"*

He recoiled from me. "Giuliano is still at the piazza, trying to quiet the crowd." At the fury on my face, he added in a rush, "It was his idea; I didn't want to leave him. He knows if things get bad to meet me at the San Gallo gate. . . ."

I turned away, disgusted. As I walked toward the stable, I began to form a plan.

"Leave with us!" Piero called after me. "They're fetching my things now. . . . Are you packed?"

I ignored him. There was a long line of stalls, as far as I could see, and almost every one of them empty. An elderly man was arguing with a pair of soldiers; I shouted louder than any of them. "A horse! I need a horse, at once!"

"Here now," said the older man, who was no doubt master of the stables. His tone started out imperious; I think in the excitement he mistook me for one of the chambermaids, but a second glance at my dress changed his demeanor. "Forgive me, Madonna—you are Giuliano's new wife, yes?" He had no doubt arranged the carriage that brought me to this palazzo. "You have need of a mount? Does Ser Piero know of this? I thought he had judged a carriage more defensible, and able to carry your belongings—"

"He has changed his mind," I said. "I have no belongings. He said I must have a horse *now.*" My stare challenged him.

A group of six armed men entered. "Are the wagons filled?" one of them asked the stablemaster. "Ser Piero wants plenty of hay and water for the long ride."

The old man lifted a hand at them, then turned to me. "See here, Madonna, I have only so many horses . . ." He turned to the soldiers. "And only so much hay and water . . ."

Furious and shaking, I turned my back to him and walked away, brushing past the soldiers without seeing them. I walked past stall after stall as the stablemaster argued with the men. Stall after empty stall.

But one—at the far end—contained a mare, perhaps the mount the stablemaster was saving for his own escape. She was already saddled, with the bit in her mouth, and when I moved toward her, she snorted. Her coat was gray, save for a spot of black on her muzzle. As I opened the gate and stepped inside the stall, she took a step back, bowing her head and regarding me with eyes that were worried and dark, with the whites showing.

"Here now," I said, unintentionally echoing the stablemaster. "If anyone is frightened, it's I." I set a tentative hand upon her soft, twitching muzzle; her quick breath was warm on my skin.

"Can I mount you?" I asked. The prospect made me nervous. I was used to traveling in carriages; my father believed women were poorly suited to ride. In my case, perhaps, he was right. It was a difficult business. We were both anxious, and I too short; I had to stand on an overturned bucket before I could swing awkwardly up into the saddle. My long skirt, with its train, made the venture even more difficult. Once up, I tucked my gown round my legs as best I could, and let the overdress furl out around me.

The mare was used to a firmer hand than mine, but I gave her her head, knowing she would take the shortest way out of the stables; luckily, her preferred route did not lead us past the stablemaster.

Once we were out in the yard, I continued to let her lead, since she knew the way out to the Via Larga.

Armed guards milled about in front of the bolted gate topped with deadly sharp spikes and lined with iron bars thick as my arm. Through the bars, I could see the black shapes of soldiers standing in the flickering play of firelight and shadow. The men moved little; not yet engaged in battle, they were the rear guards, the last line of protection against the mob.

On my side, one soldier stood directly next to the bolt.

I rode up to him and leaned down. "You there. Open the gate."

He looked up at me; even the dim light could not hide the fact that he thought me mad. "Madonna, they'll tear you to pieces."

"Everyone's confused out there. No one will notice where I've come from; no one knows who I am. I'm not armed; who will attack me?"

He shook his head. "It isn't safe for a lady."

I felt around in the pocket of my overdress—pushing the heavy sheathed dagger aside—and pulled out one of the medallions without looking to see which it was. It caught just enough torchlight to shine. "Here. It's worth more than a florin. Perhaps a lot more."

He took it, frowned at it, then realized what it was. He glanced guiltily about him, then without another word, quietly slid the bolt and pushed the gate open—only a crack, since the press of bodies outside kept it from swinging very far. The mare and I sidled out, barely squeezing through; the rough iron skinned my bared shins and snagged the fine threads of my gown and overdress.

The instant I cleared it, the gate clanged shut behind me; the bolt slid locked with grim finality.

I found myself amid a group of perhaps forty men guarding the gate. They stood shoulder to shoulder; as the mare picked her way past them, their sweat-soaked bodies pressed against me.

"Mother of God!" one swore.

Another cried, "Where in Hell's name did she come from?"

Their unsheathed swords caught on my train, shredded my skirts, nicked my skin—and the mare's flank, too, for she whinnied in complaint. But I guided her firmly, relentlessly, toward the front line.

There, men fought in the light of torches hung from the palazzo walls. The guards cast looming shadows on the rebellious citizens; the black outlines of their upraised swords extended far beyond reality, appearing to pierce men standing a good distance away.

I urged my reluctant mount beyond safety, into the fray. The air was cold but foul, redolent of smoke and burning rancid fat. The cacophony was maddening: The Signoria's cow still tolled, horses screamed, and men cursed, while others shouted Messer Iacopo's rallying cry.

But I could hear no countering *Palle! Palle!*

Bodies danced about so quickly, in such uncertain light, that it was difficult to judge friend from foe. There were no colored banners here, no neatly arrayed forces with clearly marked enemies and orderly rows of lances; there was certainly no hero leading the charge. A sword swiped the air just behind me, barely missing my exposed leg; I felt the rush of air stirred by the blade.

My mount and I surged forward; our place was quickly filled by a peasant.

I could not see the soldier behind me dealing the blows, but I saw their result. The blade came down and bit into the man's flesh between his neck and shoulder with a thud. The peasant screamed, so shrill and wild it was horrible to hear. Blood spilled from the wound and spread, dark and swift, down the front of his robe until it merged with the shadows. He fell to his knees shrieking, the sword still buried in him; the unseen soldier struggled mightily to free it. At last it came out with a sucking sound, then came down again, this time on the peasant's head, with such force that—for the blink of an eye—a spray of blood, a fatal red halo, hung suspended in a beam of light.

The man fell forward, grazing my mare's hooves.

I turned my head to glance behind me and met the gaze of the murderer: a Medici soldier, barely Giuliano's age, his eyes filled with an odd, unfocused terror. He did not notice that I was a finely dressed woman, without a weapon, or that I had come from the direction of the palazzo. He seemed only to know that he should heft his sword again and bring it down. And I was now in his path.

I ducked my head and goaded the mare into a gallop. We tore through the crowd; my knees and elbows banged against flesh and bone, metal and wood.

Soon I broke free and made my way east down the Via Larga, passing the loggia and the palazzo's front entrance, where only a few years before Lorenzo had escorted me over the threshold. Medici guards still fought in small scattered groups, but the great entry doors had been abandoned, and a group of rioters were attempting to batter their way in with a heavy wooden beam. I rode through the alleyway Giovanni had taken to elude the crowd. From there, I made my way past the church of San Lorenzo down to the Baptistery of San Giovanni and the Piazza del Duomo. Small groups roamed the streets—a group of three riders, a pair of monks, a poor father and mother, running with squalling children in their arms.

Only when I reached the Duomo did the growing crowds force me to slow. Abruptly, I was completely encircled by men, two of them holding flaming branches. They lifted them higher to get a better look at me.

They were *giovani,* street ruffians.

"Pretty lady," one called snidely. "Pretty lady, to be out riding with her skirts pulled up to her waist! Look, such delicate ankles!"

I scowled at them, impatient, and glanced about me. There were many people within earshot, true, but the tolling of the Signoria's bell was much louder here, and everyone was shouting and running toward the piazza. There was no guarantee they would notice the cries of a solitary woman.

I did not want to cry out—not yet.

"Let me pass," I snarled, and drew the dagger from my overdress; it came out fully sheathed.

The *giovani* laughed scornfully; they sounded like barking dogs.

"Look here!" one cried. "Why, Lisa di Antonio Gherardini has teeth!"

He was sharp chinned and scrawny, with wispy blond curls that thinned to bare flesh at his crown.

"Raffaele!" I lowered the dagger, relieved. It was the butcher's son. "Raffaele, thank God, I need to pass—"

"I need to pass," Raffaele echoed, in a mocking singsong. One of his mates giggled. "Look on her, boys. She's one of *them*. Married Giuliano de' Medici not two days ago."

"A merchant's daughter?" someone asked. "You lie!"

"God's own truth," Raffaele said firmly. His words, and the look in his eye, made me draw the dagger from its sheath. "What happened, Monna Lisa? Has your Giuli already forsaken you?"

I clenched the dagger. "I *will* pass. . . ."

Raffaele smiled wickedly. "Let's see you try."

Something whizzed past me in the darkness; my mare shrieked and reared. I held on desperately, but a second pebble stung my wrist like fire. I let go a wordless cry and dropped my weapon.

I felt another pebble, then another. The world heaved. I lost my reins, my sense of orientation, and went tumbling—against horseflesh, against cold air, against hard flagstone.

I lay on my side, sickened from pain, terrified because I could not draw a breath. Firelight flared overhead; I squinted as it spun slowly, along with the rest of my surroundings. Soon it was eclipsed by Raffaele's face, half obliterated by shadow, half leering.

"Aren't we the sheltered princess?" he said bitterly. "You don't know how to stay on a horse or hold a weapon. Here." The dagger appeared before my eyes. "Here is how to grip a knife." A pause; the blade turned so that the tip, not the flat, pointed at me. "And here is how to use it. . . ."

Air. I was frightened less by the dagger and more by my inability to breathe; my ribs, my chest, would not move. The world darkened a bit more, grew indistinct.

I heard a different voice, plaintive: "Can't we have some fun with her first?"

Another: "Out here, in public?"

"No one cares! Look, they aren't even watching!"

Raffaele now, disgusted: "And her, freshly done by a Medici?"

The dagger, a blur of silver, moved until I felt the tip rest against my throat; if I swallowed, it would cut me. I could see Raffaele's hand and the black leather hilt.

Then hand and dagger disappeared as light faded to darkness.

XLVIII

ave I died? I wondered. But no—my pain had resolved into a fierce headache and agony in my shoulder.

All at once, my chest gave a lurching heave, and I sucked in air as frantically as a drowning man.

Thus preoccupied, I noticed little more than blurry shadows, caught only an occasional intelligible word above the clatter of horses' hooves, the tolling of the bell, and the noise of the crowd.

Above me, men on horseback bore torches—in my disorientation, there seemed to be hundreds of them, elongated black giants bearing flames that sparkled like huge orange diamonds.

One of the riders spoke; his voice bore the dignity of high office. "What are you doing with that lady?"

Beside me, Raffaele replied timidly: "She is the enemy of the people . . . the bride of Giuliano . . . a spy."

The mounted man made a brief reply. I caught only ". . . della Signoria . . . protect . . ."

I was lifted. The stabbing pain from my injuries made me cry out.

"Hush, Madonna. We don't mean to harm you."

I was slung over a horse, my stomach pressed against the leather; my head and legs dangled against the horse's flanks. A man nestled into the saddle behind me, pushing against my waist and hip; the reins brushed against my back.

We rode. The weight of my hair caused it to work its way free of Alfonsina's golden net, which fell, a treasure for some lucky soul to find. My face bounced against hot lathered horseflesh until my lip cracked; I tasted salt and blood. I saw only dark stone, heard the bell and the shouting. Both grew louder—the bell at last so loud and insistent, my skull throbbed with each peal; we were in the Piazza della Signoria. I tried to straighten, to lift my head, thinking, in my confusion, to call out Giuliano's name. But the rider pushed me firmly down.

As I crossed the piazza, excitement traveled swift as a lightning bolt through the crowd. Their shouts were high-pitched, wild.

"Look—there he goes, the bastard!"

"Up there! The third window! See him swing!"

"*Abaso le palle!* Death to the Medici!"

I thrashed like a fish on the hook, my hair spilling forward, covering my eyes; I clawed at it, trying to see from my upside-down vantage, but it was no use. I could make out only shadowy figures, pressed close together.

I panicked as I thought of Francesco de' Pazzi, hanging naked from a high window with the teeth of Archbishop Salviati's corpse buried in his shoulder. I thought of my father saying, *Eighty men in five days . . . heaved out the windows of the Palazzo della Signoria.*

I hung limp. "Giuliano," I whispered, knowing that, in such an uproar, no one would ever hear me. "Giuliano," I repeated, and began to weep.

They put me in a cell in the Bargello, the prison adjoining the palazzo. Mine was a small, dirty room, windowless, with stained floors and three walls, the corners silvery with spiderwebs. The fourth wall consisted of stone up to my waist, then thick, rough iron bars that ran up to the ceiling; the door was made of iron. Some straw had been scattered on the floor and in the center of the room rested a large wooden bucket that served as a communal privy. The room itself admitted no light, but depended on the sconced torch in the corridor outside.

There were three of us there: me, Laura, and a lady thrice my age, stunningly dressed in aubergine silks and velvets. I believe she was one of the Tornabuoni—the noble family to which Lorenzo's mother had belonged.

When the guard brought me in—groaning with pain—I pretended not to recognize Laura. Even for hours after the man had left, we did not look at each other.

We were ignored the first night. The gendarme who brought me in disappeared. After a time, the bell—deafeningly close, in the campanile next door—finally ceased ringing. I was grateful for only a short time. Afterward, hour upon hour, we heard the crowd outside suddenly hush . . . and then, after a brief silence, cheer raucously.

I imagined I could hear the song of the rope as it snapped taut.

The Tornabuoni woman, white and delicate as a pearl, twisted a kerchief in her hands and wept continuously. Ignoring the spiders, I lay propped in a corner, my bruised legs spread out in front of me, covered by my tattered skirts. Laura sat beside me, chest pressed to her knees, one arm coiled about them. When the crowd had briefly fallen silent, I asked, in a low voice, "Giuliano . . . ?"

Her answer was anguished. "I don't know, Madonna; I don't know . . ."

Another shout went up, and we both cringed.

In the morning they took Laura, and never brought her back.

I told myself they never executed women in enlightened Florence unless they were the vilest murderers . . . or traitors. Surely they had let Laura go, or at worst banished her.

I drew comfort from the fact that the crowds no longer roared outside. The quiet had to mean that the killing had stopped.

Rising unsteadily to my feet, I sucked in my breath at the pain in my stiff shoulder. The slightest movement stabbed. My limbs were numb from cold; the stone walls and floor were like ice. But I was far more distraught by the fact that I had lost my wedding ring and the remaining gold medallion.

I passed the Tornabuoni woman to stand at the rusting iron door. She had ceased crying and now stood swaying on her feet, having been upright most of the night; her eyes were two bruises in the whiteness of her face, stark against her deep purple gown. I glanced at her and in return got a look full of hopelessness and rage; I turned quickly away.

I listened for the guard. While Laura had been with me, I had not wanted to utter Giuliano's name lest I incriminate her, but now it was on the tip of my tongue. When the jailer finally appeared, I called out softly.

"What news? What news of Giuliano de' Medici?"

He did not answer at once, but came and stood in front of the door. He fingered through the jangling keys, muttering to himself, until he decided on one, then tried it. It didn't work, and so he fished out a similar one, dark and dull from disuse; it clanged and grated in the lock, but at last the door swung open with a lingering screech.

"Giuliano de' Medici." He sneered. "If you have any news of that scoundrel, best sing out when your time comes."

He took no notice at all. "Madonna Carlotta," he said, not unkindly. "Will you accompany me? It's a simple matter. The Lord Priors want to ask you a few questions. They mean you no harm."

Her gaze, her tone, was pure viciousness. "No harm . . . they have already caused me the greatest possible harm!"

"I can summon other men to help me," he offered simply.

They stared at each other a moment; then the old woman walked out and stood beside him. The door was slammed behind them and locked.

I did not care. I did not care. *If you have any news of that scoundrel, best sing out. . . .*

I hugged myself, not even feeling my injured shoulder. Such things were said only of the living. Giuliano was gone, and they did not know where.

. . .

I returned to my corner and settled into it as comfortably as I could, propping myself so that the cold wall numbed the pain in my shoulder. I heard church bells, but I dozed a bit and could not remember how many chimes had sounded.

When I woke, I made a decision: I would admit to having married Giuliano. Such a crime would not necessarily mean my death—even Lorenzo, in his vengefulness, had spared the Pazzi women—but more likely my exile, which would free me to find my husband.

I thought of how I should phrase my confession to the priors. I would speak eloquently of Giuliano's concern for Florence; I would point out how he had married me, a merchant's daughter—proof of his sense of commonality with less wealthy citizens.

Finally I heard the jailer's step, and the jangle of keys, and forced myself awkwardly to my feet. Despite my sense of determination and my fine plan, my hands shook, and my tongue adhered to the dry inside of my cheek.

Beside the nearing jailer walked Zalumma, her eyes wild and wide. When her gaze found me, her mouth opened with a gasp of relief, of joy—of horror. I suppose I looked a sight.

The jailer led her up to the bars of my cell, then took a step back. I reached for her, but the space between the bars was wide enough to admit only my fingers.

"No touching!" the jailer growled.

I dropped my hand. The sight of her made me let go a sob so loud and wrenching it startled even me. Once I began, I felt I could not stop.

"Ah, no." She reached tenderly toward me; the jailer's scowl made her pull away. "No, no. This can't help matters. . . ." Even as she said it, tears slid down one side of her perfect, straight nose.

I struggled to compose myself. "I'm all right. They'll just want to ask a few questions. And since I know nothing, it'll go quickly."

She glanced away, her eyes unreadable, then looked back at me. "You must be brave."

I stiffened.

"He's in the jail here, with the men. They set fire to the house last night, but the servants managed to put it out, finally—a lot was saved. But . . ." She ducked her head; I saw her swallow tears.

"My God! Giuliano—only tell me—is he unhurt? Tell me he is unhurt!"

She looked up at me, her expression odd. "I know nothing of Giuliano. The gonfaloniere came last night and arrested your father."

XLIX

N o." I took a step backward.

"The gonfaloniere and his men searched the palazzo. Tore the rooms apart. They found your letters from Giuliano—"

"No."

"—and with the fact that Lorenzo was your father's best customer for so many years—they have charged him with being a spy for the Medici." She dropped her gaze. Her voice shook. "They have tortured him."

In my selfishness, I had thought only of myself and Giuliano. I had known my marriage would break my father's heart, but I had deemed it worth the price. Now my stubbornness had cost him far more.

"Oh God," I groaned. "Tell them—tell them to question *me*. Tell them he knows nothing of the Medici, and I know everything. The crowd—" I struggled to my feet, suddenly inspired, and lurched at the bars in an effort to catch the jailer's jaded gaze. "The crowd in the Via Larga, on Saturday after I was married! They saw my father shout at me, in the middle of the street. I called to him from the Palazzo Medici, from the window. He begged me to come home; he disapproved of my marriage, of the Medici— Ask Giovanni Pico! My father is loyal to Savonarola. Ask—ask the servant, Laura! She can tell them!"

"I will tell them," Zalumma promised, but her tone was sorrowful; the jailer had moved between us and nodded for her to leave. "I will tell them!" she called, as she made her way down the corridor.

I spent the next few hours alone in my cell, without even the jailer's presence to distract me from the fact that I was the most monstrous of daughters. How could I have behaved differently? How could I have protected my father? I waited, miserable, straining for the sound of footfall, of men's voices, of the metallic ring of keys.

At last they came, and I rushed to the door of my cell and worried the iron bars with my fingers.

The jailer accompanied a man dressed in rich, somber blue to mark his importance; a Lord Prior or perhaps a *Buonomo,* one of twelve elected to advise the Signoria. He was tall and thin, very serious in his manner, perhaps forty; his hair showed quite a bit of gray, but his brows were thick, very black, and drawn tightly together. His nose was long and narrow, and his chin sharp.

As I stared at him, he soberly regarded me. I realized I had seen him before, in church, when Savonarola was preaching; when my mother's fit had knocked me to the floor, he had lifted me to my feet, and cleared the way for us.

"Madonna Lisa?" he inquired politely. "Di Antonio Gherardini?"

I nodded, cautious.

"I am Francesco del Giocondo." He gave a small bow. "We have not been introduced, but perhaps you will remember me."

I had heard the name. He and his family were silk merchants and, like my father, quite wealthy. "I remember you," I said. "You were there in San Lorenzo when my mother died."

"I was very sorry to hear of that," he said, as if we were making conversation at a dinner party.

"Why have you come?"

His eyes were pale blue—the color of ice reflecting sky—each with a dark circle at the outer edge, and they narrowed slightly as they focused on me. The neck of his tunic was edged in white ermine, which brought out the sallowness of his complexion. "To speak to you about Ser Antonio," he said.

"He is innocent of all charges," I said swiftly. "He did not know I was planning to go to Giuliano; he only delivered wool to the Medici; everyone knows how devoted he is to Fra Girolamo's teachings. . . . Have you seen their servant, Laura?"

He raised a hand for silence. "Madonna Lisa. You need not convince me. I am quite certain of Ser Antonio's innocence."

I sagged against the bars. "Then has he been freed?"

"Not yet." He let go a contrived sigh. "His situation is quite serious: Certain Lord Priors believe he is overly connected to the Medici. A sort of madness has seized everyone, unfortunately even those highest in our government. Last night, the priors—quite against my advice—hung Ser Lorenzo's accountant out a window of this very building. It seems that the gentleman had assisted Lorenzo in swindling the city out of the major portion of its dowry fund. And I understand you have discovered for yourself how the people are determined to destroy anything, anyone, that reminds them of the name Medici. The gonfaloniere's men are doing their best to control them, but . . ." He gave another sigh. "Many palazzi were vandalized, even set afire. All along the Via Larga, and other places, as well."

"My father is close to Giovanni Pico," I said, angry that my voice shook. "He can verify that my father is no friend of the Medici."

"Pico?" he murmured. His gaze flickered before returning to me. "He was an associate of Lorenzo's, was he not? Alas, he suffers desperately from a wasting ailment. Too sick, I am told, to leave his bed, even to speak; he is not expected to survive much longer."

"Laura, then, the servant who shared my cell. She saw—"

"You cannot ask the Lord Priors to take the word of a Medici servant."

"What must I do? What *can* I do? My father is entirely innocent."

"I have some influence," he said, with maddening calm. "Over

Corsini and Cerpellone, those who are most hostile to Piero. I could speak to them on your father's behalf."

"Will you?" I grasped the bars, eager, even as a distant, quiet thought puzzled me: *Why has he not done so already?*

He cleared his throat delicately. "That depends entirely on you."

I let go of the iron bars and took a step back. I stared at him until the long silence obliged him to speak.

He was a cold man. Only a cold man could have said what he did without blushing.

"I am a widower," he said. "I have been too long without a wife. I have been waiting for God to direct me to the right woman, one of fine character, from a good family. A young, strong woman who can bear me sons."

Aghast, I stared at him. He gave no sign of discomfort.

"I have watched you for some time. All those times you went to listen to Fra Girolamo. You are very beautiful, you know. Sometimes you would glance over your shoulder at the crowd, and I thought you might be looking in my direction, at me, because you knew I was there. Because you had noticed me.

"I know you are a woman capable of great passion, Madonna. I have your letters to your prospective husband. No one connected to the Signoria has any knowledge of them, yet. And I saw to it that the young lady who shared the cell with you will remain silent. No one need know that *you* had anything to do with the Medici. I can destroy the letters; I can protect you and your father from any reprisals."

He paused, apparently waiting for a sign from me to continue, but I was struck dumb. He showed the first signs of genuine emotion then: His cheeks colored slightly as he stared down at his slippers. His feet moved nervously, scuffing softly against the stone.

Then he regained his absolute composure and looked levelly at me. "I want to marry you. I have feelings for you, and I had hoped—"

"I can't," I interrupted; surely he understood why.

His expression hardened. "It would be a terrible thing for your father to undergo any more suffering. A terrible thing, if he were to die."

Had the bars not separated us, I would have leapt on him like a man, put my hands upon his throat. "I would do anything to save my father! But I cannot marry you. I am already married, to Giuliano de' Medici."

He gave a soft, indignant snort; his eyes were pitiless. "Giuliano de' Medici," he said, his tone absurdly flat, "is dead. Thrown off his horse while crossing the Ponte Santa Trinità, and drowned in the Arno."

L

e must have been searching for me. He must have broken free of the hostile crowd in the Piazza della Signoria and made his way back to the Palazzo Medici. Perhaps Piero had already left, perhaps not—but Giuliano must have somehow gotten the notion that I had returned to my father's house.

Ser Francesco said that a patrolling guard had fished his body from the river. It had been taken immediately to the Lord Priors, who identified it and buried it outside the city walls before anyone had a chance to desecrate the corpse. The grave's location was secret. Even the Lord Priors did not discuss it among themselves, lest a search for the remains provoke fresh riots.

I cannot tell you what I did then. I cannot tell you because I cannot remember. They say that God, in His wisdom, causes mothers to forget the pain of childbirth so that they will not fear bearing more young. Perhaps that is what He did for me, so that I would not fear loving again.

The one thing I do remember of that night is greeting my father. It was dusk, and a haze of smoke further darkened the sky. The Piazza della

Signoria was empty save for a solitary coach and soldiers hired by the Signoria, patrolling on foot and horseback.

Someone had splattered dark paint across the morbid portraits of the conspirators Francesco de' Pazzi, Salviati, and Baroncelli. As their marred, life-sized images looked on, I clutched Ser Francesco's forearm and staggered down the steps of the palazzo into a horrific new world.

At the end of those steps, the coach—ordered by Ser Francesco and occupied by my father—yawned open. As Ser Francesco steadied me on the step—his hand on my elbow, his gaze suddenly as timid as a youth's at the outset of courtship—he said, "There is food and drink waiting for you. I have seen to it."

I stared at him, still too numbed to react. I had not eaten in a day, but the notion of doing so now was offensive. I turned away and climbed into the coach.

My father sat, one shoulder pressed hard against the inner wall, his body slumped diagonally; he gingerly held one hand out to his side. The skin over his cheekbone was tight, violet, so puffed up that I could not see his eye. And his hand . . .

They had used the screws on him. His right thumb, protruding from the hand at a full right angle, had swelled to the size of a sausage; the nail was gone, and in its place was an open red-black sore. The same had been done to the forefinger, which was also grotesquely bloated and extended straight ahead, perpendicular to the thumb.

When I saw him, I began to cry.

"Daughter," he whispered. "Thank God. My darling, my child." I sat beside him and wrapped my arms about him, careful not to brush against the injured hand. "I am sorry." His voice broke. "Forgive me. Oh, I am sorry . . ."

When he uttered those words, all of my resistance toward him, all of my anger, melted.

"I am sorry, I am sorry . . ."

I understood. He did not just regret our current situation or the promise I had been forced to make Ser Francesco in order to win his freedom. He was sorry for everything: for striking my mother, for taking her to San Lorenzo, sorry that Fra Domenico had murdered her, sorry that he had not taken up her cause. He was sorry for my sorrowful wedding day, and for the fear I had felt for him the previous night, and for the pity I was feeling for him now.

Most of all, he was sorry about Giuliano.

The next morning, when I woke safe in my own bed, I found Zalumma standing over me. She wore a look of such guardedness and complicity that I repressed the urge to speak, even before she lifted a finger to her lips.

The sunlight streamed through the windows behind her, causing a glare that made it difficult to see what she held in her hand.

I frowned and pushed myself up to a sitting position—grimacing at the soreness of my body. She thrust the folded papers at me. "I came upstairs," she whispered, so softly I had to strain to hear her over the soft rustling as I unfolded my gifts. "As soon as the gonfaloniere came with his men, I rushed in here to try to hide your letters. But there wasn't enough time. I only managed to save these."

I smoothed them out—one a larger piece of paper, folded many times, the other small, creased in half. And I stared for a long time at my lap, at the image of myself, beautifully rendered in silverpoint, and of a brown ink drawing of Bernardo Baroncelli, swinging from his noose.

Order was restored fairly quickly throughout the city, though by then, every statue of Lorenzo de' Medici had been toppled, every stone crest of the Medici *palle* adorning any building chiseled away. Four days after Piero's flight, the Signoria overturned the law exiling the Pazzi, and encouraged all the offspring of Giuliano's assassins to return. A bill was passed stating that Francesco and Iacopo de' Pazzi had acted on behalf of "the people's freedom."

The day after the Medici left Florence, Savonarola met with King

Charles to negotiate terms of his entry into Florence. A week after my wedding, King Charles marched triumphantly into the city, where he was welcomed as a hero. Ser Francesco wanted badly for me to go with him, for the Lord Priors ordered that all in Florence who were able to should attend, and wear their best finery.

I did not go. All my fine clothes had been burned the night of the riots, and my wedding dress was ruined. More important, I was needed at home. My father's hand was red and putrid, and he shook from fevers. I sat at his bedside day and night, pressed damp cloths to his head, and applied poultices to the festering sores. Zalumma stayed to help me, but my father's new chambermaid, Loretta, went to the spectacle on our behalf.

I liked Loretta. She had a keen eye and wit, and told the truth even when it was impolitic.

"Charles is an idiot," she reported. "He does not have enough sense to keep his mouth closed. He stands with it gaping open, breathing in air through great crooked teeth. He is ugly—so ugly! A hooked nose so bumpy and large as to make Fra Girolamo shudder."

Zalumma laughed softly; I hushed her. We stood in the doorway to my father's bedchamber. Behind my back, my father slept quiet as the dead after a restless, pain-filled night; I had closed the shutters to keep out the glare of the morning sun.

"Oh, but it was grand, though," Loretta said, "when he rode through the San Frediano gate yesterday. The Signoria stood on a platform, dressed in crimson coats with ermine at their necks. It was so loud! Every bell in the city was tolling, and then when the drummers began, I thought my ears would burst. And I never heard of an army dressing so beautifully—why, the footmen themselves wore velvet embroidered with thread of gold, and the calvary's armor was engraved with beautiful designs, and they all carried gold embroidered banners. . . .

"Then Charles came. We knew it was him, because he rode a great black stallion and his armor was covered with gemstones. Four knights rode beside him—two on each side—and held a silk canopy over his head.

"It was lovely, just lovely—until Charles finally stopped, and got off his horse, and joined the Lord Priors on the platform. He's the strangest-looking man I ever saw. A great head, covered with hair the color of fresh-polished copper, almost pink, and a tiny body— he looked like a walking baby. A walking baby with shoes like horses' hooves. I don't know what is wrong with his feet.

"He was so comical. Everyone was waiting for Charles or the Lord Priors to speak, and over the silence a little girl near me cried out, 'But he is so *small*!' And the people around me laughed—not too loud, though. No point in starting trouble.

"So that is the man who has kept us in mortal fear all this time. A small man. And the Signoria addressed him in Latin—he didn't understand a word! One of his attendants had to translate every word into French.

"Do you know what a man in the crowd told me? An educated nobleman, very intelligent. He said—very quietly of course, because you don't know who's listening these days—that Charles wanted to invade Naples because he heard the hunting was good there and the weather always nice, and he loves to hunt. And then he got wind of what Savonarola was saying about him, so he figured he may as well take a little trip south."

Zalumma was fascinated by all this, but I turned away and went back to sit with my father. I did not want to hear that Charles was a buffoon who had blundered his way into Tuscany, who for foolish reasons had caused the death of my husband and the downfall of the Medici family.

I did not let myself think of much of anything outside of my father. He was all I had left now, besides Zalumma. I had nothing else.

I honestly feared my father would die. There were nights his teeth chattered and he shook so violently that I crawled into the bed and held him, hoping the warmth of my body would soothe him. I slept in his room, abandoning mine.

Slowly, he improved, though his right thumb and forefinger remained misshapen; dark scabs had formed in place of the fingernails.

Zalumma haunted me like a ghost. I was only peripherally aware of her presence, as she worried over my lack of sleep and food, my lack of any pursuit other than nursing my father. She was the only one I told about Giuliano's death. The Lord Priors kept the public uninformed, lest the graves outside the city walls all be dug up in the anti-Medici frenzy that had consumed the city.

We had two French soldiers camping at our palazzo then; the Signoria had insisted that the well-to-do families house and feed Charles's soldiers. I did not go to market or out into the city at all, so I saw little of them. I only glimpsed our houseguests from my father's windows or in passing, when I had to leave the room.

Occasionally I saw them when Ser Francesco came to visit. He did not come often in those first days, when the city was in turmoil and my father was gravely ill. But when it became clear that my father would survive, Ser Francesco came to pay his respects. I admit, when my father greeted him with wan cordiality, I was inwardly seething.

But I reminded myself that my father smiled at the man who had saved his life. Ser Francesco, too, supported us: My father's *bottega* had been incinerated, and all his wools stolen or consumed in the blaze; and our palazzo had been vandalized. All the furniture on the ground floor and most of our clothing, drapes, tapestries, and linens had been burned. Ser Francesco had the best food delivered to our kitchen, had the apothecary deliver unguents and ingredients for poultices, had the barber come to lance my father's sores, and had sent his own physician to apply leeches. All this he did without asking for time alone with me— indeed, without referring once to our bargain. The one time he managed a private word with me, as I led him to the door of my father's chamber, he said, in a low voice so my father could not hear:

"I have left funds in Zalumma's care, for the replacement of furniture and other things that your father lost during the rioting. I did not want to be presumptuous and choose them myself; you know your father's taste better than I." He paused. "I am sorry to relay that Count

Giovanni Pico died recently. I know such news will be difficult for your father. Perhaps it would be best to wait to tell him until he is well."

I nodded. And I looked into his face—into those eyes of icy blue— and saw something very like affection, very like the desire to please. But they were not Giuliano's eyes, and the difference left me bitter. The slightest reference to Lorenzo, or Cosimo, or anything even distantly related to the Medici scalded my heart.

When Loretta casually mentioned one day that King Charles had demanded that Piero de' Medici be returned to power, I turned on her, furious, and ordered her to leave the room. The next day, after I had lain awake that night, burdened by the knowledge, I apologized to Loretta and asked for more news.

"The Signoria would not hear of it," she said. Savonarola had gone to Charles and told him God would smite him if he caused the Medici to be returned.

A fortnight passed. Charles and his soldiers grew increasingly demanding and abusive; Florentines no longer welcomed them as heroes, but came to see them as a great nuisance.

On the twenty-seventh of November—eighteen days after I became Giuliano's wife—Savonarola again went to King Charles. This time he told the monarch that God demanded the French army move on or risk divine wrath. And Charles, stupid Charles, believed him.

The next day, the French were gone.

December came. My father grew hale enough to leave his bed, though he became morose and silent when told of Giovanni Pico's death. Even Ser Francesco's visits, with their attendant discussions of preparations for our June wedding, failed to cheer him.

I, on the other hand, grew ill.

I thought it was grief at first: It made sense that the ache in my heart should spread outward. My limbs were heavy; at times, the slightest exertion made me gasp for air, made me long to lie down. My breasts hurt. Food became increasingly repugnant, until I could no longer bear to go into the kitchen.

One evening I eschewed supper and instead took to my bed, wrapping myself in furs because the cold seemed to pierce me with especial vengeance that winter. Zalumma brought me up one of my favorite dishes: quail roasted with onions and leaves of sage. As a special temptation, she had added some warm stewed figs.

She presented it to me as I sat up on my bed, and held the tray under my nose. I looked down at the little bird, gleaming and crisp, with juices visible swirling beneath its skin. The pungent scent of sage rose up with the steam . . . and I rose up from my bed, quite desperate, overwhelmed by a nausea swifter and more urgent than I had ever known.

Zalumma moved out of the way quickly, but I never made it to the basin. The smell of smoke and burning wood from the nearby hearth mingled with that of the quail; I fell to my knees and retched violently. Fortunately, I had taken nothing more than water and a little bread that day.

Then, while I sat on my haunches against the wall, eyes closed, gasping and trembling, she quickly took the tray out of the room. In an instant, she returned, cleaned the floor, and pressed a cool cloth to my forehead.

When I finally took it from her, opened my eyes, and wiped my face, she demanded, "When was your last monthly course?"

I blinked at her, not understanding. Her expression was very grave, very severe.

"Two weeks," I began, then broke into tears.

"Hush, hush." She put an arm about my shoulder. "Then you have nothing to fear. You are just tired, tired from sorrow and sick from not eating . . ."

"Let me finish." I struggled, my voice catching on almost every word. "Two weeks . . . before my wedding."

"Oh." As tears streamed down my cheeks, I watched her do a quick calculation. It was almost mid-December; I had consummated my marriage to Giuliano on the ninth of November.

It had been five weeks.

"You are pregnant," she said implacably.

We stared at each other for a very long, very silent moment.

I let go a sudden laugh, and she caught my hand and smiled.

Just as abruptly, I turned my face and stared, melancholy, into the fire.

"I want to see my mother," I said.

LI

*T*wo days later, Zalumma swaddled me against the chill. With my father's leave, she and I rode to the churchyard at Santo Spirito. Had I not been feeling unsteady, we could have walked.

The driver waited inside the narthex while we women went outside to the churchyard. The cold air stung my nose and eyes and made them water; the tip of Zalumma's nose, the edges of her nostrils, were bright pink. We both raised the hoods of our capes—new ones, courtesy of Ser Francesco.

The dead grass and leaves were frosted and crackled beneath our feet as we walked to where my mother was buried.

My mother lay in a crypt of pink and white marble that gleamed like pearl where the feeble sunlight struck it. Per my father's wishes, her marker was plainer than most: Two curly-haired marble cherubs adorned it. One sat upon the marker, an arm and his face directed upward, as if contemplating her destination; the other gazed solemnly at the viewer, the index finger of his dimpled fist pointing at her name:

ANNA LUCREZIA DI PAOLO STROZZI

Had the weather not been bitter, I think I would simply have sat down next to her, on the ground, and rested in her presence. As it was, I stood none too steadily and thought, *Mother, I am going to have a child.* I put a gloved hand on her tomb; it burned like ice, and I thought how very cold her bones must be, lying there.

"Three years ago," I said aloud to Zalumma. "Three years ago this very day, she took me to the Duomo." It had been cold that day, too, though it did not make me ache so.

"On your birthday," Zalumma said. Her voice was taut; I thought she would cry. "She wanted to do something special for you that day."

Grief, I thought, had made her forgetful. I clucked my tongue gently, made my tone light. Zalumma cried very rarely, and I could not have borne it that day. "Silly. Where is your head? You know my birthday is in June. The fifteenth, like today."

Zalumma bowed her head beside me. "Your mother always tried to do something special for you on this day. Something no one else would notice, but I always knew."

I turned my face toward her. She knew exactly what she was saying. She stared straight ahead at my mother's grave, unable to meet my gaze.

"That's impossible," I said slowly. "Everyone knows my birthday falls in June."

"You were born at your grandmother's country estate. Your father sent Madonna Lucrezia there when she began to show. And she stayed there for almost a year after you were born." Her face was flushed. She, who had always been supremely confident, now spoke timidly, stumbling over her words. "She and your father were agreed on this. And she swore me to secrecy. If it had been only for *him* . . ." Her handsome features contorted briefly with hate.

I had entirely forgotten the cold. "What you're saying makes no sense, Zalumma. No sense. Why would so many people—"

"Your father had a wife, before your mother," she said swiftly. "A young thing. He was married to her four years before she died of fever. And she never conceived. They blamed it on her, of course. They never question the man.

"But then he married your mother. Three years passed, and again, no child. No child, until . . ." She turned to me, suddenly herself again and filled with exasperation. "Oh, child! Go look in a mirror! You look nothing like Antonio! But everyone else could see it—"

"See what?" I had made myself intentionally stupid, I think, because I did not want to understand what she was saying—but in retrospect, I must have understood it all along. I was near crying. "I know I don't look like my father, but . . . what does everyone *see?*"

She put her hands upon my shoulders at last, in a gesture of comfort, as if she had finally realized that what she was saying would hurt me. "Madonna, forgive me. Forgive me. Your mother loved Giuliano de' Medici."

"Giuliano—" I began, then stopped. I had been going to say that Zalumma *was* mad, that Giuliano—*my* Giuliano—had never met my mother, so to say that she loved him was insane.

But then my mind returned to that point in time when I had stood in Lorenzo's courtyard with Leonardo, and the artist had asked me to pose in front of Giuliano's statue, with its oddly familiar features.

I thought of Leonardo's skillful, trained eye, how he had so faithfully reproduced my image in a sketch after meeting me only once. I thought, too, of Lorenzo, staring through the window, waiting. I knew then he had been watching the artist for a sign.

My mother had to have known I was Giuliano's child from the start. My father, in his jealousy, had shunned her for months before I was conceived, and continued to do so long after I was born. That same jealousy caused him to strike her when she confessed she was pregnant.

There were rumors of the affair, of course. Once Giuliano died, my mother and Antonio agreed upon a deception, to spare my father shame: She would deliver me in secret, in her mother's house in the country, and return with me when my age made the lie feasible.

I was baptized late; my false birthdate was recorded in the city ledger.

That way, no one would suspect me of being Giuliano de' Medici's daughter. No one except perhaps for the astrologer, paid by Zalumma in secret so that she and my desperately curious mother could learn the truth about my destiny.

No one, except Leonardo and Lorenzo, who had recognized their loved one's features from afar.

Zalumma and I rode home in silence.

Why, I had demanded of her in the churchyard, *did you not tell me this earlier? Why did you wait until now?*

Because your mother made me promise to keep this secret from you, she had replied, almost shouting from the grip of strong emotion. *And then—you were so miserable living with your father, there seemed no point in making you more miserable, until you were free of him. I had planned to tell you the day you married Giuliano.*

I speak now because you deserve to know the truth about the child you carry.

I wanted to weep, for many reasons, but the tears remained trapped in my tightening throat. I remembered Lorenzo, whispering, *I love you, child;* I remembered my mother, giving me the medallion as a keepsake. And now it was gone, and I had nothing to remember my real father or my husband—my cousin—by.

Perhaps I should have felt angry with my father—with Antonio—for striking my mother because she carried me. But I could only remember his crushed hands, his bleeding fingers where the nails had been torn away. I could only remember my father's words, as I left to attend the dying Lorenzo:

No matter what he says to you, you are my daughter.

He must have been terrified that I would learn the truth that night; yet he had let me go.

When we returned home, I went up to my chambers and did not go down for supper; I couldn't have eaten anyway. Zalumma brought me bread and salt to settle my uneasy stomach.

We still did not speak. My mind was racing, reinterpreting the past, and Zalumma seemed to understand that. I blew out the lamp and lay down that night upon my bed, but my eyes stayed open. I stared into the darkness for an hour, for two, for three.

And then I sat up abruptly, my heartbeat quickening. I thought of the ink rendering of Bernardo Baroncelli; suddenly, I understood why Leonardo had given it to me. And I remembered some of the last words I had heard my husband speak.

Leonardo. Leonardo saw him; my uncle died in his arms.

Leonardo saw him: the man who killed my real father, Giuliano. The man the dying Lorenzo had called "the third man."

For my mother's sake, for my own, I wanted revenge.

To Leonardo da Vinci, at the Court of Ludovico Sforza, the Duke of Milan:

Ser Leonardo,

> *I am writing you because I have recently learned a certain fact—about myself, specifically in terms of my mother's relationship with Lorenzo de' Medici's murdered brother, Giuliano the elder. I feel, because of your actions the evening we were in the Medici courtyard, that you have long been aware of said fact.*

> *Forgive my boldness, but I feel I can trust you as a friend. Giuliano had told me that you were present in the Duomo the day of the assassination, and that you are privy to information—specifically, regarding the identity of a particular man who was also in the cathedral that day. It is my understanding that this man has never been found.*

> *He is now of especial interest to me. Please, Ser Leonardo, could you tell me all that you know about him?*

If you are able to describe him—or even to sketch him from your recollection—I would be very grateful.

If he still breathes, I am determined to find him. I have little else to live for.

> *May God keep you well,*
> *Lisa di Antonio Gherardini*
> *Via Maggio*
> *Santo Spirito, Florence*

LII

I wrote the letter at dawn. And from the instant I handed it to
Zalumma, I impatiently awaited a reply and hoped desperately that my letter would not be confiscated because it made
reference to the Medici.

That same morning, I forced myself to consider a very unpleasant
fact: Francesco and my father had set the wedding for June. My
husband-to-be insisted that I should have a proper wedding dress of
his design, and that Zalumma and I have some time to restock my new
cassone, my wedding chest, with new clothes and linens we embroidered ourselves. My old *cassone* had been destroyed in the fire, along
with its contents.

Besides, Francesco wanted to give me a full, traditional wedding,
as if I were a virgin bride—as if Giuliano had never existed, as if I had
never ridden away from my father's house to be with him. Summer
was the favored season for weddings, since the weather was best for
the slow bridal procession through the city, particularly as the girls
were accompanied by their families on foot.

But there was no denying that by the time I sat upon a bride's
white horse in June, I would be seven months pregnant. Francesco
would know I had lied to him about remaining a virgin. Worse, he

would know the baby was Giuliano's; when a widow remarried, her children were often unwelcome in her new husband's home. And I could not bear the thought of being separated from Giuliano's child.

I knew of only one solution: to convince Francesco the child belonged to him. And there was only one terrible way to accomplish that.

A day passed before my opportunity came.

A traditional family gathering was held at my father's house to discuss the details of my wedding gown. Francesco's aged father, Ser Massimo—a grim, quiet man—and his widowed sister, a colorless ghost named Caterina, attended. My groom's three brothers all lived in the countryside, too far to travel on such short notice, though they assured Francesco they would come to the city in June. There were even fewer members in my family, for my father's siblings all lived in Chianti and could not attend, and my mother had lost two sisters at birth and two older sisters to plague. That left only my uncle Lauro and his wife, Giovanna Maria. They brought with them two older boys, a nursemaid, and three howling little children. Giovanna Maria was again pregnant. She was moonfaced and bloated; Lauro looked haggard and exasperated, with the beginnings of a receding hairline.

I had requested the event take place later in the day—at supper, since most of my retching occurred at morning and midday. By evening, I rallied somewhat, and though I could eat little and found the smell of certain foods unsettling, I was less likely to empty my stomach in the presence of guests.

But I was no less likely to cry. The thought of preparing for another wedding barely a month after losing Giuliano ravaged me. I spent the entire morning and day weeping. When my new relatives arrived at dusk, I graced them with an empty smile and red, swollen eyes.

My father understood. He had entirely recovered by that time and, thanks to Francesco's intervention and recommendation, had revived his business by, ironically, selling woolen goods to members of the returned Pazzi family.

Stalwart and serious, he wound his arm around mine and stood beside me as we greeted our guests. At the supper table, he sat next to me, as my mother would have, and answered questions directed at me when I was too overwhelmed to think of replies. When I rose once and hurried into the kitchen—after Francesco's father asked what flowers should comprise the garland he would place upon the street—my father followed. And when he saw me dabbing at tears, he put his arms about me and kissed my hair, which made me cry in earnest. He thought I wept only for my dead husband; he did not realize that I also wept for myself, for the terrible thing I was about to do.

I had insisted that no sage be used in the dishes, and managed to eat a bit, and drink a little wine when the toasts came. By the time the meal ended and the plates were cleared, I was hoarse from shouting replies at Francesco's deaf father.

At that point, the discussion about the gown began. Francesco presented a sketch of his idea: a high-waisted gown with a square bodice. The sleeves lacked the customary bell shape; they were narrow, closely fitted, with the emphasis on the *camicia* being pulled through several slits and ostentatiously puffed. The neckline was quite low, so that a great deal of the *camicia* showed there as well.

This surprised me. My husband-to-be was supposedly a staunch *piagnone*, yet he had just presented me with a design of the latest Spanish fashion, fresh from the decadent Borgia papal court.

Sitting on my other side, Francesco laid a bundle of fabric swatches on the table. On the top of the pile lay a gleaming silvery damask and a gossamer red and yellow *cangiante*, "with, if you like, garnets and pearls for the headdress."

None of the colors or gems suited me. "Ah!" he said. "She is reticent! This will never do, then." And he folded the cloth and immediately set it aside.

This irritated his father. "It is not hers to choose."

"Father," Caterina said sharply. "Francesco is here to listen to everyone's opinion."

Giovanna spoke up. "Something fresh, like spring blossom, or the delicate flowers of early summer?" she said. "Pinks and whites. Velvets and satin, with seed pearls."

"She has olive skin," Caterina countered. "Pale pinks will make her look sallow."

My father took my hand beneath the table and squeezed it. He behaved now toward Francesco with the same odd reserve he had shown Pico after my mother had died. "The design is lovely," he said. "I know that Lisa likes it, too. Over the years, I have noticed that the colors that flatter her most are blues and greens and purples, the more vibrant, the better. And sapphires . . ." His voice faltered only a moment, then regained its strength. "Sapphires were her mother's favorite, and hers. They suit her. And diamonds."

"Thank you," Francesco said. "Thank you, Ser Antonio. Then Lisa must have sapphires and diamonds. And deep, rich blues to go with them, with perhaps a touch of purple."

"You need not please her," Ser Massimo huffed, and would have said more, but his son silenced him with a finger.

"I need not, but I will," Francesco replied firmly. "I had only hoped for a modest bride, with a fair enough face. But I had never dared hope to win one both modest and brilliantly beautiful. Any woman so lovely must *feel* lovely in her wedding dress. I owe her no less."

I stared down at the table; perhaps others judged this response as demure.

"A pretty speech," his sister Caterina said. Only in retrospect did I hear the faint sarcasm in her tone.

"You are so lucky, Lisa!" Giovanna Maria exclaimed, with a pointed look at her husband Lauro. "So lucky to have a man who flatters you so, who cares for your opinion."

The event was agonizing, but at last it ended, and only my father and Francesco remained at the table, which held only the candelabrum and our goblets. The time to begin my deception was fast arriving. I raised my goblet to my lips, then set it down quickly when I noticed the trembling of my hand.

My father and Francesco were speaking quietly, leaning forward on either side of me, so that I was less of a barrier. Francesco had his sketch spread before him and was pointing to the gown's skirt. "Not so heavy a fabric, I think now," he said. The general consensus had been velvet for the skirt—but on reflection, Francesco decided the choice had been prompted by the fact that this particular December night was exceptionally cold. "June can be warm. Lisa, what do you think?"

My voice sounded astonishingly cool to my ears. "I think," I said, "that my father is tired and should retire for the evening."

"Lisa," my father admonished mildly. "Ser Francesco is still discussing the gown. And he has a right to enjoy his wine."

"I agree. He should continue to enjoy his wine. And you should retire."

Francesco turned his face sharply toward me and lifted a black brow.

My father blinked and drew in a soft breath. For a moment he studied me intently. "I . . . am tired," he said at last. The statement was altogether believable. He sat with his arms folded on the table, his elbows bracing him as he slumped forward beneath an invisible weight. The firelight caught the gold in his hair, but there was now silver there, too. His gaze guarded secrets; I knew one of them.

He stood up and put a hand on Francesco's shoulder. "God be with you." He uttered the words like a warning. Then he leaned down and kissed my cheek sadly.

I gripped the stem of my goblet and listened to his steps as he left the room, crossed the great hall, and ascended the stairs.

The sound had not yet faded when Francesco spoke. "I brought a gift for you." His hand worked its way beneath the pile of fabrics and drew out a small square of red satin, tied with ribbon. "Would you like to see it?"

I nodded. I expected him to pass it to me, to let me open it, but instead he pulled the ribbon and drew out something bright from the shining satin.

Francesco's eyes were shining, too, with a light intense and strange. He held my gift up to the glowing candles: an emerald pendant. The chain rested over the fingers of his upturned hand as the gem revolved slowly, the gold glittering. His eyes were tensed, his lips parted. "You were so eager to have your father leave. Was there a reason you wanted to be alone with me?"

"Perhaps there was." I kept my voice soft; he might have thought it intentionally alluring, but had I spoken louder, it would have shook. I ventured a small smile to keep my lip from curling.

"Were you ever with him?" Francesco asked. His gaze pierced me. "Your father said you were there less than a day."

I stared down at my goblet and shook my head. It was the first of many bold lies.

My answer pleased and excited him. "Look up at me," he said; he dangled the jewel in front of me. "Do you want it?"

"What?"

"The necklace." He leaned forward, his breath upon my face; his voice grew hard, flat, dangerous. "Tell me you want it."

My mouth fell open. I stammered. "I . . . I want it."

"What will you do for it?" The words lashed like a whip.

I submerged my anger and stared at him. I thought, *I will get up and tell you to leave. I will call for the servants. I will tell you never to set foot in this house again.* I thought, *If I disappoint him, he will leave, and the world will know I carry Giuliano's child. If I disappoint him, he will turn my father back over to the Signoria for questioning.*

"Anything you wish," I whispered.

"Say it louder. Like you mean it. Look me in the eye."

I looked him in the eye. I repeated the words.

He rose quickly, went to the doors, and pulled them shut. In another few strides, he stood next to me and pulled my chair away from the table with a sharp movement. Then he moved in front of me and bent over to swing the necklace in front of me.

He was on fire, his chest heaving, his eyes bright and feral. "On your knees," he said. "Beg for it."

I burned with hate. I looked down at the floor and considered what I was willing to do to protect Giuliano's child. Our child. What I was willing to do to protect my father. I slid from the chair onto my knees.

"Give it to me. Please."

"So." He was flushed, trembling, exhilarated. "This is your price, then. This is your price." He tossed the necklace aside carelessly; it landed on the carpet in front of the hearth.

He yanked me to my feet. I expected him to kiss me, but he wanted nothing to do with my face. He set me upon the dining table and swept away the goblets. One fell and shattered on the stone floor.

He pushed me down against the hard oak; my legs hung down and the toes of my slippers brushed against the floor. Instinctively, I pressed my palms to my thighs, holding down my skirts, but he moved between my legs and pulled the fabric up with such force that my *camicia,* of fine French lawn, ripped with a stark sound.

Frenzied, he pulled down his black leggings with one hand and pushed his underblouse away; he wore no *farsetto* beneath his tunic. My struggling only fueled his ardor; at this realization, I forced myself to lie back, limp, submissive, even when he pulled my arms over my head and held my wrists with crushing force.

His manner was loveless, animalistic. He entered me so roughly that I cried out in pain.

I left myself then. I was no longer in my body, but in the light and shadows that played upon the ceiling. I was in the smell of candles burning menacingly close to my head, in the warmth emanating from the hearth.

I became a fortress; he was a beam trying to shatter me. In the end, I held. Giuliano and our child remained safe on the other side.

I came to myself with the sensation of hot liquid flowing into me, out of me. I gasped as he pulled away as quickly as he had entered. I put my hand between my legs and realized that I had been wounded.

Slowly, I righted myself and settled unsteadily onto my feet. Still breathing hard, he stood efficiently tucking his underblouse back into his leggings, adjusting his tunic, his belt. He saw me staring at him and smiled. He was cheerful, brisk, his tone playful.

"Lisa, Lisa. What a fine Jezebel you make. Go and fetch your payment."

My face hardened; I turned it from him.

"Go," he said, with a hint of danger. "Or shall I summon the servants now to come fetch the goblets? Better yet, shall I call for your father and tell him what you have done?"

Silent, closed, I walked slowly to the necklace and picked it up from the floor. The gem was warm from the fire. It was deeply colored, glittering evergreen.

I had never seen anything so ugly.

He walked over and clasped it around my neck. Once the transaction was accomplished, he transformed. He was gentle, solicitous.

"Here, then," he said kindly. "Before you call for the servants"— he nodded at the shards of glass on the floor—"let me help. It is my fault that your hair and gown are in disarray."

I let him touch me; he tucked errant locks back into my silk hairnet, smoothed my skirts. "I am so sorry your lovely *camicia* is torn. I shall have it replaced at once with one even finer."

I called for the kitchen maid in a voice that shook. As she swept up the glass, Francesco joked about his own clumsiness. I said nothing.

When we were alone again, I would not walk him to the door. I did not respond when he bowed and softly wished me a good night.

I went upstairs to my room and pulled off my clothes with Zalumma's help. The *camicia* I threw in a corner. I was glad it was torn; I would have thrown it out anyway. It stank of Francesco.

Zalumma had brought a basin and cloth so that I could wash myself; at the sight, I began to cry. She held me and stroked my back, the way my mother had when I was a child.

Zalumma did not let me throw away the stained *camicia*. Instead, she pricked her finger and squeezed drops of blood onto its lap, front and back, bright scarlet against dazzling white. She folded it carefully, wrapped it in a square of cloth, tied it, and had it delivered to Francesco's *bottega* in town.

LIII

*F*rancesco called again two days later, ostensibly to discuss progress on the gown and to arrange a fitting. This time it was he who hinted that my father should leave us alone.

I did not protest; I had known it would happen. I had already discussed this with Zalumma, who had agreed that, for the child's sake, I had no choice but to comply. The more often I offered myself to Francesco, the more convinced he would be that the child was indeed his.

This time he brought me earrings, of diamonds and opals that spilled down the sides of my neck like tears.

Francesco soon gave up finding pretexts for his visits and became a regular at our supper table. I collected a good deal of jewelry, though the gifts grew increasingly modest. My father knew to leave the dinner table early without being prompted. We did not speak to each other of Francesco. We suffered separately, in our own lonely spheres.

· · ·

After two weeks, immediately following another brutal encounter with Francesco, I mentioned casually to him that I had missed my monthly course.

He snorted like a man who had a great deal of experience with such things, but he had been sated and so was not ungentle. "It's too soon to know, Lisa. You shouldn't worry. Nerves are no doubt the cause. You'll see."

I let another week pass. And then I had Cook prepare my favorite dish: quail with sage and onions. I sat beside Francesco at dinner, and when my plate arrived, I leaned over the little bird, with its crisp golden skin, and inhaled deeply.

The result was gratifying. I cupped my hand over my mouth and dashed from the table; I didn't make it out of the room in time. There, before my father and Francesco, I leaned against the wall and retched violently.

Even in my desperate state, I could hear the screech of a chair being pushed back quickly from the table. When, gasping, I was finally able to turn my swimming head to look, I saw my father standing, fists clenched, staring across the table at my future husband. This time, he did not try to hide his fury or his hate.

A servant came to clean the mess and wash my face; my father ordered the plates removed and the chamber aired. Once we were all reseated and I felt well enough, I said, "I don't want to be married in June. I would prefer March."

My father's eyes darted up and to the side; he was calculating. And then his gaze lit upon Francesco and bored through to the man's very soul. I fancied Francesco shuddered ever so slightly.

"The fifth of March," my father said, his tone so ominous and unyielding that neither my betrothed nor I had anything further to say about it.

For a week, my father refused to leave us alone after supper—but soon after, he apparently reached an agreement with Francesco, for I was once again at the mercy of my intended.

Now that Francesco knew I was pregnant, the gifts stopped. Now he demanded I beg for the sexual act itself, since my condition was clearly the result of my wanton craving. I called myself terrible names: whore, harlot, slut.

I feared being broken. I looked on the fifth of March with dread.

It came all too soon, on a day that was damp and cool and uncommonly warmer than the rest of that bitter winter; fat clouds floated in a gray-blue sky. I could easily have ridden a white horse over the bridge to Francesco's palazzo, but we had anticipated a cold day and so I, my father, and Zalumma rode in a carriage, with Uncle Lauro, his wife and children all riding in a wagon behind us.

My gown was of vivid bright blue velvet, with a broad belt of the same color brocade; because of my thickening waistline, I wore the belt just below my breasts. Zalumma insisted it looked as though it were meant to be worn that way. Francesco had given me a necklace of gold and sapphire, and a headdress so expensive, its presence made me nervous; it was a net of small diamonds woven into the finest gold thread. Every time I turned my head, the sun caught the diamonds, and in the corner of my eye I saw flashes of rainbow light. It was mid-morning. I was queasy and leaned out of the window to breathe in the chill air.

We left the Via Maggio and headed east on the Borgo Sant'Iacopo, leaving behind my neighborhood of Santo Spirito. From there, we rolled over the bustling Ponte Vecchio. Men and boys saw our carriage, draped in white satin, and called out, some jesting, some congratulatory, some lewd.

I had chosen the route. It would have been more convenient for the driver to cross the Ponte Santa Trinità, but it was hard enough for me to turn my face in its direction and gaze at the waters of the Arno, and think of how Giuliano had died.

We made our way into the city quarter of Santa Maria Novella, onto the Via Por Santa Maria, then east onto the Via Vacchereccia, home to the silk *botteghe,* including Francesco's. The stalls stood in the shadow of the Arte della Seta's, the Silk Guild's, tower.

My husband's palazzo lay on a side street behind black iron gates; it had been built expressly for him and his first bride. It was classically Roman, hewn from gray stone so pale it shone white in bright sun. Rectangular, strong, and starkly elegant, it rose four stories into the air, its face turned north, its back to my family home. This was the first time I had set eyes upon it.

As we approached the gates, I heard a shout. Francesco stood out in front, his palm thrust forward, fingers spread out, indicating that we should stop. Beside him, draped in dark *mantelli,* stood his stooped father and three middle-aged dark-haired men: his brothers.

I peered out the window at the road. A braided garland of satin ribbons, gleaming white and dark blue, lay upon the flagstones, stretching all the way from one edge of the street to the other.

There were no flowers to be had in March.

As his brothers cheered and catcalled, Francesco—smiling abashedly—went out and pulled a single strand. The garland was suddenly undone in the center, and as the men clapped, he hurried to pull the two halves far enough on either side to permit our carriage to pass through.

He was quite talented at it; after all, he had practiced it enough. I was his third spouse. The first had died in childbirth, the second of fever. I could certainly understand their eagerness to quit life.

The iron gate swung open. Francesco and his brothers emerged on horseback, followed by two wagons holding his family. Like those of my two predecessors, my nuptial carriage headed east, toward the looming vast brick-orange cupola of Santa Maria del Fiore. Once again, I leaned out the open window, grateful for the air, which had steadily cooled as the minutes passed. The sky was filling with heavy damp clouds.

My father repeated the old saying, "A wet bride is a happy bride." A rainy wedding day supposedly brought luck.

At last we rolled into the great Piazza del Duomo and stopped. We waited a time while Francesco and his family preceded us into the Baptistery of San Giovanni, built upon an ancient temple dedicated to

Mars. Here, all good Florentines were baptized as infants, wed as adults.

As my intended and the guests took their places inside, I waited an interminable time, fighting nerves and nausea; just when I was certain I would be ill, the signal was given, and I was forced to compose myself. Zalumma held my train as I stepped out. My father, haunted and loving, took my arm.

I walked with him past Ghiberti's amazing doors. I had lived all my life in the city, yet had only once set foot inside that octagon of stone. I walked across marble floors adorned with images of gryphons and spirals, beheld golden walls, and stared up at the gilded cupola, the blazing candelabra.

The priest and Francesco—dignified, reverent, tender—stood waiting in front of the white marble altar.

The walk was a blur of sensations: the pull of the long velvet train behind me, the sparkle and flash of diamonds, the intense blue of my sleeve, the shimmering white of puffed gossamer silk. The glittering mosaics of Christ in blues and reds and brilliant saffron at the Last Judgment, of sinners cringing in Hell, tormented by devils.

My father held on to me tightly—so tightly—until the time came for him to give me away. As he handed me to Francesco, then stepped back, he wept.

An interminable Mass followed. I fumbled over prayers I had known since childhood, listened to the priest's sermon without comprehending a word. The longer I stood, the more I feared I would faint; each time I knelt, I felt certain I would never again be able to stand.

"Will you?" the priest asked at last.

Francesco smelled of rosemary. I looked at him, at his deceptively gentle expression, and saw my bleak unhappy future. I saw my child being born, my father growing old. I saw Giuliano's memory paling to a whisper.

"I will," I said. My voice surprised me with its strength, its steadiness. I will, until my father dies. Until my father dies, and my child and I can escape.

A ring appeared—another plain and slender ring of gold—and caught the candles' glow. This one was too tight, but Francesco used force to make it fit. I did not allow myself to flinch.

Francesco's kiss was reserved, timid. There were other kisses, then, many kisses from many faces and many murmured words.

With my husband beside me, I stepped outside into the great piazza and drew in a breath. The afternoon was gray; mist hung in the air. Soft as steam rising from water, it settled on my face, but its touch was cold.

LIV

fterward, our party returned to my new home. This time my carriage rumbled through the open black iron gates onto a circular drive of new flagstone that took us past a copse of young laurels. The entry doors, of intricately carved wood, were taller than any I had ever seen. To their east lay a large formal loggia for receiving guests in better weather.

The carriage stopped, and Francesco helped me out while Zalumma worried with the great trail of fabric that followed me. Crouched upon high pedestals, a pair of majestic stone lions guarded the threshold. We walked between them and the doors opened for us as if by magic.

A servant led us to the room on our left: a vast hall, the walls pristine white, the floor gleaming pale marble with black inlay of classical design. Beyond, past an archway, was a dining chamber, the surface of its long table entirely obscured by platters heaped with food. The size of the rooms was better suited for a prince and his court than our small gathering. Indeed, the fire in the dining chamber could not quite dispel the chill. This was a cold, formal place.

My new husband was a very rich man.

I had lived my life in a house more than a century old, with an interior of bland walls and plain furniture. I was used to uneven stone floors, worn by the tread of generations, to stairs that dipped in the middle, to doors whose edges were darkened by the touch of countless hands.

This house had seen barely a decade of wear, with floors that were perfectly flat and smooth and shining, with unscarred doors that sported bolts and hinges of bright metal. I did not like it at all.

None of my father's relatives had chosen to come from the country, but Francesco's brothers had brought their wives and children with them. Once his family had followed us inside, along with Uncle Lauro's brood, the building seemed less empty, though the chatter echoed off the walls. When the wine was poured, a great deal of laughter followed, some of it loud and raucous.

Custom dictated that I ride a white horse to my wedding, then return from it on foot to my father's house, where I would spend the night, alone and chaste. The wedding was not to be consummated until the second night, following a day of feasting.

But I flouted custom for my first wedding and my second. I did not ride the white horse. Nor did I walk back to my father's house, a decision that had been reached due to three factors: I had suffered from fever the week before and was still weak, the weather was inclement, and I was pregnant. This last was not discussed openly, but my waist had so thickened that it was obvious to most. It caused only a passing concern, for formal betrothals were considered as binding as marriage. Many a Florentine bride had to let out her wedding gown before riding to San Giovanni, and no one thought worse of her for it.

I greeted more guests, Lord Priors and *Buonomini,* Francesco's peers. A wedding meal soon followed, one that Savonarola would have frowned on for its excesses: whole roast mutton, two whole roast pigs, three geese and a swan, countless pheasants, several rabbits and dozens of fish, soup and cakes and pretty candies, six different types of pasta in broth, cheeses, nuts, and dried fruits.

The smell of the food left me dangerously close to gagging. Yet I smiled until my cheeks ached. I was told a hundred times that I was the most beautiful bride ever seen in Florence. I answered mindlessly, always giving the proper, courteous reply while meaning none of it.

There were toasts, including a popular one for newlyweds, that I should become pregnant on my wedding night. I lifted my goblet to my lips but kept them pressed together; the smell of the wine so nauseated me that I held my breath.

I ate nothing but some bread and a small piece of cheese, though my plate was full. I maneuvered the food artfully so it would appear I had taken more.

After the food came dancing, with music from a quartet of players Francesco had hired. With the ritual and the meal behind me, I felt a temporary relief. I was exhausted, but I laughed and played and danced with my new nephews and nieces, and looked on them with newfound wistfulness.

I turned once to find my father watching me with the same emotion.

But when the sun began to set, the revelers left, and my father went home to his house, empty of family—even Zalumma had left him. And my bravado waned with the light.

I was numb as Francesco introduced me to some of his servants: his chambermaids, Isabella and Elena; his valet, Giorgio; the cook, Agrippina; a kitchen maid, Silvestra; and the driver, Claudio. Most of them slept across from the kitchen, on the ground floor in the southwest wing, which opened onto the back of the palazzo. I repeated the names aloud even as I knew I would not remember them long; my heart was beating too loudly for me to hear even myself clearly. There were others I did not meet—stablehands and the stablemaster, a second cook who had taken ill, an errand boy.

Elena, a sweet-faced woman with chestnut hair and the serene gaze of a Madonna, led Zalumma and me up the stairs to the third floor, past Francesco's rooms on the second, to the vast chambers that now belonged to me. Holding a lamp aloft, she led me first to the nursery, with its forlorn cradle beneath a painting of a stiff Mary and her manlike child, and its empty nursemaid's quarters; the room was so achingly cold I decided no fire had ever been built in its hearth.

We then toured my sitting room, which had chairs, a table bearing a lit lamp, a desk, and a shelf with books suited to a lady's taste: love poetry, psalms in Latin, primers on classical languages, volumes of advice on how the mistress should run her household, how she should conduct herself in regard to her husband and guests, how she should treat common ailments. No fire burned here, either, but the room was warmer, given that it rested two floors above the dining room's blazing hearth, and one floor above Francesco's chambers.

The sitting room and nursery sat at the front of the house, with windows that faced north; Zalumma's quarters (which she shared with Elena and Isabella) and mine sat at the back, facing south. Elena took us to the servants' chambers and allowed me a swift, cursory glance inside; my own bedroom at home had not been as large or well appointed.

Then we crossed the corridor and Elena opened the door to the bridal chamber, my chamber.

The room was unabashedly feminine. The walls were of white, the floor of variegated cream, pink, and green marble, the mantel and hearth made from white granite that glittered in the light of a generous fire. Two delicate lady's chairs, their padded seats covered in pale green brocade, faced the hearth; on the wall behind them was a large tapestry of a pair of women plucking oranges from a tree. The bed was covered by scattered dried rose petals and an embroidered tasseled throw of the same blue velvet as my gown. Matching curtains, trimmed with gold, hung from an ebony canopy; the inner curtains were made of armloads of sheer white chiffon, cunningly draped. French doors opened onto the south and, I assumed, a balcony.

On either side of the bed stood tables; one held a white basin, painted with flowers and filled with fragrant rosewater. Above it hung an oval mirror. The other table held a lamp, a silver plate of raisins, a flagon of wine, and a silver goblet.

The room's appointments were so new, so clearly made expressly for me, that it was hard to believe I was not the first owner.

Elena showed me the iron chain hanging from the ceiling near the bed, which, if pulled, would sound a bell in the servants' quarters across the hall.

"Thank you," I said, by way of dismissing her. "I have everything I need. I will undress now."

The small smile on her lips, which had never wavered during our tour, did not change. The lamp still in her hand, she curtsied, then left, closing the door behind her. I stood and listened to the scuffle of her slippers on the marble, to the sound of the door across the hall opening and shutting.

Zalumma unlaced my sleeves and my bodice. The cumbersome gown with its heavy train dropped to the floor and, clad only in the shimmering *camicia,* I stepped out of it with a low groan, exhausted.

I sat fidgeting at the foot of the bed and watched as Zalumma carefully folded the sleeves, the gown, and set them upon a shelf of the large wardrobe. She gently removed the diamond hairnet and put it in the trunk, along with my other jewelry. Then I took my place in front of the mirror and let her unloose my hair. I stared at my reflection and saw my mother, young and terrified and pregnant.

Zalumma saw her, too. She tenderly lifted the brush and brought it down, then smoothed the hair with her free hand. Each stroke of the brush was immediately followed by another stroke of her hand; she wanted to comfort me, and this was the only way she had.

At last, the brushing stopped. I turned to face Zalumma. Her expression now reflected my own: falsely brave, intent on cheering the other.

"If you need anything—" she began.

"I will be fine."

"—I will be right by the door, waiting."

"Will you come afterward?" I asked. Despite my dread, I had noticed that Francesco had ignored one of my requests: There was no cot here for Zalumma. While it was the fashion for servants to sleep apart from very wealthy masters, Zalumma had always slept on a cot near my mother's bed, in case she suffered a fit. After my mother died, Zalumma's presence was a comfort to me. And it would be my one comfort now, in this heartless house. "This room is too large, and this bed; I cannot bear to sleep alone."

"I will come," she said softly.

I nodded. "I will call for you."

I turned away so that she could leave.

Francesco arrived a quarter of an hour later. His knock was hesitant, and when I did not come at once, he opened the door and called my name.

I was sitting on the stone hearth staring into the fire, my arm wound round my legs, my cheek resting on my bent knees, my bare feet pressed against the warm, rough granite. Had I been any closer, the heat would have burned my skin, but it could not dispel the cold that enveloped me.

I rose and walked toward him. Still dressed in his wine-colored wedding clothes, he smiled sweetly, shyly, as I stopped two arm's lengths away. "The festivities went quite well. I think our guests were pleased, don't you?" he asked.

"Yes," I replied.

"Do you find your rooms satisfactory?"

"They are beyond my expectations."

"Good." He paused. "I have a gift for you." He drew a silk pouch from his pocket.

I reached for it, took it. I fumbled with the drawstring, my fingers clumsy, numb, as if I had been swimming in icy water. Francesco laughed softly and loosened the drawstring for me; the contents spilled into my hand.

It was a lady's brooch. A large one, made of an acorn-sized garnet surrounded by seed pearls and set in silver.

"It's . . . a family tradition," Francesco said, suddenly uncomfortable. He folded his hands behind his back. "It was my mother's . . . and my grandmother's."

The stone was clouded, dull, the piece unremarkable, except for the fact that it was very old. Black tarnish stubbornly surrounded each pearl, despite the fact that the brooch had recently been polished.

A tradition, I thought. *For all of his brides.*

"Thank you," I said stiffly, bracing myself for the cruelty that would certainly follow.

But something entirely impossible and remarkable occurred; Francesco's expression remained mild, almost bored. He stifled a yawn.

"You're certainly welcome," he said, his manner diffident. "Well, then." He glanced around awkwardly, then smiled again at me. "It has been an exhausting day for you, I am sure. I'll see you come morning. Good night."

I stared up at him in disbelief. He was uncomfortable, anxious, eager to be done with me. "Good night," I said.

He left. I quickly set the brooch down, put my ear to my closed door, and listened to him move down the hall and descend the steps. Once I was sure he had gone, I opened my door to call Zalumma— and started to find her already there.

Her gaze was fastened on the dark stairs. "Is he coming back?" she whispered.

"No." I pulled her into the room.

Her jaw went slack; her mouth opened and her eyes opened wider. "What happened?"

"Nothing." The realization that my performance this night was finished overwhelmed me. I felt suddenly exhausted, and barely made it to the bed before my legs gave out entirely. I sat, my back against the sturdy wooden headboard, my legs spread out before me, and mindlessly picked up a rose petal and fingered it. Zalumma tipped the flagon of wine and filled the silver goblet, then handed it to me. Its aroma was surprisingly appealing, given that I had felt so ill earlier in the day. I took a small, careful sip and savored it on my tongue; it was as delicious a wine as I had ever tasted, as good as any served by the Medici.

For the first time that day, I relaxed enough to notice her. She stood at the bedside and frowned, watching me carefully to make sure the drink appealed, that I would not become ill. She was quite handsome that day; her worrying over me had caused her to lose weight recently, which made the cheekbones beneath her dark, upward-slanting eyes more prominent. The ink-black hair around her face had been finely braided, the bulk of it pulled back into a veil of creamy silk; her gown was of rich brown wool edged with gold-colored ribbon.

"What did he say?" she demanded, when she could no longer bear my silence.

"He gave me a gift." I nodded at the garnet brooch on the bedside table. "He gave me a gift and said I must be tired, and then he excused himself."

She stared at the brooch. "He's mad."

"Perhaps he's ill," I said. "Or perhaps he's tired himself after so many preparations. Look at the bed." Her gaze went to the embroidered velvet cover, the matching hangings. "He had all this done for me."

"It's the least he could do," she said, her tone hard.

I took another cautious sip of wine and realized I was ravenous. I looked at the plate of dried grapes beside me and frowned. The servants had assumed I would be stuffed after feasting all day and had left these as sweet morsels to be enjoyed with the wine; they did not yet know I disliked raisins.

Zalumma noticed at once. "Are you hungry? You've eaten nothing today."

"I would love some bread and cheese."

"I'll find some."

I paused. "Bring another goblet—for yourself. And whatever else you wish. I don't want to eat alone." Francesco would think it improper, but I didn't care. I was giddy with relief and, despite my weariness, suddenly in the mood for a small celebration. For at least one night I was free of Francesco's brutal attentions.

"Are you sure, Madonna?"

I clicked my tongue in disgust at the question and waved her off.

While she was gone, I sat with my eyes closed. I was grateful beyond words to be left alone on my second wedding night; I had not wanted to profane the memory of the first. Aloud, I promised Giuliano: "I will tell your child everything I know of you, of your goodness, and of your father's. I will tell him of your uncle—my father. And I will teach him everything I know of love and kindness."

I closed my eyes and saw Giuliano kneeling on the floor of the chapel after parting the garland of flowers, smiling up at me.

I smiled, too. And when Zalumma appeared at the door with a tray balanced on one hand, my lips were still curving. On the tray were three different cheeses and half a round loaf of bread. I was glad to see she had brought a second goblet.

"You're feeling better," she said, pleased. "I never saw such a kitchen. You would think they had expected an army today." Her tone carried a curious undercurrent.

"What is it?" I demanded. I knew she had discovered something, seen something. "What has happened?"

She carefully pushed the lamp aside and set the tray down on my bedside table. "Ser Francesco," she said, her tone puzzled. "When I went down to the kitchen, I could see lamps outside the front door, and hear men's voices."

"And?"

"I went to the window; I had no candle, so they couldn't see me. The stableboy was opening the gate. Ser Francesco was on horseback, alone. He was speaking to the boy. I think he was telling him when to expect him back. He kept glancing about as if he were worried that someone might see him."

"He left," I said to myself, trying to fathom what it could mean. Perhaps I should have been concerned, but I was simply happy that he was gone. "It doesn't matter," I pronounced. "Here." I lifted the flagon of wine. "Drink with me, and have some food. I've survived my first night here."

We ate and drank. When we grew tired, I insisted Zalumma lie down beside me. As a slave, she found the liberty of lying down upon her mistress's bed uncomfortable; she did not want it thought she had forgotten her place, and she knew Isabella and Elena would notice if she had not slept in her bed in the servants' quarters. But at last she fell asleep.

I dozed for a while, too. I dreamed that I was in the wrong house, with the wrong man; the grief of it woke me. I sat up to find Zalumma snoring softly beside me, still dressed in her wool gown, her veil askew, the wood in the fire now reduced to glowing ash.

It came to me clearly, then, that I was truly married to Francesco, that Giuliano was dead, that these facts could never be undone. I realized that I was going to cry, and violently—and I did not want to be seen or heard.

I slipped from the bed and, shivering from the cold, hurried quickly, quietly, out of the room. I closed the door behind me and ran halfway down the stairs, then sat upon a step.

Before I could release the first hoarse sob, a sound stopped me: clumsy footsteps coming in my direction. Yellow lamplight wavered far below me, then gradually lit up the wall like a spreading stain.

I knew before he appeared that it was my husband. Swaying, he paused to orient himself on the second-floor landing, only a few steps below me.

"Francesco," I said softly. I meant only to think it; I did not want to be noticed, least of all by him.

But he heard and looked up at me, startled.

"Lisa," he slurred. He was very drunk. He held up the lamp and squinted at me. He was swaddled carelessly in a black *mantello;* as he lifted the lamp, the end of it slipped down to reveal his wedding tunic and leggings.

Near his right hip, the hem of his tunic was bunched up, and his leggings bunched down; and the white wool of his undershirt protruded like a flag.

I let go an amused, soft snort at the sight, and when I breathed in again, I noticed the sharp smell of cheap lavender. I had detected it before a few times at market on bawdily dressed, brightly rouged women, the sort that Zalumma always steered me away from.

I heard Francesco's voice in my mind, saw his lecherous, glittering gaze. *Whore. Slut. Harlot.*

But as of that morning, I was a respectable married woman.

And I was free.

"I wasn't able to sleep," I said swiftly. "But I think I can now. Good night."

"Good night," Francesco said drowsily, and as I ran up the stairs, I heard him groan.

When I arrived back in my room, I closed the door behind me, leaned against it, and laughed so hard that I woke Zalumma.

LV

*S*pring came, and the weather warmed. During the days, I opened the French doors and sat on the balcony. To my left were the stables, and the kitchen garden, bordered by hedges of lavender and rosemary. Directly before me lay a formal garden with cobblestone paths, young laurel trees, and carefully sculpted boxwood. In the mornings, I walked alone through the garden, past a roaring stone lion, his jaws releasing a cooling spray of water into a stone well. Beyond lay an arching trellis covered with thorny rose-bushes, which led to a small grotto of the Virgin, her hands spread to welcome petitioners.

The child in my belly grew. By April, I had thickened unmistakably; the lines of my jaw, my cheeks softened. My nausea was replaced by a hunger so demanding that I kept plates of food beside my bed and often woke during the night to eat. Francesco doted on me like a parent; each day he instructed Agrippina to bring me a bucket of milk, frothy and still warm from the animal's body.

My husband never touched me. We behaved toward each other like distant but cordial acquaintances; he gave me whatever I asked for. He did not protest when I ordered that a cot for Zalumma be put at the foot of my bed. But to a great extent, I was his prisoner: I was no longer to go to market. I could attend Savonarola's sermons and, if I wished, go to our family chapel at Santissima Annunziata. All other outings required my husband's express permission.

Francesco and I usually saw each other once daily, at supper. My father joined us. He seemed to take special joy in my company and brightened at any mention of the coming child. But he lost weight, so much so that I worried for his health; and when he sat at the table listening to Francesco, I detected a silent misery gnawing at him. I doubted he would ever be happy again.

Nor would I, though my life had not become as hellish as I had feared. Francesco heard Savonarola preach in the mornings and visited his whores at night; if he worried over the discrepancy between his public and private life, he did not show it. After a day of work at the *bottega* and the Palazzo della Signoria, where he served as a *Buonomo,* he relished his supper and his attentive audience. My father and I listened but said little as Francesco related the news of the day.

Many changes had come about because of Fra Girolamo, who had decided that God should be deeply involved in the workings of the Signoria. Laws were passed: Sodomy brought a fiery death at the stake, a low décolletage brought public disgrace and a fine. Poetry and gambling were outlawed. Adulterers quaked in fear of death by stoning. (Francesco related this with all seriousness; never mind that he was chief among them.) Men and women who dared sport jewels risked losing them, for the streets were now patrolled by young boys loyal to the friar and determined to seize any "unnecessary" wealth as a "donation" to the Church. Citizens ventured out furtively, worried that a thoughtless act might call attention to themselves, that a chance remark might be taken as proof of indifference toward God.

We all grew afraid.

Meanwhile, the Lord dictated that Florence should no longer be governed by the rich. He preferred a Great Council in the style of Venice, and if one was not created, He would smite the city. The Mother of God was also interested in politics. She appeared to the friar and spoke eloquently in Tuscan of the need for reform.

Savonarola began to preach vehemently against Rome and the

scandalous behavior of Pope Alexander, who had brought his teenaged mistress to live with him in the Vatican.

Francesco taught me a new term: *Arrabbiati*, the mad dogs. These were the men who snarled at Savonarola, who said that a friar had no business meddling in politics. Francesco had nothing but disdain for them.

My father, who had once been an outspoken proponent of the friar, now smiled palely or frowned at the appropriate times, but said little. The fire had altogether left him, though he went with Francesco to hear Savonarola preach.

Talk of the prophet annoyed me. His sermons now excluded women—given that he spoke mostly of political matters—except on Saturdays, when he preached directly to members of the gentler sex. I was obliged to attend; my husband was a *Buonomo*, after all. Zalumma and I sat and listened in rigid silence.

But at times I spoke to God. I had forgiven Him, to some extent, after my father's recovery. But I only prayed at our family chapel at Santissima Annunziata, where I was comfortable. I liked the fact that it was old, and small, and plain.

During this time, King Charles of France made his way to Naples, only to be ultimately defeated there. His army retraced its steps northward, passing unimpeded again through Rome, until at last it arrived barely two days' ride from Florence.

Savonarola warned us all to repent, else God, in the form of Charles, would strike us down. At the same time, the friar went to Siena, heard Charles's confession, fed him the Host, and threatened him in person with God's wrath if he did not deliver Pisa into our hands.

Charles remained mute on the subject; Savonarola returned home without an answer, and we Florentines grew anxious as the French lingered in Siena.

I couldn't trouble myself, however. I sat on my balcony and watched the white lilies bloom.

In May, a flood drowned all the tender young corn growing on the banks of the Arno. A sign of God's displeasure, the prophet said; if we did not repent, He would send Charles next. I watched the laurel trees grow full and flutter, silvery, in the wind; I watched them bow to the gray rains.

In June, I stared out at the roses, vividly red against deep green; I inhaled their scent, carried on the breeze. Water flowed from the lion's mouth with a soothing, repetitive gurgle.

August was sultry and I was miserable. I could not sleep because of the heat, because of the restless child, because of the ache in my back. I was uncomfortable lying down, sitting, standing; I could no longer see my feet, could not remove my own slippers, could hardly get up from the bed or a chair. My wedding ring grew so tight my finger ached. Zalumma generously applied soap, and when she finally succeeded in wrenching the ring off, I shrieked.

Zalumma and I counted. We expected the baby to arrive the first or second week of the month. By the last week, Zalumma was pleased—the child's tardiness would only serve to convince Francesco it was his—but I was too desperate to appreciate my good fortune.

By the first of September, I was unpleasant to everyone, including Zalumma. I had given up coming down to supper; Francesco sent up small gifts, but I was too irritable to acknowledge them.

That week, on one particularly hot night, I woke abruptly, filled with a strange alertness. I was sweating. I had balled up my night-gown and pushed it beneath my pillow; the damp linen sheet clung so tightly to my belly that I could see the child stirring.

I rose awkwardly and pulled on my gown. Zalumma was snoring lightly on her cot. I moved as lightly as my bulk allowed and slipped quietly out the door. I was thirsty and thought to go downstairs where it was cooler, to get some fresh water to drink. My eyes had adjusted to the lack of light, and so I took no candle.

As I began to descend the stairs, I saw light advancing from the opposite direction—Francesco, I assumed. Like a good wife, I turned, intending to go back up discreetly; but a feminine giggle made me stop, press my back firm against the wall to keep my body clear of the arc of looming light, and look down.

On the landing below stood Isabella—young, pretty Isabella—in a white linen *camicia*, with a key in one upraised hand and a candle in the other. She leaned backward into the grasp of a man who had wound his arms beneath her breasts and pulled her against his chest, then pressed his face against her neck. As he kissed her, she fought to repress her laughter—and when she failed, he shushed her, and she pulled away from him to open the door to my husband's chambers. A lamp burned there in anticipation of his return.

Francesco, I thought, and Isabella. He had returned an hour or two early; perhaps one of his strumpets had fallen ill, because his schedule was otherwise predictable. I was not at all surprised or offended by the thought of his dalliance, though I was somewhat disappointed in Isabella.

But the man who raised his face was not my husband.

I caught only a glimpse of him, of his flashing smile, before he took the key from Isabella's hand. He was dark-haired, perhaps my age, around sixteen. I had never seen him before. Had Isabella admitted a thief?

I stood, motionless save for the kicking of the child. For reasons I still do not understand, I was not afraid of him.

Isabella turned and gave him a passionate kiss; as she left him to go back down the stairs, taking the candle with her, he slapped her bottom soundlessly. Then he went alone into Francesco's rooms, guided by the lamp shining there.

I listened to his unfamiliar footfall. With all the awkward grace I could summon, I moved stealthily down the stairs, past the intruder, who had paused in my husband's study.

I went to the kitchen hearth and took the large iron poker, then moved quietly back up the stairs, to Francesco's study.

Draped in shadow, I watched as the stranger stood in front of Francesco's desk, where he had placed a burning lamp taken from my husband's bedroom. The drawer was open, and the key placed beside it; the stranger had unfolded a piece of paper and was frowning at it, his mouth silently forming words as he read. He was a pretty young man, with a large, strong nose and sharp eyes limned by coal-colored lashes; brown-black curls framed his oval face. He wore an artisan's clothes: a gray tunic that fell almost to his knees, covering patched black leggings. If he had borne my husband's jewels, or our gold or silver, or anything of value, I would have called out for the servants. But he was interested only in what he was reading.

He didn't see me until I stepped forward out of the darkness and demanded, "What are you doing?"

He stopped, his chin lifting in surprise, and when he turned to look at me, the paper fell from his fingers. Miraculously, I reached out and caught it, fluttering, in the air before it reached the ground.

He moved as if to take it from me, but I raised the poker threateningly. He saw my weapon, and his full lips curved in a crescent smile. There was lechery in it, and good humor. Like me, he was fearless. And, like me, he was aware that he simply needed to move a few paces back in order to reach the poker set beside the cold hearth. He glanced swiftly at it, then dismissed the notion.

"Monna Lisa." His tone was that of someone mildly startled to find a friend he knew well, but not in the place he had expected. He looked like a poor apprentice, and his speech was that of a tradesman.

"Who are you?" I demanded.

"The Devil himself." His smile never wavered; his gaze grew bemused and challenging, as if I were the one who had trespassed, not he. He was a brazen, cheerful criminal.

"How do you know my name?"

"You husband will be coming home soon. I should leave, don't you think? Or else we both will be in a good deal of trouble. It's awfully soon for you to be caught in your nightgown with a young man." He eyed the poker, decided I wouldn't use it, and reached for the folded paper in my hand. "Your timing is unfortunate. If I could only have another moment with that letter, please—nothing more—then I shall happily return it to you and be on my way. And you can pretend you never saw me. . . ."

His fingers grazed the paper. He was an instant away from taking it; I made a decision.

"Help!" I cried. "Thief! Thief!"

His smile broadened to show white teeth, with a slight gap between the two front ones. He did not—as I expected him to—make another attempt to seize the letter; instead, his eyes were bright and approving of my tactic.

I shouted again.

"I will say good-bye, then," he said, and dashed down the stairs, his step surprisingly light. I followed him as swiftly as my bulk allowed and watched him fling open the doors to the front entrance. He left them open behind him, and I stared after his dark form as he raced across the curving flagstone drive into the night.

I was utterly perplexed and curious. And when Claudio and Agrippina called out to me, I refolded the paper and slipped it underneath my arm so that it was entirely hidden in the folds of my nightgown.

When they arrived, breathless, frightened, I said, "I must have been dreaming. I thought someone was here . . . but it was no one."

They shook their heads as I sent them back to their rooms; Claudio muttered something about pregnant women.

Once they were gone, I went back upstairs to Francesco's study and held the paper to the lamplight. It was indeed a letter, folded into thirds, the black wax seal broken. The writing was slanted strongly to the right, and thick, as if someone had exerted a great deal of pressure on the quill. The paper itself was worn, as though it had traveled a long way.

> *Your worries about retribution from Alexander are unfounded; the excommunication is mere rumor. When it becomes more than that, we shall use it to our advantage.*
>
> *In the meantime, continue to encourage him to preach against Rome and the* Arrabbiati. *And send me the names of all* Bigi—

The *Bigi*. The gray ones, generally older and established, who supported the Medici. I had heard the term before, on my husband's lips, and my father's.

*—but do nothing more; a strike now would be prema-
ture. I am investigating Piero's plans for invasion. He has
settled for now in Rome, and I have found agents there
willing to deal with him as you did with Pico. If we accomplish that, the* Bigi *will pose little threat.*

As always, your help will be remembered and rewarded.

I refolded the letter and set it back in the desk, in the place
Francesco kept his correspondence, then locked the desk. I paused a
moment to study the key. Isabella had given it to the intruder; was it
the one belonging to my husband or a copy?

I kept it in my hand. If Francesco missed its presence, Isabella
would have to do the explaining, not I.

Then I returned to my bedchamber. Half asleep, Zalumma murmured vague words about hearing a noise downstairs.

"It was nothing. Go to sleep," I said, and she gratefully complied.

I avoided my own bed, and went out onto the balcony to think.
The air was oppressively warm, weighty as water; I breathed it in and
felt it settling heavy inside me, against my lungs, my heart.

. . . continue to encourage him to preach against Rome and the
Arrabbiati.

I thought of Francesco faithfully attending Savonarola's every sermon. Listening carefully to every word. Coming home to his lavish
palace and spoiling me with jewels. Riding out each night to visit his
harlots.

. . . willing to deal with him as you did with Pico.

I thought of Pico with the goblet in his hands, smiling at Lorenzo;
of Pico, hollow-eyed and gaunt. Of Francesco saying softly, *Pico . . . ?
He was an associate of Lorenzo's, was he not? Alas . . . he is not expected to survive much longer.*

I had thought the greatest danger to myself, my father, was for
Francesco simply to open his mouth, to reveal my connection to the
Medici. To speak.

*It would be a terrible thing for your father to undergo any more
suffering. A terrible thing, if he were to die.*

I thought I had understood my husband. I understood nothing.

The world was hot and heavy and stifling. I put my head upon my knees, but couldn't catch my breath to cry.

My body opened up; I heard the splash of liquid and realized that I was the source. My chair, my legs, my gown were all soaked, and when I stood, startled, a cramp seized me so violently I thought I was turning inside out.

I cried out and seized the balcony's edge, and when Zalumma, wide-eyed and gasping, appeared, I told her to bring the midwife.

LVI

$\mathcal{F}$rancesco named the boy Matteo Massimo: Massimo, after Francesco's father, and Matteo, after his grandfather. I accepted the patriarchial naming dutifully; I had always known I could not name him Giuliano. And I was pleased to learn that Matteo meant "gift of God." God could have given me none better.

Matteo was amazing and beautiful, and gave me back my heart. Without him, I could not have borne what I had learned in my husband's study; without him, I had no reason to be courageous. But for his sake, I kept my counsel, and told only Zalumma of the letter—a necessity, since she would notice the key I had kept, and which Francesco never mentioned.

When I recited the line about Pico, she understood at once and crossed herself in fear.

Matteo was baptized the day after his birth, at San Giovanni, where I had been married for the second time. The formal christening was held two weeks after, at Santissima Annunziata, some distance to the north in the neighboring district of San Giovanni. For many generations, Francesco's family had maintained a private chapel there. The church stood on one side of the piazza with the orphanage, the Ospedale della Santa Maria degli Innocenti, opposite. The gracefully arching colonnades of the buildings—each bearing Michelozzo's stamp—faced the street.

I found the chapel comforting. Save for the bronze crucifix of an anguished Christ, whitewashed walls rose bare above an altar carved from dark wood, braced on either side by two iron candelabra as tall and twice as broad as I. The blond glow from twenty-four candles fought to ease the windowless gloom. The room smelled of dust, of wood and stone, of sweet incense and candlewax, and echoed silently with centuries of murmured prayers.

Since my son's birth, I had kept my distance from Francesco; my hatred, my disgust, my fear, were so great I could scarcely bring myself to look at him. His manner remained unchanged—solicitous and mild—but now, when I studied him, I saw a man capable of Pico's murder and perhaps Lorenzo's. I saw a man who had helped to oust Piero, and thus brought about my Giuliano's death.

I had tried to let my maternal devotion obliterate any consideration of my husband's dark dealings with Savonarola, as if forgetfulness could magically protect Matteo from them. I had tried—but as I sat in the chapel and beamed at my child, the knowledge that Francesco sat beside me sickened me.

Uncle Lauro and Giovanna Maria served as godparents. Matteo was an impossibly content child; he slept through most of the ceremony, and when he woke, he smiled. I sat, still weary after the long labor, and watched with joy as my father held the baby and Lauro answered for him.

Afterward, as my father proudly bore his grandchild down the aisle and the others followed, I paused to take Matteo's certificate from the priest. He was young and nervous; his voice had cracked several times during the ceremony. When I took hold of the certificate, he did not let go, but glanced surreptitiously at the others; when he reassured himself they were preoccupied with the baby, he hissed at me:

"At night. Read this only at night—tonight, when you are alone."

I recoiled . . . then looked down at my hands. He had given me more than the single piece of parchment; beneath it he had tucked a piece of paper, neatly folded.

Thinking he was mad, I walked swiftly away from him and hurried after the others.

Outside, in the piazza, I had almost joined up with them when a young monk stepped into my path. He wore the black robes of the Servants of Mary, the monastic order whose convent was housed there, at Santissima Annunziata. His cowl had been raised, leaving his brow and eyes in shadow; over his arm was a large basket filled with eggs. As I swept by him, he said, in a low voice, "A beautiful child, Monna."

I turned back to smile. And found myself looking at the familiar smirk of the Devil himself.

"*You,*" I whispered.

The recognition pleased him. He leaned into the light, which revealed amusement in his eyes—tempered by anxiety that my husband might notice. "Tonight," he said softly. "Alone." Then he turned and walked briskly on.

As I joined the others, who were talking and fawning over Matteo before Francesco returned to work at his *bottega,* my husband looked up from his presumed son, his gaze gentle, absent. "Who was that?" he asked.

"No one," I said, moving to join him. I held the certificate tightly in my hand, making sure it entirely covered the smuggled note. "No one at all."

I told no one about the note—not even Zalumma. But after she went downstairs at noon to eat with the other servants and left me alone with Matteo on my balcony, I unfolded the piece of paper. The sun was overhead in a cloudless sky, but I could not wait—nor did I see any reason to. Matteo lay, warm and soft, against me. Dared I become embroiled in more deceit?

When I stared at the paper, I let go a sound of disgust. It was blank, utterly blank. The Devil had played a joke—and a poor one, at that.

Had the hearth been lit, I would have thrown it into the fire. But I curbed my temper, smoothed out the creases, and put it in a drawer. I intended to use it for correspondence, since it was of fine quality, neatly cut and bleached white.

Late that night, the sound of Matteo's wailing in the distant nursery woke me; it stopped quickly once the wet nurse rose to feed him, but I could not return to sleep. The air was unseasonably warm; I lay sweating on my bed and fidgeted restlessly while Zalumma slept on her cot.

The words of the priest returned to me: *Read this only at night—tonight, when you are alone.*

I rose. In the darkness, I moved with deliberation and care, despite the fact that Zalumma was difficult to wake. I lit a candle, opened the drawer beside my bed very slowly, and retrieved the paper given me by the priest.

Feeling both foolish and frightened, I held it up to the flame.

I stared into the white blankness and frowned—until inspiration struck. I brought the paper closer to the heat, so close that the flame flared toward it and began to darkly smoke.

Before my eyes, letters began to appear, transparent and watery brown. I drew in a silent, startled breath.

> *Greetings.*
>
> *I regret I could not respond to your earlier letter.*
> *Tomorrow at sext, go unaccompanied to ask God for the answer.*

For centuries, the faithful had divided the day into hours of prayer: The most familiar were matins, at dawn, and vespers, in the evening. After dawn, there came the third hour of the morning, terce, and the sixth hour, sext, at midday.

I stared at the writing, at the perfectly vertical letters, with the long, flourished *f*'s and *l*'s, the squat *n*'s, the careless spelling. I had seen it only twice before in my life, but I recognized it at once.

Greetings, Madonna Lisa, from Milan. . . .

LVII

*F*or the remainder of the night I did not sleep, but lay in my bed pondering the letter. Go pray, it had said. *Unaccompanied.* Surely this meant I should leave the palazzo; but there were easily a hundred churches in Florence. Where had he meant for me to go?

In the end, I decided only one place was logical: Santissima Annunziata, our family chapel, where I could easily go to pray at matins or sext without arousing suspicion, where I had last encountered the Devil.

In the morning, I rose without saying anything to Zalumma, but she sensed my agitation and asked me what was troubling me. When I told her of my intention to pray—alone—she scowled. I rarely went anywhere without her.

"This has to do with the letter," she said. Her words gave me a start, until I realized she was referring to the letter the devilish young intruder had dropped, the one I had told her about. "I know you don't mean to frighten me, Madonna, but I can't help worrying. I would not like to think you are becoming involved in dangerous matters."

"I would never be so foolish," I said, but even I heard the uncertainty in my tone.

She shook her head. "Go alone, then," she said darkly, pressing against the limits of what a slave might say to a mistress. "Just remember that you have a child."

My answer held a trace of heat. "I would never forget."

The driver took me to Santissima Annunziata. I directed him to wait in the open square in front of the church, across from the graceful colonnades of the Foundling Hospital. Just as the bells began to call the faithful, I stepped over the threshold of the narthex, passed the monks and worshipers moving into the sanctuary, and made my way to our little chapel.

The room was empty, which both disappointed and relieved me. No priest awaited; the candles were unlit, the air unclouded by incense. I had made no arrangements, had told no one save Zalumma and the driver of my coming. Uncertain, I went to the altar and knelt. For the next few minutes, I calmed myself by reciting the rosary. When I at last heard light, quick footsteps behind me, I turned.

The Devil stood smiling, in his guise as Servite monk. His cowl covered his head; his hands held folds of black fabric.

"Monna Lisa," he said. "Will you come with me?" He was trying to play the role, to be polite and circumspect, but he could not entirely mask the slyness in his voice, his eyes.

In answer, I rose. As I approached him, he proffered the black fabric; the folds came loose, revealing a cloak.

"This is silly," I said, more to myself than to him.

"Not at all," he replied, and held the cloak open for me, his gaze darting all the while at the chapel door. "It will make sense shortly."

I let him drape the cloak over me, let him raise the cowl and pull it forward so that my cap and veil were covered, my face obscured. The black cotton hung low, trailing on the floor so that it hid my skirts.

"Come," he said.

He led me back out onto the street, a safe distance from where my carriage waited; the plaza was busy, filled with men and children and vendors, so that no one noticed two friars. He steered me to a rickety wagon tied to a post and harnessed to an aging, swaybacked horse.

"Let me help you up." He gestured for me to climb into the seat.

"No." I realized suddenly that this young man had been capable of breaking into my house like a thief. How could I be certain that he did not mean to abduct and question me about my husband's secret activities?

He raised his hands in a show of disgusted innocence. "Then don't come. Go back to your pretty palace. Close your eyes."

He meant what he said; he had taken a step away from me. If I wanted, I could leave him and go back into the chapel. I could walk across the piazza to my driver. "Help me up," I said.

He did so, then untied the reins and climbed up beside me. "A few precautions first." He reached for a bit of cloth on the seat between us. Quickly, deftly, he shook out the folds and reached inside my raised hood. His fingers, so fast and nimble, teased the fabric around my eyes, around the back of my head, and tied it before I understood what he was doing.

I was blindfolded. Panicked, I raised my hands.

He clicked his tongue as if he were soothing an animal. "Hush. No harm will come. This is for your safety, not mine." I shuddered at the feel of something soft brushing against my cheek and pulled back again at the sensation of it being stuffed into my ears. All sound was dulled—the noise of the crowd in the plaza became an unintelligible thrum—but I could hear the Devil speaking, no doubt loudly for my sake.

"It's all right. We'll be there soon. . . ."

The cart jerked and began to move; I swayed and held the edge of the seat to keep my balance. We rode for several minutes. I did my best to listen to where we were going, but I understood why I had been summoned precisely at midday. All the church bells had already sounded; there were none singing—each in its own peculiar voice—to indicate what part of the city we were in.

At last the wagon rolled to a stop. The young Devil's voice instructed me to turn to the right. I heard movement, felt hands reaching for me; with their help, I climbed blindly from the wagon. He took my elbow, and urged me to move quickly, just short of a run; I lifted my skirts, fearful of tripping. Even with the unspun wool in my ears, even without sight, I sensed the change as we moved from the sun-warmed air inside, where the air was closer and cool.

Fingers gripped my arm, forced me to stop; my guide gave a low whistle. A pause, then the sound of a different whisper, low and muffled, unintelligible through the wool. A warm body stood before me, then turned. The Devil and I followed. We walked a short pace, then climbed a flight of stairs. I was made again to stop, and listened to the groan of heavy wood sliding against stone, as if a wall were being pushed aside. A faint breeze stirred as a door opened.

I was led at a more leisurely pace for a moment, over a floor gritty from a dusting of sand. I had passed by enough artists' *botteghe* to recognize the pungent smells of boiling linseed oil and caustic lime. I was pressed to sit upon a low-backed chair. In a smug, cheery tone, the Devil addressed a third party, loud enough so that I could clearly distinguish each word.

"Ask and you shall receive."

"Will you bring what I asked for?"

"If I must. After that, how long do I have to myself?"

"Give us no more than half an hour, to be safe." The voice was masculine, soft. "Make sure we don't run over the time."

At the sound of the voice, I reached for the blindfold and pulled it up and off my head.

The Devil was already gone, his steps sounding in the corridor. The man standing over me, reaching for the piece of cloth at the same time I removed it, was clean-shaven, with softly waving shoulder-length hair streaked brown and iron, parted in the middle. He, too, wore the habit of a Servant of Mary.

For an instant, I failed to recognize him. Without the beard, his chin appeared sharply, unexpectedly pointed, his cheekbones and jaw more angular; the stubble that glinted in the diffused light was now mostly silver. He was still handsome; had his features been any more perfect—the eyes less deep-set, the bridge of the nose less prominent, the upper lip less stingy—he would have been merely pretty. Leonardo smiled gently at my confusion, which made the creases in the corners of his light gray eyes more noticeable.

I pulled the wool from my ears and said his name. Instinctively, I rose. The sight of him evoked memories of my Giuliano, of Lorenzo.

I remembered his letter to Giuliano, advising him of the Duke of Milan's intentions, and felt grateful. I wanted to embrace him as a dear friend, as a family member.

He felt the same. I saw it in his brilliant if uncertain smile, in his arms, which hung determinedly by his sides but tensed with the desire to rise, touch, enfold. Had he been able, he would have lifted his fingertips to my face and read the contours there. He loved me, and I did not understand why.

Behind him was a window covered by a piece of canvas, cut to the window's precise dimensions, hung from a rod and attached to ropes which served as pulleys to raise or lower it. At the moment, the canvas was raised, revealing a thick layer of oiled paper—opaque enough to bar all scenery, translucent enough to permit yellow filtered light.

"Please sit," he said, then gestured to a stool. "May I?" When I nodded, he pulled it across the stone and sat down in front of me.

Behind him stood an easel bearing a large wooden slate; I leaned forward and caught a glimpse of cream-colored paper folded over the top edge of the slate and pressed against the easel to hold it in place. To the left of the easel, a lamp burned on a small table bearing scattered pieces of charcoal and a small pile of downy chicken feathers. On the floor beside it was a basket of eggs, a stoppered bottle of oil, and a few crumpled, stained rags.

"Madonna Lisa," he said warmly. The robe's severe black emphasized the hollows of his cheeks. "It has been a long time." Abruptly, an odd reserve overtook him. The smile faded; his tone grew more formal. "Please forgive the secrecy. It protects you as well as us. I hope Salai did not frighten you."

Salai: Little Devil. The perfect nickname. I let go the briefest of laughs. "No. Not much."

He brightened at my amused expression. "Gian Giacomo is his given name, but it hardly suits him. Incorrigible, that boy. He came to me as a street urchin; over the past several years, I have done my best to educate him. He has learned his letters, albeit badly, and makes a passable artist's apprentice. Still, I despair, sometimes, of ever teaching him more civilized ways. But he is loyal to the death, and thus very

useful." His tone grew kindly. "You look well, Madonna. Motherhood suits you. Salai says you have a fine son."

"Matteo, yes." I bloomed.

"A good name. And is he healthy?"

"Very!" I couldn't contain my enthusiasm. "He eats all the time
and wants more. And he is always moving, except when he
sleeps. . . ."

"Does he take after you?"

"I think so. His eyes are blue now, like agates, but they'll darken
soon enough, I'm sure. And he has so much hair, so soft, with little
curls—I take my finger, like so, at his crown, and make it all twist together in a big ringlet . . ." I faltered as I caught myself. Francesco's
eyes were icy blue, his hair quite straight. I had almost admitted that
my son looked like his father—with curling hair, and eyes that would
certainly be dark. I had been on the verge of describing the sweet dimple in his cheek—Giuliano's dimple.

My tone cooled. "It seems you know a great deal about me and my
husband," I said. "Are you back in Florence? I thought you were at
Ludovico's court in Milan."

His expression was indecipherable. "I am. But I have come to
Florence for a little while, on holiday."

"And you have brought me here, with all this secrecy,
because . . . ?"

He did not answer because Salai arrived with a tray bearing wine,
and cheese, and nuts. Leonardo rose and took it, then banished his assistant; he took the tray over to a long, narrow table that covered almost the entire expanse of the wall behind us. He had a good deal of
difficulty making enough space to set it down.

I turned, thinking to offer help, and was so fascinated by what I
saw that I rose and went over to investigate. On the table were levels
and wooden slices with long, sharp edges; heaps of gray-white minever pelts, with holes where the hairs had been painstakingly plucked,
one by one, were arranged in heaps next to a pair of scissors. There
were piles, too, of feathers—the largest, darkest ones from vultures,
the paler ones from geese, the smallest, most delicate from doves—and

of translucent, wiry pig bristles. On the far end was a wooden bucket, streaked with lime and covered with a cloth; the floor beneath was speckled with plaster. Near it, in neat, careful rows, small, rolled pellets of color—white, black, yellow-tan, warm pink—lay drying on a cloth beside a large pestle and mortar, which held a few tiny nuggets of brilliant malachite. There was also a large slab of red stone which held a pile of dark yellow-brown powder, a palm-sized grinding stone, and a thin wooden spatula with a sharp edge. A number of paintbrushes were in various stages of construction: a vulture feather had been plucked, the tip cut away. A thick bunch of pig bristles had then been carefully inserted into the opening and tied firmly in place with waxed thread. There were a number of very slender spindle-shaped wooden sticks; one had been inserted into the barrel of the quill so that it could withstand the pressure of an artist's hand.

"This is a painter's studio," I said to myself, delighted.

Leonardo had set the tray down and studied me, amused, as he poured wine into a goblet. "After a fashion; it's only temporary. The one in Milan is much nicer. Go ahead, touch whatever you like. Please."

I drew in a breath. I reached for a half-finished brush that wanted a handle. It was made from a dove's stripped feather; the creator had carefully inserted white minever fur, strand by strand, into the cutaway quill, and trimmed the brush to an impossibly sharp point. I touched the silky tip with my finger and smiled. It was an instrument for painting the finest detail: a single hair, an eyelash.

I set it down and pointed to the dried pellets. The colors were amazingly uniform. "And how are these made? And used?"

He set one goblet down and filled another; my questions pleased him. "You see the ocher there, on the porphyry?" He indicated the powder on the red stone slab. "The best ocher is found in the mountains. I found this in the forests outside of Milan. There, if you dig, you can find veins of white and ocher and sinoper of all shades, from black to a light reddish brown. The mineral is many times washed, then many times ground, until it's brilliant and pure. Then it is worked up with linseed oil—or water, if one prefers—and dried. This particular black here isn't sinoper, but from burned almond shells, which makes a very nice, workable color."

"And this? Is this sinoper?" I pointed at a pink pellet.

"The *cinabrese*? It's made from a mixture of lime white and the very lightest shade of sinoper. For painting flesh. When I'm ready to paint, I crush a bean with linseed oil, as much as I need." He paused and gave me a strangely curious, shy glance. "I know we have many things to discuss, Madonna. But I had hoped . . ." He handed me a goblet of wine. I was too nervous to want it, but I accepted it out of courtesy, and took a sip so that he felt free to drink from his own glass. He took a token swallow and set it down. "I had hoped we might relax a bit before launching into difficult subjects. And I had hoped you might consent to sit for me, if only for a little while today."

"Sit for you?"

"For your portrait."

I let go a short laugh of disbelief. "What would be the point?" I challenged. "Lorenzo is dead. And Giuliano . . ." I didn't finish.

"I would still like to complete the work."

"Surely you are doing this for some reason other than a sense of obligation to dead men."

He did not answer at once. He turned his face toward the viewless window, bathing his features, his hair, in the buttery glow. His eyes were clear as glass, almost colorless, filled with light. "I saw your mother," he said.

He spoke so softly I was not sure I had heard aright. I jerked up my head. "What do you mean? You knew my mother?"

"I was acquainted with her. She and your . . . her husband, Ser Antonio, were often guests at the Medici palazzo in those days. Before she became infirm. I was never introduced to Ser Antonio—he was quite shy and often remained out in the garden, or speaking to the stablehands. But I sat twice beside your mother at banquets. And I spoke to her often at Carnival celebrations. Like you, she had a good eye for art. She appreciated it, understood it."

"Yes." I could not speak beyond a whisper. "So she was often at the Medici palazzo?"

He gave a slow nod. "Lorenzo was quite taken with her—as a friend. He showed her his collection, of course. He respected her opinion greatly. Her family had always been friends with the Tornabuoni—the family of Lorenzo's mother—and that was how they met. Through Lorenzo, of course, she met Giuliano."

"Was she—did everyone know she was having an affair with him?"

His eyelids lowered. "No, Madonna. Your mother was a woman of great virtue. I honestly don't believe that she and Giuliano—" He broke off; to my surprise, he flushed.

"You don't believe they were . . . together . . . until?" I prompted. I did not want to embarrass him, but I had waited for years to learn the truth about my mother's life.

He lifted his gaze, but would not look directly at me. "The night before Giuliano was murdered—I saw her on the Via de' Gori just outside the Medici palazzo. She was going to see him; she was radiant with joy, so happy. And . . . the light was very tender, very gentle. It was dusk, and she stepped from the shadows. I . . ." His voice trailed; he was overwhelmed by the task of trying to convey what he had seen, something numinous and fleeting. "There was no harshness of line, no clear delineation between her skin and the air that surrounded it. She emerged from the darkness, yet she was not separate from it, not separate from the sky or the street or the buildings. And it seemed as though . . . she were outside time. It was an amazing moment. She looked to be more than a woman. She was a Madonna, an angel. The light was . . . remarkable." He stopped himself; his tone became practical. "You must forgive me for such foolish ravings."

"They're not ravings. They sound like poetry."

"You know how beautiful she was."

"Yes."

"Imagine her a hundred times more beautiful. Imagine her lit from within. I wanted very badly to paint her, but . . . Giuliano was murdered, of course. And then Anna Lucrezia fell ill."

"She wasn't ill," I said. "Her husband couldn't father children. He struck her when he learned she was pregnant." It felt odd to speak of my father so distantly, so coldly, when I loved him despite all his sins.

Leonardo's eyes flickered with anger and pain, as if he had been struck himself. "So. He always knew."

"He always knew."

It took him a long moment to gather himself. "I am sorry for it. That night, I had resolved to paint your mother. I had wanted to capture that beautiful essence and show her as joyful. As content. The way she was then, going to Giuliano, not the way she became. She had a natural radiance—and you have it, too, Madonna Lisa. I see her in you. And if I could be permitted to record it . . ." He broke off. "I know it is terribly awkward to have you sit now, but I have learned the capriciousness of fate. She was with Giuliano that night; she was happy. And the next day, he was gone. Who knows where you or I will be tomorrow?"

He might have said more in an effort to make his argument, but I silenced him by laying a hand upon his forearm. "Where," I asked, "would you like me to sit?"

He let me look at the charcoal sketch upon the easel first, the *cartone*, or cartoon, as he called it. It was made from the drawing done in the garden at Santo Spirito, the day after Lorenzo's funeral. No longer was I glancing over my unfinished shoulder at the artist, as I had been in the silverpoint drawing; now I sat with my full face shown directly to the viewer, with my shoulders and body turning only slightly away. No longer was I only a head with the merest intimation of shoulders and headdress; I had hair, long and free as a young girl's. I had a décolleté that would bring down the wrath of Savonarola's militant cherubs. I had hands, and enough of a body to convey the fact that I was sitting.

As I stood beside Leonardo, gazing at the drawing on the easel, he glanced at me, made a small sound of disgust, and at once retrieved a chicken feather from the little table and very lightly swept it over the paper. The feather's edge darkened; the charcoal beneath it disappeared.

"Sit," he said, utterly distracted. "The chin. I must get it right."

I went and sat. Feather still in his hand, he followed me and, with meticulous fussiness, arranged me just so: chin perfectly straight, with no tilt up or down, head turned at a precise angle away from my body. He did not care, at the moment, about the positioning of my hands. In fact, he gave me my wine goblet and insisted I have some before he started.

I sat in silence as he finished erasing his crime; then he took up the charcoal fastened to its wooden stick and, with a deft, flourished move, corrected the chin. And then he stared at me. Stared and checked my nose against the drawing, my right eye, my left, each eyebrow, and my nose. I grew restless and let my gaze wander: It lit upon the wall near the easel—on a small panel of wood that had been coated with plaster and was drying. Next to it was a sharp wooden slice which had obviously been used to scrape the panel's surface smooth.

"Is that what you will use—for the painting?" I asked.

He frowned, faintly annoyed at the interruption. "Yes. It needs to dry for a few days."

"Is the surface made of just plaster?"

"Plaster," he said, "of a sort. Very fine *gesso sottile,* plaster of Paris with some of my own adulterations. First comes the white poplar. Then good linen is glued to it, to make a base for the gesso. Then it is made very smooth, like ivory. When it dries, I'll transfer this sketch to it."

"You'll copy it?"

"I'm far too lazy for that. I prick the *cartone,* attach it to the gessoed panel, and sprinkle powdered charcoal over it. It goes on very quickly that way. Then we start the painting. Which we will do the next time we meet, if fate permits." He gave a small sigh. "Please take some more wine, Madonna."

"You are trying to get me drunk," I said. I meant it as a joke, but when I caught his eye, he did not smile.

"We have enough difficult things to talk about, don't you agree?"

In answer, I took an earnest sip of my wine. It was cheap and slightly sour. "Why don't we talk about them, then? I'm tired of appearing content and angelic." I stared up at him. "You didn't bring me here just to paint my portrait or speak of happier times."

His tone darkened. "Very well. Tell me the truth, Madonna. I . . . saw you with Francesco del Giocondo—"

He was going to say more, but I interrupted. "When?"

"At your child's baptism."

So. He had been watching when Salai arranged for me to get the note.

He continued. "Do you love him?"

His tone was bitter. My cheeks burned; I stared down at the stone floor.

He let go a barely audible sigh, then softened. "Am I mistaken, or are relations between you strained—at least, on your part?"

I raised my face. "How do you know that?"

My answer seemed to please him. "Through casual observation. It is very difficult to completely conceal one's emotions. And I did not detect much affection in your gestures. This is not the first time I have successfully divined such . . . unhappiness between husband and wife."

"I . . ." Guilt surged through me. I remembered those horrible days when I had sacrificed myself to Francesco for Matteo's sake, when I had permitted myself to be called a whore. "My father had been arrested. Francesco offered to save him, if . . ."

I could not finish. He nodded to indicate I did not need to. "Then I must ask you whether you are still loyal to Giuliano. To the Medici."

I suddenly understood. He had had no way to know that I had been forced into marriage with Francesco; he had no way of knowing whether I was privy to Francesco's political schemes, whether I approved.

"I would never betray Giuliano! I loved him. . . ." I cupped a hand against my cheek.

He stood unmoving in front of the easel, the stick of charcoal frozen above the drawing. "Do you not love him still?"

"Yes," I said. Tears welled in my eyes and overflowed; I did nothing to stop them. "Of course, yes. When he died, I wanted to die. I would have, by my own hand, had I not carried his child. . . ." I panicked at my unintended admission. "You must tell no one—not even Salai! If Francesco ever knew, he would take him from me—"

"Giuliano . . . dead." Very slowly, he set the charcoal down on the little table, without looking at it. "Few people have heard this. Most believe he is still alive."

"No. Francesco told me. His body was found in the Arno. . . . The Lord Priors took it and secretly buried it outside the city walls. They were afraid because of what happened to Messer Iacopo."

He digested this. "I see. This explains a great deal." For a long, uncomfortable moment—a moment in which I struggled to regain my composure, to suppress all the grief I had never been allowed to express fully—he was silent. Then he said, very carefully, "So you are still loyal to the Medici. And you would not shrink from helping Piero to recapture Florence? And you can guard your tongue?"

"Yes, to both questions. I would do anything—so long as it brings my son Matteo no harm." I wiped away my tears and looked up at him. His gaze was troubled, but the barrier between us was beginning to crumble.

He had not known, I realized. He had not known that *I* knew Giuliano was dead. Perhaps he had thought me capable of betraying him, of marrying Francesco when I thought my first husband might still be alive. Yet he had still been cordial; he had even asked me to sit.

"Believe me when I say that I understand your concerns about your child. I would never ask you to do anything that directly endangered him." He paused. "I was rather surprised when I received your letter," he said, his tone soft in deference to my weeping. "I . . . had reason to think you had perished the night the Medici brothers fled Florence. I did not, you see, know your handwriting. So I did not respond. Later, I learned you had married Francesco del Giocondo—"

"I read the letter Salai dropped," I interrupted. "The one written to my husband. I . . . had no idea he was somehow involved with Savonarola until that night. I don't even know who sent him the letter." I studied him. He still watched me with peculiar intensity; he wanted to believe me, but something held him back.

"It is true," he said, more to himself than me. "When you saw Salai at the christening, you could have told your husband that Salai took the letter from his desk. But it seems you have not."

"Of course not. What do you want me to do? You brought me here for a reason."

"Piero de' Medici wishes to speak to you," he said.

I gaped at him, thunderstruck. "Piero? Piero is here?"

"He intends to retake the city. And he needs your help. Will he have it?"

"Of course."

He stepped away from the easel and moved over to me. "Good. Go to the Duomo in three days' time, at midday precisely. He will meet you in the north sacristy."

I considered this. "A woman alone, in the sacristy . . . The priests' suspicion will be aroused. If I was seen waiting there—"

"The priests know what to do. Tell them Gian Giacomo sends you. They will take you to a secret passage accessible only from the sacristy."

"Why did Piero not simply tell you to relay his message to me? Why would he risk meeting with me?"

"I am merely an agent, Madonna. I do not presume to understand him."

He rose and called for Salai, then dismissed me with a bow. Salai tied the cloth around my eyes once more, and I was taken back to Santissima Annunziata in the same manner I had left.

Zalumma was waiting for me in my chambers. I knew better than to try to disguise my unease; she could smell the encounter with Leonardo on me as surely as if it had been attar of roses. But I had already decided to share no details, for her sake. Before I could speak, she said, very quietly so that no one standing in the hall could hear: "I know that you have gone to meet someone, and that this has something to do with the letter the intruder found. It is not my place to ask questions. But I am here. In whatever way I can help, I will. Instruct me as you wish."

I took her hands and kissed her as if she were my sister and not my slave. But I said nothing of Leonardo or Piero; such names could cost her her head.

And they could cost me mine. I went to the nursery and sat a long time with Matteo in my arms, ran my hand over the tender, vulnerable skin of his crown, over the wisps of impossibly fine hair. I kissed his soft cheek and smelled milk and soap.

Three days passed quickly.

Claudio lifted a brow at my unusual request to be driven to the Duomo. I did so casually, as if it were a whim, as if it had not been years since my first and last visit there.

Just before noon, as the bells chimed deafeningly, I crossed beneath the massive, impossible cupola and knelt a short distance away from the high altar, carved from dark wood and limned with gold.

I mouthed prayers along with the others, fumbling for words I had known since childhood; I knelt and stood and crossed myself at the appointed times. Attendance was sparse, as most worshipers now favored San Marco and her famous prior, or San Lorenzo, where he often preached.

The instant the ritual ended, I rose and went quickly to the cathedral's north end, where the main sacristy lay—the room where the young Lorenzo had sought safety the morning of his brother's murder. The doors were engraved bronze, very tall, and so heavy that when I went to open them, they scarcely moved.

Just as I made my second attempt, I heard steps behind me and turned. Two priests—one young, one gray-headed and worn—approached the sacristy bearing the gold chalice and the crystal decanter of water for the wine.

"Here now," the older one said. "Do you seek the counsel of a priest, Madonna?" His tone held a note of reserve; it was odd for a woman to loiter near the sacristy, but as I was clearly wellborn, he was polite.

I had to clear my throat before the words would leave me. "Gian Giacomo directed me to come here."

"Who?" He frowned, mildly suspicious.

"Gian Giacomo," I repeated. "He said you would understand."

He shook his head, and shared a swift, uneasy glance with his companion. "I'm sorry, Madonna. I don't. Why would someone send you here?"

"Gian Giacomo," I said, louder. "Perhaps there is another priest who can help me. . . ."

Now both priests were frowning. "We know no one by that name," the older priest said firmly. "I'm sorry, Madonna, but we have tasks to attend to." With his free hand, he pushed open the heavy door to admit his fellow, then entered himself and let it close on me.

I paced there a moment, hoping that another priest might come by. Had no one gotten the message? Had Piero been captured? Surely Leonardo had no reason to draw me into a trap. . . .

The priests emerged from the sacristy to find me still there. "Go home!" the younger commanded, exasperated. "Go home to your husband!"

"This is unseemly, Madonna," the elder said. "Why have you come here asking about a man? Where is your escort?"

It occurred to me then that it might be assumed Gian Giacomo was the name of my lover, whom I intended to meet for a tryst. In these days of Savonarola's reign, an accusation of adultery would be as dangerous as my true mission; I apologized and hurried from the church.

I rode home, unnerved and angry. Leonardo had just made a fool of me, and I had no idea why.

LVIII

*O*nce home, I went straight to the nursery and sat with Matteo
in my arms. I did not want to see Zalumma, to face her
silent scrutiny when I was angry and liable to talk. I ordered
the wet nurse to leave and rocked my son. When Matteo reached up
and pulled a tendril of my hair—so hard that it caused real pain—I
permitted myself to cry a bit.

I had not realized until then just how badly I had wanted to do
something that would permit me to honor Giuliano's memory. Since
his death, I had been forced to keep silent about him, to behave as
though my marriage to him had never occurred. Now, my hopes had
been turned into an ugly joke.

I had been alone with my son for almost an hour when Zalumma
arrived quietly and stood by the door. "I thought you might be hungry," she said softly.

I shook my head. She turned to leave, then stopped and glanced beyond the door to make certain no one stood out in the hallway.

"Someone left a letter," she said quickly. "On the table by your
bed. Elena or Isabella is bound to notice it soon."

I handed Matteo to her without a word, went to my room, and
closed the door behind me.

The paper was pristine white, with neatly trimmed edges, and, as I knew even before I unfolded it, completely blank.

The morning had been cold, and a feeble fire still burned in the hearth. I walked over to it and held the paper low, close to the flames, and crouched so that I could read the pale brown letters as they emerged:

Forgive me. God will explain tomorrow, when you go at noon to pray.

I threw the paper onto the fire and watched as it burned.

I said nothing to Zalumma. The next day at noon I went to the chapel at Santissima Annunziata to pray.

This time, when the Devil-cum-monk named Salai approached me, I glared at him. Once in the wagon, he tied the cloth around my eyes and whispered, "This time, it truly *is* only for your protection, Monna." I did not speak. When the blindfold was at last loosed and I sat looking into Leonardo's face, I did not smile.

His voice and manner were hushed and sympathetic. "I am sorry, Madonna Lisa," he said. Lean and tall in his loose monk's robes, he stood in front of the paper-covered window. The stubble was missing; he had shaved recently, and his sculpted cheek bore the red nick of the razor. The easel was empty; the wooden slate with the drawing now lay, covered with a layer of black soot, on the long table. "It was a cruel trick, but our situation is uncommonly dangerous."

"You lied to me. Piero was not at the Duomo." I faced him with cold fury.

"No. No, he was not." He walked over to stand an arm's length in front of me; in his pale eyes, I saw honest sympathy. "Believe me, I did not relish being so unkind. But I had to test you."

"Why? Why would you not trust me?"

"Because you are married to a great enemy of the Medici. And because, though I have known you for a long time, I do not know you well. And . . . there is also the fact that I cannot trust my own judgment concerning you. I am not . . . a disinterested party."

I made a sound of disgust. "Please. Don't think you can fool me by pretending you have feelings for me. I know you can never love me— that way. I know what you were charged with. I know about you and Salai."

His eyes widened abruptly, then narrowed again, bright with fury. *"You know—"* He caught himself; I watched his fists clench, then slowly uncurl. "You are speaking of Saltarelli." His voice was coiled.

"Who?"

"Iacopo Saltarelli. When I was twenty-four, I was accused of sodomy—a simple word you seem to have trouble saying. Since you are so interested in specifics, let me give them to you. I was arrested by the Officers of the Night and taken to the Bargello, where I learned that I had been implicated in an anonymous *denuncia.* It was alleged that I and two other men—Bartolomeo de' Pasquino, a goldsmith, and Lionardo de' Tornabuoni—had engaged in various sexual activities with Iacopo Saltarelli. Saltarelli was all of seventeen. He was licentious, to be sure, and probably earned the charges—but he was also apprentice to his brother, an enormously successful goldsmith on the Via Vaccarechia. Pasquino also owned a *bottega* on the same street, and I frequented both shops because I was often hired by them as a painter.

"I'm sure you've heard of unsuccessful business owners getting rid of their rivals by a well-timed *denuncia?"*

"I've heard that it's done," I said, not kindly.

"According to shop owners on the street, my *denuncia* was written by one Paolo Sogliano. He happened to be the painter for and assistant to a goldsmith on the Via Vaccarechia named Antonio del Pollaiuolo. The charges were dropped for lack of evidence, although many possible witnesses were questioned. And a few years afterward, Sogliano was out on the street."

"There was no truth to it, then." I looked down at my hands.

"There was no truth to it. I ask you to consider how you would have felt in my situation. How you would have felt, being taken from your bed at night to the jail for questioning. How you would have felt, telling your father. How you would have felt, having to rely on your connections with Lorenzo de' Medici—asking him for help—so that you could be freed and go sleep in your own bed instead of in prison. Dante says that sodomites are doomed to wander forever in a fiery desert. I tell you, there can be no worse desert than the inside of a cell in the Bargello." The anger left his tone; the next words came out hesitant, shy. "That does not mean I have never fallen in love with a man. Nor does it mean I have not fallen in love with a woman."

I kept looking down at my hands. I thought of what it had been like for a young man to tell his father he had been arrested for such a crime. I thought of his father's fury, and I flushed.

"As for Salai . . ." Indignance welled up in him again; the words lashed the air. "He is a *boy,* you may have noticed. Oh, he is your age, to be sure, though he might as well be ten years your junior; you can see for yourself that he has the maturity of a child. He is not yet old enough to know what he wants. And I am a grown man, and his guardian. To hint that there is anything more to our relationship— outside of a great deal of irritation on my part—is reprehensible."

When I could finally speak, I said, "I apologize for my terrible words. I know what the Bargello is like. They took me there the night Giuliano died. My father was there, too. We were freed only because of Francesco."

His face softened at once.

"Did you really believe I would bring Francesco with me?" I asked, but my tone held no heat. "To arrest Piero? To arrest you?"

He shook his head. "I did not honestly think you would. I judged you to be trustworthy. As I said, I had to test my own judgment. I have . . ." A glimmer of pain crossed his features. "My swiftness to indulge my instincts and feelings has led to great tragedy. I could not permit such a thing to happen again." He stepped over to me and took my hands. "What I did was hurtful, but necessary. And I apologize with all my heart. Will you forgive me, Madonna Lisa, and accept me again as your friend?"

Your friend, he had said, but the emotion in his eyes spoke of something deeper. Before I fell in love with Giuliano, I might easily have given my heart to this man; now I was too damaged even to consider it. Gently, I extricated my hands. "You know I loved Giuliano."

I expected the words to sting slightly, to quell the affection in his eyes. They did not. "I do not doubt it," he said cheerfully, and gazed expectantly at me.

"I forgive you," I said, and meant it. "But before today, I had only my son. Now I have this, too. Do you understand? So don't deny me usefulness."

"I won't," he said softly. "You can be of great use to us."

"Piero is not here, in Florence?"

"No, Madonna. And if your husband thought that he was, he would certainly have tried to arrange for his murder."

I refused to let the words frighten me. "So what shall I do?" I asked. "To be of help?"

"First," he said, "you can tell me what you remember of the letter Salai was reading when you encountered him in Ser Francesco's study."

I told him. Told him that my husband had been ordered to collect the names of all the *Bigi* and to encourage Fra Girolamo to preach against Rome. Salai, it seemed, was a poor reader with a poorer memory. I would make a far better informant.

I was to search Francesco's desk on a nightly basis, if possible, and, if I discovered anything of import, was to signal my discovery by setting a certain book from my library on my night table. I did not ask why: It was obvious to me. Isabella, who had provided Salai with entry into the study, also cleaned my bedchamber each morning and lit the fire each night. I doubted she had full knowledge of what she was involved in, or that Salai told her; she probably thought it was no more than one *Buonomo* spying on another.

The day after I gave the signal with the book, I was to go at sext to Santissima Annunziata, ostensibly to pray.

I was possessed of two hearts: One was heavy with grief at memories stirred by talk of the Medici; the other was light, relieved at last to be able to work toward the removal of Savonarola, the fall of Francesco from power, the second advent of Piero.

"There is a second thing you can do to be of help," Leonardo told me. He led me over to the long table littered with a painter's detritus. The gessoed poplar panel lay flat atop it, covered with the charcoal *cartone* of me. The corners of the paper were weighed down against the panel with four smooth stones; the entire drawing had been sprinkled with glittering pulverized charcoal.

"A bit of magic," Leonardo said. "Don't breathe." He moved the stones aside, and very deliberately caught hold of the upper left and lower right corners of the paper and lifted it straight up off the panel. With extreme care, he moved away from the table and let the powder slide off the drawing into a bin on the floor; swirls of dark dust settled onto his face and clothing like a fine layer of soot.

I remained in front of the panel on the table, still holding my breath. There I was upon the panel's smooth ivory surface, my features blurred and gray and ghostly, waiting to be born.

I sat no more than half an hour lest Claudio become suspicious. Leonardo carried the outlined panel over to the easel. He wanted me to sit on my stool right away, but I demanded the right to examine the tools first. The little table beside the easel now bore three slender brushes of minever fur—each with very fine points of differing size—set in a small tin dish half filled with oil. Upon a small wooden palette lay dried pellets of color, some half crushed; there were three tin dishes, one holding black, the other two each holding two values of a muddy greenish brown.

"Those are almond-shell black and *verdaccio,*" he said, "the black for outlining the features, the other for adding shadows. The *verdaccio* is a mixture of dark ocher, *cinabrese,* lime white, and a dash of black, just enough to cover the very tip of a palette knife."

"If you're painting the outline," I asked, "why should I sit?"

He looked at me as if my question were mad. "I must see how the shadows fall. How the contours of your features are brought forward, how they recede. And I must see your face alive—with a thousand different expressions as your thoughts move—otherwise, how can I make it seem alive for the viewer?"

I let him settle me on my stool then and arrange my hands, my head, my torso at precise angles with a skilled, light touch. When he was satisfied, he went back to stand in front of the easel, and frowned at it.

"Too dark," he said. "I am not in favor of harsh light, which steals softness, but we must have more. . . ." He stepped over to the window and, using a pulley, raised the canvas shade all the way up. Once the degree of brightness suited him, he wondered aloud whether I might take down my hair, for he could not be sure how it now appeared—but an arch look from me silenced him. I could well imagine what Claudio would think if I returned from the chapel with my hair unruly.

At last he took up his brush. I remained still a long time, listening to the whisper of the wet fur against the dried plaster, doing my best not to scratch my nose, not to fidget. Leonardo was intense and impervious; his full attention was focused on the work in front of him. He stared at my face, seeing each curve, each line, each shadow, but he did not see *me*. At last I asked:

"Is this for Piero? Will you give it to him?"

He lifted a brow but did not allow the interruption to affect his concentration. "I am not yet sure whom I will give it to. Perhaps I will give it to no one at all."

I frowned at that. At once he chided softly, "No, no . . . only smiles now. Think only of happy things."

"What happy things? I have none in my life."

He looked up from his work with a look of faint surprise in his pale eyes. "You have your son. Is that not enough?"

I gave a short, embarrassed laugh. "More than enough."

"Good. And you have memories of your Giuliano, yes?"

I nodded.

"Then imagine . . ." His voice grew faintly sad. "Imagine you are with Giuliano again," he said, with such wistfulness that I felt he was speaking to himself as much as to me. "Imagine that you are introducing him to his child."

I let go of my sadness. I imagined. I felt my features melt and soften, but I could not quite smile.

I left eager to do whatever I could to facilitate Piero's advent, but for days after my meeting with Leonardo, my surreptitious nocturnal searches were in vain: The old letter had disappeared from Francesco's desk, but no new one appeared in its place.

On the seventh night, however, I found a letter folded into thirds, with a broken seal of black wax. I opened it with unsteady hands, and read:

> *Piero has been in touch with Virgines Orsini, his soldier-cousin from Naples. He appears to be gathering troops, ostensibly in response to Pope Alexander's request for an army to protect the Pisans from King Charles's return. But who is to say that, once gathered, such a force might not well make its way to Florence, with a different aim?*
>
> *Cardinal Giovanni is of course arguing his brother's case. He has the Pope's ear—but so do I. His Holiness has written a brief, by the way, which shall soon be delivered to the Signoria. He has threatened King Charles with excommunication if he and his army do not leave Italy, and threatened Florence herself with the same if she continues to support Charles. He has also ordered the prophet to cease preaching.*
>
> *Ignore this last, and trust in me. In fact, our prophet should now redouble his fervor, specifically against the Medici. I will ensure that His Holiness eases his stance. As for Charles—it would be best for the friar to begin to distance himself.*

*I have written Ludovico. We cannot trust him but may
need to rely on him for men if Piero decides to make an attempt on the city in the near future.*

*I appreciate your invitation, but my coming to Florence
would be premature. Let us see first what Piero plans.*

*Send my cousins my regards—how sweet it is to see
them home again after so many years, and Messer Iacopo
avenged. Florence has always been, and will ever remain,
our home.*

My cousins . . . Messer Iacopo avenged.

My memory traveled back through the years, to my mother standing in the Duomo, weeping as she spoke of her beloved Giuliano's
death. To the moment I stood staring up at the astrologer, as he sat in
his carriage.

*In your stars I saw an act of violence, one which is your past and
your future. . . . What others have begun, you must finish. . . .*

LIX

*T*he one who writes the letters—he is one of the Pazzi," I said. Leonardo was master of his emotions. Yet as I spoke on that rainy autumnal day, two days after finding the letter, I could clearly see his unease.

Carefully posed, I sat on the chair while he bent over the easel. I had insisted on seeing the beginnings of the portrait before I settled down to sit for him. My features were outlined in black, the edges softened by layers of muddy *verdaccio;* pools of shadow had collected beneath my right jaw, in the hollow of my right cheek, beneath my right nostril. I stared out at the viewer with unsettlingly blank white eyes. My hair had been filled in with flat black. I was surprised to see that—although I always wore it coiled and pinned up, usually veiled—Leonardo had remembered exactly how it appeared years ago, when I wore it loose and flowing to the Palazzo Medici. It hung with just the right amount of waviness and the little hint of curl at the ends.

Five small tin dishes were set out on the little table today: one of oil to hold the brushes, one of the *verdaccio,* and three of varying shades of a grayish color called *terre verte*. These last colors he administered to the panel with a delicate, fluid motion, to create, as he said, "Shadows between shadows between shadows." Dark colors were to come first, followed by the medium tones, then the lightest, layer upon layer upon layer.

I had recited from memory the text from Francesco's mysterious correspondent. I was cold and shivering; my skirts were damp from rain, despite the black cloak Salai had wrapped around me. The room was dark, even at midday, though a lamp cast yellow light against the oiled paper covering the window. The hearth was lit, but even that could not dispel the chill or the gloom. Winter threatened.

Leonardo lifted his gaze and stroked his chin thoughtfully, as if his beard were still there. "It is dangerous," he said at last, "for you to interpret what you have read."

"Am I wrong?"

"The answer to your question is unimportant. What *is* important is your safety."

"I don't care," I responded. "Piero is coming. He's gathering an army. And when he is here, everything will change."

"Perhaps he is coming. Perhaps not . . . Do you really think he would let the Pazzi become aware of his movements?" He lowered the hand which held the brush and looked intently at me.

He was going to say more, but I interrupted him. "This all began long ago, didn't it? With Lorenzo?"

He blinked, and I saw the reticence, the disapproval, in that tiny gesture. "Lorenzo made a grave mistake, giving full vent to his hatred when his brother was murdered. It came to haunt him in his final years. Even after his death, it haunts his sons. The question is whether the cycle of violence can be halted."

"You know who I am," I said. "You told Lorenzo. You gave him a sign, that night at the Palazzo Medici, when you showed me the sculpture of Giuliano."

He lifted a brow at that. "You are far too perceptive, Madonna."

"Did . . . did *my* Giuliano know?"

"Not when you married him, but—" He caught himself. "You should take care that your emotions don't reveal themselves to others." He lifted his brush again, then said, very softly, as if to himself, "Sometimes I wish you had never discovered Salai that night."

"I won't be caught."

"Perhaps not. I realize now you are as clever as your father. Too clever. Again, I urge you not to meditate overlong on your discoveries. Doing so may well lead to your detection, which could cost you your life. Do you understand?"

"I can hold my tongue," I answered, a bit sharply. "I am, as you say, clever. I won't be discovered. After all, I live with a man I despise—and he doesn't know how I feel."

"But I do. I saw it on your face, in your every gesture. Who is to say others have not noticed?"

I fell silent.

His tone eased. "Here. I am not helping matters by speaking glumly. And worse, I have caused you to lose your smile. I know that you are wise and will be discreet. Let us speak about something more cheerful. Your son, perhaps? I'm sure he must resemble you."

His words had the intended effect; I remembered Matteo and softened at once. "He's getting so big. He crawls," I said proudly. "Faster, sometimes, than I can walk. And he looks like me. Dark-eyed, with great long lashes, and his grandmother's full lips. . . . And when I look at him I see his father, of course . . . his hair is softer and curlier, like his."

He looked up from his easel, smiling faintly.

"Do you?" I asked suddenly.

"Do I what?"

"When you look at me, do you see my father? My *real* father?"

His expression darkened, grew unreadable. At last he replied, "I see him. But most of all, I see your mother. You have the same kind of sadness I saw in her when . . ."

"When? Did you ever see her outside of the Palazzo Medici?"

He blinked; his gaze lowered. He looked at the portrait, not at me, as he replied. "I saw her, some time after he died. At Santo Spirito."

I leaned forward, intrigued. "What were you doing on the other side of the Arno?"

He shrugged. "I had commissions all over the city, at many churches. I was going to speak with the Dominican prior about an altarpiece for a chapel. . . ."

"Was she praying? At Mass?"

"Leaving Mass. Her husband was not with her, but her maid—"

"Zalumma."

"The one with the amazing hair? I so wanted to draw it. . . . Yes, her maid was with her. She was pregnant with you."

I was entranced. "How did she look?"

"Beautiful. And broken," he said softly. "Broken, yet somehow hopeful. You gave her reason to continue, I think."

I turned my face away, toward the papered window and the drab light.

"I am sorry," Leonardo said, looking up at me again. "I did not mean to make you sad."

I shrugged, still gazing at the window. "I can't help wondering whether he let her go to Giuliano's funeral."

"He could not stop her," he answered, with such sudden vehemence that I turned my head to stare at him.

"You saw her there?"

"Yes." His cheeks flushed.

I thought of the two of them there—two people in love with the same man—and wondered whether my mother had known, whether they had ever spoken of the fact. I opened my mouth to ask another question, but Leonardo set his brush down carefully into a little dish of oil and stepped from behind the easel. "Nearly an hour has passed; you dare not stay longer," he said firmly. "Madonna, I will be returning to Milan for a time. I am obliged to my patron, the Duke, and I have a commission to paint a Last Supper scene for a refectory. . . ."

"You are leaving?" I could not keep the disappointment from my voice; I rose. Salai's damp black cloak slipped from my shoulders onto the chair.

"I'll be returning, of course, though I cannot say precisely when. In the meantime, Salai will remain here. You will continue just as you have before, except that you will now tell him the content of any letters you discover. And he will relay that content to me."

"But . . . what if Piero comes? What should I do?"

He smiled gently at that. "If Piero comes, you'll have no worries. Your safety, and your child's, will be assured.

"In the meantime . . . you may well learn many things that disturb you, or even anger you. Please understand that there are many things I don't tell you now because it would increase the danger to you . . . and those you love most dearly."

"If you are to return to Milan," I said, "and we may not meet again for a long time . . . I must ask you your response to the letter I sent you so long ago."

He knew precisely what I meant, but was reluctant to reply.

"The assassin in Santa Maria del Fiore, the day Giuliano died," I prompted. "The first man to attack him, the man who escaped. My Giuliano, my husband, told me about him. He said that you told Lorenzo about this man. That you had been in the cathedral when Giuliano the elder was murdered."

"He was wearing a penitent's robes," Leonardo answered shortly. "With a hood. I couldn't see his face clearly."

"But you must have seen part of it. My Giuliano said that you saw him. That his uncle died in your arms."

"I . . . saw a part of it. But it happened more than fifteen years ago; I saw him only for an instant. You can't expect me to remember."

"But I can," I said. "You remembered my face when you saw me only once, at the Palazzo Medici. You sketched it perfectly, from memory. And you told me exactly *how* to remember a face: Surely you used the same technique to remember this one. You carry your little notebook everywhere. I can't believe you never sketched his face—at least the part of it you saw."

Footsteps sounded in the corridor; I turned to see Salai standing in the doorway. "She cannot stay long. The clouds have grown black; a hard rain is coming."

"Understood," Leonardo said, and dismissed the lad with a nod.

He looked back at me and drew in a breath. "I must take my leave of you now."

Unkindly, I said, "When you first met me here, you told me that Piero wanted to see me. And I wanted so badly to believe you that I didn't notice you were lying. But now I see very clearly that you aren't being truthful. You *have* sketched the penitent, haven't you? You must have been looking for him for years. I have the right to see the face of the man who killed my father. Why won't you show it to me?"

His expression grew stony; he waited for me to finish, then after a long moment asked, "Has it occurred to you, Madonna, that it might be better for you *not* to know certain things?"

I began to speak, then stopped myself.

"Giuliano was murdered a long time ago," he said. "His brother Lorenzo is dead. The Medici have been banished from Florence. The assassin—if he still breathes—will certainly not live much longer. What good will it do to distract ourselves with finding one man? And what do you think we should do if we find him?"

Again, I had no answer.

"No noble cause would be served by revenge. We could only stir up old pain, old hatred. We are already trapped in circumstances born of distant mistakes. We must hope not to repeat them."

"I still deserve to know," I countered evenly. "And I don't want to be lied to."

He raised his chin sharply at that. "I will never lie to you. You can trust that. But I *will*, if I deem it best for you, hide the truth. I do not do so lightly. Do not forget, you are the mother of a Medici heir. That is an enormous burden. You and the boy must be protected. And I am sworn to do so, even if my heart did not already demand it."

I stared at him. I was angry, frustrated; yet I trusted him as deeply as I trusted the man who had raised me as his daughter.

"You need to leave," he said softly. "Your driver mustn't become suspicious. And there is the rain."

I nodded. I lifted the damp cloak from my chair and slipped it over my shoulders, then turned to him. "I don't want to say good-bye on unpleasant terms."

"There is no unpleasantness; there is only goodwill." He nodded at the painting. "I will take it with me and work on it, if I am able. Perhaps you will have the chance to sit for me again."

"I know I will." I stepped forward and took his hand; his grip was warm, with the perfect degree of firmness. "Be safe. And well."

"And you, Madonna Lisa. I know that these are difficult times for you. I can only promise that great happiness awaits you at their end."

His tone carried conviction, but I took no comfort in it. My Giuliano was gone; happiness was, for me—as it had been for my mother—buried in the past.

Once again, Salai fastened a dark cloth over my eyes; once again, he stuffed bits of uncarded wool into my ears. With his guiding hand on my elbow, I walked slowly, unsteadily, down a short corridor, then paused as a large piece of wood—a door, I decided, or a large panel—was slid aside for me, rumbling, scraping against the stone floor.

We moved down a flight of stairs—I uncertainly, one hand worrying with my long skirts, my heavy overdress, the sweeping hem of the cloak. There came our usual pause as Salai waited for word from a lookout that the path was clear. The signal was given, and we trotted across smooth floors.

Then, for the first time, we hesitated—in a doorway, I am certain, for beyond, rain crashed down violently, only inches from my face. Errant darts, driven by the wind, grazed my cheeks. Thunder roiled so powerfully, the earth beneath my feet shuddered.

Beside me, Salai tensed, readying himself, and gripped my upper arm. *"Run,"* he commanded, and pulled me with him.

Blindly, I ran. And gasped as sheets of icy water pummeled me. The rain lashed down at a fierce diagonal under my hood, directly into my face; I angled it away and down, trying to shield it, but my blindfold quickly became soaked; the water stung my eyes. I put my free hand to them.

As I did, my shoe caught the soggy hem of my cloak. I lost my footing and fell, torn from Salai's grasp, and came down hard on my free elbow, my knees. I struggled to push myself up; my palm pressed against cold, slick flagstone. At the same time, I raised the back of my wrist and wiped my burning eyes.

The soaked blindfold slipped and fell away. I found myself staring up at Salai's handsome young face, now stricken with panic.

Near us, the horse and wagon waited. And behind him stood the massive walls of a great monastery, one I recognized quite well. He reached for me, tried to restrain me, but it was too late: I turned my head and glanced through the gray downpour at the piazza in the distance behind me.

The graceful colonnades of the Ospedale degli Innocenti, the Foundling Hospital, looked back at me from the other side of the street. Farther down, so far to my left that he appeared no larger than a fly, my driver Claudio had sought refuge beneath a loggia.

Salai and I were on the northern side of the church; Claudio waited for me on the western side, which faced the piazza.

Each time I had met with Leonardo, I had been at Santissima Annunziata the entire while.

LX

*S*alai and I did not speak; the crashing downpour made communication impossible. He pulled me to my feet, pulled the cowl of the cloak back over my head, and we ran again, this time back into the shelter of the monastery. There, in the entry hall of what I presumed was a dormitory, we caught our breaths. My knees and left elbow ached and were no doubt badly bruised, but no real damage had been done.

Salai made no effort to replace my blindfold; indeed, he motioned for me to pull the wool from my ears. He stood so close that our bodies touched, and said, his lips close to my ear, "Now you have the power to betray us all. Wait here. No one should come. If someone does, don't speak—I'll think of something when I return."

I waited. In a moment, Salai returned with a large cloth. He helped me out of the sodden black cloak, then watched as I dried myself off as best I could.

"Good," he said, when I handed the cloth back to him. "I was worried as to how you would explain your . . . damp condition to your coachman."

"You need not tell Leonardo," I said. "About my knowing where we are."

He snorted. "It's not as if we had any hope of hiding it from him, Monna. He can smell a lie as surely as we can smell blood on a butcher. Besides, I'm tired of driving you through town. Come."

He led me up a flight of stairs, through a maze of corridors, and down, until we arrived at the narthex leading to the main sanctuary. There he left me, without so much as a backward glance.

I walked out beneath the shelter of an overhang, and waved at the loggia where Claudio waited.

That night, after Matteo had at last fallen asleep in the nursery, Zalumma unlaced my sleeves. I was curious, in the mood to talk.

"Did you know Giuliano?" I asked. "Lorenzo's brother?"

Her mood was already troubled; I had come home shaken, with my hair inexplicably wet. Like Leonardo, she had a nose for deceit. And when I asked about Giuliano, her mood darkened further.

"I didn't know him well," she said. "I met him, on a few occasions." She glanced up and to her left, at the far-distant past, and her tone softened. "He was a striking man; the few images I have seen of him don't really show it. He was very happy, very gentle, like a child in the very best sense. He was kind to people even when he didn't need to be. Kind to me, a slave."

"You liked him?"

She nodded, wistful, as she folded my sleeves and set them in the closet, then turned back to me and began unlacing my gown. "He loved your mother dearly. She would have been very happy with him."

"There was a man. In the Duomo," I said. "The day Giuliano was killed. Someone . . . someone saw it happen. It wasn't just Baroncelli and Francesco de' Pazzi. There was another man, a man wearing a hood, to cover his face. He struck the first blow."

"There was another man?" She was aghast.

"Another man, who escaped. And he has never been found. He might still be here in Florence." My gown dropped to the floor; I stepped from it.

She let go an angry noise. "Your mother loved Giuliano more than life. When he died, I thought she would . . ." She shook her head and gathered my gown into her arms.

Very softly, I said, "I think that . . . someone else, someone in Florence . . . knows who he is. And the time will come when *I* learn who he is. On that day, he will finally meet justice—at my hand, I hope."

"What good will it do?" she demanded. "It's too late. Giuliano's life is gone, and your mother's destroyed. She was going to him that night. Did you know? She was going to leave your father to go with him to Rome. . . . The night before he was murdered, she went to tell him so. . . ."

I went and sat in front of the fireplace to warm myself. I said nothing more to Zalumma that night. I thought of my mother's ruined life as I stared into the flames, and promised myself silently that I would find a way to avenge her, and both our Giulianos.

Winter passed slowly. In Leonardo's absence, I went to pray almost daily in the little chapel at Santissima Annunziata. I missed the artist: He had been my one link to my real father and my beloved Giuliano. I knew that, like me, he grieved over their loss.

Almost every evening, when the way was clear—that is, when Francesco was off whoring—I stole down to his study and searched his desk for letters. For several weeks, I found nothing. I fought off disappointment by reminding myself that Piero was coming. Piero was coming, at which point I would abandon Francesco and—with Matteo, my father, and Zalumma—seek refuge with the Medici.

But Piero did not come.

As wife of a high-ranking *piagnone,* I was obliged to continue attending Savonarola's Saturday sermons for the women. I went with Zalumma to San Lorenzo and sat close to the high altar and the lectern, the place reserved for those with ties to the prophet. I endured the sermon by imagining myself going to Leonardo and commissioning a beautiful monument for my Giuliano. But my attention was captured by Fra Girolamo's ringing voice, filled with vitriol as he addressed his hushed congregation:

"Those lovers of Piero de' Medici and his brothers, Giuliano and the so-called Cardinal Giovanni—"

Zalumma and I stared straight ahead; I dared not look at her. Pain and anger blinded me. I heard the prophet's words, but I could not see his face. *Fool,* I thought. *You don't know that Giuliano is dead. . . .*

"God knows who they are! God knows their hearts! I tell you, those who continue to love the Medici are just like them: the rich, the idolatrous, who worship pagan ideals of beauty, pagan art, pagan treasures. And all the while, as they glitter and gleam with their gold and jewels, the poor starve! God tells me this—I do not speak for myself: *Behold, those who worship such idolaters deserve to feel the bite of the executioner's blade upon their necks. Like headless men they behave, without consideration of God's law, without compassion for the poor. And so, they* shall *become headless, indeed!"*

I remained silent, but inwardly I seethed as I remembered a line from the most recent letter discovered in Francesco's study:

In fact, our prophet should now redouble his fervor, specifically against the Medici.

I seethed. And I trembled. And I prayed to Piero to come.

I found only one letter in Francesco's study at that time—again, in the same heavy-handed script.

> *Your fears of excommunication are unfounded. I told you before to have faith. Let him preach without fear! Do not hold him back. You will see. Pope Alexander will relent.*

One year faded into the next. On the very first day of 1496, Ludovico Sforza, Duke of Milan, betrayed Florence.

One of the gems that King Charles of France had stolen from Florence, on his march south, was the fortress of Pisa. Pisa had always been ruled by Florence, but had long yearned to be free. Since the invasion, the city was controlled by the French.

But Ludovico bribed the keeper of Pisa's fortress to hand over the keys to the Pisans themselves. And with that single move, Pisa gained her freedom—from Charles and from Florence.

Ludovico, the crafty man, worked to keep his involvement secret. As a result, Florentines believed that King Charles had given the Pisans self-rule. Charles, hailed by Savonarola as God's champion who would bring Florence great glory, had instead betrayed her.

And the people blamed Savonarola. For the first time, their praise turned to discontent.

It was Salai who—unable to restrain his enthusiasm—whispered the truth of it to me one day, as I left my prayers at the family chapel. I smiled. If this was the result of Leonardo's work, then I could more cheerfully accept his absence.

Winter yielded to spring, which brought relentless rains. The lower-lying areas of the city flooded, damaging many workshops, including those of many dyers, which in turn delayed profits for Francesco's silk and my father's wool businesses.

But for the time, we had more than enough food to eat—especially given Francesco's connections.

My husband's mood was exceptionally cheerful during those days. I did not learn why until one evening at supper, when he was feeling particularly loquacious.

The storm outside had eased to constant heavy drizzle. After weeks of gloom, our palazzo was drafty and cold, so the three of us— my father, Francesco, and I—sat as close as possible to the fire.

Francesco had spent the afternoon at the Palazzo della Signoria; as a result, he was dressed in his best *lucco,* the long burgundy tunic trimmed with brown sable at the sleeves and neck. He came home smiling, and his cheerfulness only seemed to increase after his arrival. By the time we all sat down at the table—at the instant the wine was poured—Francesco could no longer contain himself.

"Good news, Ser Antonio!" he said, addressing himself to my father—my wan, faded father, who was Francesco's age but looked far older. Francesco's eyes were bright; his cheeks and the tip of his nose were still flushed from his ride home through the chill, damp air. Tiny beads of moisture had collected in his silver hair and gleamed with firelight. "You will remember, of course, the Pope's brief last year, which called for Fra Girolamo to stop preaching?"

"I do," my father replied, without enthusiasm. Savonarola's sermons had continued in defiance of the order. There were those who said excommunication could not be far behind.

"His Holiness has, after investigating the matter, realized the unfairness of this request. Today, the Signoria received notice from him that Fra Girolamo can continue to preach, so long as he does not excoriate Rome, and specifically His Holiness." Francesco beamed, then leaned his head back and took a long swallow of wine.

I listened but maintained a polite, disinterested expression. Secretly, I wondered whether Francesco had in fact learned this from the Signoria, or from his mysterious correspondent. I decided to search his desk that night if possible.

"Well," my father said, "it's just as well that he doesn't anger Rome. People were beginning to worry, you know."

"Such worries are unfounded," Francesco said. "And people are too quick to forget all that Fra Girolamo has done for Florence. Charles might have razed the city, were it not for the friar's intervention."

My father nodded faintly, then stared distractedly into the fire.

"But what of the rumor," I began, with feigned innocence, "that a letter was intercepted long ago, on its way to France . . . from Fra Girolamo to King Charles?"

My husband turned sharply on me. "Where did you learn such a thing?"

"Agrippina said she overheard it at the market. They say the friar begged Charles to come to Italy so that Florence would believe his prophecy."

"I know what it says. How can you repeat such an obvious lie?"

"I mentioned it because I knew you would know the truth," I said, so smoothly I astonished myself. "I have also heard the Pope was thinking of leaving the Holy League." Pope Alexander had formed the League—which was backed by Naples, Milan, and the Holy Roman Emperor—in order to oust Charles from Italy. Savonarola of course opposed it, but Florence had been under great pressure from Rome to join.

This calmed Francesco. "That I had not heard. It is very possible. It would certainly be good news for us." He paused and took another gulp of wine, then shot my father a sly glance. "Ser Antonio," he said. "I was thinking that it's high time you had another grandchild to enjoy." His gaze flickered at me briefly before he smiled down into his goblet. "I am not a young man. I need sons who can take over the family trade. What do you think?"

Sickened, I lowered my eyes and stared down at the wine in my own cup. I yearned to drown myself in it.

"I think," my father answered slowly, "that I had only one child. And I never felt lacking. I am very proud of my daughter."

"Yes, we all are," Francesco replied swiftly; his expansive mood could not be darkened. "And of course, it is wrong of me to discuss such things without first consulting my beloved wife." He finished his goblet of wine and called for more, then abruptly changed the subject to the implications of the foul weather.

"High prices are coming," my father said. "This happened before, when I was a boy. If the rains don't stop, we won't have any crops. And if that happens, I guarantee you, the starving will riot."

"We need have no worry," Francesco said firmly. "God smiles on Florence. The rain will stop."

My father was unimpressed. "What if it doesn't? What if there are no crops at all? Savonarola had best intercede if the sun is to shine on us again."

Francesco's smile faded a bit; he turned his careful gaze on my father. "It will, Ser Antonio. I promise you, it will."

"Floods bring plague," my father said. "Hunger brings plague. I have seen this before. . . ."

Thinking of Matteo, I started. My father saw it and, chastened, took my hand. "I did not mean to frighten you. Plague would never affect us, Lisa."

"Indeed not," Francesco said, with a hint of warning. "We are in no danger of floods here, nor of hunger. No one in my house will ever go hungry."

My father nodded by way of acquiescence before lowering his gaze.

We ate mostly in silence, except for Francesco's complaint that the peasants were still too ignorant to realize the truth of the matter: that the Duke of Milan, Ludovico Sforza, and not Fra Girolamo, had given the Pisans the keys to their fortress. An unfortunate confusion, since it made men speak out against the one who loved them the most and prayed to God fervently on their behalf. It was, Francesco insisted, the only possible reason for the growth of the *Arrabbiati,* who were very close to becoming a formal political party opposing Savonarola and the *piagnoni.*

Afterward, Francesco hinted broadly that he and I were tired and would retire early; my father—who normally stayed later and enjoyed his grandson's company—took the hint graciously and left.

As I excused myself to retire to my chambers, Francesco rose and gave me a pointed look.

"Go to your room," he said, not ungently, "and tell Zalumma to undress you. I will be up shortly."

I did so with a disgust so profound it verged on nausea. As Zalumma unlaced my gown, we studied each other with the same fear we had experienced on my wedding night.

"If he hurts you . . ." Zalumma murmured darkly.

I shook my head to silence her. If he hurt me, there was nothing I or she could do about it. I watched her put my gown in the wardrobe, then stood patiently as she brushed out my hair and braided it. At last, I sent her away. Dressed only in my *camicia,* I sat on the bed and apologized to Giuliano. *Francesco touches only my body,* I told him. *He'll never touch my love for you.*

I waited alone on my bed for a miserable half hour. When the door opened, I looked up to see Francesco, his eyes red-rimmed and glittering, his balance unsteady. In his hand he held a goblet of wine.

"Beloved wife," he murmured. "What do you say to my desire to have another son?"

I didn't meet his gaze; perhaps he would think it modesty. "You are my husband. I cannot fight your wishes."

He sat down beside me, letting his full weight drop carelessly onto the bed, and put his goblet down on the night table; the wine sloshed over the rim and perfumed the air. "Don't you have wishes yourself? Surely *you* want more children. What mother doesn't?"

I couldn't look at him. "Of course I want more."

He took my hand; I let it go limp in his grasp. "I am not a fool, Lisa," he said.

The words caused the hairs on the back of my neck to prick. Did he know? Had my searches in his study been detected? Had Claudio seen something?

But he continued, "I know that you don't love me, though I had hoped you would learn to. You are a very beautiful woman and an intelligent one. I take pride in calling you my wife. And I had hoped you would repay my kindnesses by giving me many heirs."

"Of course," I repeated.

He stood up. His tone grew businesslike, cold, faintly threatening. "Lie down, then."

I lay down.

It was an impersonal procedure. He remained completely dressed, and lowered his leggings only as far as necessary. With care but not tenderness, he crawled between my legs, lifted my *camicia,* and inserted himself. But he was not altogether ready; in fact, his proximity to me quenched all ardor and he shrank. He remained still for a moment, breathing hard, then suddenly pushed his palms against the mattress, raising his upper torso.

I thought he meant to extricate himself. Immediately I stirred, hopeful that he would proclaim defeat and leave.

"Lie down, I said!" He lifted one hand, turned the back of it toward me as if preparing to strike. I flinched and turned my face away.

This pleased him. He grew inside me; as he did, he closed his eyes and began to whisper to himself. "Whore. Insolent bitch!"

I thought of nothing. I let my head strike the wooden headboard. I listened to it hammer against the wall.

This continued long, painful moments; it was difficult for him, but he goaded himself on with foul words until at last he achieved his aim.

When he was done, he pushed himself away from me, quickly arranged himself, and left without a word, closing the door behind him.

I called for Zalumma. A good wife would have lain in the bed and allowed herself to become pregnant. But I rose at once, and when Zalumma arrived, I said, my voice shaking: "I won't bear his child. Do you understand? I won't!"

Zalumma understood. The next morning, she brought me a flagon of tea and instructed me on how to use it.

LXI

My father's warning had been prophetic: The rain never abated. At mid-month, the Arno flooded, washing away all the crops. In early June, the Rifredi River spilled over its banks, destroying what few fields were left.

By the time the sky dried up in summer, the city suffered from an outbreak of fever. For Matteo's sake, I permitted no visitors to the nursery, nor did I allow him to leave the palazzo. He was just starting to take his first clumsy steps; the more I looked into his face, the more I saw his father's.

I left the house rarely. Once the fever became widespread, I forbade Zalumma to go with Agrippina to market, and I went to Santissima Annunziata only irregularly, owing to the fact that I found no new letter in Francesco's desk during those weeks.

But, wishing to appear a good wife and allay suspicion, I continued to attend Savonarola's Saturday sermons for the women. His ranting against the Medici and their followers continued, but was combined with another obsession: Alexander's cohabitation, in the Vatican, with his young mistress, Giulia Farnese, and his penchant for inviting prostitutes to his parties.

"You leader of the Church!" he railed. "Each night you go to your concubine, each morning you go take the sacraments; you have provoked God's anger. You harlots, you miserable pimps, you have turned your churches into stalls for whores!" And when the cardinals grumbled that he ought not speak so of the Pope, he proclaimed: "It is not I who threaten Rome, but God! Let her do what she wills, Rome will never extinguish this flame!"

Several nights later, after my husband had gone to visit his own concubines and the servants had all retired, I made my way to Francesco's study.

The letter hidden in the desk was plaintive.

> *Let him rail against the Medici, I said. But I did not encourage him to attack Alexander—far from it! He is undoing all my careful work here in Rome. Make it exceedingly clear to those involved: If they do not stop this foolishness at once, they will pay dearly!*
>
> *In the interim: The people's hunger could lead to grumbling. Rally them. Focus their attention not on their bellies, but on Heaven, and Fra Girolamo.*

I silently repeated the words to myself, emblazoning each one in my mind so that I could summon them again at will.

The next morning, I left the book for Isabella to see. The following day, I rode to Santissima Annunziata just as the bells announced sext.

Salai made no further attempt at subterfuge. The Servants of Mary were all at prayer and would soon be supping at the refectory; our way was clear. We walked from the chapel to a narrow corridor, then up a flight of spiraling stone stairs. At the top was a blank wooden wall; Salai went to the corner and hooted, soft as a dove, and a panel hidden in the wall slid open. We stepped inside.

A young artist wearing the long, paint-stained tunic of his craft closed the panel behind us. We walked down a corridor that opened onto three rooms: a monk's cell with a cot; a larger chamber where a pair of young men, fresh plaster streaked on their cheeks, their hands, and their long aprons, were preparing a fresco; and the room where I had met with Leonardo.

The portrait of me still rested on the easel; Salai informed me that in his haste, Leonardo had forgotten to take it. I studied it: Except for the outlines and shadows, my skin was represented by the stark white of the gesso panel. I looked like a half-materialized ghost.

I smiled at the painting.

And I smiled at Salai as I recited the contents of the letter to him. He wrote the words down slowly, laboriously, stopping several times to ask me to repeat myself.

I left the church feeling lighthearted. Leonardo's efforts were bearing fruit, I thought. The Pope would surely silence Savonarola now. The Medici's enemies were flailing, and it was only a matter of time before I would greet Piero again.

I smiled because I was ignorant. I smiled because I did not realize that the letter in fact threatened all that I held dear.

In the fall, plague came. Savonarola still preached, but Francesco allowed me to remain home. No new letters arrived for him from Rome requiring me to venture out to the family chapel. I was deprived of my forays to Santissima Annuziata, and with the worsening weather, I could neither sit out on my balcony nor walk in the garden. I chafed.

The loss of the spring crops devastated Tuscany. Farmers and peasants left the barren countryside and swarmed into the city seeking food. Men and women lined the streets, begging for scraps and alms. They slept on the steps of churches, in the doorways of the *botteghe;* Francesco went to his shop one morning to find a mother and two children propped against his door, all dead. As the nights grew colder, some froze to death, but most died from starvation and plague. Each morning brought so many new corpses, it was impossible to remove them all. Florence began to stink.

Despite Francesco's wealth and connections, we felt the lack. Agrippina ran out of bread first, then flour, so we went without our customary pasta in broth; the hunters brought us fowl, which we ate until we could no longer bear the sight of it.

By winter, even we rich had grown desperate.

Christmas passed, then the New Year. Carnival came—once a time of celebration, with parades and parties and feasting, but under Savonarola's guidance, the new Signoria outlawed such pagan displays.

At last word came that the Signoria had elected to allow stores of government grain to be sold at a fair price to the people at the Piazza del Grano on the morning of Tuesday, the sixth of February, the last day of Carnival. Lent began on the morrow.

The cook, Agrippina, had lost a nephew to plague only a few days before. For fear of bringing *la moria* back to the house, she had not attended his funeral—but she opined, loudly, that she would find comfort if only she could go to the nearby Duomo to light a candle and pray for his soul.

Of course, it was her duty to go buy grain and bread for us. It made sense that she should go to the Duomo and offer her prayers, then go the short distance to the Piazza del Grano and make her purchases.

And I, restless as I was, presented to Francesco my argument for accompanying Agrippina to the Duomo. It was not far at all; there would be few crowds; I was anxious to pray. To my delight, he relented.

And so, on the appointed Tuesday, I climbed into the carriage with Agrippina and Zalumma, and Claudio drove us east, toward the orange-brick dome.

The sky was clear and fiercely blue. The air was still, and as long as I could sit motionless in a pane of sunlight, I felt its feeble warmth; but any shade brought bitter cold. I stared outside the carriage at the shops, the houses, the churches, the people moving slowly through the streets. Before Savonarola had seized the heart of Florence, Carnival had been a beautiful time; as a child, I had ridden through the streets and gaped at the façades of the buildings—formerly bland and gray, they had been transformed by red and white banners, by gold-shot tapestries, by garlands of bright paper flowers. Men and women had danced through the streets wearing painted masks adorned with gold and diamonds; lions and camels from the Medici menageries had paraded past for the amusement of the citizens.

Now the streets were again quiet and dull, thanks to the prophet's hatred.

Zalumma and the cook did not speak. Agrippina was a gray-haired woman of peasant birth, not given to conversation with those she considered her betters. She was squat, with a broad face, thick bones, and few teeth. One brown eye was clouded and blind, but with her good one, she gazed out of the window, like me hungry for new scenery.

We had agreed that it would be best to pray later and buy the food first, before supplies ran scarce. And so we rolled past the Duomo and headed south, toward the great toothy battlements of the Palazzo della Signoria's tower. The Piazza del Grano, a modest-sized square, stood behind the palazzo, on its eastern side. Abutting the palazzo's rear wall were large bins of wheat and corn, behind sturdy wooden fences; in front of those stood makeshift stalls, with scales for the transactions. In front of the stalls was a low gate, which remained locked until there was business to be done.

Claudio pulled the carriage up to the outer perimeter of the square; we could go no farther. I had expected a crowd, but I had not expected what I saw: The square was crammed with bodies, so many that not a speck of ground was visible. There were hundreds of bareheaded peasants with dirt-smudged faces and blackened hands, their shoulders wrapped in shreds of wool as they cried out for mercy, for alms, for a handful of grain. Beside them recoiled noblewomen in furs and velvets, who had not trusted their slaves to bring home food, and grim-faced servants, elbowing past the equally determined poor.

I leaned my head out the carriage; from my high perspective, I could see several men inside the stalls, heads pressed together, conferring in front of the still-locked gate. They had sensed the growing unease, as had our horses, who began to pace nervously. None of us had expected such a crowd so early.

Claudio swung down from the driver's seat and put his hands upon the carriage door, but did not open it. He was scowling.

"Perhaps I should go," he said. "Agrippina is small; she'll never be able to fight her way to the gate."

She snorted and looked down her nose at him with her good eye. "I've seen this family fed for forty years. No crowd can stop me."

Claudio kept his gaze on me. "Both of you go," I said. "That way, your chances are better. Zalumma and I will wait in the carriage."

Claudio gave a curt nod and opened the door for Agrippina, who clambered out with some difficulty; only half his height, she turned and walked toward the crowd beside him and he rested a hand on the hilt of his long knife.

I watched them disappear into the throng—until a face appeared abruptly in the carriage window, startling me.

The woman in the window was young, no older than I; her uncovered hair was matted, her blue eyes bulging, wild. Her sunken cheeks were streaked with soot. A silent infant was slung in a scarf at her breast.

"Pity, Madonna," she said, in a thick rustic accent. "Have pity, for the sake of Christ! A coin, a bit of food for my baby . . . !"

Zalumma's face was hard; her hand went to her bodice. "Go away! Get away from our carriage!"

The beggar's red-rimmed eyes and nose streamed from the cold. "Madonna, God has sent you here to me! For the sake of Christ . . ."

Had it not been for the baby, I might have been more wary. As it was, I fumbled for the purse at my waist; I pulled out a soldi. I meant to put it in her filthy, ungloved hand, but the thought of Matteo and the plague made me instead toss it in her direction.

She tried to catch it with numbed, clumsy fingers; it fell just outside the window, and she dove to find it. She was not alone. Another nearby peasant had seen, and fell on her; she started shrieking, and soon others were attracted to the row.

"Get away!" Zalumma shouted. "Leave us be!"

Still others came, men and young boys. One began to beat the young beggar woman until she squalled, then fell abruptly, ominously silent.

"She had one coin—there are more!" someone said. Our horses shrieked and lunged forward; the carriage jerked and began to rock.

"Death to the wealthy!" a man shouted. "They take our food and leave us nothing!"

Dirty faces filled the window; arms reached through, strange hands plucked at us. Someone pulled open the door.

Beside me, Zalumma reached into her bodice and withdrew a slender, two-edged knife. She slashed out at the flailing arms; a man yelped and cursed.

And then, from the direction of the crowd came thunderous shouts, the lightning crack of wood splitting, and a rumble that sounded like the earth heaving. The beggars assaulting our carriage turned like flowers to sunlight; in an instant they, too, were running toward the sound, leaving us quickly abandoned.

I clung to the frame of the open carriage door and stared out.

The crowd had broken through the locked gate and rushed past the stalls; as I watched, they swarmed the fence that guarded the bins of grain and tore it down. Two men—one still a lad—scrambled up the sides of the bins and scattered handfuls of grain onto the desperate crowd below.

A tide of starving indiscriminate flesh surged forward; countless hands clawed at the sky, grasped at the succoring rain. Screams rose in the midst of the madness, as the swift and strong trampled the slow and infirm.

And as the laughing men on the pinnacle pelted the sea of pinched faces below, I heard a low, rhythmic chant, soft at first, then growing louder and louder, spreading swift as fire through the frenzied crowd:

"Palle, palle, palle . . . !"

I seized Zalumma's arm and gripped it hard; I sobbed aloud, but shed no tears.

That day, dozens were killed—trampled or suffocated—in the rush for food. Every soldier, every gendarme, was called out to quell the riot and send people back to their homes—if they had them. Agrippina's chest and legs were crushed; Claudio came limping back to the carriage with her in his arms. Amazingly, he had managed to collect some of the pilfered grain in a pouch. I half expected Francesco to demand that he return it—it was, after all, stolen—but my husband said nothing.

News of the crowd's call for the Medici was everywhere, even on our servants' lips, and when Francesco returned from his shop that afternoon, he was stone-faced and uncharacteristically silent. Upon learning of Agrippina's injuries, he went straightaway to her bed, murmured a few sympathetic words, then sent for his own physician.

But I had never seen him in such foul temper. When Elena dared ask timidly whether he had heard about the cry of *"Palle!"* he turned to her and said, quite nastily: "Utter that word again in this house, and you will find yourself on the street!"

That evening, my father failed to come for supper and Francesco chose to forgo it, instead leaving—he claimed—to meet with the Signoria.

Zalumma and I spoke little. But when we had retired for the night in the bedchamber—when she lay on her cot, and I on my bed—I said softly, in the darkness:

"You had a knife. I would like one, too."

"I will give you mine," she said.

And in the morning, she made good on her promise.

The following day was Ash Wednesday. At noon, Francesco, my father, and I went to San Lorenzo to hear Fra Girolamo deliver a sermon open to all.

I looked up at the prophet in the pulpit, at his gaunt, homely face with its hawkish nose, and wondered whether he understood that his inspiration did not spring from a heavenly source.

He said nothing about Pope Alexander, but he spoke of "those vile prelates who mewl about God yet adorn themselves with jewels and furs." And he vehemently denounced women who paraded about in "immodest" gowns made of fabrics so fine that the sale of even one would feed many of the starving beggars who were, at that very instant, dying of hunger in Florence's streets.

I shot a sidewise glance at my husband. Francesco seemed to be listening intently, his brow furrowed in sympathy, his eyes soft with calculated innocence.

At sunset, Zalumma dressed me in a drab gray gown with a plain headdress. I eschewed all jewelry; I had not worn any in months for fear of the *fanciulli*. These were the members of Savonarola's "army": boys ten years of age, perhaps younger, who dressed in white robes and patrolled the streets of Florence looking for women who flouted the laws prohibiting immodest dress. Any bodice that hinted at the presence of breasts, any glint of gold or gems, was a crime. Necklaces, earrings, brooches, all were confiscated as "offerings" for the poor. In the preceding months, the unforgiving cherubs had gone from house to house throughout the city, seizing paintings, statuary, curios— anything that might serve, on this Ash Wednesday, as a lesson to those who indulged in ostentatious displays of wealth.

But they never came to our palazzo.

Once I was dressed and ready, I waited until Francesco called for me. As I came down the stairs, he studied my dull attire, my unremarkable coiled braids, my modest black veil, and said merely: "Good."

Then he handed me a painting the breadth of my arm from elbow to fingers. "I would like you to offer this tonight."

I glanced at it. I had seen it before, on the wall in the corridor near the nursery. Rendered on a wooden panel was a portrait of Francesco's first wife, Nannina, costumed in the guise of Athena. Her bust was shown in profile; on her head, she wore a small silver helmet from which spilled long, carefully crimped black locks. The artist's style was crude, lacking any depth. Her skin was unnaturally white, her eyes lifeless, her posture stiff when it was intended to be dignified.

We had many paintings in the house with pagan themes—one in

Francesco's study portrayed a nude Venus—yet he had chosen this innocuous one, perhaps to suggest to the public that this was the most sinful item we could find.

And he had taken it out of its wrought silver frame.

I took it without comment, and we rode in silence—Francesco was still in ill sorts—to the Piazza della Signoria.

It was a starless, moonless night, thanks to the clouded sky, but I could see the glow as we approached the crowded piazza. As our carriage rolled in front of the Signoria's palace, I saw torches everywhere: torches next to the high platform where the prophet and his army of white-robed *fanciulli* sat; torches flanking either side of the entry to the Palazzo della Signoria; torches in the hands of the onlookers; torches flanking, on all four sides, the great Bonfire of the Vanities. Every window in the palazzo, every upper-floor window of the surrounding buildings, glowed with candlelight as people gazed down to watch the spectacle in the square.

Francesco and I climbed from the carriage and joined the crowd standing before the pyre. My husband was an important man in the government; those who recognized him made way so that we could join the innermost circle.

The bonfire was a massive wooden structure—almost the height and breadth and depth of a two-story *bottega*, or a humble merchant's house—consisting of eight tiers hammered together like a great makeshift open staircase, so that the children could easily make their way from the bottom level to the top. At its apex stood a straw-stuffed effigy of fat King Carnival, with a painted canvas head. His face was not that of the benevolent monarch I had seen in Carnivals past, but rather that of a gruesome demon, with fangs protruding from his mouth and blood-red eyes.

Crowded together upon the freshly constructed, unpainted wooden tiers were all the vanities collected by the friar's little soldiers in the preceding months: golden necklaces, heaps of pearls, piles of embroidered velvet and satin and *cangiante* silk scarves, gilded hand mirrors, silver hairbrushes and combs, spun gold hairnets, fringed tapestries, carpets from Persia, vases and ceramics, statues, and paintings.

Statues of Zeus, Mars, Apollo, Eros, Athena, Hera, Artemis, Venus, and Hercules, symbol of Florence's strength. Painting after painting, on wood and canvas and stone; sketches on paper in silverpoint, red chalk, pencil, and ink. The crimes contained therein were all the same: pagan themes and nudity. I felt as I had upon first entering Lorenzo's study: awed by the sheer magnitude of so much beauty, so much wealth.

Trumpets sounded; lutes began to play. Francesco nudged me, nodded at the painting in my hands.

I stepped up to the bonfire alongside other prominent citizens eager to make a public display of piety. The tiers were crowded with items, the raw planks soaked with turpentine; I averted my face from the fumes and wedged Nannina's portrait in sideways between a pair of tall, heavy candlesticks whose cast-bronze bases were nude women with upstretched arms.

As I turned away, I brushed against a moving body and glanced up to see a bulky older man in a high-necked gown of black; the sight of him gave me pause. He was in his sixth decade of life, with red-rimmed eyes set in a pale, bloated face; a wattle of flesh hung beneath his prominent chin.

Sandro, I heard Leonardo say, and at once, I envisioned this man several years younger, holding the leg of a roasted quail to his lips, grinning and quipping archly: *Alas, sweet bird . . .*

Sandro was not smiling now; the glittering torchlight in his haggard eyes reflected infinite misery.

He looked at me and did not know me; his attention was consumed by the painting he clutched in his arms. It bore the image of a woman—slender, with elongated limbs and skin of incandescent pearl. She was naked save for a lock of amber hair that flowed down over one breast. One arm reached for an unfinished sky.

He stared down at it, tenderly, grieving—and then with a spasm of determination thrust it from himself, onto the nearest tier, atop a large urn, where it rested precariously.

I watched him disappear into the crowd, then went back to my husband.

As the bell in the tower of the palazzo began to chime, four leaders of the *fanciulli* came down from the platform and took up waiting torches. Wads of straw and tinder had been stuffed beneath the bonfire at four locations: two front and back near the center, two near either end.

Trumpets blared, lutes sang, cymbals crashed; as the crowd fell silent, the white-clad boys gathered beside the prophet and lifted their young, sweet voices in a hymn.

The straw went up quickly, black tendrils writhing in a bright blaze. The planks caught fire more slowly, emitting a pungent, resinous smell; the vanities smoldered, emitting narrow streams of black smoke.

For two hours, I stood beside Francesco and watched as the pyre burned, watched as Botticelli's pearl goddess darkened and melted away. At first, I stamped my feet to ward off the cold, but as the upper tiers charred and collapsed, the fire surged upward with a gasp. I loosened my *mantello*; my cheeks grew so hot I pressed my ungloved hands against them for relief.

In the end, the heat forced us back. Francesco touched my elbow, but I remained frozen for a moment, staring up at the roiling flames, orange-red against the pinkening sky. The vanities lay dark and writhing at their heart.

I was sweating when we returned to our carriage. As we rode home, the wind stirred; red cinders sailed through the air and swarmed like glittering fireflies on the façades of buildings.

"There will likely be fires tonight," Francesco said.

I did not answer. I sat with my face against the window and watched the ash float down, pale and silent as snow.

LXII

An attack from Piero is imminent. Word is that he plans to approach from the north; Siena again seems likely. Prepare for this—but do not be too overly alarmed. He has only the Orsini and mercenaries, perhaps thirteen hundred men all told. Not enough.

When he does fail, use the opportunity to make the new council public. The Arrabbiati *have grown too noisy, as have Bernardo del Nero and his* Bigi. *The council must bring them down.*

Inside the hidden studio at Santissima Annunziata, I recited the letter to Salai. He wrote it down as I dictated—clumsily, with maddening slowness, asking me several times to repeat what I had said. When I moved to take the pen myself, he pulled away.

"No, Monna! Your hand might be recognized."

When he had at last finished and rose to escort me out, I stood my ground. "Do you think—do you think there is a chance Piero will succeed? That he will be able to retake Florence?"

Salai's expression turned wry; with mock exasperation, he ran a hand through his short black curls. "I care nothing for politics and know even less about military affairs. But I do know that if anyone wants to dethrone this lunatic preacher and his fire-wielding brats, I'll take up arms and join them."

"Do you know how to use a knife?" I asked, and he grinned.

"I was born with one in my hand."

Awkwardly—taking care I did not cut myself—I drew Zalumma's double-bladed knife from the sheath tucked into my bodice.

Salai made a face. "So like a girl. If you don't cut yourself to ribbons first, your opponent will be doubled over laughing by the time you get your weapon out."

"Don't make fun of me. Show me how to use it."

"Leonardo would never approve, you know." He was teasing; his eyes still smiled. "I've never been able to convince him even to pick one up. He's worse than a woman about such things."

"Leonardo isn't here."

"An excellent point." He laughed. "First, don't keep it in your bodice. That's sloppy and slows you down. See, you have to reach *up* to get hold of it. You want to keep it in your belt, near your waist."

"But I don't always wear a belt."

"You will if you want to carry a knife. A nice wide one—isn't that the fashion? Just tuck it underneath. But please, don't hold it like you're going to eat with it."

I blinked down at the weapon in my hand.

"With your permission," he said. He came to stand behind me, at my right shoulder, and put his hand over mine. My grip on the knife was tight, stiff; he jiggled my wrist until my grip loosened a bit. "Now," he ordered, "you're holding it overhanded, with the tip pointing down. Do the exact opposite: underhanded, with the tip pointing *up*. But just slightly up. Here."

He turned my hand over and guided the tip up; his breath was warm on my ear. He smelled of wine and linseed oil. I glanced back at him and realized, for the first time, that despite his immaturity, he really was a young man, my age, and good-looking; his body was hard and strong. When my gaze caught his, he grinned flirtatiously. I flushed, embarrassed by the flash of heat between us, and looked away. But I now understood how Isabella had been taken in.

"That's right," he said softly. "It's good that it's double-edged; less for you to worry about. Now, show me how you attack. Go ahead, kill someone."

I took a step forward and stuck the knife out in front of me. Salai snickered.

"That's all well and good, if they're holding completely still and you want to give them a nick and let them run away. Here."

He moved up beside me and, in a flash, produced from the depths of his robe a long, slender knife. Before I could flinch in surprise, he took a step forward and thrust the knife out low in front of him; then, with a savage gesture, he hoisted it straight up in the air.

"You see?" He turned toward me, the knife still raised. "Get them low, in the gut; that's their most vulnerable spot. And it's easy for a weak girl to penetrate. The heart, the lungs—too much bone there, too much effort. Just aim for the gut, almost down to the groin, and then—to make sure they don't have a chance to give you any more trouble—bring it up *hard*. All the way up until the ribs stop you. Tears up the vitals. That's all you have to do to kill a man. They'll bleed to death, almost as fast as if you slit their throat." He smiled and tucked his own knife away. "Now, you do it."

The words were not entirely out of his mouth when I surged forward, so fast that he started. I kept the tip slightly up. I remembered to thrust low, to pull up, straight and hard and brutal.

Salai clicked his tongue in astonished approval. "And you, supposedly a noblewoman, from a good family? You're a quick study, Monna Lisa. You handle it as if you'd been born on the streets."

I went out alone on the balcony that evening after supper. I held the weapon in my hand, tip slightly up, and I practiced. I lunged on one foot, I jabbed forward with the knife; I jerked it up and listened to the blade whistle through the air.

Again and again I lunged. I wielded the knife. I wounded and killed. I thrust repeatedly at the bowels of the Pazzi, at the bowels of the third man.

Piero never came. A fortnight after I delivered the message to Salai, Zalumma came to my chambers wearing an expression of abject defeat. The news was spreading all over the city. Piero and his men had come from Siena and headed as far south as San Gaggio. But the sky had opened up en route, and a violent rain had forced the army to seek shelter and wait out the storm, with the result that they lost the cover of night. The delay allowed word of them to reach the Florentine troops stationed in Pisa, to the north. Piero was forced to retreat in order to avoid being overpowered.

Savonarola's followers said, of course, that God had spoken. The rest of us were downcast and afraid to speak.

And I was bitter. Bitter because I knew we would never know the full truth of it, thanks to my husband and the Pazzi. By day, I held my child in my arms; at night, I cradled the knife.

Given the failure of the Medici invasion, I had expected Francesco to be in good spirits—indeed, I expected him to gloat. But the following evening at supper, he was in a noticeably preoccupied mood and said nothing whatsoever about Piero's disastrous attempt on the city.

"I hear," my father said neutrally, "that the newly elected Signoria is all *Arrabbiati*. Fra Girolamo must be sorely frustrated."

Francesco did not directly meet his gaze, but murmured, "You know better than I." And then he pulled himself out of his quiet mood and said, more loudly, "It doesn't matter. The Signoria always ebbs and flows. For two months, we suffer with the *Arrabbiati*. Who knows? The next group might all be *piagnoni*. At any rate, the Signoria won't be able to cause too much trouble. We succeeded just recently in creating a Council of Eight, thanks to our recent threat."

My gaze flickered down to the dish of food in front of me. I knew he meant Piero; perhaps he did not say my brother-in-law's name aloud for fear of offending me.

"Eight?" my father asked conversationally.

"Eight men, elected to police the city against the threat. They will keep a special eye on Bernardo del Nero and his *Bigi* party. And they will take stern measures to stop all espionage. All letters going to and from Florence will be intercepted and read. The Medici supporters will find familiar avenues closed to them."

I addressed myself to the piece of roasted hare in front of me. Grain was still dear, and Agrippina—crippled now, with a permanent limp after that terrible day at the Piazza del Grano—relied heavily on local hunters to fill our larder. I picked the flesh from the bones, but ate none of it.

"What does Fra Girolamo say of this?" my father ventured. I was surprised he asked the question. He went daily to hear the friar preach; he sometimes spoke to him after the sermons. Surely he would have known.

Francesco's tone was terse. "Actually, it was his suggestion."

We finished the meal in silence. Francesco's usual bland smile did not appear once.

That night, I left Zalumma to go down to Francesco's study. I was glad for the fact that my husband had not visited my room again after his one effort to impregnate me; apparently, his distaste for sanctioned intimacy was great.

It was late spring, and the weather was pleasant; the windows were all open, and the air was alive with the smell of roses and the clicking of insects. Yet I could take no pleasure in the night's beauty; I was sleepless over the prospect that Piero might never succeed in taking the city, that I might grow old and die with Francesco in a city ruled by a madman.

I entered my husband's study—dark, save for the lamp that flickered in the next room—and unlocked the desk quickly, expecting to find nothing and to return quietly to my own bed.

But there, in the drawer, was a letter I had not yet seen, with a freshly broken seal. I frowned; I would have preferred to find none. I was in no mood to discuss Piero's failure with Salai. But I was obliged to take it and to steal into my husband's bedchamber—since there was no fire in the study—and hold it to the lamp.

> *It seems our prophet still vehemently denounces Rome from the pulpit. His Holiness is displeased, and there is little more I can do at this point to assuage him. Our entire operation falters! At whose feet shall I lay this monstrous failure? Giving the prophet free rein against the Medici alone was my intent—how could you misunderstand? You know I have worked for years to gain papal access, papal trust . . . and now you would see it all undone? Or shall I give you the benefit of the doubt and credit Antonio with this? If he truly has the prophet's ear, he must be forceful. Exhort him to use all his powers of persuasion. If he fails—because the prophet no longer trusts him, or because he has lost his resolve—it is your decision as to whether to dispose of his services altogether, or make use of the daughter and grandchild. I defer to your preference in this matter, as you are hardly a disinterested party. If Antonio quails, rely again, as you did so long ago, on Domenico, who has proven he can do whatever needs to be done.*
>
> *If Pope Alexander does in fact act against the friar, we have little choice but to resort to extreme measures. Perhaps Bernardo del Nero and his Bigi shall need to serve as examples to the people.*

"Antonio," I whispered. I reached out and steadied myself against the night table. I stared at the letter, read it again and again.

I had honestly thought Francesco had married me because I was beautiful.

If Antonio quails, rely again, as you did so long ago, on Domenico—

I thought of my father, miserable and wasting. I remembered that terrible moment so long ago in San Marco's sacristy when Fra Domenico had stood over my mother's body. When he had caught my father's eye, then looked pointedly at me.

A threat.

And my father had knelt. Choking on his fury, but he had knelt.

I remembered him begging later for me to go with him, to listen to Savonarola preach. When I had refused, he had wept. Just as he had wept the day of my marriage to Giuliano, when he had told me frantically that he could not keep me safe.

I remembered my father's cooling friendship with Pico after my mother died. I thought of Pico's death, and my father's current unhappy friendship with my husband.

—make use of the daughter and grandchild—

I could not cry. I was too horrified, too hurt, too frightened.

I pushed myself upright; breathing hard, I stared at each separate word, emblazoning it on my memory. When I was done, I went back to my husband's study, replaced the letter in the desk, and locked it.

Then I stole up to my chambers, found the knife, and slipped it inside my belt. Once armed, I crossed the corridor to the nursery. Matteo was asleep in his crib. I did not wake him, but sat on the floor beside him until I heard Francesco return, until I heard him settle into his bed, until the house fell quiet again, until the sun rose at last and it was dawn.

LXIII

*E*arly that morning, I sent Zalumma on foot to see my father at his workshop and let him know that I wanted to see him alone. She returned less than two hours later to say that my father felt unwell, that he was going home directly, and hoped I would visit him there.

He was of course not unwell; and as Zalumma—with Matteo balanced on her knee—and I sat in the carriage on the way to my father's house, she stared unflinching at me until at last I said, "My father is involved."

There seemed no point in trying to evade the truth. I had already told her the contents of the first letter I had discovered in Francesco's study; she knew my husband was involved with Savonarola, knew that he was somehow involved in Pico's death. She had found me asleep that morning by Matteo's crib and was not stupid. Ever since I had sent her to speak to my father, she had been waiting for me to explain what was going on.

My words did not seem to surprise her. "With Francesco?"

I nodded.

Her expression hardened. "Then why are you going to him?" The distrust in her tone was plain. I looked out the window and did not answer.

My father was waiting for me in the great room where he had greeted Giuliano the day he came to ask for my hand, the same room where my mother had met with the astrologer. It was just past midday, and the curtains had been drawn back to admit the sun; my father sat in a ribbon of harsh light. He rose when I entered. There were no servants attending him, and I sent Zalumma off to another room to mind Matteo.

His face was pinched with concern. I don't know precisely how Zalumma worded my request, or what my father had expected. He certainly did not anticipate what I said.

The instant Zalumma closed the door behind her, I drew myself up straight and did not even bother with a greeting. "I know that you and Francesco are involved in manipulating Savonarola." I sounded amazingly calm. "I know about Pico."

His face went slack; his lips parted. He had been moving forward to embrace me; now he took a step back and sat down again on his chair. "Dear Jesus," he whispered. He ran a hand over his face and peered up at me, stricken. "Who—who told you this? Zalumma?"

"Zalumma knows nothing."

"Then one of Francesco's servants?"

I shook my head. "I know you go to Savonarola. I know you're supposed to tell him to preach against the Medici, but not against Pope Alexander. But you are not doing a very good job."

"Who? Who tells you this?" And when I remained silent, his expression became one of bald panic. "You're a spy. My daughter, a spy for the Medici . . ." It was not an accusation; he put his head in his hands, terrified by the thought.

"I'm no one's spy," I said. "I haven't communicated with Piero since Giuliano died. I know only what I just told you. I came by the information accidentally."

He groaned; I thought he would weep.

"I know . . . I know you have done this only to protect me," I said. "I'm not here to accuse you. I'm here because I want to help."

He reached for my hand and squeezed it. "I am so sorry," he said. "So sorry you had to learn about this. I still . . . Fra Girolamo is a sincere man. A good man. He wants to do God's work. I truly believed in him. I had such hope . . . but he is surrounded by evil men. And he is too easily swayed. I once had his confidence, his trust, but I am no longer so sure now."

I held on to his hand tightly. "It doesn't matter. What matters is that you've displeased your masters. You're in danger. We have to leave. You and Matteo and I—we have to leave Florence. There's no reason to stay here any longer."

"You've never been safe." My father looked up, hollow-eyed.

"I know. But now you aren't safe, either." I sank to my knees beside him, still holding his hand.

"Don't you think I thought of leaving? Years ago—after your mother died, I thought I would take you to my brother Giovanni in the country, that you and I would be safe there. They found out. They sent a thug to my brother's house to threaten him with a knife; they did the same to me. They watch us. Even now, when I take you out to the carriage, Claudio will study your face. If you are upset, he'll tell Francesco everything, everything." He drew in a sharp, pained breath. "There are things I can't tell you, do you understand? Things you can't know, because Claudio, because Francesco, will see it in your eyes. Because you'll behave rashly and endanger us all. Endanger Matteo."

I hesitated. "I don't think Francesco would truly permit anyone to harm Matteo." My husband showed genuine fondness for the boy; I had to believe it in order to remain sane.

"Look at him," my father said, and at first I did not know of whom he spoke. "He is still a baby, but even I can see his true father in his face!"

The words pierced me; I grew very still. "And when you look at me, whose face do you see?"

He looked on me with pain and love. "I see a face far more handsome than mine. . . ." He drew my hand to his lips and kissed it; then he stood and drew me up with him. "I don't care if they threaten me, but you and the baby—I will find a way. They have spies everywhere, all over Florence, in Milan, in Rome . . . but I will find us a safe place, somewhere. You can say nothing of this; you can speak to no one. We will talk again when it is safe." He thought for a moment, then asked, "Did anyone see Zalumma come to speak to me?"

I shook my head. "Claudio was at home. We told everyone she was going to the apothecary's for me." It seemed a reasonable alibi; the apothecary's shop was on the same street as my father's.

He nodded, digesting this. "Good. Then tell them that Zalumma passed by and learned I was ill and had gone home—and you came to see me. Make sure Zalumma says exactly the same. And now you are happy because you have seen me and learned it wasn't serious."

He gave me a sudden, fierce hug. I held him tightly. I was not his blood, but he was my father more than any man.

Then he pulled away and forced his expression and tone to lighten. "Now smile. Smile and be happy for Matteo's sake, for mine. Smile and be cheerful when Claudio looks at you and when you go home, because there is no one in that house you can trust."

I nodded; I kissed his cheek, then called for Zalumma. When she came, shooing Matteo along, I told her we had only to remain with Francesco a little while longer—and in the meantime, we should appear happy.

And so we went out to the carriage, Zalumma and I, with Matteo tottering precariously beside us. I smiled up at Claudio, baring my teeth.

That day I had no choice but to leave a book on my night table where Isabella would see it. As much as I dreaded seeing Salai, the information I had learned was too important to ignore: Our enemies were losing their influence over the Pope and the friar—and, more important, they were considering taking action against the *Bigi*.

But I had no intention of relating the entire truth. That night I lay awake, silently reciting the letter to myself, omitting all reference to Antonio, to the daughter, to the grandchild. There would be no harm done; Leonardo and Piero would still learn everything of import.

And Salai, careless lad, would never know the difference.

In the morning, my thoughts clouded and dull, I informed Zalumma I would need Claudio to drive me to Santissima Annunziata. She asked me nothing, but her dark, serious manner indicated she suspected why I was going.

It was the first week in May. In the carriage, I scowled, squinting at the sunlight, and leaned heavily against the door frame until we arrived at the church.

Salai appeared in the door of the chapel; I followed him at a safe distance down the corridor, up a twisting staircase, and waited with him as he tapped on the wooden panel in the wall, which slid aside to permit us entry.

I had determined to make my recitation quickly, to spend no time at all in conversation, but to plead exhaustion and then hurry home.

But Salai broke with our custom, which was for him to sit immediately at Leonardo's little table—cleared of painter's supplies and outfitted with a vial of ink, a quill, and paper—and serve as scribe while I dictated what I had learned the previous night.

Instead, he gestured at my low-backed chair, smiling and a bit excited. "If you would, Monna Lisa. . . . He will come to you right away."

He. I drew in a startled breath and looked about me. My portrait was again on the easel; beside it stood the little table, covered now with new brushes, small dishes of tin, a crushed pellet of *cinabrese* for painting faces, a dish of *terre verte*, and a dish of a warm brown.

I lifted a hand to my collarbone. *Nothing is different,* I told myself. *Nothing is changed. Leonardo is here, and you are glad to see him. And you will smile, and you will recite exactly what you planned. And then you will sit for him.*

In less than a minute, Leonardo stood smiling in front of me. He looked refreshed; his face had seen a good deal of sun. His hair was longer, sweeping his shoulders, and he had regrown his beard; it was short, carefully trimmed, almost entirely silver.

I smiled back. The gesture was slightly forced, but certainly more genuine than it had been for Claudio.

"Madonna Lisa," he said, standing over me, and took my hands. "It is wonderful to see you again! I trust you are well?"

"Very, yes. You look well yourself; Milan must agree with you. Have you been in Florence long?"

"Not at all. And how is your family? Matteo?"

"Everyone is fine. Matteo just keeps growing and growing. He's running now. He wears us all out." I gave a little laugh, hoping that Leonardo would assume my exhaustion was the result of motherhood.

He let go my hands and took a step back, assessing me. "Good. All good. Salai says you have something to report today. Shall we get it over with quickly, then?" He folded his arms. Unlike Salai, who wrote everything down, Leonardo simply listened to my recitations.

"All right, then." I cleared my throat; I felt a slight surge of heat on my face and realized, to my utter disgust, that I had blushed. "I'm sorry," I said, with a sheepish little smile. "I didn't sleep well last night and I'm rather tired, but . . . I'll do my best."

"Of course," he said. Watching.

I drew in a determined breath and began. The first seven sentences of the letter came easily; I could see it in my mind, in the dark, thick handwriting, just as it had appeared on the page. And then, without intending to, I began: *"And now you would see it all undone? Or shall I give you the benefit of the doubt—"*

I broke off, absolutely panicked. I knew how the phrase should be finished: *and credit Antonio with this?* But I dared not say my father's name; yet I was obliged to complete the thought. "I'm sorry," I said again, then continued, *"and credit our friend with this?"* At that point, in order to make the letter seem all of a piece, I recited all the lines that referred to my father, taking care to replace his name with the phrase *our friend*. And I exerted my full concentration so that I would not stumble when I omitted the line *or make use of the daughter and grandchild.*

When I was finished, I looked to Leonardo. He reacted not at all; he simply stood gazing at me, his face composed and neutral, his eyes intense.

The long silence left me dizzied; I lowered my gaze and was sickened to realize my cheeks were reddening again.

At last, his voice soft and free of reproach, he spoke. "You are a poorer spy than I gave you credit for, Lisa. You can't hide the fact that you are lying."

"I'm not!" I said, but I couldn't look at him.

He sighed; his tone was resigned, sad. "Very well. I'll put it another way: You are hiding the truth. I think you know who 'our friend' is. Perhaps I should ask you to recite that particular line for me again and again . . . until you finally tell it to me as it was written."

I was furious with myself, ashamed. Through my own stupidity, I had betrayed the man who most needed my trust. "I've told you what you need to know of the letter. You can't—you think you know everything, but you don't."

He remained calm, sad. "Madonna . . . you won't be telling me something I don't already know. I understand that you want to protect him, but it's too late for that."

I closed my eyes. When I opened them again, I said, "You must promise me that no one will hurt him. That no harm will come to him. . . . If I thought that you, that Piero, was a danger to him, I—"

"Lisa," he said. His tone was sharp. "You are trying to protect someone who isn't worthy of your protection." He turned his face toward the window. "I had hoped this moment would never arrive, that you would be spared. I see now, of course, that it was only a matter of time."

"If you hurt him, I won't help you." My voice shook.

"Salai!" he called, so loudly that I started, thinking at first that he was shouting at me. "Salai!"

In a moment, Salai appeared in the doorway, grinning; at the sight of us, his good humor evaporated.

"Watch her," Leonardo commanded. He left the room. After a moment, I could hear him shuffling about in the next chamber, searching for something.

When he returned, he held a folio in his hand; he dismissed Salai with a curt nod. Then he took the folio over to the long table against the far wall, and opened it, and began going through the drawings—a few done in charcoal, some in ink, most in meltingly delicate red-brown chalk—until he found the one he sought.

He laid his forefinger on it firmly, accusatorily.

I moved to stand beside him; I looked down at the drawing.

"You were right," he said. "I made a sketch immediately after the event and kept it for a very long time. This is one I made recently, in Milan. After you asked me, I realized the time might come for you to see it."

It was a fully rendered drawing of a man's head, with a hint of the neck and shoulders. He was in the act of turning to look over his shoulder far, far behind him. He was draped in a cowl, which hid his hair, his ears, and left most of his face in shadow. Only the tip of his nose, chin, and mouth were visible.

The man's lips were parted, one corner drawn lower as his face turned; in my mind, I could hear his gasp. Although the eyes were hidden in blackness, his terror, his spent anger, his dawning regret were conveyed surely in the one brilliant, horrified downward turn of the lower lip, in the straining muscles of his neck.

I looked at the man. I felt I knew him, but I had never seen him before. "This is the penitent," I said. "The man you saw in the Duomo."

"Yes. Do you recognize him?"

I hesitated and at last said, "No."

He cleared a space upon the table, took the drawing from the portfolio, and set it down. "I did not learn what I am about to show you until recently." He took up a piece of crumbling red chalk and beckoned for me to stand close beside him.

And he began to draw with the same natural ease that another man might use to walk or breathe. He made light, staccato strokes over the jaw first, and the chin; it took me a moment to realize he was drawing hair, a beard. As he did, the penitent's jaw softened; the upper lip disappeared beneath a full mustache. He drew a pair of lines, and the corners of the man's mouth were suddenly braced by age.

Slowly, beneath his hand, appeared a man I knew, a man I had seen every day of my life.

I turned away. I closed my eyes because I did not want to see more.

"You recognize him now." Leonardo's voice was very soft and unhappy.

I nodded, blind.

"His involvement was not born of innocence, Lisa. He was part of the conspiracy from the beginning. He joined not out of piety, but out of jealousy, out of hate. He does not merit anyone's protection. He destroyed Anna Lucrezia. Destroyed her."

I turned my back on him, on the drawing. I took a step away.

"Did you go to him, Lisa? Did you say anything to him? Did you speak to him of me, of Piero?"

I went to my chair and sat. I clasped my hands and leaned forward, elbows on my knees. I wanted to be sick. I had worn my knife that day, hungry for the moment I would meet the third man.

Leonardo remained next to the table, the drawing, but he faced me. "Please answer. We are dealing with men who do not shrink from murder. Did you go to him? Did you say anything to him, to anyone?"

"No," I said.

I had told Leonardo half the truth—that I had said nothing about him or about Francesco's letters. Perhaps it was the half truth that showed on my face, in my aspect, for Leonardo asked me no further questions. But even he, for all his charm, could not convince me to sit for him that day, nor could he interest me in conversing about all that had happened since we last had met. I returned home early.

Francesco was late returning from his *bottega*. He did not stop at the nursery to greet me and Matteo; he went into his chambers and did not venture out until summoned to supper.

My father was also late in arriving for the meal, and he, too, did not come to the nursery first, as was his custom. I arrived at the table to find Francesco stone-faced, defeated, gripped by cold, powerless rage. He uttered my name and gave a curt nod in greeting, but his features never stirred.

My father did his best to smile—but given what I had learned from Leonardo, I found it difficult to meet his eyes. Once the food was served, he inquired after Matteo's health, after mine; I answered with awkward reserve. After those pleasantries were dispensed with, he began to speak a bit about politics, as he and Francesco so often did, after a fashion that I might understand and be educated.

"Fra Girolamo is working on an apologia, *The Triumph of the Cross*. There are those who claim that he is a heretic, a rebel against the Church, but this work will show just how orthodox his beliefs are. He is writing it expressly for His Holiness, in answer to charges brought by his critics."

I glanced sidewise at Francesco, who addressed his *minestra* and revealed no trace of an opinion on the matter. "Well," I said tentatively, "he has certainly preached strenuously against Rome."

"He preaches against sin," my father countered gently. "Not against the papacy. His writings will show his absolute respect for the latter."

I knew better, but I looked down at my plate and did not answer.

"I think it is wise of Fra Girolamo to address such questions," he said; and when neither I nor Francesco replied immediately, he surrendered, and the three of us ate in silence.

After a few moments, Francesco surprised me by speaking—suddenly, with cool bitterness. "Let the prophet write what he will. There are some who believe he has little chance of placating His Holiness."

My father looked up sharply from his food; in the face of Francesco's icy gaze, he soon looked down again.

Supper ended without another word. My father took his leave immediately afterward—a fact for which I was glad, as I was far too troubled by my new knowledge to be comfortable with him. Francesco returned to his room. I went up to the nursery and played with Matteo in an effort to cheer myself, to blot out the image of my father plunging his blade into Giuliano's back.

It was not until I had put my son to bed and returned to my chamber that I understood Francesco's anger. Before I could reach for the door, it opened before me, and Zalumma seized my arm and pulled me inside. She closed the door quickly behind us, then leaned against it, her eyes bright, her manner excited but furtive.

"Did you hear? Did you hear, Madonna? Isabella just told me—the news is spreading quickly tonight!"

"Hear what?"

"Savonarola. The Pope has done it at last: He has excommunicated him!"

LXIV

*S*ummer brought with it a second, fiercer outbreak of *la moria,* the Death. Florence was hard hit: Stretchers were seen everywhere, carrying to the hospitals those pedestrians who had collapsed en route to their homes, their shops, their churches.

My visits to Santissima Annunziata came to a halt. Even if I had wanted to venture out onto the plague-ridden streets, I had no news to share with Leonardo, since I no longer had access to my husband's letters. Fearful of contagion, Francesco had given up his nightly prowling and stayed in his chambers, often sitting in the study; he went out only to his nearby shop, and more rarely, when the most important business called, to the Palazzo della Signoria. Yet despite *la moria,* he received more visitors than ever: Lord Priors, *Buonomi,* and other men who were never introduced to me, about whom I never asked. Savonarola was in political danger, and Francesco was desperate to save him.

To avoid the danger of traveling back and forth over the Arno, my father came to stay with us for a time. After Francesco's visitors departed, he often called my father into his study, and the two men would speak together at length. I did not try to spy on these meetings, but there were times I could hear their low voices, the pitch and timbre of their conversations. Francesco always sounded argumentative, imperious; my father sounded simply unhappy.

After an oddly early and lengthy visit from one Lord Prior, Francesco and my father came down in the morning to eat. I was at the table, with Matteo squirming in my lap; I had never before brought him downstairs to eat, but he was almost two years old, and I dreamt of teaching him to eat with a spoon. When the two men arrived, Matteo was happily pounding the utensil against the surface of Francesco's fine, polished table. I expected my husband to be displeased, to speak sharply, since he had been in foul temper of late. But Francesco, for the first time in days, smiled.

My father stood beside him, grim and cautious.

"Wonderful news!" Francesco exclaimed, raising his voice just enough to be heard over Matteo's drumming; he was in far too good a mood for the noise to irritate him. "We have just captured a Medici spy!"

I tried to draw a breath and failed; I sat up straight, barely averting my head in time to avoid Matteo's wildly flailing arm. "A spy?"

My father seemed to sense my sudden fear; he pulled out a chair and sat beside me. "Lamberto dell'Antello. You've heard of him: He was one of Piero's friends," he said quietly, next to my ear. "He even went with Piero to Rome. He was discovered trying to get into Florence with a letter. . . ."

Francesco stood smiling across from us; I put a restraining hand on Matteo's wrist and ignored him when he complained. "Yes, Lamberto dell'Antello. He was captured yesterday, and is being interrogated now. This will be the end of the *Bigi*. Lamberto is talking, giving names." He moved toward the kitchen. "Where is Agrippina? I need some food, and quickly. I must leave for the Palazzo della Signoria this morning. They're holding him at the Bargello prison."

"Do you think it's safe to go out?" I asked out of concern for appearances' sake, not for Francesco.

"It doesn't matter if it is or isn't—this is far too important to miss!" He disappeared into the kitchen. "Agrippina!"

In the instant he was gone, my father studied me searchingly. I tried my best to appear mildly interested in the news about Lamberto, mildly and pleasantly distracted by my wriggling child. I tried, but I suspected my father saw my fear.

I know I saw his.

Once Francesco had eaten and left in the carriage, my father and I took Matteo out to run in the gardens behind the palazzo. The garden was green and lush, the mist rising from the lion fountain soft and cool. I strolled beside my father, letting my son run slightly ahead of us, calling out to him not to trample the boxwood, not to touch the thorny rosebushes. I might as well have told him not to be a little boy.

I was still angry at my father. I knew he would never cause me harm, but each time I looked on him, I saw the penitent. Even so, I worried for his sake. "I am afraid," I told him. "The excommunication—Francesco will say that you've failed him."

He gave a little shrug to make light of it. "Don't worry about me. I have spoken with Fra Girolamo—I, and others. He is finally convinced that he must make amends. He knows he has been foolish— that he has failed to control his tongue and that he speaks like one possessed in the pulpit. But he will write his apologia. And he has already sent private letters to His Holiness, begging for forgiveness. Alexander will be soothed."

"And if he isn't?"

My father stared ahead at his sturdy grandson. "Then Florence will be placed under papal interdict. No Christian city will be allowed to do business with us unless we turn over Savonarola for punishment. But that won't happen." He reached for my hand to comfort me.

I did not mean to pull away, but could not stop myself. His eyes filled with hurt.

"You have been angry with me. I don't blame you, for all I've done—terrible things. Things I pray God will forgive, though I long ago gave up any hope of Heaven."

"I'm not angry," I said. "I want only one thing: for us to leave Florence with Matteo. I can't bear it here any longer. It's growing too dangerous."

"It's true," he admitted sadly. "But right now, it's impossible. When they found Lamberto dell'Antello, the Lord Priors became crazed. Every one of them is a *piagnone* now and out for blood. They've closed all nine gates of the city: No one can come in, no one can go out; every letter is intercepted, read by the Council of Eight. They are questioning everyone, looking for Medici spies. Were it not for my usefulness to Francesco, they would question us." His voice grew hoarse. "They will destroy the *Bigi*—every man who looked kindly on Lorenzo or his sons. And they will have Bernardo del Nero's head."

"No," I whispered. Bernardo del Nero was one of Florence's most revered citizens, a longtime intimate of Lorenzo de' Medici. He was a strong, clearheaded seventy-five years of age, childless and widowed, and so he had devoted his life to the government of the city. He had served with distinction as gonfaloniere, and was irreproachably honest. So well liked was he that even the Signoria respected and tolerated his political position as head of the *Bigi*. "They wouldn't dare hurt him! No citizen would stand for it."

But I was even more worried for Leonardo, who was effectively trapped within the city, unable to communicate with the outside.

My father was shaking his head. "They will have to stand for it. The appearance of Lamberto dell'Antello has filled every *piagnone*'s heart with fear. After the food riots in the Piazza del Grano, the Signoria is desperate to stifle any more cries of '*palle, palle.*'"

"But when Piero was ousted," I said, "Savonarola called for mercy for all the friends of the Medici. He insisted that everyone be forgiven and pardoned."

My father looked out across the garden, down the cobblestone path lined with blooming rosebushes and sculpted boxwoods, at his grandson, currently distracted by an unfortunate beetle. The sight should have gladdened him; instead, his eyes grew haunted.

"There will be no mercy now," he said, with the conviction of a man who held secrets. "And no hope. There will only be blood."

I wanted desperately to go to Santissima Annunziata, to warn Leonardo of the imminent peril to Bernardo del Nero and his political party, but Francesco would not hear of me leaving the house to pray—especially when it meant going to the family chapel, which stood across from the Ospedale degli Innocenti, where many of the sick were housed. And no amount of arguing could convince Claudio to disobey his master's orders.

So I remained housebound. Francesco's letters had all spoken of the *Bigi* as enemies who must be contained; now it was clear that they must be destroyed. I trusted Leonardo knew more about the danger than I did.

In the meantime, I stole onto my balcony alone and unsheathed my knife. My opponent was no longer the third man, the murderer of my true father. He was Francesco; he was the writer of the letters—the murderers of *my* beloved Giuliano. Night after night, I wielded my blade. Night after night, I killed them both, and took comfort in it.

Arrests were made; the accused were tortured. In the end, five men were held and brought before the Signoria and the Great Council for sentencing: the august Bernardo del Nero; Lorenzo Tornabuoni, Piero's young cousin, who, though titular head of the *Bigi,* was nonetheless a much-loved citizen and a pious *piagnone;* Niccolò Ridolfi, an older man whose son had married Lorenzo's daughter Contessina; Giannozzo Pucci, a young friend of Piero's; and Giovanni Cambi, who had had many business dealings with the Medici.

Pity! supporters cried, certain that the sentences would be light and, in the case of Bernardo del Nero, commuted. The accused were all admired, upright citizens; their confessions—that they were actively involved in arranging for Piero de' Medici's return as the city's self-proclaimed ruler—had been elicited under the most brutal torture.

The people looked to Savonarola for guidance. Surely the friar would once again call for forgiveness, forbearance.

But Fra Girolamo was too distracted by his efforts to placate an angry Pope. He could no longer be bothered, he said publicly, with political matters. "Let them all die or be expelled. It makes no difference to me."

His words were repeated thousands of times by followers whose eyes were troubled, whose voices were hushed.

Three hours before dawn on the morning of the twenty-seventh of August, Zalumma and I were startled from slumber by pounding on my chamber door. Zalumma rolled out of her cot and opened the door to find Isabella, disheveled and squinting in the light shed by the taper in her hand. Still bewildered by sleep, I moved into the doorway and stared at her.

"Your husband summons you," she said. "He says, 'Dress quickly, for a somber occasion, and come downstairs.' "

I frowned and rubbed my eyes. "And Zalumma?" I could hear her behind me, fumbling for the flint to light the lamp.

"Only you are to come."

As Zalumma laced me into a modest gown of gray silk embroidered with black thread, I began to worry. What possible "somber occasion" required that I be wakened in the middle of the night? Perhaps someone had died; I thought at once of my father. Savonarola's excommunication left him in his masters' bad graces. Had they decided at last to be rid of him?

The air was heavy, warm, and still; I had slept fitfully because of the heat. By the time I was fully dressed, my breasts and armpits were damp.

I left Zalumma and went down the stairs, stopping one level below to visit the guest chambers, where my father now slept. At the closed door, I paused—but my desperation overcame all notions of courtesy. I opened the door just long enough to peer past the antechamber into the bedroom and confirm that my father lay sleeping within.

I closed the door quietly, gratefully, and went downstairs to Francesco.

He was pacing by the front entrance, fully alert and restless. I could not have described him as happy, but in his expression and eyes I saw nervous triumph, a dark joy. It was then I realized that we were waiting for Claudio, that something so important was happening that Francesco was willing to risk exposing himself and his wife to plague.

"Has someone died?" I asked, with a good wife's gentle concern.

"There is no point in discussing it with you now; you will only become agitated, as women do about such matters. You will see soon enough where we are going. I ask only that you contain yourself, that you exert as much bravery as you are able. I ask that you make me proud."

I looked at him with dawning fear. "I will do my best."

He gave a grim little smile and escorted me out to the carriage, where Claudio and the horses waited. The air outside was stifling, without hint of coolness. We did not speak during the ride. I stared out at the dark streets, my dread increasing as we rolled east toward the Duomo, then relentlessly south.

We pulled into the Piazza della Signoria. In the windows of the Palace of the Lord Priors, every lamp burned—but this was not our destination. We rumbled to a stop in front of the adjoining building: the Bargello, the prison where I had been held, where Leonardo had been taken by the Officers of the Night. It was a forbidding square fortress crowned by jagged battlements. Great torches burned on either side of the massive entry doors.

As Claudio opened the door, my heart quailed. *They have captured Leonardo,* I thought. *Francesco knows everything. He has brought me here to be questioned. . . .* But I showed no outward sign of my turmoil. My face was set as I took Claudio's arm and stepped lightly onto the flagstone. I thought fleetingly of Zalumma's knife, at home beneath my mattress.

Francesco stepped from the carriage after me and gripped my elbow. As he directed me toward the doors, I saw wagons waiting nearby—five of them, in a cluster, attended by small groups of grim black-clad men. A keening sound made me turn my head and look at them more closely: A woman, veiled in black, sat atop a wagon, sobbing so violently that she would have fallen had the driver not clutched her.

We made our way inside. I expected to be led to a cell, or to a room filled with accusatory priors. Armed guards scrutinized us as we passed through the entry hall, then outside into a large courtyard. In each of the four corners stood a large pillar, of the same dull brown stone as the building; on each of these pillars were affixed black iron rings, and in each ring burned a torch, which cast wavering orange light.

Against the far wall was a steep staircase leading down from a balcony, and at the foot of those stairs stood a broad, recently constructed platform. Mounds of straw had been scattered on its surface. Beneath the smells of fresh wood and straw was a faint, fetid undercurrent of human waste.

Francesco and I were not alone. There were other high-ranking *piagnoni* present: seven sweating Lord Priors in their scarlet tunics, a handful of *Buonomi*, and members of the Council of Eight. Most prominent was the gonfaloniere Francesco Valori, who was serving for the third time in that capacity; a hard-eyed, gaunt man with streaming silver hair, Valori had stridently called for the blood of the accused *Bigi*. He had brought his young wife, a pretty creature with golden ringlets. We nodded silent greetings, then joined the crowd waiting in front of the low platform. I let go a shuddering breath; I was here as a witness, not a prisoner—at least for now.

People had been murmuring to one another, but they fell silent as a man mounted the scaffold: an executioner bearing a heavy single-edged axe. With him came another man, who set down a scarred wooden chopping block upon the straw.

"*No*," I whispered to myself. I remembered my father's words about the *Bigi;* I had not wanted to believe them. If I had found a way to see Leonardo, could I have prevented this?

Francesco inclined his head toward mine, to indicate that he had not heard me, that I should repeat myself, but I said nothing more. Like the others, I stared at the scaffold, the executioner, the straw.

The clink of the chains came first; then the accused appeared on the balcony, flanked by men wearing long swords at their hips.

Bernardo del Nero was first. He had always been a dignified white-haired man, with large, solemn eyes and a straight, prominent nose. Those eyes were now puffed almost entirely shut; his nose, twisted and crusted with black blood, was enormously swollen. He could no longer stand straight, but leaned heavily on his captor as he took each halting step down. Like his fellows, he had been forced to surrender his shoes and meet death barefoot.

I did not recognize young Lorenzo Tornabuoni; the bridge of his nose had been crushed, and his face was so bruised and swollen he could not see at all, but had to be led down the stairs. Three other prisoners followed: Niccolò Ridolfi, Giannozzo Pucci, Giovanni Cambi, all of them broken, resigned. None of them seemed aware of the assembly gathered to watch them.

When they at last stood upon the scaffold, the gonfaloniere read the charges and the sentence: espionage and treason, death by beheading.

Bernardo del Nero was granted the mercy of dying first. The executioner asked his forgiveness, and was told, in a frail, thick-tongued voice, that he was forgiven. And then Bernardo squinted out at our small assembly and said, "May God forgive you, too."

He was too weak to kneel without aid; a guard helped him settle his chin properly into the chopping block's darkly stained cradle. "Strike neatly," he urged, as the executioner lifted the axe.

I did not care if I made Francesco proud; I averted my face, closed my eyes. But I opened them again immediately, startled by the warm spray and the collective gasp of the crowd. I caught a sidewise glimpse of Bernardo's kneeling body falling to one side, of blood spurting in a thick upward arc from its headless neck, of a guard moving forward to retrieve something red and round from the straw.

And suddenly I remembered. Remembered a day years before, in the church at San Marco, when my mother, her gaze fixed and terrible, had stared up at Savonarola in the pulpit. And she had cried out:

Flames shall consume him until his limbs drop, one by one, into Hell! Five headless men shall cast him down!

Five headless men.

I stepped backward, treading on the slippered foot of a Lord Prior. Francesco caught my arm and held me steady. "Nerves," he whispered to the offended man. "Forgive her; it is only nerves. She is young and unused to such things; she will be fine."

Guards came and took the corpse away; Tornabuoni was pushed forward, forced to murmur words of forgiveness, to kneel, to die. Two more followed. Giovanni Cambi was last. He collapsed from fear and had to be dragged to the block; he died screaming.

In the end, the straw was sodden. The smell of fresh wood was eclipsed by the tang of blood and iron.

By the time Francesco and I rode home, the darkness had not yet begun to ease. We sat in silence until Francesco abruptly spoke.

"This is what becomes of Medici supporters." He was watching me curiously. "This is what becomes of spies."

Perhaps my pallor seemed suspicious; perhaps he spoke simply out of a desire to relish his political victory. In any case, I did not answer. I was thinking of my mother's words. And I was thinking of my father, and what would happen to him when the prophet was cast down.

LXV

s the weather cooled, the plague's grip on the city eased. My father returned to his house, Francesco took up with his prostitutes again, and I went to the marketplace and church as often as I could. One morning I placed the book on my night table, even though I had found no new letter in Francesco's desk, and the next I day went to Santissima Annunziata.

Leonardo was well, to my relief. He had even worked on the painting. The bold outlines and shadows of my features had been softened by the application of light *cinabrese,* a translucent curtain of flesh. I was beginning to look human.

But when I told him of my father's warning that the *Bigi* would pay with their blood—of my anguish that I had not been able to come and warn him—he said, "You bear no guilt. We knew of the danger, well before your father spoke of it to you. If there is any fault, it is mine. I was unable—I could not—bring influence to bear in time. And the horror of it was, even had we been able to arrange a rescue . . ." He could not bring himself to continue.

"Even if they could have been rescued—they should not have been," I finished.

"Yes," he murmured. "That is the horror of it. It is better that they

have died." It was true; the executions had outraged everyone in
Florence, even most of the *piagnoni,* who felt that the friar should
have extended the same forgiveness he had freely dispensed in those
days shortly after Piero was banished. Isabella, Elena, even the devout
Agrippina, who had never dared risk my husband's disapproval, now
criticized Fra Girolamo openly.

"My mother said—" I began, and stopped, confused as to how to
express my thought without sounding insane. "Years ago, my mother
told me . . . that Savonarola would be brought down. By five headless
men."

"Your mother? Your mother spoke to you years ago of Savonarola?"

"I know it sounds very strange. But . . . I believe what she said was
true. I think that this will cause Savonarola to be defeated. I think that
he might even die."

He grew motionless, intensely interested. "Did she ever say anything else about Fra Girolamo?"

"I believe she was speaking about him. She said, 'Flames shall consume him until his limbs drop, one by one, into Hell! Five headless
men shall cast him down!' "

What he said next astounded me. "He will die by fire, then. And
these executions shall be his undoing. We will expect it, prepare for
it."

"You believe me," I said.

"I believe your mother."

I stared at him for so long that he lowered his gaze and said, with
unexpected tenderness, "I told you that I had seen your mother once
when she was pregnant with you."

"Yes."

"She told me she was carrying a daughter. She told me I would
paint your portrait." He hesitated. "I gave her the medallion, then, of
Giuliano murdered. I asked her to give it to you, as a keepsake."

I wanted suddenly to cry. I reached for his hand.

. . .

The Signoria tried desperately to win back the people's love for Savonarola. It commissioned a medal to honor Fra Girolamo, with his alarming profile stamped on one side and on the other the image of a bodiless hand wielding a sword beneath the legend *Ecco gladius Domini super terram cito et velociter.* Worse, they encouraged him to defy the papal command that he should not preach. And so Francesco announced that he and I would go together to hear the prophet speak. My father was unwell and chose to remain at home.

The Lord Priors had decided that the most appropriate place for Savonarola's return to the pulpit should be the Duomo, in order to accommodate the anticipated crowd; but when Francesco and I entered the cathedral, I was startled to discover it less than half full. Not everyone, it seemed, was eager to risk the possibility of excommunication by a wrathful Pope.

Francesco's decision to attend the sermon provoked my curiosity. After the execution of the five *Bigi,* he had grown guarded where the subject of Savonarola was concerned. He no longer crowed about the successes of the *piagnoni* or spoke glowingly of the prophet, and when Agrippina let slip a critical remark about the friar, he said not a word. But our attendance at this defiant sermon was a show of the most fervent support. Or, more likely, a show of Francesco's desire to monitor his mouthpiece and public reaction to him.

There was no weeping that day in the Duomo, no emotion in the air; the citizens were sober-eyed and cautious, and when Savonarola ascended to the lectern, they fell expectantly silent.

Fra Girolamo's appearance was disturbing. He had been fasting during his months of silence and was even more haggard than before, his eyes dark, glittering holes in a face of yellowed ivory. He gripped the sides of the podium and stared out at the crowd; he exuded a vibrant misery, a desperation so profound he was compelled to share it or go mad. His breathing came so hard and furious that I could see the heaving of his chest from where I sat.

When he at last spoke, I was startled: I had forgotten how shrill and grating his voice was.

He began with his tone low, basely humble, as he recited the text. "Lord, how my tormentors are increased. How many are they that rise up against me."

He bowed his head and, for a full minute, was too moved to speak. At last, he said, "I am merely a tool of the Lord. I seek no fame, no glory; I have begged God that I might live the simple life of a monk and take the vow of silence, never to darken the pulpit again. Those of you who have criticized me, who have said that I should have inter-vened in Florence's politics of late: Do you not see that I held myself back out of humility, not cruelty? It was not I who wielded the axe, not I. . . ." He squeezed his eyes shut. "O Lord, let me close my eyes and lay me down! Let me enjoy a silent season! But—God does not hear me. He will not let me rest!"

And the friar took a gulp of air that produced a ragged sob. "God will not let me rest. It is His will that I speak—speak against the princes of this world, without fear of retaliation."

Beside me, Francesco tensed.

"Do I disrespect the papacy?" Fra Girolamo asked. "No! It is God's own institution. Did not Jesus say, 'On this rock I shall build my Church'? And indeed, all good Christians must honor the Pope and abide by the Church's laws.

"But a prophet—or a pope—is merely an instrument of God, not an idol to be worshiped. And a prophet who lets his tongue be stilled can no longer be an instrument. . . .

"Just as a pope who flouts the laws of God is a broken tool, a worthless instrument. If his heart is filled with wickedness, if his ears will not hear, how can God use him? He cannot! And so good Chris-tians must discriminate between God's laws and man's.

"Alexander is a broken tool, and his excommunication of me heretical. You who have come today recognize this in your hearts. Those who have stayed away for fear of the Pope are cowards, and the Lord shall deal with them."

I glanced over at my husband. Francesco's eyes were cold, staring straight ahead. The Duomo was unusually silent and Savonarola's words echoed off the high vault of the cupola.

The preacher sighed and shook his head ruefully. "I try to speak well of His Holiness, but when I come here—to God's holy place—I am obliged to speak the truth. I must confess what God Himself has told me.

" 'Girolamo,' He said, 'if you are banned on Earth, then you will be blessed a thousandfold in Heaven.' "

The prophet lifted his arms to the ceiling and smiled up as if listening to God; and when God had finished speaking, the friar cried in answer: "O Lord! If I should ever seek absolution from this excommunication, send me straight to the bowels of Hell!"

I heard a rush of air in the cathedral. It came from the listeners, each letting go an outraged gasp. Francesco was among them.

Then the friar humbly bowed his head. When he looked back up at his congregation, he spoke in a reasonable, gentle voice. "But how shall I address my critics, who say I do not speak for God? I tell you now, the Lord in His infinite wisdom shall soon give a sign to silence them forever. I have no desire to tempt God—but if compelled, I will give Florence her miracle."

Francesco was intense and distracted during the walk back to the carriage. He was so absorbed by his thoughts that when I spoke to him, he glanced up at me and for an instant seemed not to recognize me.

"Fra Girolamo needs a miracle," I said, with cautious respect. "Let us hope God provides one soon."

My husband gave me a searching look, but did not reply.

> *Damn Ascanio Sforza and his brother Ludovico! And damn the prophet's letter to the princes! One of Ludovico's agents procured it, and Cardinal Ascanio delivered it directly into the eager hands of the Pope. Our control of the Signoria cannot last. Even the* piagnoni *are divided now. If the friar continues as you say, a papal interdict of Florence is unavoidable.*
>
> *I have tried to deal with His Holiness as with Pico. But*

Alexander is too canny, too well guarded. There is no hope we can replace him with one more sympathetic to our aims.

The prophet's time is waning too quickly, and my own has not yet come. I can no longer rely on papal troops; I have not enough friends in the Signoria. But I will not surrender my hopes! There is still a way. Give the prophet his miracle.

If that fails, then we must find a way, quickly, to be palatable to the Signoria and the people. If Savonarola is cast in the role of devil, then I must be presented as a savior. Consider this, and give me your thoughts.

In the studio at Santissima Annunziata, I stared at the portrait on the easel. The paint was still drying—a coating of the palest shell pink, which brought a gentle bloom to my cheeks and lips—so I dared not touch it, though my finger hovered, yearning, over a spot in the hollow of my neck.

"There is a bit of blue there," I said. And green; the merest hint of a vein lurking beneath the skin. I followed the line with my finger; I felt that if I could set it down on the panel, I would feel my own pulse. "It looks as though I'm alive."

Leonardo smiled. "Have you not noticed it before? At times, I think I can see it beating. Your skin is quite translucent there."

"Of course not. I have never stared in the mirror that long."

"A pity," he said, without a trace of mockery. "It seems that those who possess the greatest beauty appreciate it the least."

He spoke so honestly that I was embarrassed; I changed the subject at once. "I will sit now."

And, as always, before I sat for him, I recited the letter. He listened, frowning slightly, and when I finished, he said, "They have grown desperate. If Savonarola does not get his miracle, they will feed him to the wolves and try another strategy. He will never give up."

"And he—whoever he is—wants to seize control of Florence." I paused. "Who *is* he? I already know that he is one of the Pazzi, but I want to understand why he craves power."

Leonardo did not answer immediately.

I pressed. "How can it hurt for me to know these things? If I'm captured, I'm already likely to be killed because I know of these letters. After all, I know that this man wanted to kill the Pope; I know that Ascanio Sforza and his brother Ludovico are involved."

He studied me a moment, then let go a small sigh. We both knew that I was right. "His name is Salvatore. He is the illegitimate son of Francesco de' Pazzi," he answered. "He was perhaps ten years old at the time of Giuliano's murder, when many of his family were executed by Lorenzo and the rest were exiled. They lost everything: their possessions, their lands. . . . He and his mother fled to Rome.

"Most of the Pazzi are good, honorable people; they had been horribly wronged by Lorenzo, and there was a good deal of bitterness. But they simply wanted to return to Florence, to their ancestral home.

"In the case of Salvatore, however—his mother instilled him with intense hatred and bitterness from an early age. He was very precocious and ambitious; he decided, early on, to take Florence for the Pazzi, out of revenge."

"It all repeats," I said. "Lorenzo took his revenge, and now the Pazzi want theirs."

"Not all of the Pazzi. Just Salvatore. He took advantage of the family's position as papal bankers in order to ingratiate himself with the Pope."

I leaned forward, perplexed. "Then why . . . why would he get involved with Savonarola?"

Leonardo took the chair across from mine. "That," he said, "is a very long story. It began with Giovanni Pico. As a young man, he was a womanizer and a fair philosopher. The Pope was eager to excommunicate him—and was even considering burning him—for his rather un-Christian syncretism.

"It was Lorenzo de' Medici who used diplomacy to save him in 1490, well before the Medicis' relationship with the papacy soured.

Pico, however, had a short memory. He took a Pazzi mistress, who turned him against Lorenzo. When Giuliano died and Lorenzo took his horrible vengeance on the Pazzi, Pico began looking for ways to influence the people against the Medici, to bring the Pazzi back.

"When Pico went to hear Savonarola speak in Ferrara, he saw a very charismatic man who disapproved of the wealthy and corrupt. He saw an opportunity for swaying the people against Lorenzo. And Fra Girolamo is an enormously gullible, impetuous man. Pico guessed correctly that he would be able to convince Savonarola to preach against the Medici, and make the friar believe it was his own idea."

I interrupted. "Does Savonarola know about the Pazzi? About this Salvatore?"

He shook his head. "Not at all. Savonarola listens to your father, and to Fra Domenico. But that is another part of the story.

"As for Pico . . . through his mistress, he knew of Francesco de' Pazzi's son Salvatore. And when the Pazzi were expelled from Florence, Pico exchanged letters with Salvatore. He fueled the boy's rage with tales of the Medicis' excesses, of their pilfering from public funds. By the time Salvatore was a youth, he wanted to wrest Florence from the Medici. And so he consulted Pico as to how the city might be won.

"Pico suggested the use of Savonarola to sway public opinion— and came up with the notion of using slow-acting poison on Lorenzo. Pico was intimate enough with the Medici to know that Piero had never nurtured his father's political connections, and so would be weak and easily removed. The original plan was to kill Lorenzo, oust Piero, and install Salvatore as the new ruler of Florence.

"Unfortunately—or fortunately, as you prefer—Lorenzo died before Salvatore was able to muster enough troops, or enough support in the Signoria.

"But Salvatore had managed to find one stalwart supporter in the government: a Pazzi advocate, one Francesco del Giocondo. And he put Francesco in touch with Giovanni Pico. Together, they concocted a plan to turn Florence against the Medici. I'm sure it worked far better than they ever dreamt it would.

"After a time, though, Pico's guilt over Lorenzo's murder overcame him. He actually began to take Savonarola's words to heart, to repent. This made him dangerous and liable to confess. For that, he was killed."

"By my father," I said miserably.

"By Antonio di Gherardini," he corrected, not unkindly. "Antonio had his own reasons for supporting the Pazzi. He never meant to become entrapped in a political scheme."

I looked down at my hands. Out of habit they rested one on top of the other, the way Leonardo preferred to paint them. "And Francesco married me so that he could control my father."

Leonardo's reply was quick in coming. "Don't underestimate yourself, Lisa. You are a beautiful woman. Your husband knows it; I saw how he behaved in your presence at the christening."

I shrugged off the flattery. "What of the 'prophet's letter'? How did it ruin things for them?"

He smiled faintly. "Savonarola is a very difficult man to contain. In a moment of self-aggrandizement, he wrote to the princes of Europe—to Charles of France, Federico of Spain, and Emperor Maximilian, among others—urging them to unite and depose the Pope. He said that Alexander was not a Christian and did not believe in God."

I gaped. "He is mad."

"Most likely."

"And you must have been involved," I said. "Someone gave the letter to Duke Ludovico, who then gave it to his brother, Cardinal Sforza, who then gave it to the Pope."

He did not answer. He merely regarded me pleasantly.

"But if," I said, "this so-called miracle fails . . . if the people refuse to unite behind Savonarola . . . then what will happen?"

"Violence," he said.

"If they have no choice but to let Savonarola be ruined—if they murder him or arrange for him to die—then they'll have no use for my father. For Antonio . . ."

His expression softened; he felt sorry for me. But I could see, too, his reserve.

"What can I do?" I believed wholeheartedly in my mother's prophecy that death was coming for the prophet. "The longer I stay, the more dangerous it is for my father. You must help us. Take us out of Florence. Take us with you to Milan."

"Lisa . . ." I heard pity in his tone. "If I could have, I would have done so long ago. But it is not so easy. There are you, and your father, and your child . . . and your slave, I assume. Four people. And you re-alize, of course, that your comings and goings are watched. That is why I have stayed here, at Santissima Annunziata, because you can come here regularly without arousing suspicion. But you will never make it past the city gates so long as your husband retains any influence."

"So I am to stay," I asked bitterly, "until it is too late, and my fa-ther dies?"

My words hurt him, but his voice remained gentle. "Your father is not a helpless man. He has survived this long. And the time will come soon enough for you to leave. I promise you that. It will come."

"It will never come soon enough," I said.

I wish now I had been wrong.

LXVI

*F*lorence became hungry for Savonarola's proffered miracle, and thus came about the event known as the Trial by Fire.

During Fra Girolamo's silence, Fra Domenico had replaced him in San Marco's pulpit. He was not as popular as his master, being stubborn and somewhat dim-witted—but he was extraordinarily tenacious and fanatically devoted to Savonarola. He doggedly maintained that each word that fell from Fra Girolamo's lips had been placed there by God.

Others had begun to preach as well—including an outspoken Franciscan at Santa Croce, Fra Francesco da Puglia, who offered a bold challenge:

"I will walk through the fire with any man who wishes to prove that Savonarola is a prophet who speaks God's truth. For I believe Fra Girolamo to be a liar and a heretic—and that anyone who walks through the fire believing otherwise will die. I would not expect to survive, myself . . . but certainly, anyone who walked successfully through the flames, believing and trusting in Fra Girolamo, could then be assured he speaks the truth."

Domenico learned of the challenge. And one Sunday he announced, from his lectern in San Marco, that he intended to enter the fire. His vehement proclamation so moved his congregation that each man and woman enthusiastically offered to enter the fire with him.

A wild enthusiasm swept the city. For once, both the *Arrabbiati* and the *piagnoni* were in agreement: Savonarola should take the challenge and prove beyond question whether he was or was not anointed by God.

Both parties presented the suggestion to the Signoria, who approved the event at once, and announced that a stage would be constructed in the Piazza della Signoria, and the spectacle would be held on a Saturday, the seventh of April, at the hour past midday. Everyone was eager to see the contest take place. As the respected *Arrabbiato* Leonardo Strozzi put it: "We require speedy clarification as to Savonarola's inspiration: God, or the Devil."

Everyone was eager but Savonarola. He regretted the fact, he said, that his followers were eager to indulge in a test which might result in another's death; surely they already had ample proof of his inspiration and should need no more. He publicly rebuked Domenico for putting him in a position "that might prove dangerous to others." He tried—and failed—to convince the *piagnoni* that the trial was a useless, prideful display.

But he could not stop it. "If my master will not enter the flames," said Domenico, cleverly, "then I will enter them myself and prove he is God's chosen one."

And so, on Saturday, the seventh of April, at ten o'clock in the morning, my husband and I rode in our carriage to the Palazzo della Signoria. Extraordinary precautions had been taken: Foreigners had been expelled and all of the city gates had been locked. Florence was patrolled by small neighborhood armies, and her streets filled with *piagnoni* making their way on foot to the square. All but three approaches to the piazza had been blocked, and those three were guarded by the Signoria's own soldiers.

Women were not permitted to view the spectacle—at least, those women without powerful husbands and a carriage. My husband was now one of the most influential men in Florence: He had finally been elected Lord Prior for the current session. We had thrown a party to celebrate the event—quite a lavish one, though none of his *piagnoni* associates seemed to mind.

Francesco took great pride in wearing the long scarlet tunic of the prior, and this morning was no exception. The instant the guards saw the tunic, they bowed. Francesco greeted the guards with a courteous, condescending gesture, and we were waved on. Half the time, my husband graced me with his benign, calm smile; half the time, he was silent and frowning. I believe he nursed hope that somehow circumstances would resolve themselves in Savonarola's favor.

Our destination was the palazzo, where Francesco excused himself to join the other Lord Priors, who sat in the *ringhiera,* a railed, covered patio in front of the palazzo which gave the best view of the square. I sat a short distance away, in a discreet little loggia outfitted with comfortable chairs for wives of government officials, of which there were four. My companion was Violetta, the golden-haired wife of Francesco Valori, he who had rabidly called for the head of Bernardo del Nero. It was a cool morning, but Violetta had brought a fan and waved it nervously, as she spoke of the miracle that was surely coming. How wonderful, she said, to see the *Arrabbiati* silenced at last.

I occupied myself with the surroundings. The Lord Priors, including Gonfaloniere Valori and my husband, sat next to the massive stone lion, the regal *Marzocco* sculpted by Donatello. Near the lion rested one end of a long wooden platform. Raised high off the ground, it was not quite wide enough for two men to walk along it side by side. Beneath it was a trench filled with limbs and brush; atop these lay neat stacks of unbaked bricks, to prevent the platform from being consumed by the fire. This contraption spanned a respectable distance, from one end of the piazza almost to the other.

The atmosphere was rather like Carnival. The weather was bright, cloudless, and exhilarating. Those pedestrians who had entered the piazza early were jubilant. The *piagnoni* indicated their loyalties by carrying little red crosses and singing hymns; the *Arrabbiati* and the uncommitted sang bawdy songs and called out jokes to one another.

Though Savonarola had called on the faithful to fast, servants emerged from the palazzo and offered us ladies bread and cheese and wine, as if we were at a joust.

At last two men appeared with jugs and began heavily dousing the wood and brush with oil. Other men appeared bearing torches and set the trenches ablaze; the crowd cheered. Dark smoke billowed heavenward. For about an hour, the people remained cheered and excited as the fire caught hold and grew—but then the excitement faded to restlessness.

After another hour, our boredom was eased by the appearance of the Franciscans: They arrived together, gray-robed and disorderly, a scattered flock of pigeons. Their spokesman went at once to the priors in the *ringhiera,* and they all huddled together, conferring. In the meantime, the rest of the Franciscans took their place in a loggia adjacent to ours.

Violetta startled us all; she set down her fan and went over to our stone railing and hissed down at the Franciscans: "Why does he speak to them? Will your brother not enter the fire?"

This drew the disdainful gaze of a young monk, who against the advice of his elders turned around to answer her. "He will enter. He is not afraid. But we have reason to believe that Fra Domenico"—for it was he and not Savonarola who steadfastly maintained he would enter the fire—"wears garments that are bewitched."

"Lies!" Violetta countered. I and a *Buonomo*'s wife pulled her back to her seat.

The Dominicans were late in arriving; the Signoria reluctantly sent a mace-bearer to escort them to the piazza. They arrived most dramatically: Fra Domenico led the way, carrying on his shoulder a martyr's cross almost as tall as he. Savonarola followed, bearing a small silver receptacle containing the Sacred Host, for he had insisted that Domenico would not be safe unless he carried the Host with him into the flames. Behind them came the men of the congregation of San Marco, bearing torches and more of the little red crosses, and then came the rest of the friars.

The crowd erupted with hisses and catcalls, shouts of joy and sobs.

Men screamed curses, blessings, prayers, and insults. Monks, both Franciscan and Dominican, began to sing.

At last San Marco's entourage took their places at a safe distance from the Franciscans; and then Francesco Valori, the gonfaloniere, beckoned for Domenico and Savonarola to come to the *ringhiera*.

I watched rather than heard the discussion: Valori spoke to Savonarola, who made an exasperated gesture. Domenico—who by then had abandoned his cross—put a hand upon his master's shoulder to calm him. And then Valori and my husband led Domenico into the Palazzo della Signoria.

The crowd grumbled. They had waited a long time and did not understand Domenico's sudden disappearance. But we women did, and I was not surprised to see Domenico emerge shortly afterward in a Franciscan robe. Violetta nudged me, and said, in a voice loud enough for the nearby Franciscans to hear: "You see? If his clothes had been bewitched, he would not have so quickly and graciously removed them. *He* is not afraid to enter the fire."

Fra Domenico and Savonarola began to make their way to the entry of the trial platform, where two soldiers and Fra Giuliano, the young Franciscan who had volunteered to enter the fire with Domenico, stood. And then the young Franciscan monk stepped forward and interrupted—which caused Domenico and Savonarola to hurry back to the *ringhiera*.

The crowd sighed in irritation.

Valori, my husband, and two other *piagnoni* intercepted Domenico and explained something rapidly to him. Domenico shook his head in disgust, but once again let himself be led into the palazzo.

Beside me, Violetta snapped her fan shut, dropped it into her chair, and went to the railing that overlooked the loggia. "What is it now?" she challenged. "I suppose you are going to tell me that Domenico himself is bewitched, and so cannot enter the fire!"

An older Franciscan turned to her. "Of course not, Madonna. But is it not possible that Fra Domenico's undergarments might also be as bewitched as his outer ones? Perhaps it is hard for you to understand, but there are those of us who believe sincerely that Fra Girolamo's power does not spring from God, but from a far more sinister source."

"This is absurd!" Violetta leaned low over the railing. "You are just stalling because you are afraid!"

"Of course we are afraid," the monk answered calmly. "We know that Fra Giuliano will die when he enters the fire. We have but one question."

Violetta waited, frowning, for the answer.

"If Fra Girolamo is not afraid—and he knows that God will spare him and prove him a prophet—why does he not enter the fire at once and settle the matter?"

Violetta drew back; she retook her seat and fanned herself frantically, muttering about the unfairness of the Franciscans. But I saw a glimmer of doubt in her eye. A cool breeze caused my veil to flutter. I looked out and up at the once-clear sky. Sudden winds had gathered swift clouds that smelled of rain.

Once again, Domenico emerged, presumably having surrendered the possibly accursed undergarments. At last he went to gather up the large cross he had carried into the square.

Gonfaloniere Valori tapped him on the shoulder and gestured for the cross to be laid down. Domenico obeyed wearily.

A few men in the crowd booed in disgust.

Another monk had joined the young Fra Giuliano by this time, and the two went together a third time to the government officials in the *ringhiera*. Savonarola was waiting there, next to the silver receptacle containing the Host, which had been set reverently upon a table. When the two Franciscans starting speaking to the officials, Savonarola began to shout. He pointed vehemently at the silver receptacle, at the other monks, at my husband and Francesco Valori. Savonarola turned then to Domenico, and it became clear, from Domenico's shaking head, that an impasse had been reached.

"What is it, what is it?" Violetta called.

The monks below us did not answer, but I looked at Savonarola's emphatic gesture at the silver receptacle and said, "They do not want to let Domenico carry the Host."

It was a point everyone had agreed on from the beginning. A Dominican friar had dreamed that Domenico successfully traversed the fire because he had been holding a consecrated wafer; Savonarola insisted that Domenico be allowed to do so. Before now, the Franciscans had offered no objection.

Furious, Domenico strode into the piazza and stood stubbornly at the entrance to the trial platform, staring into the flames; his angry demeanor contrasted with the sweet hymns being sung by his brothers. The wind whipped his robe about his legs, his torso. Overhead, the sky was darkening.

The older Franciscan who had spoken to Violetta earlier turned and faced us women. "Why," he asked kindly, "is Fra Domenico afraid to enter the fire without the Host? Is not his faith enough to preserve him? And why does not Savonarola put an end to the arguments? If he grows impatient with our demands, why does he not simply walk through the flames himself?"

Violetta did not answer. She frowned at the *ringhiera,* where her husband and the Franciscans stood arguing with Fra Girolamo.

"Coward!" someone shouted.

A few scattered drops of rain began to fall. Safe beneath the shelter of the loggia, I watched them strike the railing.

"Coward!" another voice cried. "Enter the fire!"

"He is afraid!" a man called. "Don't you see? He is afraid!"

Thunder boomed, frighteningly close; Violetta started and seized my arm. Domenico stood, solid and thick and relentless, in the quickening rain, while Savonarola continued to argue with the Priors.

Thunder, again, then a shriek: "He lied to us! He has always lied to us!"

Torrents of water crashed down in gray sheets, quickly flooding the piazza. Lightning dazzled. We wives left our seats and scurried to the center of the loggia. I peered out at the square: Domenico had not budged. Amazingly, neither had the crowd. They had come to learn the truth about the prophet, and would not leave without satisfaction.

The fire, which had blazed fiercely an instant before, was quenched; the wood and the brush were sodden with water rather than oil.

The people's enthusiasm was just as quickly extinguished. Men shouted over the roar of the rain.

"God Himself disapproves!"

"Fra Girolamo conjured up the storm, lest it expose his lies!"

My husband and Valori sent a representative dashing into the rain to speak to the commanders of the soldiers. They began to urge the crowd to disperse and go home. But the men in the piazza—most of them men who had cast their little red crosses to the ground—would not leave.

"Why would you not enter the fire?"

"Sodomite!"

"Heretic!"

"Liar!"

The wives grew frightened; they hurried to the *ringhiera,* to their husbands' sides. I went to stand beside Francesco. Savonarola was nearby, quite dry, but trembling as though the rain had soaked him through.

"I cannot leave without an escort! The Franciscans have turned the people against me!"

"I will arrange for one," Valori said, and disappeared inside the palazzo. Francesco sent a page out into the piazza to summon Claudio.

While we were riding home, the deluge let up as quickly as it had come. Francesco looked out the window and let go an odd, catching sigh.

"It is over."

LXVII

*W*e returned to the palazzo and Francesco did not venture out again that day. He ordered the gate closed and locked, and set stablehands armed with swords to guard it; then he went into his study and did not come out, even for supper.

My father failed to come to supper as well, which concerned me. I had not seen him in several days, but Francesco had forbidden anyone to leave the palazzo that night. Our street, fortunately, was quiet, but I could see the glow of torchlight coming from the west, where the monastery and church of San Marco lay.

Earlier that morning, Isabella had been nervously waiting with the women of San Marco—out of curiosity, not faith—to hear the outcome of the Trial by Fire. When Savonarola arrived, she said, he told the women that the Franciscans had delayed for so long that they angered God, Who sent the storm. The women were skeptical—even more so when their husbands arrived, furious with their prophet. Isabella reported that the parishioners had actually begun to battle the monks, and so she had left out of fright.

The next day was Palm Sunday. Francesco did not attend church, but chose again to remain home and forbade the rest of us to leave. This day, however, he had visitors, all at different times. The head of the *piagnoni*, Francesco Valori, called early in the morning and spoke privately to my husband in his study; he came and left wearing the stricken expression of a man who had discovered all his gold turned to sand. The second caller was a young messenger with a letter; my husband insisted on taking delivery of it personally.

The third caller was a prominent member of the *Arrabbiati*, one Benedetto de' Nerli. He arrived at night, after supper, and apologized for the lateness of the hour, but said that he had pressing need to speak to Ser Francesco.

My husband received him in our great sitting room. I had heard the disturbance and came down; although I was not invited to sit with the men, I hovered near the open door and listened. Ser Benedetto had a deep, resonant voice and spoke very clearly, for which I was grateful.

"I come bearing bad news," Ser Benedetto began.

Francesco's voice was faint, slightly sarcastic. "I can't imagine how the situation could grow worse."

Ser Benedetto ignored the comment and continued, steady and forthcoming. "The *piagnoni* have lost their leader. Francesco Valori was killed tonight."

There came a silence, as my husband digested this tragedy. "How did it happen?"

"He was attending vespers at San Marco. A group of roughs disrupted the service and threatened to burn his house. It grew ugly; they took him by force, but he managed to escape. When he got to his house, he hid in a cupboard; the group followed and shot his wife in the forehead with a crossbow. Then they found Valori and started to drag him to the Signoria—"

"A foolish course, if they wanted to harm him," my husband interjected. "He would find safety there."

Ser Benedetto's tone turned abruptly cool. "Perhaps not." He paused to let his innuendo sink in, then continued. "On the way to the Signoria, they came across Vicenzo Ridolfi and Simone Tornabuoni . . ."

I knew the names. These men were relatives of two of the beheaded men, Lorenzo Tornabuoni and Niccolò Ridolfi.

"They can hardly be blamed for wanting revenge on Valori, who spearheaded the campaign to behead their loved ones. They had taken to the streets, as have so many others who hope for Savonarola's arrest. Tornabuoni wielded a pruning hook . . ."

I closed my eyes.

". . . and split Valori's skull in two, while Ridolfi cried, 'You will never govern again!' As far as I know, Valori's body is still lying out in the street."

"Why are you telling me this?" my husband asked. His tone was not cold or defensive, as I would have expected; there was a hint of receptiveness in it.

"For the current session, as you know, the Signoria is split evenly between your party and mine. If it remains equally divided, there will be no legal way to resolve the question of Savonarola. It will be decided in the streets, with bloodshed, and all the citizens suffering.

"But if—"

My husband interrupted. "If just one *piagnone* prior were to change his loyalties and side with the *Arrabbiati* . . ."

"Precisely. Justice could be administered swiftly, and many lives spared."

"Ser Benedetto," my husband said, with the same warm graciousness he extended to any honored guest. "I shall think on what you have said. And I shall give you my answer in the morning, when the Signoria convenes."

"Let it be no later," Ser Benedetto said, and I heard the warning in it.

I heard the warning, and was happy. I wanted Fra Girolamo to burn. Even more, I wanted Domenico to burn with him.

On Monday morning, my husband told me to have the servants prepare the house for a prestigious guest, who would be coming to stay with us for a few weeks; then he left for the Signoria. Even though the streets were calmer, thanks to the small battalions of neighborhood troops maintaining the peace, he did not travel alone: He requested that Claudio drive him, and he had two armed men accompany him in the carriage.

I was stranded at home, without a driver. Zalumma and I could always ride on horseback together, if we desperately needed to leave the house—but it was always safer to have a male companion, and that was under normal circumstances, not uncertain times like these. And every servant that might act as chaperone was far too busy obeying Francesco's orders to ready the palazzo for our guest.

I chafed to see my father. I decided that as soon as Francesco returned, I would insist on going to visit my father, to be sure that he was well. I envisioned the conversation with Francesco in my mind: his refusal, saying it was not safe, and my insistence, saying that I would have Claudio and the two armed men to protect me.

Zalumma and I fetched Matteo from the nursery and took him down to the garden, since the day was pleasant. We chased him and giggled, and I clasped his hands and wrists and whirled him round in a circle until his feet lifted off the ground.

I intended to exhaust us both. I knew of no other way to brighten my thoughts. But for the first time, Matteo tired first. Head lolling, he slept in my arms—almost too heavy now to hold—and I walked beside Zalumma past the rosebushes.

Zalumma kept her voice low. "What do you think will happen to Savonarola?"

"I think that Francesco will join the *Arrabbiati*," I said, "and that Savonarola will die. Be burned at the stake, just like Mother said. She was right about the five headless men, don't you remember?"

"I remember." Zalumma gazed at a distant olive grove on a hill, at some secret memory. "She was right about many things." Her tone hardened. "I'll be glad when he dies."

"It won't change anything," I said.

She snapped her head about to look at me in disbelief. "What do you mean? It will change *everything*!"

I sighed. "The same people will be running Florence. It won't change anything at all."

Afterward, when Matteo was asleep in the nursery and the servants were all downstairs eating in the kitchen, I went to Francesco's study.

It was foolish, going in the middle of the day, but I was consumed by restlessness and a mounting sense of worry. And I had not even considered how I would get to Leonardo if I found a new letter.

> *It is time to join the* Arrabbiati *and sacrifice the prophet. We have already translated into action your suggestion of luring Piero to Florence and making public example of him. The people are still angry; we will give them a second scapegoat. Otherwise, with Savonarola gone, they might soften too much toward the Medici. We are taking Messer Iacopo's plan as our model: I shall expose the traitor in the midst of his crime, take him to the piazza for public spectacle, and rely on mercenary troops as reinforcement. Those mercenaries failed Messer Iacopo years ago—but ours, I assure you, will not fail us.* Popolo e libertà!
>
> *Seek out Lord Priors who will support us in this move. Recompense them generously. Guarantee them important roles in the new government to come; but only you will be my second.*
>
> *Let us not confine our public spectacle to Piero. We must dispense with all Medici brothers—for if even one survives, we are not free of the threat. Cardinal Giovanni presents the least danger, and my agents will try to deal with him in Rome, where he will surely stay.*
>
> *But the youngest—he is the most dangerous, having all the intelligence and political acumen his eldest brother lacks. And in your house sleeps the perfect lure to bring him to Florence.*

I dropped silently to the floor as if downed by an assassin's blade and sat, gasping, my skirts furling about me, the impossible letter in my lap. I was too stunned to embrace its contents. I dared not. My father had been right: If I knew the full truth, Francesco and Claudio would read it in my face, my every gesture.

For the sake of my father and my child, I chose to become numb. I could not let myself think or feel. I could not let myself hope or rage.

I rose on trembling legs, then carefully refolded the letter and slipped it back into the envelope. I went up the stairs to my room. Slowly, deliberately, I took a book from the trunk and set it on my night table, where Isabella would be sure to see it.

Rapid footsteps sounded on the stairs, in the corridor; as I went to open the door, Zalumma pulled it open first.

She did not notice that I was stunned, wild-eyed, pale. Her black brows, her lips, were stark, broad strokes of grief.

"Loretta," she said. "From your father's house. She is here. Come quickly."

He was dying, Loretta said. Three days earlier, his bowels had turned to blood, and he had not been able to eat or drink. Fever left him often delirious. Not plague, she insisted. Plague would not have brought the bloody flux. For two days, he had been asking for me.

And each time Loretta had come, Claudio or Francesco or one of the armed men had sent her away.

Loretta had driven herself in the wagon. I did not stop or think or question; I said nothing to anyone. I went immediately to the wagon and climbed in. Zalumma came with me. Loretta took the driver's seat, and together we left.

It was a terrible ride over the Arno, over the Ponte Santa Trinità, over the murky waters where Giuliano supposedly had drowned. I tried to stop the words repeating in my mind, to no success.

But the youngest—he is the most dangerous. . . .

And in your house sleeps the perfect lure.

"I can't," I said aloud. Zalumma looked worriedly over at me, but said nothing. The letter had to be a trap; Francesco must have discovered me rifling through his desk, or else Isabella had lost her nerve and told all. It was impossible, of course. The world could not have known he was alive and not told me.

I drew a deep breath and remembered that my father was dying.

The ground beneath my feet had tilted sideways, and I was clawing for purchase.

For the first time in my life, I entered my father Antonio's bedchamber. It was midday; a cool breeze blew outside. In my father's room, it was dark and hot from the fire, and the air stank of unspeakable things.

Antonio lay naked beneath a worn blanket, on a bed damp from cleaning. His eyes were closed; in the light filtering through the half-closed shutters, he looked grayish white. I had not realized how thin he had become; below his bare chest, his ribs thrust out so prominently, I could count each one. His face looked as though the skin were melting off the bone.

I stepped up to the bed and he opened his eyes. They were lost and glittering, the whites yellowed. "Lisa," he whispered. His breath smelled vilely sweet.

"Father," I answered. Loretta brought a chair. I thanked her and asked her to leave, but asked Zalumma to stay. Then I sat down and took my father's hand; he was too weak to return my grip.

His breath came quick and shallow. "How like your mother you look . . . but even more beautiful." I opened my mouth to contradict him, but he frowned. "Yes, more beautiful . . ." His gaze rolled about the room. "Is Matteo here?"

Guilt pierced me; how could I have denied him his one joy, his grandson? "I am sorry," I said. "He is sleeping."

"Good. This is a terrible place for a child."

I did not look at Zalumma. I kept my gaze on my father and said, "They have poisoned you, then."

"Yes. It happened faster than I thought. . . ." He blinked at me. "I can hardly see you. The shadows . . ." He grimaced at a spasm of pain, then gave me an apologetic look once he recovered. "I wanted to get us out of Florence. I had a contact I thought could help us. . . . They gave him more money than I did. I'm sorry. Can't even give you that . . ." All the speaking had wearied him; gasping, he closed his eyes.

"There is one thing you can give me," I said. "The truth."

He opened his eyes a slit and gave me a sidewise glance.

"I know you killed the elder Giuliano," I said. Behind me, Zalumma released a sound of surprise and rage; my father began to mouth words of apology. "Please—don't be upset; I'm not asking you to explain yourself. And I know you killed Pico. I know that you did whatever Francesco told you, to keep me safe. But we are not done with secrets. You have more to tell me. About my first husband. About my only husband."

His face contorted; he made a low, terrible noise that might have been a sob. "Ah, daughter," he said. "It broke my heart to lie so cruelly."

"It's true, then." I closed my eyes, wanting to rail, to give vent to my fury and joy and grief, but I could not make a sound. When I opened my eyes again, everything in the room looked changed, different.

"If I had told you," he whispered, "you would have tried to go to him. And they would have killed you. They would have killed the baby. And if he had tried to come to you, they would have killed him."

"*Giuliano,*" Zalumma whispered. I turned to look at her. "I did not know," she explained. "I was never sure. Someone in the marketplace once said something that made me think perhaps . . . but I decided he was mad. And few people in Florence have ever dared breathe the name Medici, except to criticize. No one else ever dared say anything around me, around you, because you had married Francesco. And Francesco told all the other servants never to mention Giuliano's name, for fear of upsetting you."

My life with Francesco, I realized, had been limited: I saw the servants, my husband's guests and associates, the insides of churches. And no one had ever spoken to me of Giuliano. No one except Francesco had ever spoken at length to me about the Medici.

I looked back at my father and could not keep the pain from my voice. "Why did he not come to me?"

"He did. He sent a man; Francesco killed him. He sent a letter; Francesco made me write one, saying you had died. I don't think even then he believed it; Francesco said someone had gone to the Baptistery and found the marriage records."

Salai. Leonardo. Perhaps Giuliano had heard of my marriage and had it confirmed; perhaps he had thought I wanted him to think me dead.

Imagine you are with Giuliano again, Leonardo had said. *Imagine that you are introducing him to his child. . . .*

"You want the truth. . . ." Antonio whispered. "There is one thing more. The reason I was so angry with your mother . . ."

His voice was fading; I leaned closer to hear.

"Look at your face, child. Your face. You will not see mine there. And I have looked at you a thousand times, and never seen Giuliano de' Medici's. There was another man. . . ."

I dismissed the last statement as the product of delirium; I did not consider it long, for my father began to cough, a low burbling sound. Blood foamed on his lips.

Zalumma was already beside me. "Sit him up!"

I reached beneath his arm and lifted him up and forward; the movement caused a fountain of dark blood to spill from his mouth into his lap. Zalumma went to call for Loretta while I held my father's shoulders with one arm and his head with the other. He gagged, and a second, brighter gush of blood followed; this seemed to relieve him, and he sat, breathing heavily. I wanted to ask him whose face he saw in mine, but I knew there was no time.

"I love you," I said into his ear. "And I know you love me. God will forgive your sins."

He heard. He groaned and tried to reach up to pat my hand, but he was not strong enough.

"I will leave soon with Matteo," I whispered. "I will find a way to go to Giuliano, because Francesco has little use for me now. You mustn't worry about us. We will be safe, and we will always love you."

He shook his head, agitated. He tried to speak, and started, instead, to cough.

Loretta came in with towels, then, and we cleaned him as best we could, then let him lie down. He did not speak coherently again. His eyes had dulled, and he did not react to the sound of my voice. Soon after, he closed his eyes and seemed to sleep.

I sat with him through the afternoon. I sat with him at dusk, when evening fell. When Francesco came, his indignation over my escape from the palazzo constrained by false sympathy, I would not let him in my father's room.

I stayed beside my father until the hour past midnight, when I realized he had not been breathing for some time. I called Loretta and Zalumma, and then I went downstairs, to the dining room, where Francesco sat drinking wine.

"Is he dead?" he asked, kindly.

I nodded. My eyes were dry.

"I shall pray for his soul. What did he die of, do you know?"

"Fever," I said. "Brought on by an ailment of the bowels."

Francesco studied my face carefully, and seemed satisfied by what he saw there. Perhaps I was not such a bad spy after all. "I am so sorry. Will you be staying with him?"

"Yes. Until after the funeral. I will need to speak to the servants, find them placement with us or a new family. And there will be other matters to deal with . . ."

"I need to return home. I am awaiting word on our guest's arrival, and there are still many matters to take care of in regards to the Signoria."

"Yes." I knew that Savonarola had been arrested, thanks to

Francesco's timely defection to the *Arrabbiati*. At least I would no longer have to pretend that my husband and I were pious folk.

"Will I see you, then, at the funeral?"

"Of course. May God give us all strength."

"Yes," I said. I wanted strength. I would need it, to kill Francesco.

LXVIII

I stayed at my father's house that night and slept in my mother's bed. Zalumma went back to Francesco's palazzo and fetched me personal items and a mourning gown and veil for the funeral. She also brought, at my request, the large emerald Francesco had given me the first night I had sullied myself with him, and the earrings of diamond and opal. Matteo remained at home, with the nursemaid; I did not have the heart to bring him to such an unhappy place.

I did not watch Loretta wash my father's body as I waited for Zalumma to return. Instead, I went to his study, and found a sheet of writing parchment, and a quill, and ink.

Giuliano di Lorenzo de' Medici
Rome

My love, my love,

I was lied to, told you were dead. But my heart never changed toward you.

A warning: Salvatore de' Pazzi and Francesco del Gio-condo plan to draw you and Piero here to kill you. They are amassing an army in Florence. They want to repeat—this time, with success—Messer Iacopo de' Pazzi's plan, to rally the people in the Piazza della Signoria against the Medici.

You must not come.

I paused. After the passage of so much time, how could he be sure of my handwriting? What could I say so that he could be certain of the letter's authenticity?

I only ask, as I did before: Give me a place, in some other city, and a time. Either way, I am coming to you soon. You dare not communicate it by regular correspondence—your letter would be confiscated and read, and I and our child, your son, endangered.

I have been separated from you because of a monstrous falsehood. Now that I know the truth, I cannot tolerate the distance between us an instant longer than I must.

Your loving wife,
Lisa di Antonio Gherardini

When Zalumma returned, I handed her the folded parchment. "I cannot send this as correspondence," I said. "The Council of Eight would intercept it, and have my head. I will have to buy someone willing to hide the correspondence on his person and ride all the way to Rome with it, and see it personally delivered." I showed her the emerald and the earrings, and handed them to her.

"You are the only one I can trust," I told her. I had thought I could trust Leonardo; now, I could not speak his name without venom. He had knowingly kept from me the one truth that would have healed my heart.

Giuliano . . . dead. Few people have heard this. Most believe he is still alive.

Do you not love him still?

He had been reticent on our first meeting because he thought I had married another man while my first husband still lived. He had thought me capable of complete betrayal—because he was capable of it himself.

Zalumma took the jewels and nestled them carefully in the pocket hidden in the folds of her gown. "If it is at all possible," she said, "I will see it done."

We agreed that she would go early in the morning to search for a trustworthy courier. The lie: I was so grief-stricken that she had gone to the apothecary's in search of something to soothe my nerves. It was so early, and I so desperate, that I did not want to wait for the stable-hand to wake and ready the horses, and so I sent her off on foot.

I was terrified to send her off on such a dangerous hunt; one thing especially worried me. "I did not bring my knife," I said; if I had, I would have given it to her.

Her smile was small but wicked. "I did."

I did not mourn that night. I lay in my mother's bed, with Zalumma at my feet in the cot that my father had never been able to bring himself to remove, and did not sleep. Now that Antonio was dead, Francesco had no more use for me—except as a lure, a role I would not play. The time had come to escape; my ultimate destination was Rome. I considered a dozen different ways to try to make it past the city gates—but none were safe or feasible when a restless two-year-old boy was involved.

I resolved only one thing, that we three—Zalumma, Matteo, and I—would leave in the hours before dawn, after Francesco had returned from his revels, so that I could kill him as he lay drunk in his bed.

In the quiet of morning, when everyone was still asleep, the time came for Zalumma to go. I took her hands and kissed her cheek.

"You will see me again," she promised, "no later than your father's burial. If I am late, I will find you at the church." She moved to the door, her step light; and then a thought stopped her and made her look back over her shoulder at me. "You forgave your father many things," she said. "Too many. But perhaps I will try to forgive him, too."

Once she was gone, I went into my father's bedroom. He looked cold and unhappy in his white linen shift, with his hands folded around a little red cross. I took it from his grasp and hid it in the wardrobe, under a pile of tunics where Loretta would not find it; and when I did so, I came across a gold-handled stiletto—neat and deadly—and hid it in my belt.

The funeral was just after *none,* mid-afternoon, at Santo Spirito. Loretta had gone early to make the arrangements; since the plague was no longer widespread, it had been easier than she expected to hire gravediggers.

The Mass said for my father was short and sad. Francesco came and sat impatiently through the service, then left abruptly, saying there was an emergency at the Signoria. I was relieved; it had grown almost impossible to hide my infinite loathing for him.

Few stood at my father's graveside: only Uncle Lauro, his wife and children, Loretta, my father's stablehand, my father's cook, and me. Matteo remained at home with the nursemaid. As I cast the first handful of earth onto my father's coffin—nestled beside my mother's sweet stone cherubs—I shed no tears.

Perhaps fear stole them from me: Zalumma had not returned. It had been a mistake, I told myself, to send her out alone with such expensive jewels, especially so early when the streets were empty. If she had encountered a thief, who would have heard her cries for help?

The time came to return to my father's home for a funeral supper. Uncle Lauro and the others tried to coax me into walking back with them to my parents' house, but I refused. I wanted a private moment with my father and mother; I wanted to remain in case Zalumma finally returned.

When the others left, I was alone only briefly. One of Santo Spirito's Augustinian monks approached, in his order's traditional habit, with a capuchin's gathered folds around his shoulders and his cowl raised.

I kept my eyes focused on my father's grave; I wanted no conversation. But he came to stand directly beside me and said, softly, "Madonna Lisa. I am so terribly sorry."

The sound of his voice disgusted me. I turned my face away.

"You signaled with the book that you had found a letter," he said, "but when you did not come I became concerned. I am saddened to learn that Antonio's passing is the cause."

"Go away." My voice was ragged. "Go away and never come back."

In the periphery of my vision, Leonardo bowed his head. "You are right to be angry: I could not save him, though you begged me to. But I could find no way. No way short of endangering you and Matteo. Perhaps when your grief eases, you will understand—"

"I understand that you are a liar, that you have been one from the beginning. You *knew*—" I tried to utter the words and choked; I wheeled on him. "Giuliano is alive. And you let me live in grief, in agony, all this time. Like a good spy, you used me without heart!"

He lifted his chin; he straightened. "I told you long ago that I could not tell you everything because it would endanger you. I have not used you. I care more for you than you know."

"The hell you care! You look at me so you can moon over your dear lost Giuliano."

He colored at that and had to compose himself. "How did you learn he was alive? From the letter, then?"

"And from my father, before he died."

Inappropriately, with the familiarity of a husband, a brother, he seized my arm at the elbow. I resisted, but he would not let go. "Tell me, then, whom did you speak to of this? Does Francesco have any idea that you know Giuliano is alive?"

I tried to shake my arm free; he tightened his grip. "No," I said. "I'm not that big a fool. *Why* didn't you tell me? Why have you let me suffer all this time?"

"Look at you," he said, with a sharpness and a coldness I had never heard in him. "You're answering your own question. People kill and die because they cannot control their emotions. You did not know me very well, the first time we met at Santissima Annunziata. You had no reason to trust me. If I had told you Giuliano was alive, you would have written him immediately. Or you would have tried to go to Rome to find him. Nothing I might have said could have stopped you. And you, or he, or both of you, would have died as a result. If I ever told him that you married Giocondo because you thought he was dead, he'd—"

"He'd have come to me, wouldn't he? So you've lied to him, too. Why should I ever trust you now?" My face contorted; the tears that had been so long suppressed suddenly streamed unchecked down my cheeks. "Why should I tell *you* the contents of the letter? I'm warning him myself of the danger—"

"*God,*" he whispered, his face so slack with fear that I fell silent. "Lisa—swear to me you have not tried to contact him!"

"I'll swear nothing." My voice was ugly. "They mean to entice him here, and Piero, then kill them. They want to make it all repeat— rally the people against the Medici, as Messer Iacopo meant to do— and this time succeed. Do you think I am such a child that I would let Giuliano endanger himself? I told him not to come. I told him to stay." I shook my arm. "Let go of me!"

He reached for me again; I took a step away, back toward the gravediggers. "Lisa . . . They will discover this. They will kill you."

"They won't find out. I've seen to it."

In the distance, someone called my name. I turned, and saw Loretta, half running toward us.

"Lisa, *please.*" I had never heard such desperation in his voice. "You cannot go back with her—they will trap you, try to kill you, or use you against Giuliano. What must I do to convince you . . . ? Everything I have ever done has been for your safety, and your child's." His eyes glittered; I realized, to my surprise, that they were filling with tears.

A brilliant performance, I told myself. Loretta was still too distant to hear us, but close enough for me to see panic on her face; he was forced to drop my arm, lest she see a monk behaving so suspiciously. "You'll have to convince me quickly, because I am going home." And I turned my back to him and took a step toward Loretta.

"Lisa, I love you," he said quickly.

I glanced at him over my shoulder. "Not so much as you loved Giuliano," I said nastily.

"More," he said. "More, even, than I loved your mother."

I slowed. I stopped. I looked up at him.

"Giuliano de' Medici was not your father," he said. "I am."

"Madonna Lisa!" Loretta called. She was breathless, red-faced, at the gate of the churchyard. "Matteo is sick! He is sick; they think it is *la moria*! Claudio is here, waiting to drive you home!"

"Matteo is sick," I said to him. He opened his mouth and reached for me again, but before he could touch me, before he could speak, I lifted my skirts and ran to meet Loretta.

I rushed into the front entry of our palazzo and would have run up the stairs, but my husband called out from the dining hall.

"Lisa! Come and meet our guest!"

Francesco emerged, wearing his typical benign smile, and took my arm. "Come," he said, and drew me with him before I had time to protest.

A man sat at the middle of our long dining table; at the sight of me, he rose and bowed. He was a good head shorter than Francesco and twenty years younger. His short tunic, sharp goatee, and accent smacked of Rome. "Madonna Lisa, is it?"

"Sir," I said, "you must forgive me. My son is very ill. I must go to him."

Francesco's little smile did not waver. "There is no hurry. Come sit with us."

His placid expression was entirely out of place; I panicked. Had my child died, and was Francesco now going to attempt to soothe me?

Was this stranger a physician, here to comfort me? "Where is Matteo?" I demanded.

"Safe," he said, and that single, sharp word was double-edged.

He did not try to stop me as I fled up the stairs, stumbling over my skirts, frantic. When I threw the door to the nursery open, I saw the room was empty—neatly cleaned of Matteo's things—and the nursemaid's room was empty, as well. There were no linens on his little bed, in the crib.

I went back down the stairs, a madwoman. Francesco stopped me on the second level, on the landing in front of his chambers.

"Where is he?" I demanded, seething, trembling. "Where have you taken him?"

"We are all in the study," he said calmly, and took my arm the instant before I reached for the knife.

I scanned the study: My baby was not there. Instead, our guest was sitting at the little round table in the center of the room, in front of the fireplace. Two men flanked him: Claudio and one of the soldiers who had guarded our palazzo immediately after Savonarola's trial by fire.

The soldier held a knife to Zalumma's throat.

"How can you do this?" I hissed at Francesco. "How can you do this to our son?"

He made a soft sound of disgust. "I have eyes. He is like his mother: of questionable heritage." My cold Francesco.

He guided me to a chair across from our guest; I sank into it, my gaze fastened on Zalumma. Her face was stony, her stance unrepentant. I looked down. On the table in front of me was the letter to Giuliano, unfolded and open so that it could be easily read. Beside it rested a quill and inkpot, and a fresh piece of parchment.

Francesco stood beside me and rested his hand on my shoulder. "There is a problem with this letter. It needs to be rewritten."

I balked. I looked at Zalumma's eyes: They were unfathomable black mirrors. Our esteemed guest nodded faintly at the soldier, and he pressed the tip of the knife against her white throat until she gasped. A dark trickle escaped the flesh there and collected in the hollow at the base of her neck. She looked away; she did not want me to see her face and how frightened she was, to see that she knew she was going to die.

"*Don't,*" I said. "I will write whatever you want." I sized up the soldier, Claudio, and the goateed man, all on the other side of the table; I glanced at Francesco, standing beside me. If I reached for the stiletto hidden in my belt, I would be stopped before I ever got around the table, and Zalumma would be killed.

Francesco made a gracious gesture to the goateed man. "Ser Salvatore," he said. "Please."

Salvatore put his elbows on the table and leaned forward on them, toward me. "Copy the first two lines," he said. "The letter must sound as if you wrote it."

I dipped the quill in the pot, and scratched out the words:

> *My love, my love,*
>
> *I was lied to, told you were dead. But my heart never changed toward you.*

"Very good," Salvatore said, then dictated the next lines.

> *Your son and I are in mortal danger; we are captured by your enemies. If you and your brother Piero do not appear at Santa Maria del Fiore for High Mass on the twenty-fourth of May, they will kill us. Send troops, or anyone else in your place, and we will die.*
>
> > *Your loving wife,*
> > *Lisa di Antonio Gherardini*

"*Giocondo,*" he had said, but I stubbornly would not add it.

Francesco folded the letter and handed it to Claudio, who pocketed it. "Now," my supposed husband said, turning to me. "Let's talk about your spying."

"I didn't mean to spy," I said. "I was curious, and read just the one letter. . . ."

"Curious. That's not what Isabella says. She says that you leave a book on your night table as a signal, for her to tell a certain Giancarlo that you will be going to pray the next day."

Salvatore's tone was casual, almost friendly. "Who do you meet at Santissima Annunziata, Lisa?"

"Just Giancarlo," I answered quickly. "I go to tell him what the letter says."

"She's lying." Francesco's tone was brutal; he had used it before, when he had uttered the word *whore*.

Salvatore was very, very still. "I think your husband is right, Madonna Lisa. And I think that he is right when he says that you are very fond of your slave. She was your mother's, yes?"

I stared down at the table. "I go to meet a spy," I said. "An older man, with gray hair. I don't know his name. I found Giancarlo in your study one night, with the letter, and I was curious. I read it."

"How long ago?" Salvatore asked.

"I don't know—a year, perhaps two. He said he worked for the Medici. I decided to do what he told me—to go to Santissima Annunziata and tell the old man about the letters."

Salvatore glanced back at the soldier who held Zalumma. Simply glanced, and lifted a finger.

I followed his gaze. The soldier's knife made a quick, small movement beneath Zalumma's jaw. Quick and small and simple; I heard the sound of fluid spilling. She would have fallen straight down, but he caught and lowered her. She went to the floor languid and graceful as a swan.

"Call a servant," Salvatore told the soldier. "Get something to clean this up."

I screamed and reared up; Francesco pushed me straight back down.

Salvatore faced me. "You are lying, Madonna Lisa. You know that the young man's name is not Giancarlo; it is Gian Giacomo. And you know the old man's name."

I sobbed, hysterical, unable to stop, to speak. Zalumma was dead and I wanted to die.

Francesco had to speak very loudly to be heard over my weeping. "Come, now, Lisa, shall I send for little Matteo? We can bring him in here, as well. Or will you tell us the name of your old man?"

"Bring him," I gasped. "Bring him, and show me he is alive. Because if he is not, you will have to kill me."

Francesco let go the most irritated of sighs, but Salvatore nodded to him to leave the room. He returned moments later, followed by the frightened young nursemaid, stooping as she led Matteo in by the hand.

He laughed and wanted to come to me; he held out his arms for me. But when he saw Zalumma on the floor and his mother sobbing, he began to cry himself. I reached for him as Francesco lifted him up and handed him back to the nursemaid; my fingers grazed the dimpled back of his hand.

"All right," Francesco clucked, and closed the door over them.

He and Salvatore turned to me. "The name, Lisa," Francesco said.

I could not see Zalumma where she had fallen behind the table, but I sensed her body the way one might sense the warmth of a fire. I bowed my head and looked down at my hands, and said very softly, "Leonardo da Vinci."

LXIX

I did not look at Zalumma as they led me out; I did not want to remember her as I remembered my mother, dull-eyed and spattered with blood. Francesco and Salvatore were speaking as Claudio led me away; Salvatore's tone was heated. "Now shall we have to amend the plan? If she has told this to others, to this Leonardo . . ."

Francesco was cool. "Isabella said she has had no time to go to Santissima Annunziata. She discovered the letter before she went to see her father; she has been nowhere since then, except to his house and to his funeral."

They were drifting words which meant nothing to me at the time. They would make a difference later.

For the next few weeks, I was confined to my chamber. Different men stood guard in the corridor outside my door. Francesco told the servants that I had been discovered spying for the Medici, and that the Signoria had not yet decided whether to bring charges; out of kindness, they had permitted him to keep me under close watch at our palazzo.

On the first day they locked me in my room, I was alone for an hour and, despite crippling grief, I realized that I should hide my father's stiletto before I was searched or undressed. I slid it deep into the feather layer of my mattress, on the far side by the wall; and when, that night, Elena came with a tray of food and the intention of unlacing my gown, I faced her without concern.

Elena's ever-serene gaze and smile had vanished; she was troubled in my presence and could not meet my eyes.

I struggled very hard to speak coherently, without tears. "I want to wash her," I said.

Elena set the tray down on the table near the hearth and glanced at me, then swiftly dropped her gaze to the floor. "What's that, Madonna?"

"I would like to help wash Zalumma's body. She was very dear to me. And . . ." My voice began to break. "I want to see her properly buried. If you would ask Francesco—he could send a guard with me. She helped birth me. Please . . . if you would ask him . . ."

Saddened, she bowed her head. "I will ask him, Madonna. He has no heart and will refuse, but I will ask."

I sat in a chair in front of the cold hearth, closed my eyes, and pressed steepled hands to my lips, but I was too overwhelmed to pray. Elena moved beside me and gently, briefly, touched my forearm.

"I will do my best to convince him, Madonna." She hesitated. "It is terrible, what they did to Zalumma. . . . They say she was a spy, that she was dangerous, but I know better. I was not always with Ser Francesco's household. I came with my mistress, Madonna Nannina. I loved her so, and when she died . . ." She shook her head. "I wanted to go to another house. I wish now I had. I am afraid of him."

"And Matteo," I said, anguished. "If I could know whether—"

Her expression lightened; she looked in my eyes then. "Your child is well. They haven't hurt him—I suppose that is too heartless even for Ser Francesco to consider. They are keeping him downstairs, near the servants."

The ache in my chest eased; I put a hand to it. Emboldened, I asked, "And Isabella?"

"Gone. Escaped—" She broke off and said no more, realizing that she might be endangering herself. She unlaced my gown and put it in the wardrobe, and I was left alone. Outside in the corridor, I heard the scrape of a chair against the floor, and a heavy body settling into it. Claudio, I supposed, or the soldier.

I was dazed that first night, overwhelmed. I had lost so many: my mother, Giuliano, my father . . . but Zalumma had always been there, caring for me. Zalumma, who would have known how to comfort me now that Matteo had been taken away. I told myself repeatedly that Salvatore might want to hurt Matteo, but Francesco would never allow it. But my hope for my child was a fine thread; if I clung to it tightly, it would break.

I would not go to my massive feather bed with the dagger hidden in it. Instead, I crawled onto Zalumma's little cot and wept there until I fell asleep.

Francesco, of course, would not hear of my assisting with Zalumma's burial or attending the service; he let the disposition of her corpse remain a cruel mystery.

Until my father and Zalumma died, until Matteo was taken from me, I had not realized how thoroughly hatred could usurp a heart. As my father Antonio had been at the thought of losing his wife to another, I was consumed. I dreamed of murder; I knew I could never rest until I saw my father's dagger buried in Francesco's chest, up to the hilt.

Your temper is hot, the astrologer had said, *a furnace in which the sword of justice must be forged.*

I cared nothing for justice. I wanted revenge.

During the long, solitary hours, I drew out the stiletto and felt it, cold and heavy, in my hand; I convinced myself that this had been the instrument of the elder Giuliano's murder, that my father had kept it as a reminder of his guilt. *It all repeats,* my mother had whispered, and at last I understood. She had not meant that we would both fall in love with men named Giuliano, or bear children who were not the spawn of their ostensible fathers, or feel imprisoned by our husbands.

You are caught in a cycle of violence, of blood and deceit. What others have begun, you must finish.

I put my finger to the dagger's tip, deadly fine and shining, and let it pierce me, silent and sharp. Blood rilled, a dark pearl, and I put my mouth to it before it dripped onto my skirts. It tasted like metal, like the blade; I wished it had been Francesco's.

What was to repeat? How was I meant to finish it?

I recalled, as best I could, what my mother had told me of Giuliano's death; I contemplated each separate step.

In the Duomo, the priest had lifted the wine-filled chalice, offering it to God for blessing; this was the signal for the assassins to strike.

In the adjacent campanile, the bell had begun to chime; this was the signal for Messer Iacopo to ride to the Piazza della Signoria, where he would proclaim the end of the Medicis' reign, and be joined by mercenary soldiers who would help him seize the Palazzo della Signoria—in effect, the government.

Messer Iacopo's plan was foiled because his hired soldiers had failed to join him, and because the people had remained loyal to the Medici.

In the Duomo, however, the plan was partially successful.

In the instant before the signal of the raised chalice was given, my father Antonio struck, wounding Giuliano in the back. Baroncelli's blow followed; third came Francesco de' Pazzi's frenzied, brutal attack. But Lorenzo—on the other side of the church—proved too swift for his aspiring assassins. He suffered only a minor wound and fought off his attackers until he was able to escape to the north sacristy.

If Piero and Giuliano came, they would play the role of the two brothers. And I had no doubt that Francesco and Ser Salvatore would ensure that there were numerous assassins awaiting them in the cathedral. Salvatore clearly dreamed of taking Messer Iacopo's role, and riding, this time victorious, into the Piazza della Signoria, to tell the crowd that he had just rescued Florence from the Medici.

But what was my role to be? I would not sit passively and wait to be killed; I knew my life was forfeit regardless of the plan's outcome. And so was my son's, unless I took measures to prevent it.

And then I realized: I would be the penitent, the one fueled by personal, not political rage. The one to strike the first blow.

I thought often of Leonardo. My tears in those days sprang from many wells; guilt over my betrayal of him was one of them. Isabella had disappeared from the palazzo, and Elena would say no more about her; I hoped that she had escaped and warned Salai and his master. I could only hope that they had left Santissima Annunziata long before Salvatore's men arrived.

I thought of his last words to me. *Giuliano de' Medici was not your father. I am.*

Lisa, I love you, he had said. His tone had reminded me of someone else's, someone who had spoken long ago, but it was not until I pondered for some time that I remembered whose it was.

Lorenzo de' Medici had lain dying, and I had asked him why he had been so kind to me.

I love you, child.

Had he believed himself to be my uncle? Or had Leonardo told him the truth?

I lifted my hand mirror and peered into it. I had lied to Leonardo when I once said that I did not often look at my reflection. When I had learned of my mother's affair with Giuliano, I had diligently searched my face for hints of the smiling young man who had posed for Leonardo's terra-cotta bust. And I had never seen him there.

Now as I looked into the mirror, Leonardo gazed back at me, haggard and owlish.

I woke late on the twenty-third of May, the day before Giuliano was to meet me in the Duomo. I had slept poorly the night before, awakened by Matteo's muffled wails downstairs; I cried, too, until well after dawn, then fell into a heavy, sodden sleep.

When I rose, I went out to my balcony and squinted up at the sun, startled to find that it had passed directly overhead and strayed

slightly to the west; it was already afternoon. The sky was exceptionally blue and cloudless—save for a long finger of dark smoke rising up
in the east.

I stared at it, entranced, until Elena entered. I went back into the
room just as she set a tray of bread and fruit on the table. She glanced
up as she straightened, her expression grave. "You saw the smoke,
then."

"Yes," I said slowly, still dazed from sleep. "Is it—"

"Savonarola," she said.

"They burned him, then." I had heard no news at all for the past
few weeks, since learning Savonarola had been arrested. But I had
known at once when I saw the smoke.

"Hung him first," she replied unhappily. "In the piazza, in the very
same spot as the Bonfire of the Vanities and the Trial by Fire. I went
this morning. Ser Francesco encouraged us all to go."

"Did he say anything?"

"Fra Girolamo? No, not a word. He was dressed only in his
woolen undershirt. It was an ugly business. They built a round scaffold for the fire, filled it full of tinder, and raised a wooden beam in its
center, so high that they had to build a long ladder to climb up to the
top. The hangman carried him up and put the noose round his neck.
He struggled a bit, didn't die right away.

"Then they lit the fire. Some fool had put firecrackers in the tinder,
terrifying everyone at first. They put chains around the monks so that
when the nooses burned away the bodies wouldn't drop down into the
fire, but would roast slowly. The Signoria wanted a spectacle." She
shuddered. "The monks started turning black; and then a *giovano*
struck one of them with a stone, and the bowels spilled out in a
bloody rush. . . . Finally, the flames got so hot and rose so high, the
bodies cooked through, and the arms and legs started dropping
off. . . ."

I closed my eyes briefly. "Yes," I said. "Yes, of course." I looked at
Elena. "You said 'the monks' . . . so he wasn't the only one executed?"

"No. The heavy friar, the one who started the Trial by Fire . . .
what was his name? Domenico. Fra Domenico died with him."

"Thank you," I said. "I will eat my breakfast now. I'll call for you when I'm ready to dress."

She left. I did not eat; instead, I went back out to the balcony to sit in the sun and watch the smoke rise to Heaven. I supposed that, with Savonarola gone, Fra Domenico had become a liability for Salvatore and Francesco.

Zalumma would have been pleased.

LXX

*T*he next morning, when Elena came to dress me, she carried a small velvet purse. When she opened it on the table, out spilled the sapphire necklace and the diamond-studded hairnet I had worn the day I married Francesco.

They had not been stored in my trunk. I had opened it on the second day of my imprisonment and discovered that all my jewels had been taken; I had looked for them with the intention of bribing Elena to flee with Matteo.

Francesco knew me well. But he did not know everything.

Elena went to my wardrobe and brought out the vivid blue velvet wedding gown and my finest chemise. "Ser Francesco says you are to look especially lovely today." So; I was to be a fine lure.

I said nothing as she laced me into the gown; this time, I wore the brocade belt low so that I could easily reach it with a swift move of my hand.

I was silent, too, as Elena brushed out my hair. But when she began to arrange it with great care in the sparkling hairnet, I said, "You will not help with Matteo, then."

I saw her face in the hand mirror; like her voice, it was stricken. "I dare not. You remember what happened to Zalumma. . . ."

"Yes," I said, my voice hard. "I remember what happened to Za-lumma. Do you think the same will not happen to me and my son?"

She lowered her face, ashamed, and would not look at me or speak to me after that. When she was finished and I was ready, she moved to open the door.

"Stop," I said, and she hesitated. "There is one very small thing you could do for me. I need a moment. Just a moment alone, to com-pose myself."

Reluctantly, she faced me. "I am not to leave you alone, Madonna. Ser Francesco said specifically—"

"Then don't leave me alone," I said swiftly. "I left my shawl out on the balcony. Would you fetch it for me, please?"

She knew. She gave a little sigh and nodded, yielding, and walked slowly to the balcony, carefully keeping her back to me the entire while.

I moved faster, more quietly, than I had ever thought I could. I pulled my father's dagger from the feathery insides of the mattress and slipped it into my belt.

Elena returned slowly from the balcony. "Your shawl is not there," she said.

"Thank you for looking," I said.

The soldier who had killed Zalumma—a hostile young man with scar-pitted cheeks—led me to the carriage, where Francesco and Salvatore de' Pazzi sat waiting. Francesco was dressed in his best prior's gown; for the first time since I had known him, he wore a long knife on his belt. Salvatore wore a *lucco* of muted dark green—the very sort of el-egant but austere tunic that Lorenzo de' Medici might have chosen. He, too, was armed with a fine sword at his hip.

"Beautiful, beautiful," Salvatore murmured at the sight of me. He leaned forward, stooping in the carriage, and offered his hand to help me up; I refused, shaking off the hold of the soldier behind me. I grabbed the edge of the door and pulled myself and my heavy gown, with its long train, inside.

"She makes a pretty picture, doesn't she?" Francesco remarked with pride, as if he had created me himself.

"Indeed." Salvatore graced us with a haughty smile.

I sat beside the soldier. Claudio drove us; a second carriage followed, and I leaned out the window to try to see who was inside. I could only make out shadows.

"Sit back, Lisa," Francesco said sharply, so that I turned back to look at him as we rumbled through the gate and onto the street. "You ought not be so curious. You'll learn more than you ever wanted to know soon enough." His eyes were bright from exhilaration and nerves. I stared at him, hard, and felt the weight of my father's knife against my body.

It was a warm day—too warm for a heavy velvet gown—yet I felt cold and numb, and the air still carried a hint of smoke from the previous day's fire. The light was too harsh, the colors too bright. The blue of my sleeve pained me so much that I squinted.

In the Piazza del Duomo, the crowds were few; I suspected they were even more spare at San Marco that morning. Flanked by Francesco and Salvatore and followed by my soldier, I walked past the octagonal Baptistery of San Giovanni, where I had been married and my son baptized. Francesco took my arm and steered me straight ahead so that I could not see those who emerged from the carriage behind us.

The Duomo's interior was dim and cool. As I passed over its threshold, the edges of the present blurred and melted into the past. I could not judge where one ended and the other began.

We moved together down a side aisle: Salvatore on my far left, Francesco to my immediate left. On my right was the murderous young soldier. Our pace was brisk; I tried to see past my false husband, past Salvatore. I searched desperately for a beloved face— praying that I would see it, that I would not.

But I saw little as we swept relentlessly toward the altar. I gleaned only impressions: A sanctuary less than a third full. Beggars, black-wimpled nuns, merchants; a pair of monks hushing a group of restless urchins of varying ages. As we walked past other nobles to take our place—second row from the altar, on the side by the wooden choir—Francesco smiled and nodded to acquaintances. I followed his gaze and saw Lord Priors, six of them in various places surrounding us.

I wondered which were accomplices, and which victims.

At last we came to rest beneath the massive cupola. I stood between my husband and the unhappy soldier, and turned my head to my right at the sight of bodies moving toward us.

Matteo. Matteo walking on strong little legs, clinging to the hand of his stooped nursemaid. Stubborn boy; he would not let her carry him. As he neared, I let go a soft cry. Francesco gripped my arm, but with the other, I reached out to my son. Matteo saw me, and with a shattering smile, he called to me, and I to him.

The nursemaid seized him, pulled him off his feet, and carried him until she stood beside the soldier, our barrier. Matteo writhed, trying to worm his way to me, but she held him fast, and the soldier took a slight step forward so that I could not touch my child. I turned away, anguished.

"We thought it best," Francesco said softly to me, "that a mother be able to see her son. To know where he is at every moment so that she is always reminded to act in his best interest."

I looked at the soldier. I had thought he came to serve as my guard and my assassin alone. Now I looked at him waiting with his great knife beside my son; hatred so pressed on me I could scarcely stand.

I had come to the Duomo with one aim: to kill Francesco before the signal was given. Now I faltered. How could I save my child and still see my tormentor dead? I had only one blow. If I struck at the soldier, Francesco would surely strike at me—and Salvatore de' Pazzi was within sword's reach of Giuliano's heir.

Your child is already dead, I told myself, *just as you are*. We had no salvation; I had only one chance—not at rescue, but revenge.

I put my hand—the one that had reached for Matteo—lightly on my waist, where the dagger lay hidden. And I marveled that I was willing to abandon my son in the interest of hate; how like my father Antonio I had become. But he had faced only one loss, I reasoned stubbornly. I had suffered many.

I fingered my belt and did not know what I should do.

Mass began. The priest and acolytes processed to the dark altar limned with gold and crowned with a carving of the dying Christ upon the cross. The swinging thurible bled frankincense-laden smoke into the shadowy dimness, further blurring shapes and the edges of time. The choir sang the *Introit* and *Kyrie*. Behind us, a scattering of giggling orphans pushed their way toward the front of the church, mixing in with the offended nobility. One of the monks followed, hissing reprimands. The smell of sour, filthy children wafted our way; Francesco disapprovingly lifted a kerchief to his nose.

Dominus vobiscum, God be with you all, the priest said.

Et cum spiritu tuo, Francesco replied.

As the priest's assistant chanted the Epistle, I detected motion in the periphery of my vision. Something, someone dark and cowled, had sidled his way through the assembly to stand behind me. I imagined I heard his breath, felt it warm on my shoulder. I knew that he had come for me.

He will not strike yet, I told myself, though the urge to reach for my weapon was strong. *He will not kill me until the signal.*

Francesco glanced sidewise over his shoulder at the hooded assassin; approval flickered in his gaze. This was part of his plan. As he turned back, he caught me watching him and was pleased by my fright. He graced me with a cold, falsely benign smile.

The choir sang the Gradual: *Arise, Lord, in Thine holy anger. Lift up Thineself against the rage of my adversaries.*

Far to my left, a ripple passed through the row of priors and nobles and flowed to Salvatore de' Pazzi. He turned to my husband and whispered. I strained to hear him.

". . . have spotted Piero. But not . . ."

Francesco recoiled and unintentionally strained his neck, peering to his left at the crowd. "Where is Giuliano?"

I tensed, agonizingly aware of the assassin at my back, at the soldier standing beside my child. If Giuliano had failed to come, they might well kill us immediately. A pair of urchins behind us hooted at a joke; the monk hushed them.

I did not hear the Gospel. I heard the priest droning during the sermon but could not interpret his words. The fingers of my right hand hovered at the edge of my belt. Had the soldier or my assassin moved, I would have lashed out blindly.

Another tide of whispers washed Salvatore's way. He murmured to Francesco and gestured with his chin at a distant point to his left. "He is here. . . ."

He is here.

Here, somewhere near me, beyond my sight or voice, beyond my touch in the moment before I was to die. I did not cry at the knowledge, but I swayed beneath its weight. I looked down at the marble beneath my feet and prayed. *Be safe and live. Be safe. . . .*

The priest chanted the *Oremus*, took the Host, and lifted it toward the crucified Christ in offering.

Offerimus tibi, Domine . . .

Salvatore rested his hand upon the hilt of his sword and leaned toward Francesco. His lips formed a word: *Soon.*

As he did so, my assassin leaned in instantly, smoothly, stepping upon my train so that I could not bolt, and pressed his lips to my ear.

"Monna Lisa," he whispered. Had he not uttered those two words, I would have taken up the dagger. "When I signal, fall."

I could not breathe. I parted my lips and took in air through my mouth and watched as the priest's assistant moved to the altar and began to fill the chalice with wine. Francesco's hand hovered at his hip.

The second assistant stepped forward with a decanter of water.

"*Now,*" Salai whispered, and pressed something hard and blunt against my back, beneath the ribs, to make it appear as though he were delivering a fatal thrust.

Wordless, I sank to the cool marble.

Beside me, Francesco cried out and dropped to his knees just as he drew his knife; it clattered beside him on the floor. I pushed myself up to sit. Salai's army of street urchins streamed forward, surrounding the soldier. One knifed him in the back and pulled him down so that a second could slash his throat.

The world erupted in a chorus of shrieks. I clawed to my feet, screaming Matteo's name, cursing my tangled skirts. The orphans had swarmed him and his nursemaid; I pulled my father's stiletto free and lurched toward them. My son was nestled in the arms of one of the monks from the Ospedale degli Innocenti.

"Lisa!" he cried. "Lisa, come with us."

The bells in the campanile began to ring. A frantic nobleman and his wife ran past, almost knocking me down. I stayed on my feet as a wave of other panicked worshipers followed. "Leonardo, take him!" I shouted. "I will follow, I will follow—only *go!*"

He turned reluctantly and ran. I held my ground despite the fleeing crowd, and turned back to Francesco.

He had fallen onto his side and hip; Salai had wounded him and kicked his knife away. He was helpless.

"Lisa," he said. His eyes were feral, terrified. "What good will it serve? What good?"

What good, indeed? I crouched down and approached him with the dagger raised overhand—the wrong way. Salai would not have approved. But I wanted to bring it down the way Francesco de' Pazzi had brought his weapon down on Lorenzo's brother: wildly, carelessly, with a spasm of fury, with a spray of crimson, with a thousand blows for each wrong done. I would have spared no piece of his flesh.

Entrapped my father
Murdered my loved ones
Stole my life and my child

"You aren't my husband," I said bitterly. "You never were. For the sake of my true husband, I will kill you." I leaned down.

And he struck first. With a small blade, hidden in his fist. It bit into the flesh just beneath my left ear and would have sliced quickly to my right. But before it reached center I pulled away, astonished, and sat back on my haunches.

"Bitch," he croaked. "Did you think I would let you ruin it all?" He sagged to the floor, still alive, and glared at me with hatred.

I put a hand to my throat and drew it away. It was the color of garnets—a dark necklace, Francesco's final gift.

I can bleed to death here, I thought. *I can have my revenge. I can kill Francesco now and bleed to death and they will find me later, here, dead atop his corpse.*

I chose not to kill him.

I heard a roaring in my ears, the sound of the tide. Like Giuliano in Francesco's lie, I was drowning, as surely as if I had fallen into the Arno from the Ponte Santa Trinità. Fallen, and sunk deep. And I had descended to a place, finally, where my emotions were still.

I did not worry for Matteo. I knew he was safe in his grandfather's arms. I did not worry for myself, I did not try to flee my attackers; I knew that I was no longer their target. I did not worry about Francesco or my hatred of him. I would let God and the authorities deal with him; it was not my place. I knew my place now.

Dear God, I prayed. *Let me rescue Giuliano.*

Through a miracle, I rose.

My body was agonizingly leaden, moving as if through water, but I willed it to do the impossible: I moved in the direction Salvatore de' Pazzi had gone, to go in search of my beloved. The stiletto was heavy; my hand trembled with the effort to hold it.

I heard his voice.

Lisa! Lisa, where are you?

Husband, I am coming. I opened my mouth to cry out, but my voice was no more than an anguished wheeze, lost in the roar of the flood.

The waters inside the cathedral were murky; I could scarcely see the wavering images of fighters against a dizzying backdrop of innocents in flight. There were orphans here—filthy lads with small glinting blades—and men with wielded swords, peasants and priests and noblemen, but I could make no sense of it. My hearing faded until the frenzied chiming of the bells sank to nothingness. In the river, all was silent.

Sunlight streamed in from the open door leading to the Via de' Servi, and in its shaft, I saw him: Giuliano. He wore a monk's robes.

His cowl was thrown back, revealing his dark curling hair and a beard I had never seen. In his hand was a long sword, the point tilted toward the ground as he rushed forward. He was entirely a man; in my absence, he had aged. His features, pleasingly irregular, were taut and limned with faint bitterness.

He was amazing, and beautiful, and gave me back my heart.

But I was no longer here to surrender to emotion: I was here to redeem the transgressions of others. I was here to accomplish what should have been done almost two decades ago: stop the murder of innocents.

And I saw him, Salvatore, Francesco de' Pazzi's son, fighting his way through the onslaught of fleeing worshipers, holding his sword at his side. He was moving toward Giuliano.

But Giuliano did not see him. Giuliano saw only me. His eyes were lights from a distant shore; his face was a beacon. He mouthed my name.

I yearned to go to him, but I could not make the mistakes Anna Lucrezia, Leonardo, the elder Giuliano, made. I could not yield to my passion. I forced my gaze from Giuliano's face and kept it fastened on Salvatore. It was impossible to walk, yet I staggered behind him. I stayed on my feet, despite the pull of the escaping crowd. God granted a miracle: I did not fall. I did not faint or die. I half ran.

As I neared both men, Giuliano's joyous brilliance faded to concern, then alarm. He now saw the blood spilling from my throat, soaking my bodice. He did not see Salvatore approaching from the side; he saw only me, following. He did not see Salvatore an arm's length away, raising his sword, ready to bring it down, to kill Lorenzo's most loved son.

But I saw. And had I possessed the strength, I would have thrown my body between the two men. I would have taken the blow meant for my beloved. But I could not reach him in time; I could not step between the two men. I could only surge forward, using all the air that remained in my lungs, and close in on Salvatore from behind.

And in the instant that Salvatore raised his blade, in the instant before he brought it down upon Giuliano, I reached farther than was possible. With the dagger, I found the soft spot beneath Salvatore's ribs and buried it there.

I remembered the painting on the wall of the Bargello of Bernardo Baroncelli. I remembered the ink drawing of him dangling from the rope, his dead face downcast, still stamped with remorse. And I whispered:

"Here, traitor."

Relieved, I let go a sigh. Giuliano was alive, standing in dappled sunlight on the banks of the Arno, waiting with his arms open. I sank into them and down, down where the waters are deepest and black.

EPILOGUE

Lisa

JULY 1498

LXXI

I did not die, nor did Francesco. The blow I dealt Salvatore de' Pazzi downed him, and as he lay bleeding, he was killed by another.

His mercenaries, who rode into the Piazza della Signoria at the chiming of the bells, were met by formidable opposition. Upon encountering Piero's men—and upon learning that Salvatore would not arrive to incite the crowd against the Medici and lead the storming of the palazzo and the overthrow of the Signoria—the mercenaries disbanded and fled.

Messer Iacopo never was avenged.

It was not time, my husband explained, for the Medici to return to power in Florence; there was insufficient support in the Signoria. Piero had learned the wisdom of patience. But the time will come. The time will come.

I have learned, to my amusement, that Francesco has told everyone in Florence that I am still his wife, that I have merely gone to stay in the country with my child because of nerves caused by the fright I experienced in the Duomo. He used his wits and connections to escape the noose, but he is disgraced. He will never serve in the government again.

At last I am in Rome with Giuliano and Matteo. It is hotter here, with fewer clouds and less rain. Mists and fog are less common than in Florence; the sun reveals everything in sharp, crisp relief.

Leonardo has come to visit us now that I have regained some of my strength. I am sitting for him again—despite the bandage on my neck—and I am beginning to think he will never be satisfied with the painting. He alters it constantly, saying that my reunion with Giuliano will be reflected in my expression. He promises that he will not re-main in Milan forever; when he fulfills his obligations to the Duke, he will come to Rome, with Giuliano as his patron.

Shortly after Leonardo's arrival, when I first sat for him in Giu-liano's Roman palazzo, I asked him about my mother. The instant he had told me I was his child, I knew it was true. Because I had always looked for another man's face in my reflection, I had never seen his. Yet I looked on his features, in feminine form, every time I smiled down at my image on the gessoed panel.

He had indeed been smitten with Giuliano—until, through Lorenzo, he met Anna Lucrezia. He never expressed his feelings to her because he had sworn never to take a wife, lest it interfere with his art or his studies. But the emotion became quite uncontrollable, and when he first realized my mother and Giuliano were lovers—that evening on the shadowy Via de' Gori, when he had first yearned to paint her—he was overtaken by jealousy. He could, he confessed, have killed Giu-liano himself at that moment.

And the following morning in the Duomo, that jealousy distracted him from sensing the tragedy about to occur.

That was why he had never told anyone about his discovery—shortly after coming to Santissima Annunziata as the Medici's agent—that my father was the penitent in the Duomo. How could he arrest a man for yielding to jealousy, when he himself had been so tormented by it? It had made no sense; nor did it make sense to pain me unnec-essarily with such news.

When the murder occurred, Leonardo had been devastated. And on the day of Giuliano's funeral at San Lorenzo, he had left the sanctuary, overwhelmed, and gone out to the churchyard to silently vent his sorrow. There he found my weeping mother and confessed his guilt and his love to her. Shared grief bound them together, and beneath its sway they lost themselves.

"And see what misery my passion caused for your mother, and for you," he said. "I could not let you make the same error. I would not risk telling you Giuliano was alive, for fear you would try to contact him and endanger him and yourself."

I looked out the window at the relentless sunshine. "Why didn't you tell me this from the beginning?" I pressed gently. "Why did you let me think I was Giuliano's child?"

"Because I wanted you to have full rights as a Medici; they could care far better for you than a poor artist. It harmed no one and gave Lorenzo joy on his deathbed." His expression grew sadly tender. "Most of all, I did not want to tarnish the memory of your mother. She was a woman of great virtue. She confessed to me that, in all the time she was with Giuliano, she would not bed him—though all the world believed she had. Such was her loyalty to her husband; and so her shame, when she lay with me, was all the greater.

"Why should I confess that she and I—a sodomite, no less—were lovers, and risk damaging the respect due her?"

"I respect her no less," I said. "I love you both."

He smiled brilliantly.

I will send the portrait back with Leonardo when he returns to Milan. And when he finishes it—if he ever does—neither I nor Giuliano will accept it. I want him to keep it.

For he has only Salai. But if he takes the painting, my mother and I will always be with him.

I, on the other hand, have Giuliano and Matteo. And each time I gaze into the looking glass, I will see my mother and father.

And I will smile.

Reading
Group
Gold

I, MONA LISA
by Jeanne Kalogridis

A Conversation with Jeanne Kalogridis
- Personal History · Literary Inspiration

Historical Perspective
- The Medici Family of Florence: A Time Line

Keep on Reading
- Recommended Reading
- Reading Group Questions

*A
Reading
Group Gold
Selection*

For more reading group suggestions
visit www.readinggroupgold.com

 ST. MARTIN'S GRIFFIN

Could you tell us a little bit about your background and when you decided that you wanted to lead a literary life?

I was a shy, scrawny, unpopular kid with frizzy hair and thick glasses; since I had no social life, I read. I adored dark fantasy and science fiction, and I was writing my own stories as soon as I could hold a pencil. My mom and sisters were always dragging me to the mall on weekends, so while they shopped, I hung in the local bookstore. I think the defining moment for me came when I picked up a copy of Ray Bradbury's *The Illustrated Man* in a Waldenbooks. His writing was so beautiful, so lyrical.... I decided then I wanted to write like that.

Who are some of your favorite authors?

Margaret Atwood, Angela Carter, Philippa Gregory, Tracy Chevalier, and Chuck Palahniuk.

Is there a book that most influenced your life or inspired you to become a writer?

The Illustrated Man by Ray Bradbury. And his *The Martian Chronicles*. When I worked on my first novel, I bought new copies of those books and consciously tried to imitate his style.

> *"Of course, I had heard of The Da Vinci Code—who hasn't?"*

*You have already authored a historical novel
about Renaissance Italy,* The Borgia Bride.
What was the inspiration for I, Mona Lisa?

Italy at the turn of the sixteenth century is pure
gold for an author. The times were turbulent,
the advances in the art world amazing, the
characters mesmerizing. I fell in love with the
period while writing *The Borgia Bride.* When I
started reading about Renaissance Florence,
I realized I had to write a novel set there. Of
course, I had heard of *The Da Vinci Code*—who
hasn't? In every bookstore, Mona Lisa's eyes
were staring at me. I began to wonder about the
woman who had posed for Leonardo's painting.
The more I read about her, the more intrigued
I became.

*Do you scrupulously adhere to historical fact
in your novels, or do you take liberties if the
story can benefit from the change?*

I scrupulously adhere to historical fact. If a fact
is recorded, I don't contradict it. I *do* take liberties in writing possible scenes behind the
scenes, and in giving the characters motivation
to explain their actions. We can never really
know what the characters were thinking or
what they really intended; that's where fiction
enters the story.

*A
Conversation
with
Jeanne
Kalogridis*

And to what extent did you stick to the facts in writing I, Mona Lisa? **How did you conduct your research?**

Let me answer the second question first. While I rely on the Internet, I don't trust everything I read online—I use the Web to direct me to published experts on the topic. Then it's off to a bookstore or a university library, where I usually check out thirty or forty titles on my subject.

Now, for the first question: I was forced to speculate more while writing *I, Mona Lisa* for the simple reason that little is known about Lisa Gherardini. While I adhered to my historical time line—to the very day, where the Medici and other historical figures were involved—I took advantage of the freedom offered by Lisa's relative anonymity. This allowed me to involve her in a conspiracy.

What is it about Mona Lisa that you hoped to reveal to your readers?

We've seen the Mona Lisa's image so often that we don't really *see* it anymore. It's been copied so inelegantly so many times that she now seems homely, even mannish. If you look at a fine print of the original and try to forget all the cartoonish rendering of it, you'll begin to see the breathtaking beauty of the woman who posed for it.

"We've seen the Mona Lisa's image so often that we don't really see it anymore."

I wanted people to lose their jaded reaction to that person. I would like them to realize that they're looking at a five-hundred-year-old image of a real woman who left her session with Leonardo and lived a real life.

Why do you think readers are so drawn to historical fiction?

Because history is fascinating—and fact is often stranger than fiction. Also, readers of historical fiction love to learn, and this permits us to do so in a very enjoyable way.

What do you see when you look at the Mona Lisa? Please share a few thoughts about your reaction to da Vinci's famous portrait.

As I mentioned above, when you stare at a fine print of the original—I have one, and I stared at it every day that I worked on the novel—you begin to see the woman's true beauty. And you see how fine and elegant and tender Leonardo's rendering was. She literally melts into the shadows. But bear in mind that we are looking at a painting that, sadly, is distorted by an ugly yellow film and was retouched by insensitive "artists" over the centuries. I read Vasari's comments about the painting, written fifty years after *Mona Lisa* was painted. He describes the fresh bloom of pink on Lisa's lips, the blush on her cheeks, the vein in her neck that seems almost to be beating. He speaks of the very pores from which her eyebrows emerge. All of those details have been lost, but when I look at the portrait now, I try to imagine them.

Who are some of your favorite historical figures?

My namesake, Joan (in French, Jeanne) of Arc—yes, she was deluded, but she kicked butt and made a man a king. I read a lot of biographies of strong women when I was growing up; I admired Marie Curie, Elizabeth Blackwell (first female M.D. in the U.S.), Elizabeth I, Boudicca (who gave the Imperial Roman army a run for its money), Jane Addams, and Susan B. Anthony.

There are, of course, fascinating men. I always adored Leonardo because he was passionately interested in *everything* and pursued knowledge without the encumbrance of a formal education. Vlad the Impaler is another favorite of mine, for much grislier reasons, as is Cesare Borgia.

"While I adhered to my historical time line—to the very day, where the Medici and other historical figures were involved—I took advantage of the freedom offered by Lisa's relative anonymity."

Are you currently working on another book? And if so, what—or who—is your subject?

Yes, I'm working on *The Bloodiest Queen,* a novel about Catherine de' Medici. When I was working on *I, Mona Lisa,* I became fascinated by the Medici family, and so did some extracurricular reading. Catherine was a brilliant, shrewd, strong woman who overcame a horrific childhood to become queen of France. I was immediately drawn to her for three reasons: first, she is arguably the most capable, intelligent person ever to rule France; second, she is blamed for the worst bloodshed in French history, the St. Bartholomew's Day Massacre; and third, she was obsessed by the occult and an intimate of Nostradamus.

*A
Conversation
with
Jeanne
Kalogridis*

Ruth Miller

The Medici Family of Florence: A Time Line

April 26, 1478

Lorenzo's brother, Giuliano de' Medici, is murdered in the cathedral of Santa Maria della Fiore

❧

December 1479

Leonardo da Vinci sketches the executed Bernardo Baroncelli

❧

March 15, 1479

Recorded date of Lisa di Antonio Gherardini's birth

❧

1482

Leonardo leaves Florence for Milan

❧

April 8, 1492

Lorenzo de' Medici dies

❧

November 8, 1494

Piero de' Medici and his brothers are expelled from Florence

Medici brothers eventually settle in Rome

❧

November 17, 1494

Charles VIII of France and his army enter Florence

March 5, 1495
Lisa Gherardini marries Francesco
del Giocondo

✐

February 7, 1497
Savonarola's "bonfire of the vanities"

✐

April 7, 1498
The infamous "trial by fire"

✐

May 23, 1498
Savonarola executed

✐

December 28, 1503
Piero di Lorenzo de' Medici drowns in
the Garigliano River

✐

August 1512
Giuliano di Lorenzo de' Medici welcomed
home as Florence's ruler

✐

March 11, 1513
Giovanni di Lorenzo de' Medici elected
Pope (Leo X)

1516
Leonardo travels to France. King Francis I
purchases the *Mona Lisa*. The painting
remains in France at the Louvre Museum to
this day.

Recommended Reading

Brucker, Gene A.
Renaissance Florence.
Berkeley: University of California Press, 1983.

Gatti, Claudio, in association with the
International Herald Tribune.
Florence in Detail: A Guide
for the Expert Traveler.
New York: Rizzoli, 2003.

Kent, F. W.
Lorenzo de' Medici and the Art of Magnificence.
Baltimore: The Johns Hopkins University Press,
2004.

Letze, Otto and Thomas Buchsteiner.
Leonardo da Vinci: Scientist, Inventor, Artist.
Ostfildern: Hatje Cantz Publishers, 1997.

Martines, Lauro.
April Blood: Florence and the Plot
Against the Medici.
New York: Oxford University Press, 2003.

Vasari, Giorgio.
The Lives of the Artists.
New York: Oxford University Press, 1998.

da Vinci, Leonardo.
A Treatise on Painting.
Amherst, N.Y.: Prometheus Books, 2002.

Reading
Group
Gold

Don't miss
The Borgia Bride
by
Jeanne Kalogridis

*Keep
on
Reading*

"From sexual passion to mortal danger, the
dramatic shift of real historical events will
keep the reader turning the pages."
—Philippa Gregory, bestselling author of
The Other Boleyn Girl and *The Constant Princess*

AVAILABLE FROM ST. MARTIN'S GRIFFIN

📖 Reading Group Questions

1. Few works of art are as romanticized, celebrated, and reproduced as the *Mona Lisa*. How did reading this book teach you about—or change your impression of—the art world's most famous face? Has anyone in the group ever seen it in person?

2. Beautiful, enigmatic, sly, foreboding...many adjectives have been used to describe Lisa's portrait. But what words would you use to describe Lisa's character? Also, take a moment to talk about her role—as an only daughter, married woman, and member of the upper class—in Florentine society. How was Lisa different from other women of her era? Do you think she was a woman ahead of her time?

3. Lisa is told by her astrologer that she is "caught in a cycle of violence, of blood, and deceit." To what extent does Lisa let fate dictate her actions? Do you believe in fate? Discuss the themes of prophecy in *I, Mona Lisa*.

4. In addition to being religious, many of those we meet in the book become fanatic—and commit acts of violence to justify their beliefs. What was it that led Antonio, Baroncelli, and Savonarola to behave the way they did? Do you condone any of their actions? Do you have any sympathy for them?

5. Who do you think bears the true responsibility for the deaths of Giuliano the Elder and Anna Lucrezia? How do the various characters—from Lisa to Antonio to Lorenzo—deal with the guilt, trauma, and mystery surrounding the deaths of those they love?

6. What is significant about the third man involved in Giuliano's murder? How does this element of mystery drive the narrative?

7. *I, Mona Lisa* is a novel about truth and beauty, art and artifice. It is also about family—in all its glory and bloodshed. How important is the notion of family to each of the main characters? Which relationships are the most "real" to you in this book?

8. Do you believe that a picture is worth a thousand words? Can a work of art—a painting, a book—ever truly capture a person's essence? Did Leonardo's portrait of Lisa capture hers?

9. When Lisa views her cartoon she remarks that Leonardo's "recall of [her] features is astonishing...more sacred, more profound than any image rendered by [a] mirror." Why do you think she feels this way? Does Leonardo see himself in Lisa? What personality traits do you think they both share?

10. Leonardo is more than just an artist: He doesn't just view society from a distance; he is a member of a powerful inner circle. What does *I, Mona Lisa* suggest about the role and function of art during the Florentine era? Was it more or less political than it is now?

11. What, do you think, is the meaning of the last sentence of the book?